QUEEN OF WANDS

BOOK FOUR IN THE TREE OF AGES SERIES

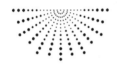

SARA C ROETHLE

D0813391

VULTURE'S EYE PUBLICATIONS

Map by Tomasz Madej

❦ Created with Vellum

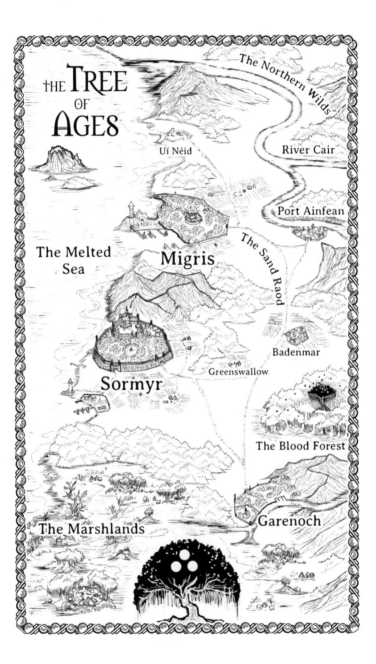

The TREE of AGES

The Northern Wilds

Uí Néid

River Cair

Port Ainfean

The Melted
Sea

Migris

The Sand Raod

Badenmar

Greenswallow

Sormyr

The Blood Forest

The Marshlands

Garenoch

CHAPTER ONE

$\mathcal{T}$he small inn room felt hot. Bedelia shifted uncomfortably, wishing she could escape.

"Stop fidgeting," Anna snapped.

Bedelia shifted again in her seat, swiping her short, dark brown hair from her face using her good arm. She glanced at the aggravated wound on her other, high up on her shoulder. "Leave it alone, it's fine."

Anna grasped Bedelia's biceps firmly, forcing her back down into her chair as she tried to stand. "If you won't let me tend your wound, you could very well slow us down on the road. If you slow us down, you will be left behind."

Bedelia bristled at the threat, then relaxed. Finn wouldn't leave her behind just because Anna was being cranky. She attempted to tug the collar of her burgundy tunic back up over her bandage free wound. "It's fine, the Aos Sí already tended it."

"Yes," Anna sighed, moving back behind Bedelia's chair to peer at the arrow wound in her shoulder. "Then they whipped you and marched you through the muck until you were near death. It needs to be *re*tended."

She ground her teeth. The cursed wound hurt bad enough without Anna prodding at it. She heard dripping as Anna wrung out the cloth, soaking in scalding hot water. The water stung like hot coals, though Anna's hands seemed impervious.

Her breath hissed out as Anna placed the wet cloth on the edge of her shoulder wound and began to dab. She clenched her fingers around the base of her chair and accepted the treatment.

She became momentarily distracted from her pain as a soft chittering sound emanated from a lump of blankets on the bed behind them. Naoki, Finn's pet dragon, had been snuggled up there all morning. The creature had taken to spending most of its time in the woods surrounding the burgh, no longer in constant need of Finn's care, but would still sneak in through the inn's windows in the morning to lie in a cushy bed.

"You probably still have shards of wood in there from them breaking the arrow like that," Anna muttered, returning Bedelia's attention to her.

She grimaced, thinking back to the Aos Sí's surprise attack. They'd ended up tending her not long after they sent an arrow through her, but it hadn't been a very clean job. Being out in the woods, the quickest option was to break the arrow near her wound, then pull it through. She was quite sure she *did* have shards of wood in there, but she wasn't about to let Anna pick them out.

A knock on the door preceded Kai peeking his head in. His shoulder-length, chestnut colored hair fell to the side as he watched them. "Are you two done yet? We'd hoped to be on the road by sunrise."

Bedelia turned in time to see Anna scowl in his direction. "Yes," Anna snarled, "then Sativola had too much whiskey and couldn't find his boots, and Finn needed private time to commune with her blasted horse! *I'm* not the one preventing our departure."

Bedelia began to stand again, ready to use Kai's distraction to escape the room, but Anna gripped her arms, forcing her back down.

"Iseult put up less fuss than you!" Anna growled at her.

She ceased her struggles, genuinely surprised. "*Iseult* let you tend his wounds?"

"Yes," Anna said more calmly.

Kai left the door ajar as he moved into the room to hover over them.

"Apparently Finn cannot provide miraculous healing to us *all*," Anna added.

Bedelia turned to see her scowling at Kai again. She found herself once more wondering about the exact details of the night Kai almost died. All she knew was that Anna and Finn had stayed near his deathbed, and in the morning he was good as new. She'd also noticed large matching scars on Finn and Kai's palms, but could not say for sure if they'd been there before that night.

The hot cloth touched down again on her shoulder. "Curse you, woman!" she hissed. "You could at least let the rag cool a bit."

Anna very deliberately placed the rag back in the water, lifting it in and out a few times like a mop, then slapped it back on Bedelia's shoulder.

"Argh!" she groaned, but bit her tongue before she could make her situation any worse.

"I think I'll just go tend the horses," Kai muttered, slowly backing away from Anna.

As he retreated quietly to the door to let himself out, Bedelia glared in his direction. *Traitor.*

The rag slapped down again.

She gritted her jaw, refusing to complain any more.

"I see you've come to your senses," Anna said haughtily. She began to dab the rag more gently.

Bedelia sighed and allowed her thoughts to wander, hoping for a distraction from the pain. Her mind meandered to their first mission, a long way off from their current location. She wished she'd told Finn about Àed's location sooner. It would be a long journey back to the island where the Archtree once stood.

FINN STROKED THE FLAT-HANDLED BRUSH GENTLY DOWN THE side of Loinnir's white neck, readying her for the long journey ahead. She hoped the unicorn would not mind carrying her all the way to find Àed.

The unicorn's horn had remained magically hidden since they reached civilization, long enough now that she sometimes questioned if she'd truly seen it at all.

Loinnir turned her neck to eye Finn with one sparkling blue orb, as if to say, *How dare you question my existence?*

She smiled encouragingly at the unicorn, then continued brushing.

The stable gate opened and shut behind her, drawing her

attention. She turned to find Iseult approaching. He'd dressed in fresh clothing in his customary black, blending in with his shoulder-length black hair, flecked with white at his temples. To her, his eyes were almost as mesmerizing as Loinnir's, though instead of sparkling blue, they were a calm gray-green, like the eyes of a hunting cat. Though his brother, Maarav, had similar eyes, she only found them interesting on Iseult.

He approached her side, then ran his fingers down Loinnir's mane. "You know," he began, "Anna seems to believe your horse is actually a unicorn."

She gasped, then turned her face to hide her furious blush. Anna could see things that others could not. Had she been able to see Loinnir's horn despite the magic keeping it hidden?

Iseult chuckled at her reaction. He rarely laughed in front of others, really, he rarely even *spoke* in front of others, but when he was alone with Finn, it was as if he could finally relax.

"It seems to me the Aos Sí knew what they were doing when they gave her to you," he continued. "You make a good pair."

She smiled bashfully, resuming her brushing. "I apologize for not telling you the truth," she glanced around to make sure they were alone, then added in a whisper, "about her being a unicorn, I mean. It just seemed the sort of thing I should keep secret."

"I understand," he replied. "It's not as if I haven't hidden things from you in the past."

His tone drew her eye, but his face was, as always, unreadable. She considered reaching out to touch him, but hesitated, unsure if her touch would be welcome. Ever since he'd refused to let her return his soul, the topic had become a sore spot between them.

She had the Faie Queen's shroud now, the thing they had been questing for all along so she could undo the curse she, as Finnur, had placed upon Iseult's people so long ago. Now he wouldn't let her right the wrong, fearing it might weaken him, and he wanted to be able to protect her. She knew he was avoiding the subject for her own benefit, but it still hurt to have that tension between them.

Although, she could not blame him for avoiding the subject, as she too had been unable to speak of her lost daughter now that her memories of the tragic death had returned. The loss felt like it had happened in a dream, or another far distant life. She feared that if she discussed it openly, it would become real once more, and she'd have to feel that pain all over again. She was already haunted by enough ghosts of the past. If she let this one in, it might break her.

"What are you thinking?" Iseult asked, shattering the silence.

She took a deep breath. "About Àed," she lied. "I hope we can find him."

He nodded, running his hand gently down Loinnir's neck. "It will be a long journey. One we can ill afford in these trying times."

"I know," she muttered, turning her gaze down to the brush clutched in her hands.

He was right. According to Sláine, Maarav's adoptive mother, she was part of an ancient prophecy. The lives of humans and Faie alike depended on her being the last of the three queens to survive. To risk everything to save the single life of an old conjurer was surely folly . . . but she was going to do it anyway. Àed was her friend. He'd taken her in when she had no clothes, no food, and no memories. She owed him her life.

Iseult gently laid his hand on her shoulder. "I'll stand with you, no matter which path you choose."

She removed one hand from the brush to place over his, appreciating his presence, even though it was a constant reminder of what she'd done to his people.

He gave her shoulder a squeeze, then moved to tend his own horse, a dappled tan mare. He'd lost his warhorse when they'd been taken captive by the Aos Sí, but never once mentioned the loss afterward. It would have bothered Finn, but if it bothered Iseult, it did not show.

Stepping away from Loinnir, she dusted the fine white hairs from her charcoal gray breeches, then turned to watch Iseult sorting through the saddles draped on wooden bars against the stable wall near his tethered mount.

Leaving his horse for a moment, he approached with a saddle for her in hand, then looked a question at Finn. "Are you sure she's . . . what Anna thinks she is?"

Finn nodded, glad he hadn't said unicorn out loud. There was no telling what some of the townsfolk might do to get their hands on a creature that was supposedly no longer in existence.

"Then should we perhaps *not* saddle her?" He gestured toward her with the heavy saddle held effortlessly in his grip.

Suddenly grasping his hesitation, her eyes widened. She glanced at Loinnir. Did being saddled like a common horse offend her? The unicorn had allowed the Aos Sí to saddle her. Perhaps she would not mind . . .

Reaching her conclusion, she nodded. A saddle was more comfortable than riding bareback, and she'd need a place to affix her supplies atop Loinnir's back.

Taking her at her word, Iseult approached the unicorn and gently laid the cushioned saddle on her back. Loinnir did not protest, except to swing her neck far enough to eye Iseult as he affixed the straps beneath her belly.

Finn jumped as the stable door swung open and shut again, settling as Ealasaid approached her. Her curly blonde hair was damp from her bath, dripping rivulets of water down the shoulders of her gray corseted dress.

"I wish we were coming with you," she groaned, reaching her side. "I want to help rescue Àed too."

"An Solas needs you," Finn comforted, though she also wished Ealasaid was coming. "You cannot leave them now."

Ealasaid sighed. "But I never *wanted* to be their leader. I've never led anyone in my life. I'm a farmer's daughter, not some sort of princess."

Finn smiled at her, truly wishing Ealasaid could accompany them. "You know, I feel the same way."

Ealasaid turned her gray eyes up to her and cringed. "Sorry, I forgot that *you're* supposed to be a queen. You have it much worse."

Finished saddling Loinnir, Iseult breezed past them and muttered, "Keep your voices down."

Ealasaid paled at the warning, turning apologetic eyes to Finn.

Finn leaned in close to her shoulder. "Do you *still* want to come with us?"

8

She turned to watch Iseult's back as he left the stables, then moved her gaze back to Finn. "Now that you mention it, perhaps I am better off remaining here in Garenoch. At least Maarav never looks at me like he might want to run a sword through my belly."

Finn laughed, turning to leave the stable. "Iseult would never do that to you."

Ealasaid followed at her side. "No, he would never do that to *you*. The rest of us mean about as much to him as a meat pie."

Finn simply smiled in reply. She knew Iseult cared more than he let on. Well, at least she thought she knew. Truth be told, she never really knew what the man was thinking. Perhaps they were all just meat pies to him . . . but, she doubted it.

KAI LEANED BACK IN HIS CHAIR, TRYING TO IGNORE SATIVOLA as he groaned about his aching head, drawing the eyes of those attempting to have breakfast in the common room.

"You knew we were departing today," he commented. "It was your choice to have so much whiskey."

Sativola groaned again, pushing his sweaty, golden curly locks back from his scarred face. "Having that much whiskey is never a choice. At a certain point, the whiskey gods just take over and have their way with you, whether you like it or not."

Kai smirked and shook his head, glancing around the common room for signs of their other companions. He was just about to get up and check on Finn in the stables, when she and Ealasaid walked through the inn's front double doors.

He waved them over, feeling a mixture of emotions as Finn spotted him and motioned for Ealasaid to approach. Finn was looking overly thin, almost sick. He'd tried to speak to her about her troubles on many occasions, but she always changed the subject back to him. He'd given up on trying.

"I'm going to look for Maarav," Ealasaid chimed as they reached the table. "Don't you dare leave without saying goodbye." She eyed Finn sternly, then Kai before turning away.

She crossed the inn and marched up the stairs to find Maarav, who was likely still in bed since he'd been the one to inspire the whiskey gods' takeover the previous night.

Finn took a seat across from Kai and peered into his eyes. "How are *you* feeling?" she asked pointedly.

He forced a smile, flexing his scarred palm beneath the table. Even though he was more worried about how *Finn* was feeling, he could admit, if only to himself, that he'd been feeling . . . odd, to say the least. Ever since Finn gave away a bit of her immortal blood to save him, he hadn't quite felt like himself. It wasn't necessarily a bad feeling, just different.

"I'm fine," he replied with a roll of his eyes. "Really, you have much more important things to worry about than my . . . condition." *If she could brush off speaking of her troubles, he could do the same,* he thought.

"Perhaps," she sighed, pawing nervously at her long, dirty blonde hair, "but I'm the one that did this to you. If you experience any more latent effects, I'd like you to let me know."

He nodded in agreement, though he had no intention of telling her next time something strange happened. It was only a small thing to begin with. He'd been out in the market procuring supplies for their journey, when the scar on his palm sent an odd tingle through his arm and down his spine. The feeling continued until he nearly fainted. Sativola had dragged him back to the inn, where he quickly recovered. That had been three days prior, and he'd had no odd experiences since.

He was saved from further questioning as Bedelia and Anna descended the stairs. He could see fresh bandages peeking out from the collar of Bedelia's burgundy tunic, and Anna was smiling, so he assumed Bedelia had finally allowed her wound to be thoroughly tended.

Silent until then, Sativola staggered up from his seat. "I'm going to see to me horse," he muttered, "before I have to hear from all these women a second time about making them late."

Anna approached, then her smile slipped into a scowl as she glared down at Kai and asked, "How's your hand?"

Finn and Bedelia both joined Anna's gaze on him as they waited for an answer, and suddenly he realized just how long their forthcoming journey would be.

He stood. "I believe Sativola needs my assistance," he muttered, then walked away. He could feel the eyes of the three women on his back as he exited the inn.

Yes, the forthcoming journey would be a long one indeed.

CHAPTER TWO

I seult inhaled deeply, glad to finally be on the road. His horse's smooth, easy gait relaxed him further. The air was cool and dry, a nice change from the perpetual dampness of the landscape. They would have no issues finding plenty of firewood that night to ward away the dark. If only they could make it as far that day as he'd hoped. After their already late start, the farewells had taken a painfully long time.

Finn rode at his side on her white *unicorn*, with Bedelia at her other side on one of the horses borrowed from the Aos Sí. He wondered if she truly missed her previous horse, Rada. Finn had explained to him that the horse had been with Bedelia for a long time, so he should be sensitive toward her when referring to their new mounts. He'd decided at that point that he would simply not refer to the horses at all. If he missed his previous horse, it was only because it had been battle hardened, and was capable of keeping its feet on a ship without panic. He had a new horse now, and that was that.

He narrowed his eyes toward the setting sun, its light gently framing Kai, Anna, and Sativola, riding ahead further down the rutted dirt road. They were riding west, and would soon veer northwest on the long road to Sormyr, the Gray City. Though they'd left ships in Migris, he held no illusions that the vessels would still be there waiting for them. They'd have a much better chance of finding a ship in Sormyr, then sailing northward toward the island where the Archtree formerly stood.

A crash sounded from within the nearby forest, then a rabbit squealed. Iseult sighed. It was fortunate the dragon was learning to fend for herself, but with her running around on her own, it would be difficult to keep her hidden. Those who didn't run at the sight of a young dragon might attack. Iseult didn't relish the thought of defending a dragon against possible attackers, but he'd do so at Finn's behest.

"Will we see any other burghs on our way?" Finn questioned, pulling him out of his thoughts. She peered at him from beneath the hood of her tattered green cloak, gifted to her by Àed. Though she'd had opportunities to procure something warmer, she always refused.

He might have found the irrational behavior irritating in others, but in Finn, he could only find it endearing. He nodded in reply to her question, then pointed northwest. "There are a few small farming villages bordering the Southern Archive. We'll be allowed in the villages, but the Archive is only for scholars and nobles."

She frowned, drawing his close observation. Her skin beneath the shade of her cloak was pale, highlighting the subtle swelling beneath her eyes. He'd been worrying about her health ever since they'd been reunited and she'd regained her memories. She'd been skipping meals more often than not, and he often heard her crying out in her dreams as he patrolled the hallways and exterior of the inn. He knew he should try to talk to her about it, but found he lacked the nerve.

"Will Anders' and Branwen's family be at the Southern Archive?" she asked, not noticing his observance. "Perhaps we should inform them what has become of their children."

Iseult sighed. Though she was correct, and the twins' parents would likely be at the Archive, she'd never get in to see them, and if she did, she'd likely be unprepared for the confrontation.

"What would you tell them?" he questioned.

Her frown deepened as she gazed in the direction he'd pointed. "Well, I suppose Branwen is as good as dead, and we have no idea where Anders is now."

"Likely dead," he grumbled, thinking back to the last time he'd seen the man. He'd fought on the side of An Fiach in the battle up North. If he hadn't died there, he likely had been killed by the Faie on his continuing travels.

Finn's expression fell. He often forgot that sometimes he was better off not pointing out the facts when around a woman who chose to always hope for the best.

Bedelia cleared her throat and guided her horse closer to Finn. "He could still be alive," she amended, "and perhaps there's hope for Branwen yet."

Iseult sighed again. Bedelia had not met either of the twins, and did not know of Branwen's situation, trapped in the in-between while her body slowly perished. Still, he appreciated her offer of optimism, since he knew she was only speaking for Finn's sake. Bedelia herself was just as pessimistic as he.

"Yes," he agreed finally. "Those are both possibilities."

Finn smiled softly at both of her companions. "Perhaps we'll find Anders on our journey to Sormyr, and maybe he'll know of a way to save Branwen."

Iseult simply nodded. He truly did not care if he saw either of the twins again, but a part of him hoped Finn's wishes would come true. She'd had enough death and disappointment in her life already, even if she chose not to acknowledge it.

ANDERS HASTILY STUFFED HIS PROVISIONS INTO A BORROWED satchel. Fresh baked bread, hard cheese, dried mutton, and enough water to last him roughly five days. He could not wait to be on his way, though he found his task daunting. Still, he would be glad to leave the fortress behind, even though he had no idea where he actually was. He and Niklas had found Keiren in a castle far to the North, but after that first night, he awoke in a different locale. The high mountains had been exchanged for low marshes and warmer temperatures, if only slightly.

The skin at the back of his neck prickled, and he whipped around to see Niklas approach. The Ceàrdaman wore his customary gray robes, leaving his snowy white bald head and long spindly fingers bare. Anders glanced around the small, stone-walled room, noting the closed door. How long had Niklas been within the room watching him?

Shaking his head, Anders sighed and returned to his task. If he never saw another one of the Ceàrdaman again, it would be too soon.

"Do you remember your quest?" Niklas purred, slinking up to his side.

Anders kept his gaze on his satchel. He did not want to look into those strange, reflective eyes as he answered, "Of course I do. It will be done as you ask, and you will finally return my sister to me."

"Yes," Niklas agreed. "Your sister will be returned to the land of the living."

Anders didn't miss the way he'd rephrased his answer. He said his sister would be returned to the living, but not to him. The Travelers did not lie, but they twisted their words until the meaning was entirely hidden. His wording left Niklas the option of killing him at any point, but it didn't matter. As long as he still saved Branwen, his vow would not be broken.

At the beginning of his journey, he might have cared to argue the slip, but he no longer feared death. He'd been on his quest for so long. He'd seen violence and destruction. He'd seen his mother's cruel gaze, blaming him for not bringing her daughter home safely. As long as he was able to save Branwen, he would willingly march into death's waiting arms.

"Remember," Niklas continued, drawing Anders out of his dark thoughts, "speak no mention of Keiren. You work with the Ceàrdaman, and the Ceàrdaman alone."

Anders nodded. Would Niklas truly know if he

mentioned the powerful sorceress, or was the threat idle at best? Part of him wanted to tell Finn what little he knew of Keiren's plan. To warn her in hopes of being saved himself.

He shook his head and slung his satchel over his shoulder. His fate was sealed the moment the Travelers took possession of his sister's dying body. They were the only ones who could save her now, which meant he would do exactly what Niklas asked of him, even if it meant betraying the last person who might actually care if he died.

"On your way now," Niklas urged. "My people will escort you through the marshes, then you will be on your own."

Anders sighed and moved toward the door, ready to leave the small stone room within the hidden fortress behind.

FINN TOSSED AND TURNED IN HER BEDROLL, JUMPING IN AND out of a fitful sleep. They'd ridden for most of the day, and had made camp not far from the road. They had a blazing fire going to ward away any of the lesser Faie that might happen upon them, and were taking turns keeping watch in pairs. Finn wished her turn would come soon.

Every time she closed her eyes she saw another memory. Memories of another life that should have no bearing on her present. She saw her daughter, like a distant phantom, blaming her for her death. Then her mother, watching Finn walk away to curse Iseult's people for what they'd done.

She saw others too. Shadowy forms, some friends, some enemies. She knew now that she had claimed the Faie

Queen's shroud, her people would never give up their hunt for her. She'd have to face them eventually, all of those shadowy forms from the past. Little more than ghosts now, according to Slàine. *Ghosts* that could kill and maim, and command dangerous Faie to hold her captive.

She forced her eyes shut. Iseult and Bedelia were keeping watch nearby. She was safe. No shadows would be creeping up on her tonight. She should rest while she still had time.

She steadied her breathing and tried to imagine happy scenes. She pictured a time when all of the danger would be over. She could return Iseult's soul and they could . . . they could what? She had no idea what life would be like when they were no longer required to fight for it, nor if he'd even remain by her side.

She turned over and buried her face into her scratchy bedding. Sleep. She needed sleep.

She wasn't sure at what point she finally drifted off, but she found herself walking through a long, stone corridor, eerily illuminated by candlelight. At first she thought she was in the in-between, but then the corridor opened up to a moonlit forest. Mist crept up from the foliage, circling wide tree trunks, only to dissipate as it reached the crisp air above.

She walked forward into the forest like there was a cord attached to her chest, pulling her toward . . . *something*. Her feet glided effortlessly through the mist, never catching on roots or brambles.

Eventually she reached a large body of water, circled by the dense mist. At the water's edge waited a small boat, just big enough for one person. She knew without a doubt that the boat waited there just for her.

She inched toward the water, then stepped into the boat. A chill wind hit her face, drawing her gaze upward. Massive fluffy white flakes surrounded her. Her eyes followed them down to the water's surface, then to where they collected in the boat's basin. Suddenly panicked, she tried to step back onto the shore, but found she could not move.

The snow increased. She sensed a presence at her back in the tiny boat, but she could not turn to see who it was. Someone whispered in her ear, "Your humans cannot help you, Finnur. You will rule, or you will die."

The boat left the shore and drifted across the dark water, carrying her and the presence at her back toward the lake's center.

Still held immobile, she narrowed her gaze past the still waters to movement on the shore across the lake. Cloaked figures had gathered there, and as one, they all knelt before the lake. Before *her*.

"I don't want to rule anyone," she croaked, forcing the words from her throat.

A woman's hand reached around her to stroke the gold locket that hung from her neck. Suddenly her mother's presence was with her, calming, comforting. She felt like she could breathe again. Then the hand turned icy cold against her skin. Fingers wrapped around her throat. The snow increased, blinding her with flashes of white.

"If you won't rule, then I will," Oighear's melodious voice hissed in her ear.

The fingers around her throat tightened, freezing her skin. She could no longer see the figures at the shore through the mist and ice. The Snow Queen continued to squeeze. Finn's vision went dark.

This was impossible. Oighear was dead. Finn had seen to it herself.

She woke gasping for breath. Slowly, she sat up in her bedroll and touched her throat. Her fingers came away slick with melting ice. Was she still dreaming?

She glanced to her side and jumped, then realized it was only Kai crouching beside her bedroll, moonlight glinting off his chestnut hair. His hand was on her shoulder, and she realized he'd shaken her awake. She looked down at the foot of her bedroll to see Naoki curled there, fast asleep.

"I just had the strangest dream," Kai whispered, regaining her attention. "Oighear was alive, and I was in a place shrouded with mist."

She met his gaze, her eyes wide with terror. She reached out and touched a lock of his hair. It was crunchy and cold. *Frozen.*

"I dreamed of her too," she breathed, lifting a hand to her throat to touch the dampness. "What do you think it means?" she asked distantly, even though something in her gut already told her the truth.

Kai shook his head, crossing his legs beneath him to sit more comfortably. He ran his hand through his hair then paused, as if just noticing the ice there. He turned wide eyes down to her. "We saw her die. We killed her ourselves."

She shivered. "But we left her body there. I never thought—"

He shook his head. "*People* don't just come back to life. Perhaps her spirit has simply lingered to haunt our dreams."

She pulled her blanket up to her throat. "People don't

just come back, but Oighear is Faie. She faded away for an entire lifetime and still came back."

He sighed. "Our goal is still the same, and if Oighear still lives . . . well, you have the shroud now. You defeated Oighear once, you can do it again." He sounded more like he was trying to convince himself than her.

She swallowed the lump in her throat. She wished she could feign confidence like Kai, but she knew she'd barely triumphed in that fight, and it was only because Kai had run an arrow through Oighear's chest to weaken her.

She reached out and gently took his hand, stroking her fingers over the prominent scar. "Do you think this is why she was in both our dreams? Have I brought you into even more danger?"

He smiled softly. "That also doesn't matter."

"You're a horrible liar," she muttered.

He gently withdrew his hand from hers. "Come now, I'll make you some tea to help you go back to sleep."

She scooted out of her bedroll, thankful for the excuse to not go back to sleep right away. She could only hope the hot tea would warm the icy lump in her throat . . . though she doubted it.

Iseult crept through the trees surrounding their camp. He'd sensed something out here, something Faie. As long as it wasn't one of those cursed Geancanach, he would scare it off then return to his companions.

He stepped forward silently, searching for whatever it was he sensed. A low, scuffling noise caught his ear and he turned. *There*. The creature was small, roughly the size of a young calf. It stood on two legs, its knees bent backward like a goat's. Shaggy fur covered most of its lower body, ending on its thin chest, and starting again on its spindly arms. As if sensing his presence, it turned a mostly humanoid face toward him, blinking spherical, milky yellow eyes.

"Bucca," he grumbled, then darted forward.

The creature shrieked, then ran, but Iseult was faster and surpassed it. Before the creature could flit past him, he landed the tip of his short sword against a tree, blocking the Bucca's path.

The little creature blinked up at him, trembling in fear.

"What are you doing here?" he demanded.

The Bucca blinked a few more times. Perhaps it did not understand him. He was about to give up and let the creature go when it hissed, "Hiding. Bucca must hide."

"From what?" he asked. He knew Bucca were among some of the least harmful Faie. Herbwives would tell stories of them stealing children, but at most all they ever stole were small farm animals for their suppers.

The Bucca blinked its strange eyes at him again. "Bucca not warrior. Bucca Light Faie, so Bucca will be made into slave."

Iseult sighed, wishing the creature would just spit out what it was afraid of so he could get back to keeping watch. "Who will make you a slave?" he asked patiently.

He heard voices coming from the camp, and reflexively turned, then cursed. He whipped his gaze back around to find nothing but empty space between him and the tree. He lowered his sword and resheathed it, then turned to see whose voice he'd heard. He'd sent Bedelia to watch the road for possible enemies, and would not be pleased if she'd returned to camp to converse with those who should be sleeping, especially Finn.

He walked on silently until the fire came back into view, and the hushed voices became clear. Kai and Finn sat side by side, whispering to each other. They both turned as he approached the camp.

"You should both be resting," he muttered, keeping his voice low to avoid waking Anna and Sativola, who were supposed to take the next watch. Naoki blinked sleepy eyes at him from the foot of Finn's bedroll.

Kai and Finn stared up at him from their shared seat on a log near the fire, guilty, like children who'd been caught sticking their fingers in their mother's pie.

They glanced at each other, then Kai explained, "Finn couldn't sleep. I heard her rustling about, so I decided to keep her company."

Iseult was quite keen at sensing lies. There was something else going on here. He met Finn's gaze. "Are you well?"

She nodded, a little too quickly. "I'm fine. Just a little nervous to be back on the road. I'm sure I'll sleep better at our next camp."

Another lie, he thought, but saw no point in voicing his suspicions. If she wanted to tell him what was going on, she would in time.

"There was a Bucca lurking around the camp," he explained. "It seemed frightened of something. Perhaps the other queen from the prophecy."

Finn and Kai met each other's gazes once more. They seemed worried.

So was he.

~

ÓENGUS WRAPPED HIS CLOAK MORE TIGHTLY AROUND himself. Blasted Snow Queen. Did she have to let her powers run amok? In front of him, Oighear addressed a gathering of Aos Sí. She seemed an inhuman goddess dressed all in white, standing in a snowfield of her own creation. He supposed the description was fitting, given she'd come back to life after a killing blow.

While he supposed if anyone could help him regain his shadow it would be a Faie goddess, he still felt a measure of remorse at abandoning Keiren. Not that he felt any love for the wicked sorceress, but she was the one who had stolen his shadow to begin with. Surely she was the best chance of restoring it. At one point he wouldn't have cared, but as he'd grown older, he began to fear what might happen if he died without his shadow. Would he end up stuck in this blasted land like a phantom, never able to truly move on?

He shook his head, lifting one foot out of the snow, then the other, though it did nothing to warm his toes.

Oighear continued addressing her warriors. They were to scour the countryside for Faie, recruiting them or enslaving them. He scowled. At least *Keiren* didn't make him stand in the snow with Faie.

Oighear glanced back at him, as if sensing his thoughts. "Gray Lord," she began, a smile curling the corners of her pale pink lips, "Please step forward and tell my men what you know of Finnur and her companions."

He cringed, both at the title, and her request. Though it

was true he was descended from Clan Liath, he'd lost any magic that accompanied his heritage long ago, and he was tired of talking about that blasted tree girl. At least he'd finally found out why Oighear and Keiren were so obsessed with entrapping her. She was the rightful Queen of the Dair Leanbh, and Oighear had let her slip through her icy fingers, right along with the Faie Queen's shroud.

He stepped forward with a sigh, prepared to divulge the paltry amount of information he possessed. If his shadow was not restored soon, perhaps he'd defect and ask Finn to help him. The girl surely was foolish enough to believe any lie he might tell her. She travelled with assassins and thieves, after all.

CHAPTER THREE

*M*aarav leaned against the side of the inn, his hand lifted to shield his eyes from the sun. Though his height and black hair made him stand out in the crowd, most of the townsfolk had grown used to his presence, so none paid him any mind.

He focused on the conversation he'd been listening to, hoping for new information.

"I saw them again last night," a woman said. She was manning a small table filled with fresh baked bread, attempting to sell her loaves to anyone who walked past.

The woman to whom she spoke took the loaf offered to her and exchanged some coin. "I haven't seen any Faie, but I heard the Alderman is planning to do something about it. It was those magic users that brought the Faie here, and we all know what the solution is."

Maarav stroked his chin in thought. He'd heard the rumors of Faie sightings over the past few days. None had neared the burgh that he knew of, but they'd been spotted around the farms on the outskirts, and livestock had started to go missing. The townsfolk would be expecting the Alderman to do something about it soon.

Ealasaid appeared from around the side of the inn, huffing and puffing. Her curly blonde hair was a staticky mess, and mud stained the hem of her simple gray dress. Though she looked a fright, he couldn't help noticing the way her dress color accented her stormy gray eyes, nor the way her freckles stood out against her pale skin in the harsh sun.

She reached his side, then leaned against the wall next to him. "What are you doing out here?" she asked. "I've been looking for you everywhere."

He held a finger to his lips to quiet her, but it was too late. The two women at the bread stall turned to glare at him, then the customer hurried off, loaves in hand.

"Ah," Ealasaid observed. "Eavesdropping again?"

He glared at her. "If you must know, yes. It seems the Alderman has grown uneasy with the recent Faie sightings. He'll be looking for someone to blame." He looked at her poignantly.

She scoffed. "What do *I* have to do with it?"

He rolled his eyes. "You're the leader of An Solas. When the Faie come around, magic users are always the first to catch the blame."

She frowned, then looked down at her feet, her lips sealed in a tight line.

He could have punched himself. Her family had been murdered by An Fiach for that very reason. "Ealasaid—" he began.

"No," she cut him off with a deep breath, returning her

gaze to his, "I understand. And you should probably get away from me as soon as possible before you end up just like my family. Being a magic user has its drawbacks, but it's nothing compared to what happens to those we care about."

They were silent for several moments. She rarely spoke of her family, and when she did, he was never quite sure what to say.

"So," he began hesitantly, "Are you trying to tell me you care about me?" He grinned and waggled his eyebrows at her.

She scowled at him and punched his arm, then laughed.

Good, he thought. *At least she's smiling.* He wasn't used to caring if women smiled, but Ealasaid was different. "I'm not going anywhere," he assured. "Being around a magic user keeps things interesting."

She snorted. "Interesting, huh? I would have chosen a different word." She paused for a moment, then continued, "So the Alderman may be preparing to finally act?" She leaned back against the wall to gaze at the growing crowd in the market. "I suppose An Solas should find a new burgh before he decides to kick us all out without supplies."

He shook his head. "I doubt there is a new burgh to find. Civilization is more spread out in the South than it is in the North. We'd have to travel halfway to Sormyr to find another burgh, and even then we cannot say what condition that burgh might be in."

She turned her gaze up to him, lifting her hand to shield her squinted eyes from the sun. "So what do we do?"

He peered out at the distant estate, surrounded by high walls and guards. He'd heard that Alderman Gwrtheryn rarely left the grounds. He'd feared the Faie long before they started showing up across the land. It would be difficult to sneak past his guards, but . . .

"I think we should have a word with our good Alderman," he explained. "Perhaps he can be reasoned with."

Ealasaid snorted. "Your kind of *reasoning* usually involves daggers and intimidation."

He laughed. She knew him well. "Yes, it's fortunate we have Slàine and her assassins at our disposal."

"Killing the man won't gain us any favor with the people," she argued. "If anything, they'll chase us off themselves."

He placed a hand on her shoulder. "Then I suppose it will be up to you to bat your eyelashes and win him over to our side."

She glared at him, but he continued to smile. An Solas had grown since word of their battle with the Cavari spread to the nearby villages. So many magic users had been displaced by An Fiach, and jumped at the opportunity to actually be accepted for what they were. Soon they would have an army. A small army, but the fact that most could wield frightening magics made them more effective than the militaries of the great cities. If Lord Gwrtheryn came to his senses, they might soon have a fortress.

He knew war was coming whether Slàine, Finn, or Ealasaid wanted it or not. When it hit, he planned to come out on top, no matter what.

~

FINN STROKED LOINNIR'S SOFT MANE AS SHE RODE, marveling at the shimmering white tendrils. White like snow. She could see why Oighear had chosen the unicorn as her prized mount, once upon a time.

She glanced at Kai riding next to her, his gaze cast down in thought. She wouldn't be surprised if he was thinking about their shared dream. She most definitely was. Kai's reminiscence had been eerily similar to hers, save her mother's presence in her dream.

Both visions had ended the same way, with Oighear's icy grip around their throats. Yet, it didn't make any sense. Oighear was dead. At least, she *thought* she was.

"Someone up ahead," Iseult muttered.

Naoki chittered nervously, looking up at Finn in the saddle as if hoping to climb atop Loinnir's back, but she'd grown too large to ride with her.

"Go play," Finn suggested, gesturing toward the tree line, but Naoki simply continued to stare, slinking along beside her.

With a sigh, Finn raised her gaze to a lone figure coming into view down the road. He was on foot, and wore a heavy brown cloak, but that was as much as she could distinguish. At least a lone man likely would not be capable of harming Naoki.

Iseult rode on ahead to intercept the man before he could reach them, while Bedelia sidled her horse up beside Finn's, opposite side where Naoki trotted. Peering toward Iseult and the man, Bedelia reached over her shoulder and partially unsheathed the sword resting across her back.

Loinnir halted without any more prompting as the rest of their party closed in around her. Perhaps they were being overly cautious, but they'd seen few travelers since embarking on their journey, and those they saw tended to travel in large groups for protection. A lone man on the road was an odd sight.

Not liking Iseult venturing forward on his own, Finn narrowed her gaze toward the distance. If the man held weapons that might cause Iseult harm, she would call up the earth around him . . . or at least she would try. Even with her returned memories, her magic still often eluded her unless the moment was dire and she could act without thinking.

The figure continued walking toward Iseult, and soon was near enough for Finn to make out his features. She gasped, then darted her gaze to Kai.

"I can't believe he's not dead," Kai mused, his gaze still on the distant figure, now intercepted by Iseult.

"What in the Horned One's name is he doing this far south?" Anna hissed.

"Likely returning to his parent's Archive," Kai suggested.

Sativola cleared his throat. "Am I supposed to know who this fellow is?"

"He's a friend," Finn blurted, feeling the need to stand up for Anders.

"More of an acquaintance," Anna corrected.

"More of an annoyance," Kai scoffed. "One that might still be a soldier of An Fiach."

Finn clenched her jaw. She'd forgotten about Anders' alleged involvement with the organization. What she hadn't forgotten was Óengus' affiliation with An Fiach. He and his men might still be hunting her, though she'd seen no sign of them since leaving Port Ainfean. What might Anders do if placed under Óengus' command?

In the distance, Iseult nodded, then turned his horse

around and trotted toward them, leaving Anders to jog in his dusty wake.

Finn's fingers trembled as she clutched the locket around her neck. Something didn't feel right. Though she was glad to see Anders, if only to inform him what had become of his sister, she could not trust his presence. She no longer believed in coincidences.

Loinnir shifted her weight from side to side as Iseult neared them. He waved his arm, gesturing for them to retreat from the road.

"We'll rest for a while before continuing on," he called out.

Finn began to obey, then tugged gently on Loinnir's reins as Iseult reached her and cut her off, keeping her behind from the others. "I implore you to trust nothing he says," Iseult whispered, leaning toward her shoulder. "We do not know where he has been, nor with whom he has allied himself. That he made it this far south alive suggests he had help."

Finn nodded, swallowing the lump in her throat before following the others off the road. Sativola and Anna had already dismounted ahead to begin rationing out their food. She hurried Loinnir forward, reaching the others, then dismounted. She handed her reins to Bedelia, then sat next to Kai on a large rock to receive her portion of food. As she took a bite of dried apple and chewed, her gaze lingered on Anders, who finally reached them, panting heavily from trying to keep up with Iseult's horse.

She was unsure how to approach him. Did he blame her for the loss of his sister? Did he blame them all for continuing on their adventure without him? His cheeks were

SARA C ROETHLE

hollow, and he moved as if his bones ached. He'd obviously not fared well in his travels.

"Erm, greetings," Anders muttered, leaving the road to stand awkwardly amongst them. He opened his mouth to say more, then sighted Naoki, who perched behind Finn, staring at the intruder.

"Is that," he began, then shook his head and rubbed his eyes. He blinked a few times, then looked at Naoki again. "Is that a *dragon?*"

Kai snorted, then took a bite of his hard piece of bread. Mouth half-full, he smirked up at Anders and asked, "Get left behind by An Fiach then?"

Anders frowned. He glanced at Naoki again, then shook his head. "I parted ways with An Fiach after learning what type of organization they truly are."

The group's gazes fell hard upon him, while Finn grew increasingly antsy. He'd been their friend once, and now they were all treating him with suspicion, when perhaps they should have been celebrating the fact that they'd all survived thus far. They could at least stand to be polite.

She cleared her throat. "Please sit," she offered, gesturing to a heavy log Sativola was dragging across the ground for seating.

Sativola frowned at her for offering his log, but simply dropped it and walked away in search of another.

Anders watched Sativola's massive back as he retreated, then sat, glancing again at Naoki.

"You claimed to have valuable information," Iseult grumbled as he approached, finished checking over the tied-off horses. "Speak it, then be on your way."

Finn watched as Anders fidgeted in his seat, smoothing

his hands across his cloak, then lifting them to run his fingers through his red hair. "I have news about Àed," he said finally.

Finn's heart fluttered, but she forced it to still. How on earth would Anders know anything about what had happened to Àed? Bedelia had known, but only because she'd been present when Keiren turned him into a tree. The only way for Anders to know such information would have been to learn from Keiren herself. Still, she found that unlikely. How would Anders have come in contact with the elusive sorceress?

"Go on," Iseult said calmly, moving to stand beside Finn, near Naoki.

How he remained so calm was beyond her.

Seeming to gain confidence, Anders lifted his gaze. "The Ceàrdaman informed me, one named Niklas, to be more precise. He is hoping to gain favor with Finn, but feared she would not give him a chance to speak if he came in person."

Iseult nodded, then looked to Finn while Kai muttered under his breath about *blasted, fork-tongued Travelers*.

"I have met Niklas before," she informed the group, seeing no reason to keep the information secret. "He approached me at Maarav's inn in Migris. He offered me partnership."

"But I was with you in Migris," Bedelia interrupted from her perch on a rock near Anna, then blushed. She'd been with Finn in Migris because she'd been working for Keiren, but Finn had forgiven her for that, even if Bedelia hadn't forgiven herself. "I was with you," she began anew, "and I never saw any Travelers. In fact, the city was up in arms over the Faie at the time, one of the Ceàrdaman would have been arrested on sight."

Anders shook his head. "Trust me, they go where they please, especially Niklas."

Iseult cleared his throat. Standing with arms crossed, he directed his icy gaze down at Anders. "Back to your information."

"Ah yes," Anders replied. "I've been told something very important. Only the caster who has imprisoned Àed can set him free."

Finn's stomach churned. Kai met her gaze and shook his head. They both knew who the caster was, and that there was only one person who might be able to find her.

They both turned to look at Bedelia.

She sighed and shook her head. "She will not free him willingly."

"Then we will kill her," Iseult stated matter of factly.

Bedelia whipped her gaze toward him, her eyes wide. "You cannot!" At his scowl, she quickly added, "Not because I would protect her, but because she would kill you. She is more powerful than anything I have ever seen. Her magic could rival even Finn's or Oighear's."

Not reacting at all to Bedelia's words, Iseult turned back to Anders. "What else did this Niklas say?"

Seeming oddly excited to relay the next batch of information, Anders began, "He hoped to arrange a meeting with Finn and her party. He believes he can be of use."

"And what would he ask in return?" Anna spat, crouching somewhat apart from the group. "Last time we dealt with the Travelers, they told Finn a story and kidnapped me in return. I'd rather like to avoid being in their care once more."

Anders' gaze rested on Finn. "Niklas believes war is coming . . . if it isn't already here. He believes you will be an instrumental force in the outcome, and would like you to favor his people in the choices you make."

Finn shook her head. The Travelers could be useful, but she did not trust them. "There must be another way," she muttered.

"At least meet with him," Anders pressed. "Hear what he has to say. I believe he may be able to change your mind."

Iseult snorted. "I imagine *you'll* be accompanying us to this meeting?"

Anders hung his head and wrung his hands, then mumbled, "Well, I *do* know the way to the meeting place. It will take another full day's journey to reach it, perhaps a little longer."

Iseult looked back to Finn.

While she appreciated him deferring to her judgement, this was not a decision she wanted to make. If it was all a trick, it would be her fault when her entire party fell to the Travelers' mercy. Yet, if it was not a trick, it just might be the only way to save Àed. After all he'd done for her, she owed it to him to try.

"Fine," she decided finally. "We will meet with him."

Anders' shoulders slumped in relief. Finn realized she was clenching her jaw again. Why was he so relieved? What did he have to lose or gain in setting up this meeting? Why was he even involved with the Travelers to begin with?

She sighed, then looked up to Iseult, hoping for some

words of comfort or advice. Instead he nodded toward the distant, forested hills, then offered her his hand.

ISEULT RELEASED FINN'S HAND AS THEY BEGAN WALKING AWAY from their temporary camp. He could hear the others begin to mutter questions, asking Anders where he'd been, and just how he'd come across the Travelers. It was information he'd like to know himself, but Bedelia could fill him in upon their return. It was odd given her traitorous start, but he'd grown to trust her more than the others.

The last thing he heard was Sativola returning with a new log, and asking what he'd missed.

Iseult turned his attention away from them. His boots hissed across the dead grass, while the smell of damp earth and decayed plant matter hit his nostrils. He was aware of everything around them, from the small animals scurrying through the underbrush, to the birds up in the trees. He sensed no Faie like the night before, aside from the other-worldly creature walking silently beside him.

They walked on until their companions were out of sight, then stopped in an open copse, partially shaded by the barren trees, their bark black with winter's cold.

He turned to face Finn, taking in her sun-kissed, furrowed brow, and the nervous twisted pout of her mouth.

"Tell me more about Niklas," he said softly, drawing her gaze up to his. The dreary light made her eyes shine dark gray from their normal deep hazel.

She frowned, crossing her cloak-wrapped arms as if cold. "There isn't much to tell. I met him briefly at Maarav's inn. He offered me partnership, then disappeared when Bedelia showed up. I had not heard from him since."

Iseult nodded. "Clearly he chose Anders because of his previous connection to you, but why wait so long to make contact? I wonder what might have distracted him."

Finn shrugged, turning her gaze to the ground. "You know as much as I."

He felt the sudden urge to do something he wouldn't normally do. He was not the type to make physical contact unprovoked, unless he was running his sword through someone's heart, but his body betrayed him. He lifted his hand to her cheek, bringing her gaze back up to his.

Her lips parted in surprise as she stared up at him, wide-eyed.

"I did not mean to frighten you," he said, beginning to lower his hand.

"No," she blurted, reaching out to grab his hand before he could retract it. "You surprised me is all."

With her guidance, he lifted his hand back to her cheek, cradling her face. "I believe Anders will lead us into a trap," he admitted, "but I will follow you anywhere you ask."

"Why?" she asked, her fingertips lingering on his hand so that he could not attempt to lower it once more.

He felt his expression harden. He was not ready for that question. "It is my duty. My people gravely wronged you, and I must set things right."

Her expression fell. "Is that truly why? Do you not care for me at all?"

He inhaled sharply, resisting the urge to pull away. Why was she suddenly asking these questions? Weren't they supposed to be discussing Anders?

At his lack of answer, she finally lowered her hands, then her gaze.

With a heavy sigh, he lifted his other hand to her chin, gently forcing her gaze back up. His heart was thundering in his ears. He wasn't sure what he was doing, but he didn't want her to think he didn't care, even though his words forced her in that direction.

"I care," he forced out. "I care *very* much. But I am a man without a soul, and you are an immortal queen. I could only ever bring you pain, when I have sworn to protect you. You must not focus your energies on me."

He had meant what he'd said to be kind, but her expression crumbled. Tears glistened in her eyes.

"Finn—" he began, but she pulled away and shook her head.

"We should return to the others," she muttered. "We've been away long enough."

He could have fallen on his own sword in that moment. He'd never possessed a way with words, and had never before cared. Perhaps Anders, as an Archive Scholar, could actually be of use. Anders was well read enough that maybe he could teach him to stop saying such idiotic things.

Finn turned away and marched dutifully back in the direction they'd come, making it clear the conversation was over.

He followed her small frame back toward their companions, wracking his brain for something to say, but as usual, the proper words eluded him.

When they returned to the camp, everyone was waiting on them, having eaten and rested. Anders stood apart from the group, a silent, ghost-like shell of the optimistic man he'd once been.

Iseult knew they should have left him there. They should have continued on with their initial plan, not allowing themselves to become entrapped in whatever web the Travelers were weaving. Yet, he kept silent as they remounted their horses. Anna shared Bedelia's horse to supply a mount for Anders.

No one seemed happy about the situation, but they would do it for Àed. Not out of any particular love for the old conjurer, Iseult suspected, but out of a knowing that if *any* of them were enthralled by dark magic, Finn would push everyone else to rescue them just the same.

They rode on into the evening, mostly in silence. Iseult tried to comfort himself with the fact that if Anders betrayed them, he would simply kill the fool, and they all could move on.

Finn didn't meet his gaze as they rode on. Even as hours passed by, she never looked at him. Once they finally stopped to make camp, she stuck by Kai and Anna, eventually going to sleep without a word to spare for him.

When it was time for first watch, he stalked off alone into the woods, feeling quite the fool indeed.

KAI ROLLED HIS EYES IN ANNA'S DIRECTION AS THE PAIR SAT by the fire, taking second watch duty for the night. It was the first opportunity they'd had to speak privately, one they eagerly seized.

"Oh, it's definitely a trap," he whispered. "The last time

we saw him, he was with An Fiach. How did he end up with one of the Ceàrdaman?"

"And what of his sister?" Anna added, her dark eyes reflecting the flickering fire. "He still hasn't even mentioned her, and we know for a fact she's stuck in the Gray Place with her body slowly withering away in our world."

Kai glanced at the sleeping forms of their companions, hoping none were secretly awake listening to them. Anders, at least, had set up a bedroll apart from the group. Kai couldn't blame him, it wasn't like they'd been terribly welcoming of his presence.

"This must have something to do with his sister," he concluded. "When we last saw him, he was still searching for her. Perhaps the Travelers know where her body is, and even where her . . . not body is trapped."

Anna sighed. "If that is his motivation, he's likely desperate. If he knows the state she's in, he will do anything to save her. He's a worthless coward, but from the time we spent with each of them, we know they have an inseparable bond. Most twins do."

One of the blanketed lumps began murmuring in its sleep. Kai listened for a moment, realizing it was Finn. Was she having another dream like they'd had the night before? Would he have one too once he went back to sleep?

"I have something else I need to tell you," he muttered, leaning close to Anna's ear.

She looked at him expectantly.

"Last night," he began, "Finn and I both dreamed of Oighear. I felt her icy grip around my throat, and when I woke, the ground around me was covered in frost."

"But she's dead," she countered. "You saw her die."

He nodded. "Yes, but I've come to realize nothing is clear cut in life and death. If Branwen can be trapped in the in-between, and the Cavari can exist as little more than ghosts, then anything is possible."

Finn's mutters increased.

He stood. "I should wake her."

Anna looked up at him and shook her head, but he moved toward Finn regardless. If she was having another dream of Oighear, he needed to know.

He crouched beside her, listening as Anna's footsteps approached behind him.

"This is because she gave you her blood, isn't it?" she whispered, moving to kneel beside him. "Now you're sharing her dreams. You are hopelessly entangled in the chaos that surrounds her."

He sighed as he reached out to shake Finn's shoulder. Anna was right. He was hopelessly entangled, for better, or for worse.

His hand was almost on her when she stopped muttering. Her breathing seemed to slow back into the normal rhythms of sleep.

"Leave her," Anna whispered. "I don't want Iseult chastising us for robbing her of rest." She peered down at Finn's now peaceful face. "And I must admit, I wouldn't argue with him. She seems . . . frailer than before."

Kai nodded as he stood, then offered Anna a hand up. He had almost pulled her to her feet when he was hit with gut-wrenching nausea. Anna caught herself before she could fall onto Finn as Kai staggered backwards. He lifted a hand to his eyes in an attempt to calm his dizziness.

"What is it?" Anna hissed, righting herself and grabbing onto his arm.

He would have explained if he wasn't about to lose his supper. Suddenly another set of hands took his other arm, and the world seemed to still. He opened his eyes to find Finn at his side with tousled hair and wide eyes.

"They're trying to find us," she rasped. "We have to wake everyone up. We need to travel far away from this place."

"*Who* is trying to find us?" Anna questioned.

"The Cavari," Finn explained. "They were in my dreams. My mother has prevented them from tracking me, so they are using Kai. They're tracking my blood through him."

"Curse you," Anna hissed, then rushed away from Kai to start gathering their supplies.

Finn helped Kai to sit, though the last of his dizziness was now subsiding. Like a dark shadow, Iseult appeared behind her. Though resting just moments ago, he now appeared fully alert.

Finn turned to him. "We have to run. I cannot face them. Not yet."

Iseult simply nodded, then looked down at Kai like it was all his fault. "Wake the others. I'll start saddling the horses."

Finn nodded, but did not immediately obey. Instead she looked down at Kai.

Realizing he likely looked quite pathetic huddling on the ground, he waved her off. "Wake everyone else. I'll be alright."

She bit her lip, but nodded, then hurried away, followed closely by Iseult.

Kai took a steadying breath, chasing away the last of his

dizziness before standing. At least he now understood why he'd fainted in the Garenoch market. The Cavari, immortal ghosts that they were, were using his tie to Finn to track them. How Finn's mother was protecting her, he did not know, but as soon as they were safe he'd implore Finn to figure it out.

He glanced around the nearly-dark campsite, but before he could move to help Anna led his horse to him and handed over the reins. "Are you well enough to ride?"

He nodded, though he wasn't sure. If the Cavari did . . . whatever *that* was again, he'd surely topple from the saddle.

Taking him at his word, Anna gave his shoulder a pat, then hurried over to climb in the saddle with Bedelia.

Sativola, the slowest to rouse, climbed into his saddle with his boots half laced, and his hair puffy from sleep.

Once they were all ready, including Anders on his borrowed horse, Finn led the way at a gallop on her swift white mount, a *unicorn* according to Anna. Naoki darted after her, a small white blur following after the larger one.

Everyone urged their horses to a gallop, reaching the road then turning westward.

The cool night air bit into Kai's flushed skin, slicing his nerves like a knife.

"There's something approaching behind us!" Anna shouted.

Kai glanced over his shoulder, but could see little in the dark. Still, he trusted Anna's judgement. He hadn't fought the Cavari outside of Garenoch, but Anna had, and her recount of events still gave him chills. They had been near immune to magic, but could be overwhelmed with physical attacks. Anna had been helped by Slàine and her assassins, but there would be no such help tonight.

"Keep going!" Finn shouted from the front of the pack, then tugged her unicorn's reins to her right.

Her mount careened off the road, quickly regaining its footing to dart back the way they'd come. Kai watched over his shoulder for a split second, then tugged his reins to slow his mount before turning in a far less graceful loop.

Not taking a moment to second guess himself, he raced after Finn. He was the reason the Cavari had tracked them to begin with, he could not let her face them alone.

Hoofbeats thundered up behind him, then Iseult was riding at his side, his piercing gaze intent on the white unicorn barely visible ahead of them.

FINN'S BREATH HISSED IN AND OUT AS SHE CLUTCHED TIGHTLY to her reins. She could *feel* the immense power ahead moments before she caught sight of the cloaked forms. They stood side by side, blocking the road.

She tugged Loinnir's reins back, hoping to grant herself extra time to consider what she was doing, but the unicorn did not slow.

Instead, it sped right toward the waiting forms, turning as she finally slowed to prance up and down the line of Cavari. Finn gazed down at the hooded figures, unable to see their faces.

"I've made it clear I want nothing to do with you!" she shouted, hating the shrill tone of her voice. She didn't want them to know just how terrified she was of them.

Loinnir stilled her prancing, taking a few steps away as the Cavari bowed their heads. A voice hissed through Finn's mind, "You have claimed the Faie Queen's shroud. You must restore what you took from us."

Her hands gripped so tightly to Loinnir's reins, her knuckles ached. Memories flashed through her mind.

Her people kneeling before her after she'd claimed the souls of those she thought her enemies. They'd worshipped *her for the act. She'd wanted none of it. These . . . creatures did not deserve power, and neither did she.*

She'd run from them. Run as far as she could until she collapsed in a small, peaceful meadow. She'd clutched the Faie Queen's shroud, begging for peace. She'd felt her magic leave her, pouring into the earth as her body stilled. She took root, transforming into a stalwart oak. She knew distantly as her magic left her, that it left her people too. She'd doomed them to walk the earth as little more than phantoms. She felt no remorse.

She shivered back into awareness, knowing something else with certainty. Her return had restored in them a measure of their power. They were dangerous once more, and it was all her fault.

Loinnir had backed further away to face the Cavari, and Iseult and Kai had joined her, their stilled horses on either side of hers.

"What would you have us do?" Iseult muttered, his gaze scanning the line of still, cloaked forms.

What *could* they do? Kill her to rob the Cavari of their magic? Was that the only way to fight these immortal creatures?

The Cavari began to chant, words vaguely familiar to Finn, like something she'd heard in her childhood. Suddenly another memory hit her. *Oighear*. When the Cavari had taken her magic away, they'd used these same words, taking advantage of the treaty she'd signed.

"Use the shroud!" someone shouted from behind them.

She whipped her gaze around to see Anna, off her horse and fighting to keep Naoki back.

"Use the shroud!" Anna shouted again. "They'll kill us all!"

A hand touched Finn's shoulder. *Kai.* "Do it now," he instructed.

A sword hissed from its scabbard at her other side, and she knew she was running out of time. Iseult would fight them all if she did not act. He would fight, and he would die.

She slid down from Loinnir's saddle, then gripped the tattered fabric tied around her waist, fighting the urge to recoil. She could still feel the souls of her victims crying out, though their torment had taken place over a century ago.

She wracked her brain as she approached. She didn't know how to shield herself from their magic. All she knew how to do was steal it.

She took a shuddering breath, calling upon the magic of the shroud, but something was wrong. She felt . . . nothing.

She looked up at the nearest cloaked form. Her face was still in shadow, but Finn could see the curve of her mouth as she smiled at her. She realized in sudden horror they'd somehow cut away her magic. She could not fight them.

She stumbled back. Why hadn't Iseult, Kai, and Anna run? Now she would be unable to protect them.

The Cavari continued to chant. As one, they stepped forward, the nearest one reaching a hand out toward Finn. She knew once they touched her, it would be too late.

The hand inched closer, then her view was interrupted by a flash of white.

Loinnir pranced in front of her, blocking her from the Cavari with her muscular white body. Her horn had reappeared, twinkling in the moonlight as if topped with tiny stars.

The unicorn turned her muzzle toward the Cavari. Her entire body seemed to shimmer as she stomped her front hooves in the dirt.

The Cavari gasped, ceasing their chanting. A hand gripped Finn's shoulder, pulling her back into Kai's waiting arms. He pulled her away as Iseult stalked forward to remain near Loinnir.

She numbly stumbled back with Kai's arm around her waist, guiding her to join Anna, Bedelia, Sativola, and even Anders. Naoki frantically paced around their feet, gazing up at Finn.

"You're all fools," Finn muttered. "I told you to run." She whipped her gaze back to Loinnir, but she and Iseult were already returning to them.

The Cavari were gone.

She held out a hand as Loinnir approached, her glimmering horn still in full sight. Her fingers stroked through Loinnir's soft mane, right between her ears.

She stared up at the creature in awe, as her friends muttered in disbelief around her. Loinnir had sent the Cavari away, all on her own.

Finn gulped. Perhaps this was why Oighear had chosen Loinnir, and why Eywen gave her to Finn. She found herself wishing she could talk to the long-dead Aos Sí warrior. Had he known she would need protection from her people? Protection only Loinnir could afford her?

She wrapped the Faie Queen's shroud back around her waist, knotting it securely, then turned her gaze to Iseult. "Let us leave this place. Kai will ride with me, just in case they try to track him again. Perhaps Loinnir will nullify their magic even from a distance."

No one argued.

Loinnir patiently allowed both Finn and Kai to climb upon her back. They continued their journey well into the night, never once discussing stopping to rest. It was clear everyone understood just how close they had come to losing everything.

CHAPTER FOUR

*E*alasaid pressed her back against the tower wall, waiting for Maarav's signal. She'd argued against a nighttime assault. She wanted to at least give Lord Gwythern a chance to negotiate, but Maarav had quickly put the argument to rest. Terrified of the Faie, Gwythern never left his estate, and allowed few to enter. No one but his closest advisors had even seen him in months.

She strained her eyes to see in the darkness, wishing she could summon a bolt of lightning to temporarily illuminate her surroundings. She pushed a lock of curly hair behind her ear and squinted in the direction of the estate's main gate.

A dark shape darted across her field of vision, then another. Slàine's assassins. Tired of lodging at the inn, they'd been more than willing to take part in Maarav's plan.

She heard an *oof* sound as one of the guards was taken down. Gritting her teeth, she resisted the urge to rush forward and verify that the assassins weren't actually killing anyone. It had been agreed upon that they would be tied and gagged, nothing more.

"You're supposed to be hiding," a voice whispered behind her.

She nearly jumped out of her skin, then whirled toward the voice.

Maarav gazed down at her, looking like a disembodied head with his black clothing and hair in the darkness.

She glared at him. "I *am* hiding," she whispered. "I just needed to be close enough to hear your signal."

He raised a dark brow at her. "And close enough to make sure no one harms the guards?"

She frowned, but could not argue. "I can take care of myself," she said instead. "There's no reason for me to hide farther away."

He leaned his face close to hers. "Yes, my girl, I am well aware of your abilities." Straightening, he gazed past her toward the gate.

"Is it time?" she whispered, unable to see whatever he'd noticed.

He turned to smile at her, then lifted his hands to his face, cupping them around his mouth. He let out a loud *hoot*, sounding remarkably like an owl, then let out a second.

From somewhere within the gates, another hoot echoed, then another from the guard tower above them.

Maarav looked down at her. "Remember what I told you. Let Slàine's people do all the work. Just stay out of sight until we find Gwythern."

She opened her mouth to argue, but he was already off, running toward the gate like a silent shadow. Cursing under her breath, she pulled the hood of her cloak up over her hair and hurried after him.

Reaching the gate, she looked around for Maarav, spotting him climbing up a rope that had been draped down from a secondary guard tower. She rushed over toward the rope, reaching it just as Maarav disappeared into the tower above.

She peered at the rope's end dubiously. She'd grown up on a farm, and was not weak for someone of her size, but she'd never climbed straight up a rope before, and the tower opening was a long way up.

"This way," a voice said from behind her, nearly startling her out of her skin a second time.

She turned to see Tavish grinning behind her, his red hair covered by a black head wrap. Silently he took her hand, then dragged her back toward the tall iron bars of the gate. Another black-clad figure waited there, holding one side of the gate open just enough for her and Tavish to slip through.

"I never did like climbing up ropes," Tavish muttered.

Dashing inside, Ealasaid had no time to observe who had let them in as they darted off into the night.

Tavish grabbed her hand and started tugging again. "We're to go around the back," he whispered as he coaxed her to run. "Rae should already be there to let us in."

"What about Maarav?" she hissed.

Tavish smirked at her as they ran. "He's more of a *barge in through the front door* type."

Panting as she tried to keep up, Ealasaid merely shook her head. If Maarav broke his promise that none would come to harm she'd . . . well, she didn't know what she'd do, but whatever it was, it would be rather unpleasant for Maarav.

They ran across the central courtyard, then scurried behind the tall shrubs lining the side walls of the estate. She could see black clad shapes darting around here and there, but no guards. The assassins had been quite thorough.

With Tavish still holding her hand, she nearly slipped on the icy grass as they reached the back of the main building. Tavish deftly pulled her out of her skid, then tugged her toward the wall of the estate.

"There may still be guards on this end," he whispered, "so keep your wits about you."

She didn't appreciate the implication that she'd lost her wits, but she was so nervous she merely nodded.

Tavish grinned, then dropped her hand to approach the large double doors at the back end of the building, leading out to expansive gardens, gray and withered from the cold.

As he crept toward the door, someone shouted from the nearby shadows. Reacting instantly, Ealasaid summoned a bolt of lighting seconds before a sword-wielding guard rushed at Tavish. The lightning hit the man in the chest, and he dropped to the ground.

Wide eyed, Tavish looked up at her as she hurried toward him, then down at the guard. The man was very, *very* still, and Ealasaid could smell burned flesh as she approached. Her lightning had hit the metal breastplate the guard wore, scorching it black.

"And here I was worried about *you* killing someone," she muttered in disbelief.

With a roll of his eyes, Tavish grabbed the man by the

arms and dragged him into the nearby bushes. Ealasaid watched on, shaken.

The body hidden, Tavish returned to her side. "Are you well?"

Guilt coursed through her. What if the man had a wife and children? He might have been innocent, *good*, and she'd taken his life.

"No," she answered. "Let's get this over with."

Not seeming to comprehend her internal conflict, Tavish hurried back toward the double doors.

Pushing away her guilt to be dealt with at a later time, she followed him. As she neared the double doors, one side swung inward, revealing Rae's dark skinned face. He wore no headwrap like Tavish, but had donned the same all-black attire.

"Way to clear out the guards," Tavish hissed. "I nearly got run through with a sword. If it weren't for little lady lightning bolt here—"

"Quiet," Rae ordered, then disappeared into the building.

Tavish shrugged, his smile never faltering, then spun his hand into a sweeping bow, admitting Ealasaid to the premises. She walked into the darkness to find Rae waiting inside, amidst several bound guards. A few appeared to be unconscious, but all seemed to be breathing.

She opened her mouth to thank Rae for following orders, but her words were stolen by a massive clattering sound somewhere upstairs, followed by frantic shouts.

Suddenly any annoyance she had with Maarav was wiped away. She rushed past Rae toward the nearest set of stairs. Tavish hissed after her to stop, but did not follow.

MAARAV CRINGED AT THE SOUND OF HEAVY CLATTERING, followed by shouts. What had those fools done now? He lowered himself the rest of the way down from the window he'd been climbing through, dropping silently to the floor. If Ealasaid was involved in the chaos, he'd skewer everyone responsible for putting her in harm's way. Tavish would be first, as he'd been entrusted with the task of looking after her.

He hurried across the ornate rugs bedecking the long hall he'd entered. Everything was dark and quiet in this wing of the estate, but that meant little. Anyone could be hiding in the dark rooms bordering the hall, and could rush out at any moment. He hoped to honor his promise to Ealasaid, but if it was a choice between his life and another's, he'd always choose his.

Knowing he was fully capable of dealing with threats as they came, he raced down the rest of the hall at full speed. At the end was a door, muffling the sound of continued shouts on the other side.

He paused for a moment to listen. Someone was barking shrill orders, partially drowned out by the sound of boots thudding and armor clinking. Perhaps the commotion hadn't been caused by any of Slàine's people. It seemed like Gwythern was desperately rousing more guards to protect him.

Maarav placed his hand on the door handle, ready to peek inside, then quickly turned at the sound of footfalls on the nearby stairs. He pressed his back against the wall and waited, ready to take down whoever was rushing toward him.

He darted out as the figure flew past, then had to stop himself from putting her in a strangle hold. Ealasaid kicked out, bruising his shin with such force she went tumbling to the floor.

His thundering heart belied his outward calm as he peered down at her. "Do you care to explain yourself?" he whispered.

Even in the darkness he could see her blush.

Sensing a change in the commotion, he darted toward the floor, gripped her upper arms, and hauled her to her feet. With no time to explain, he dragged her into a nearby room just as the door he'd been listening by thudded outward. Guards swarmed into the hall.

"I could have sworn I heard something out here," a guard hissed.

Pressing Ealasaid against the wall near the room's door, Maarav quieted his breathing. He could not be sure how many more guards waited within the adjacent room, so it was best to stay put and wait for more of Slàine's people to join them.

A fine tremble started in Ealasaid's body, pinned against his. She was so fierce half the time that he often forgot she was not used to the life of a mercenary or assassin. She was used to living a quiet life on a farm . . . before she'd been chased away, and her family slaughtered.

He lowered his face and pressed his cheek against hers, silently urging her to stay calm.

Footsteps sounded directly outside the room's open door, then passed.

"Check the guard towers outside," ordered an investigating guard. "Wilkes should have reported in by now."

Several sets of footsteps thundered away.

Maarav relaxed, then stepped away from Ealasaid, releasing her. She gazed up at him. "I killed someone," she whispered. "If I wouldn't have panicked, I could have just knocked him down, but I killed him."

He wasn't quite sure what to say. He'd taken so many lives, he felt nothing at the thought of taking another. "You fought at Uí Néid," he attempted to console.

She shook her head. "I showered lightning bolts into a crowd of soldiers. I likely only panicked them, or perhaps singed a few."

He sighed. They didn't have time for a moral crisis, but she just looked so . . . sad.

Not knowing what else to do, he kissed her cheek and whispered, "We'll talk about it later." Though when later came, he was quite sure he'd have no clue what to say.

EALASAID FOLLOWED MAARAV OUT INTO THE HALL. THE soldiers that had come to investigate had disappeared down the stairs, and the door to the adjacent room was once again shut, though murmuring voices could still be heard inside.

She looked to Maarav for instruction. She'd come to the conclusion that Gwythern was likely behind the closed door, but many other men were too. They were so close to achieving their goal, but where were the rest of Slàine's people?

As if summoned by her thoughts, Tavish appeared on the

stairs. He crept up slowly until he noticed them, then hurried up the rest of his ascent.

"You can't just go running off like that during a mission," he hissed, glaring at Ealasaid. "Have you lost your mind?"

He raised his gaze to Maarav standing behind her, then audibly gulped. She turned to observe Maarav's deadly gaze. A gaze she'd never seen him give until that moment.

"You were supposed to watch her," he growled.

Tavish began to back down the stairs.

Maarav started to go after him, but Ealasaid stopped him with a hand on his chest. "I ran off," she explained. "There was no stopping me. It was not his fault."

Maarav had no chance to reply, as the nearby door swung open, revealing a plump man with a perfectly groomed, graying beard, and hair that had once been red, but was now white at the temples. He wore a fine silk night-shirt, and held a lit candelabra in his hand. Behind him stood a few other men and women, though none appeared to be soldiers.

He looked up at Maarav and gulped. "Oops," he squeaked, then stepped back, raising his free hand and candelabra in surrender.

Maarav stepped around Ealasaid to place himself between her and the small gathering of nobles within the room. She assumed the plump man was Gwythern, judging by the jewels on his fingers, along with how those in the room yet looked to him for guidance.

Maarav stepped into the room, claiming the space Gwythern had relinquished. Ealasaid moved aside as Tavish, having gathered his courage, walked in after him.

"Stay back!" Gwythern shouted, cowering further back

into the room to stand with his fellow nobility. He held up his hands as if to ward off a blow, even though all Maarav and Tavish did was enter the room and stare at him.

Still in the doorway, Ealasaid turned as someone hurried up the stairs, then took a step further to the side of the door when she realized it was Slàine. Maarav had told her not to fear his long term mentor, but Ealasaid still found the woman unnerving. She'd seen her fight more than once, and knew Slàine could easily slit her throat in the blink of an eye.

With only her pale eyes showing from within her black headwrap, Slàine raised a gray eyebrow at Ealasaid, then strode past her into the room to address Gwythern. A few more assassins hurried up the stairs and followed her in.

"Your men have all been captured," Ealasaid caught Slàine explaining. "You will submit to our terms, or suffer a similar fate."

Ealasaid peeked back into the room as a few of the men and women gasped. Gwythern was practically trembling. "Wh-who are you?" he stammered. "What do you want?"

"We are An Solas," Ealasaid blurted, stepping into the room. If she truly wanted to make a name for her group, she needed to represent them. "And we would like to protect Garenoch while offering a safe haven to magic users."

Gwythern's eyes practically bugged out of his head. "M-magic?" He turned his gaze back to Maarav, the most imposing of the group, as if wondering what sort of magic he might wield.

Ealasaid sighed, sincerely hoping the man wouldn't wet himself. A few more assassins hurried up the stairs. They passed Ealasaid as they entered the room, then muttered to

Slàine that the mission had been fully accomplished, all guards had been captured.

Slàine turned back to Gwythern. "How big is your dungeon?"

"D-dungeon?" he stammered, his face growing increasingly flushed.

The nobles behind him began to back away, glancing about nervously for an escape route.

Slàine huffed irritably, then turned to Tavish. "Find the dungeon. Transport the majority of the guards there." She turned back to Gwythern. "I hope you have enough cells to hold everyone."

"No!" Ealasaid argued, directing her gaze to Slàine. "We only wanted to negotiate. The guards are not to be held prisoner."

Slàine raised her gray brow at Ealasaid once more. "So you would set them free to stab us in the back at their first convenience?"

"Slàine," Maarav muttered. "Ealasaid is in charge here. If we have given our allegiance to An Solas, we must defer to her wishes."

"Not if those wishes are foolish," Slàine snapped.

Ealasaid bristled, ready to argue further, but Tavish stepped forward. "Now, now, perhaps we should not argue in front of the hostages."

Slàine and Maarav both glared at him, then turned back to Gwythern. "Over there," Slàine demanded, nodding toward the a long table and chairs on the opposite end of the room.

Gwythern startled, then hurried toward the table with Slàine prowling right in after him.

Maarav looked to Ealasaid. "If you're hoping to negotiate, this is your chance. If Gwythern will not meet our terms, we'll have to go with Slàine's plan."

Ealasaid sighed, cast a wary glance at Slàine's back, then proceeded toward the table, followed by Maarav. Tavish and the other assassins remained to keep an eye on the lesser nobles.

"Lord Gwythern," Ealasaid began, approaching the table as he and Slàine sat adjacent each other. "The world is changing," she continued, "and the Faie coming forward is an inevitability. We must band together, and we must use your estate as our base. It is the most fortified location in the Southeast."

She took a seat, lacing her hands together atop the table. She hoped she looked cool and collected, but the look Slàine gave her said that she, at least, saw through the act.

While Gwythern hunched over, a woman standing with the nobles glared at her fellow captives, then stepped away from the group, drawing Ealasaid's attention. She was an entire head taller than Gwythern, with steely gray eyes, and hair just a few shades lighter. She wore a heavy red brocade coat over her dressing gown, making her appear large and stately.

"The magic users attract the Faie," the woman explained, boldly approaching the table. She stopped a few paces away, then looked Ealasaid up and down in her seat. "Scum like you are the reason we're in this whole mess to begin with."

Maarav stepped forward to her defense, but Ealasaid raised a hand to stop him. "It's alright." She turned her attention back to the woman as she stood to address her. "And *you* are?"

The woman raised her nose even higher into the air. "I am Lady Síoda, Lord Gwythern's wife."

Realizing she'd found the true ruler of Garenoch, Ealasaid rethought her approach. Lady Síoda would not be frightened into cooperating. She might, however, be bribed with the promise of power.

Acting much more calm than she felt, Ealasaid began to pace, not allowing her gaze to fall to Maarav, fearing it would make her seem weak. Síoda would not defer to her husband, and Ealasaid would not defer to her . . . well, to whatever Maarav was to her.

Síoda watched her pace with a calculating gaze.

Drawing the moment out, Ealasaid took a few more steps, before turning to face her. "Garenoch is a small burgh, is it not?" she questioned.

Síoda's brow furrowed. "What does that have to do with anything? I demand you leave our estate at once before you bring the Faie right to our door."

Ealasaid resumed her pacing. Out of the corner of her eye she could see Maarav and Slàine, the latter still lounging in her seat, watching her curiously. She stopped again. "I must say, I respect your devotion to such a small, powerless burgh. Truly, I'd expect the likes of you in one of the great cities."

Síoda's gaze narrowed. "I'm still not seeing your point."

Gwythern stood and fluttered his hands in the air near his wife, obviously hoping to stay her tongue before the scary assassins threw them all in the dungeon.

Ignoring him, Ealasaid continued. "You know, though Garenoch is small and would be conquered with ease, I see some potential here. The location is ideal for defense. With the crags to the south, and the forests to the east and west, routes of attack are limited." She began pacing again, then stopped and spun on her heel. "Of course, any hopes of defense are mere dreams without an army."

Síoda's expression grew thoughtful, though her gaze remained narrowed "And what, your mages would be that army?" she asked skeptically.

Ealasaid shrugged. "Perhaps, if our terms are met. If you can tolerate magic-wielding *scum* in your presence, then perhaps Garenoch will not be utterly obliterated when this war begins."

"War?" Gwythern gasped.

His concerns were echoed by the other nobles in the room. Perhaps she'd gone too far with her show of bravado. If she got everyone up in arms about war, they might not be willing to take any risks.

"Your mages," Síoda began, silencing the muttering. "How many of you are there?"

Ealasaid's knees went a bit weak. Should she tell her they were only twenty? Probably not.

"Our ranks are growing every day," she replied cryptically.

Maarav finally stepped forward, his hand stroking the pommel of his sword menacingly. "And they are protected by the finest warriors," he added. "Men and women capable of disabling every single one of your guards without you noticing something was amiss until we were upon you."

At Maarav's closeness, the slightest hint of fear sparked in Síoda's eyes. "I will allow your people to remain within the burgh," she said evenly, "but not within the walls of the estate."

"Not good enough," Slàine snapped, pounding her palms against the table as she stood.

Síoda raised a brow at her. "I do not remember inviting you to this negotiation."

Tavish snickered. "You didn't invite any of us."

Ealasaid resisted slapping a palm to her face. She had never negotiated a single alliance in her life, but somehow she was still better at it than any of the assassins.

She stepped forward before things could get out of hand. "We will be staying within the walls of the estate, or we will leave the burgh all together. I assure you, without our presence the Faie will still come, and you will not stand a chance against them."

Síoda's mouth hardened into a firm line. Never even glancing at her husband for agreement, she nodded curtly. "I suppose I have no choice. You have proven our defenses are limited, and I would not allow my burgh to fall to ruin as a result of my pride."

Ealasaid resisted the urge to grin. Instead she turned toward Maarav and Slàine. "Bring the guard captains so that Lady Síoda can relay their new orders, then gather the rest of An Solas. We will move onto the grounds tonight." She turned back to Síoda. "I trust you will not mind if we make use of the outbuildings?" She didn't want to stay in the main estate no matter what Maarav or Slàine might say. She wouldn't be surprised if Síoda changed her mind and attempted to knife her in the dark.

Síoda nodded curtly.

She turned back in time to see Tavish venture into the hall, then six more black-clad assassins came marching in.

"Make sure our Lord and Lady are well . . . protected," Tavish instructed as he exited.

The assassins nodded, and Ealasaid was quite sure she could hear Gwythern panting in fear. While she wanted to foster a relatively trusting relationship with the Lord and Lady of Garenoch, she would sleep better knowing they would be watched by Slàine's people.

Maarav moved to her side. "I'll accompany you to gather An Solas. They'll believe you more readily than they'll believe me."

She almost snorted, then remembered their present company. She turned and nodded to both Síoda and Gwythern. "I bid you goodnight. We can begin to plan our new fortifications in the morning."

Síoda nodded in return, while Gwythern stared at his wife like she'd just grown a second head.

Ealasaid sighed in relief as Maarav led her out of the room.

"You did well," he whispered, leaning close to her shoulder.

They entered the hallway and headed toward the stairs. She couldn't help but wonder if he was simply being nice. Had she truly just successfully negotiated with the Lord and Lady of a burgh five times the size of her own small village?

"Do you think they'll try to turn on us?" she muttered.

"Oh most certainly," Maarav said happily. "But I have faith you will lead us past that barricade without huge incident."

She stopped walking down the stairs to balk at him.

He chuckled and placed his hand at the small of her back

to urge her forward. "Too much pressure?" he mused. "We could always change our minds and do things *my* way."

She cringed and shook her head. "No, no, I will continue to navigate this new territory myself."

Maarav simply nodded and began to whistle a happy tune, giving her the impression that he was perhaps a bit mad. If Síoda only knew the fate Ealasaid had saved her from, she'd be kissing her scummy mage feet for a year.

～

"Garenoch?" Óengus questioned. "What in Tirn Ail could be interesting in Garenoch?"

Oighear sneered at him. She'd drawn together a meeting of her Aos Sí commanders, along with a few humans he did not recognize, likely drawn into her affairs just as he had been. Óengus wondered if the man and woman, both roughly ten years his seniors with the soft skin and delicate hands of the upper class, were from a magical bloodline like himself.

"There is a human magic user there who interests me," Oighear explained after a moment of seeming debate.

"One of the two queens?" he questioned, having already discovered to what he alluded from one of the Aos Sí.

She glared at him, probably still humiliated to have learned of the prophecy so late. She'd been asleep for a *long* time, and had missed much as the world of men lived on without her.

She watched his face for a moment, then smiled. "Yes, I believe you know of her. I would like you to go to

Garenoch. Be my human spy, and you will earn that which you so desire."

He peered up at her as she rose from her seat, then slunk around the table to stand before him. From within her white feathered cloak she withdrew a rough, misshapen, clear stone. She offered it to him.

He took it gingerly.

"Speak your nightly reports into this crystal," she instructed. "I must know all that happens within the burgh. Even things you may deem insignificant. Keep an eye on any visitors as well."

He gazed down at the small crystal as tension ate away at his gut. The only human magic user he could think of was Keiren. Was she one of the queens? He wondered if he should tell Oighear that Keiren would catch him the moment he began to spy, but he ultimately decided to keep his mouth shut.

He was tired of eternal winter, and thirsted for action. If Keiren *did* find him, well, perhaps he could play the two queens against each other. They each might be more eager to give him what he desired, in exchange for information on their adversary.

He tucked the crystal away into a pouch at his belt, then stood. "I shall depart immediately."

Oighear smiled, a wicked gleam in her eye. "Yes, you will."

As he exited the room, he wondered if his previous thoughts had been wise. Perhaps Oighear *wanted* him to strike a deal with Keiren. A deal that might end in the sorceress' death.

While he held little love for Keiren, life would be much

less interesting without her. In addition, while he did not make a habit of caring for the wellbeing of the common folk, even he could admit that even a crazy witch like Keiren was better than the alternative waiting in the room behind him.

CHAPTER FIVE

*F*inn shook herself, still not feeling entirely awake. She looked down at the mug of hot herbal tea in her hands, wishing the soothing liquid could somehow wash away the previous evening.

They'd ridden through the night to distance themselves from the Cavari's magic, even though Loinnir seemed able to protect them. Finn could not face the Cavari again, at least not yet. Before the encounter, her fear had waned. She'd concluded that since she was their rightful queen and now had the shroud they could not harm her. How wrong she'd been.

She looked to Bedelia and Anna, thoroughly brushing their horses' backs that no discomfort would be incurred from their saddles. Next her gaze found Kai and Sativola, sitting on a log while rubbing their tired eyes, muttering quietly to each other. Next, her gaze flicked to Anders sitting alone, waiting to lead them to their meeting with Niklas despite the previous night's events. Finally, her gaze found Iseult. His sword across his lap, he studiously sharpened it with a whetstone, either not feeling Finn's gaze on him, or simply ignoring it.

She sighed. He probably blamed her for the confrontation, for turning back instead of running away, but there had been no other choice. They were using her blood in Kai's veins to track them. Her mother had been protecting her, shielding her from the Cavari's magic, and perhaps Loinnir had been doing the same. Yet, neither of those connections extended to Kai. The Cavari had somehow figured out what Finn had done for him, and were now using it against them.

She turned her eyes back down to her tea, shivering despite the mug's warmth. Part of her wished her people *would* take her magic away. They could end her painful existence and give her peace once more.

She glanced again at her companions, knowing she could not accept such a fate. If she were gone, who would protect them from the war to come? Most of them could protect themselves with weapons, but against magic, they were sorely outmatched.

She nearly jumped when Kai appeared at her side.

Gazing down at her, he lifted his brow. "Are you sure you are well?"

Her eyes wide, she nodded.

He offered her a hand up from her perch, just as Naoki came crashing back into camp. Anders let out a shrill whimper at the sight of the juvenile dragon, then glanced around nervously, as if to determine whether or not anyone had heard him squeal.

Fighting her smile, Finn took a final sip of her tea,

dumped the rest, then put her hand in Kai's to stand. Together they joined Anna and Bedelia, now saddling the horses.

Loinnir eyed Finn as she approached, as if she too questioned her emotional health, and perhaps her sanity. Finn stroked her fingers across Loinnir's white forehead, just below where she thought her horn was, invisible once again. Loinnir's sparkling blue gaze bore straight into her soul.

"Up you go," Kai suggested, drawing Finn out of her thoughts.

Feeling oddly like she was still in a dream, she smiled gratefully to him, then hoisted herself into the saddle, tugging up her breeches as they sagged around her waist. She'd have plenty more time to organize her thoughts while they rode toward the meeting place, an encounter she was almost looking forward to. Though she did not trust the Travelers, perhaps Niklas could give her information on what her people tried to do to her.

Kai climbed up in the saddle behind her, surrendering his mount to Anders. She took comfort in his warmth at her back. Comfort in the warmth they *all* shared with her. If Niklas tried to take one of her friends as payment for the information she needed, she would kill him herself.

Anna and Bedelia both climbed into their respective saddles and moved to wait near Finn and Kai. Soon they were joined by Sativola and Anders, the latter of which rode on Kai's horse. Iseult was the last to mount after dousing their fire and covering it with dirt. She watched him mount, but averted her eyes before he noticed her. He was acting strange . . . stranger than usual, and it made her nervous. As the others guided their horses toward the road, Loinnir began to move forward, not requiring instruction.

Surprisingly, Anders moved his horse near Loinnir. Flicking his gaze first to Kai, he then settled on Finn, eyeing her expectantly.

She wondered if there was something she should say. Should she tell him about Branwen? He was yet to mention his sister, but surely he'd appreciate hearing of Finn and Anna's encounter with her.

"You've changed," he commented, surprising her further. He smiled, softening the accusation in his words. "Too much time around Iseult, I suspect."

"I'm not sure what you mean," she muttered.

He glanced around at their companions, slowly dividing into pairs as they conversed amongst themselves, then back to her. "You seem . . . colder," he explained. "World weary. After last night . . . " his gaze went distant, as if remembering the event. He shook his head. "You went back and faced them on your own. You were so brave. Today, I'm still terrified, yet the rest of you act as if nothing has happened."

She frowned. That's exactly what she'd thought when she first saw Anders, the world weary part, at least. Not really affected by anything because everything had already happened. "It's difficult sometimes to remain excitable," she commented, still wary of his intent.

"That it is," he muttered. "I never once thought when leaving my family's Archive that things would end up like this."

"Like what?" she pressed, hoping to gain information on where he'd been, and what he'd been through since they'd parted ways.

"With my sister gone, and everyone looking at me like I'm a criminal," he replied. "I'm confused on what I have done to cause everyone to distrust me so." He eyed her intently. "Especially you."

"Except join An Fiach," Kai muttered behind her.

She shook her head. "I'm slowly learning that it's best to distrust everyone until they've proven beyond a shadow of a doubt that they have earned it."

Anders smirked. "Like I said, you've changed."

They were silent for a while after that. The group had spread out further with Iseult in the lead. Their horses kicked up road dust in soft clouds around them. Finn knew before long she'd be wishing for a bath, though she wasn't likely to get one any time soon, at least not until they reached Sormyr.

Brushing back an unruly tress of hair that had fallen across her face, she glanced at Anders, warring with herself to live by her own words. He had not earned her trust, and Iseult had explicitly instructed her to be wary of him, but . . . "What do you mean, your sister is gone? You never found her?"

She felt Kai tense behind her, though he did not comment.

Anders sighed. "No, I never found her, though I searched high and low. The entire reason I joined An Fiach was to hunt down the Faie creatures who *took* her." He aimed a glare at Kai.

Finn cleared her throat, regaining his attention. "And when you did not find her, you departed from their ranks?"

Anders averted his gaze, making Finn wish she had not spoken. "I left for many reasons," he muttered. "But yes,

Branwen was part of it. After that I met Niklas, and he informed me that my sister was dead."

Finn bit her lip. Should she tell him? In truth, there was likely little hope for Branwen, even though her physical body was still alive . . . at least it had been alive when she saw Branwen in the Gray Place.

"So he informed you of Branwen's fate," she began, still mulling over her options, "and for that, you have joined the ranks of the Ceàrdaman?"

Anders, whipped his gaze up to hers, his eyes wide. "N-no, I have not joined their ranks, not in the slightest. I simply owed him a favor for the information. You know how the Travelers are."

Loinnir began to prance beneath her, nearly jostling her from the saddle. Kai wrapped an arm around her waist before she could slip off.

Finn looked around for what might have startled the unicorn, fearing the Cavari's return, but their surroundings were still, and none of her other companions seemed alarmed.

Anders eyed Loinnir cautiously. "I wonder what startled her," he commented as she seemed to calm.

Finn cast a speculative eye on Anders. By this point, she was quite sure Loinnir could understand human speech. Had there been something in Anders' words that alarmed her?

He's lying, a thought echoed in her mind.

She nearly gasped, but managed to stifle her surprise. Loinnir's peaceful gait resumed. The unicorn turned her head for a brief moment, meeting Finn's gaze with one blue eye.

"A favor?" she asked distantly, recalling Anders' words.

"Y-yes," he stammered. "In exchange for the information of my sister's fate."

She frowned, then pressed, "This seems a steep cost for information you could have figured out yourself, eventually."

Anders skin seemed to pale, and was that sweat on his brow? "I was unable to dictate my own terms," he explained. "I wanted the information, and this was the cost." He urged his horse ahead of Finn's, cutting off her next question.

She watched his back silently, wondering about the true terms of his deal with Niklas, and what he had to lose should he fail.

Kai leaned forward to hover near her shoulder. "We should reconsider this meeting."

She nodded, deep in thought, but truly felt even more motivated to attend the meeting, if only to find out exactly what sort of trap Anders had caught himself in.

ANDERS WIPED THE SWEAT FROM HIS BROW AS HE DUG HIS heels into his horse's sides. He'd never been a good liar, and he was lying more than ever. He could only hope Niklas had nothing nefarious planned for Finn and her companions, and that he'd had nothing to do with the Cavari finding them the night before. As far as he knew, Niklas genuinely desired the partnership, but then, why was he cavorting with Keiren? Keiren desired Finn's immortality to destroy the barrier to the in-between. He wasn't sure of all that

Keiren's plan entailed, but he assumed it would not be pleasant for Finn.

He felt a shiver, then turned to find Iseult watching him. He resisted the urge to gulp. Whatever might happen at the forthcoming meeting, he would be sure to get far, *far* away from Iseult.

Tearing his gaze away from Iseult, he eyed the rest of Finn's companions, including the crazed little dragon, and what perhaps was an actual unicorn. If Niklas aimed to cause Finn harm, they would *all* come after him. He was sure of that.

His shoulders slumped as he turned his gaze forward, wiping at the nervous sweat on his brow. He was no fighter, he never had been. His wits had gotten him this far, but he had a terrible feeling his time was running out. He was thoroughly caught in the Traveler's web. He could try to run, but Niklas would find him, and *definitely* would not help Branwen then.

Thinking of Branwen, he sighed. Perhaps he was doing her a disservice by returning her to these dark, ugly times.

Things were only bound to get worse.

By the time they stopped for their midday meal, Finn had thoroughly mulled over her conversation with Anders and had made her final decision about the meeting. Though Iseult had distanced himself from her, she felt she at least owed him the opportunity to voice his opinion before they reached the meeting place.

After dismounting, the party fell into their usual routine

of Anna passing out portions of food, and Bedelia boiling water over a small fire for tea.

Finn held her portion of dried apples and salty cheese in her hands, not feeling much urge to eat them. Instead, she approached Iseult, standing apart from the group as usual, and boldly met his gaze before she could think better of it.

"We need to speak," she said evenly.

He nodded, glanced down at the food in her hands, then gestured for her to lead the way.

She chose a small path through the young pine trees, walking just far enough that she could be sure their companions were out of earshot . . . though Anders' ears were the only ones she was evading.

Iseult followed her, then stopped when she did, remaining silent.

Feeling awkward with the food in her hands, she offered it to him since she hadn't seen him take any.

He shook his head. "You need to eat."

Eat? she thought. How could she even think about eating when every time she tried to relax, unsavory memories came swarming in. She inadvertently touched the shroud around her waist, covering the hips of her breeches. The tasks before her seemed too much.

"I'll eat later," she sighed. Not wanting to waste her food, she sandwiched the cheese between the apples and wrapped them in a piece of cloth from the small pouch at her belt, before placing the whole bundle back into the pouch.

Iseult observed her every movement to the point she felt uncomfortable.

With the food out of sight, she cleared her throat. "I believe Anders is lying about his intentions, but I'd like to attend the meeting regardless. After the meeting with the Cavari . . . " she trailed off.

"You feel powerless," he finished for her.

Her jaw fell open. Just when she thought he'd completely shut her out, he surprised her with his insight.

"Yes," she admitted. "I feel like I need help. Even with my memories . . . " she shook her head. "There's just too much I still don't know. I was fairly young when I gave up my magic and retreated. I don't understand the politics of the Dair completely, nor do I fully understand my role, and the power that accompanies it. I don't know if they want me to rule, or if they want to kill me and replace me with another."

He nodded. "Whatever they intend, they want to control you. They attempted to take you by force when you first returned to this land, and it seems their tactics have not changed."

She frowned. "I apologize for returning to face them. It was idiotic of me to assume I could prevail on my own."

He placed a hand on her shoulder. "I believe you still can, if you choose to remember who you truly are."

Her lip trembled. "I cannot," she rasped. "I cannot face my memories and survive. I don't want to be who I was. I want to be who I am now."

He gazed down at her, concern clear in his expression. Her tension eased. After their last conflict, she'd feared he'd never let her back in. She hadn't realized how important their closeness was to her until it was taken away.

"If you feel it will help," he began, "we will go to this meeting, but on our terms. I agree that Anders is lying. He's nervous about something. The only explanation is betrayal. He doesn't want to be found out."

She nodded. "It doesn't fully make sense though. The last time I met Niklas, he wanted to ally himself with me. I was resistant to the idea, and I haven't seen him since."

"Perhaps he found another ally in the interim," Iseult suggested.

"Yes," she agreed, "and I think it's in our best interest to find out just who that ally is. When I last met Niklas, I had neither my memories, nor the shroud. He might expect that I'm still at such a disadvantage."

"We can hope that is the case," he replied, "though I think it unwise to meet in a place of Niklas' choosing. I suggest we venture close enough, then send Anders to retrieve him."

Finn smiled. "Agreed." She was starting to wonder if the iciness she'd sensed from him was only in her imagination, she knew it was best not to press the issue, but . . .

"Iseult?" she questioned as he started to turn away.

He paused, seeming suddenly wary. "Yes?"

"I was afraid that I'd overstepped certain boundaries during our last conversation," she explained. "You've seemed . . . distant. If I did something wrong, I apologize."

He sighed. "I am the one overstepping. I'm doing it all of the time, but I just can't seem to help myself. Still, I think it's better to focus on the dangers at hand, rather than personal . . . emotions."

"I don't know if I can do that," she breathed. "It's difficult to ignore emotions when you feel like you have far too many of them. They just tend to leak out no matter what I do."

He smiled, which she appreciated since she was feeling

like a total fool. "That you can feel so much after all you've experienced only says positive things about you, and it is the reason you've formed the bonds you have. Few mortals can claim friends as loyal as yours."

She raised an eyebrow, surprised by his statement. "You believe Kai and Anna loyal? You've wanted to kill them both ten times over."

He nodded. "And yet, here they are. Two thieves, risking their lives instead of hiding like the rest of their ilk."

"And you?" she pressed. "You have been more loyal than anyone I've ever met."

He snorted, a rare show of mirth. "And I? Well I am the worst of all. That you've managed to change *me* speaks volumes."

She laughed as he began to guide her back toward their camp. If they left soon, perhaps they could have their meeting with Niklas before nightfall.

She found herself dreading it a little less than she had before. *Although*, she realized with a frown, Iseult had not denied that he'd been distant, nor had he expressed the reason for his behavior, except to say he was not upset with her due to their prior conflict.

Truly, even if she felt a bit better, she was just as confused as ever about the tall, dark-haired man walking swiftly at her side.

MAARAV PACED AROUND HIS NEW ROOM IN ONE OF THE OUTER buildings of the estate. He could get used to *this*. It was thrice the size of his room at the inn, with a wide fireplace near the door and a bed that could fit five people plus himself, though he'd happily settle for one. Of course, the one he was thinking of was currently upset with him.

They'd moved An Solas and most of the assassins to the estate, though a few chose to remain at the inn. Perhaps that was the wisest choice. The transition had not been comfortable, and arguments had ensued about Gwythern's guards being allowed to remain within the estate. Ealasaid wanted to ruffle as few feathers as possible, and believed the extra men would be useful. Maarav believed the only possible outcome was infighting and an eventual revolt. Slàine's people liked to do things their own way, and would not take kindly to any of the guards stepping on their toes.

Then there were the magic users, most of whom were simple countryfolk. Ealasaid wanted *all* of them within the estate where they would be protected, but there was no one to protect everyone else from *them*. The first night there, a fire mage had gotten bladdered on whiskey and set one of the guard towers ablaze.

A knock sounded on his door, drawing Maarav's gaze away from the barren fireplace.

"Come in!" he called out, but the door was already opening.

He'd left the door unlocked in hopes that Ealasaid would come to make amends after their last argument, but it was only Ouve, the young boy who'd become something akin to Ealasaid's second in command. Though his limbs were scrawny despite his tall height, and his sandy hair made him seem somehow more weak, he was not one to be trifled with. He could completely disable most men with his magic before they could even think about drawing a sword.

"Lady Sìoda is demanding your presence," Ouve sighed upon entering the room. "She's refusing to speak to Ealasaid on the pretense that she is *mage scum*." His thin lips puckered like he'd tasted something foul.

Maarav raised an eyebrow at him. "And Ealasaid did not attack?"

Ouve chuckled. "Not *yet*, though you should probably get up there before she ends our shaky alliance."

He sighed. His work was never done.

Ouve turned to lead the way out of the room.

Maarav followed, glancing back longingly at the ornately woven blankets on his bed. What was the point of staying within a wealthy estate if you had no chance to enjoy the fineries?

Upon exiting the room, he shut the door behind him and locked it with a slender iron key . . . not that locks did any good against magic users and multi-talented assassins, but it should at least keep Gwythern's servants out.

He followed Ouve down the narrow corridor, bordered by other occupied rooms, and out onto the terrace, then down the spiraling staircase leading out into meticulously cared for gardens.

Not even glancing at the slightly wilted, but still beautiful gardens, Ouve cut directly down the center path toward the main estate. Soon enough they were inside, and ascending the stairs toward the room where they'd initially cornered Gwythern and the imposing Lady Sìoda. Reaching the top of the stairs, Maarav paused for a moment to eavesdrop on the shouts coming from within. Ouve poised his fist to knock, then a crackling sound emanated inside the room, and the shouting ceased. The hairs prickled on the back of Maarav's neck.

Gesturing for Ouve to step aside, he let himself into the room to find Lady Sìoda and her bevy of attendants staring at Ealasaid in shock. Slàine stood at Ealasaid's side, looking bored.

Seeming to recover, Sìoda boomed, "You dare use your filthy magic in my home!"

Fury plain on her face, Ealasaid clenched her hands at her sides, ignoring the still smoking end table that must have been hit by her lightning.

"Lady Sìoda," Maarav interrupted, bowing in the impressive woman's direction. "I hope this day finds you well."

She scowled at him as he approached Ealasaid and Slàine. "Hardly," she growled. "Your pet mage wants to send *my* soldiers as messengers into the countryside."

Maarav raised a brow at Ealasaid, then turned his attention back to Sìoda. "And?"

Her plump face reddened. "*And* I will not allow you to weaken my regiment so your mages can sweep in and take over entirely. I will *not* relinquish *any* of my guards."

He turned back to Ealasaid. "A word, if you will?"

She darted her ire-filled gaze past him to Sìoda, then nodded.

He gestured for her to lead the way out of the room, leaving Slàine to smooth the ruffled feathers of Sìoda. Slàine might not be the most diplomatic woman around, but she would not allow Sìoda to get under her skin as she had Ealasaid's.

Following Ealasaid out, he shut the door behind them.

"That woman is utterly impossible," Ealasaid fumed, walking further down the hall away from the room. "I simply wanted to send a handful of her men to the distant burghs to seek out magic users in hiding, and she started hurling insults."

Maarav placed a hand on Ealasaid's shoulder to halt her advance. She stopped and blinked up at him.

"Do you blame her?" he asked calmly. "You were the one who wanted to negotiate with these people, so you must have realistic expectations. Her estate has been invaded by those who could easily eliminate her guards. She would be a fool to send away her men and worsen her situation."

Ealasaid's jaw dropped. "And here I was thinking you'd be pleased that I refused to be bullied into sending *our* people away."

He sighed. "Do you truly believe any magic users they might find will trust common men to escort them back here? Sending other magic users is the only option."

"But we're supposed to protect the magic users," she argued, her gray eyes fierce. "We cannot tell them there is safety in numbers, then split them up."

He pinched his brow, hoping to stave off his growing headache. He longed for his lavish room. "They are not children," he sighed. "They are your soldiers. Sometimes sacrifices must be made."

She glared at him. Electric pressure began building around her, raising the hairs on his neck once more. "I will *not* sacrifice those who come to An Solas seeking reprieve from persecution," she stated.

He crossed his arms and returned her glare. "Yet, you would expect Lady Sìoda to sacrifice her men for a cause she wants no part of?"

Ealasaid pursed her lips. "You are impossible to deal with," she snapped.

"As are you," he replied. "Now go back in there and inform Lady Sìoda that you will send your own people as messengers, as long as she agrees to volunteer her strongest soldiers to help Slàine's people alter the fortifications of the estate to their pleasing."

She blinked up at him, her anger dripping away. "That has been a large point of contention among the factions," she said thoughtfully, raising a hand to stroke her chin.

His shoulders slumped in relief. She was still capable of seeing reason after all.

She scowled. "I will propose those terms, but I will not take back calling her an old withered cow."

His eyes widened as Ealasaid marched away. She might have been born a farm girl, but she possessed the unwavering pride of a queen.

CHAPTER SIX

After their short break for a midday meal, the party had ridden westward without any more stops. The continued ride had been uncomfortable for Anna. Not because of her companions, nor that she was already saddle sore, but because of her own thoughts.

She was worried about Kai, and found herself grudgingly worried about Finn too. She hadn't forgotten the vision she'd had back in Garenoch. A vision she could only call a premonition . . . or a portent. She'd known from that moment on that her presence could save Finn from the death she was destined to face. She'd considered that the recent Cavari conflict was that situation, but something didn't feel right. As frightening as the Cavari were, they weren't the primary danger, at least not for Finn. That they could track Kai, however, had her worried. Would they come for him should he separate from Finn's group?

She exhaled a long sigh, shifting in the saddle, but failing to find a more comfortable position. It didn't help that her black breeches were stiff with road dust, and her tunic and vest weren't far behind.

She sighed again. Why was it *her* job to save Finn? Sure, there was the whole *prophecy* thing, and if one of these queens was going to have the fate of the land in her hands, it might as well be Finn . . . they at least knew Finn was kind hearted, and not likely to be a tyrant. Still, her thoughts always came back to Kai, thus motivating her to save Finn. In nearly dying, he had been permanently linked to her. Given that, what might happen to him should Finn perish? Would the slice of immortality she had given him be revoked? Would it matter now that his wounds had healed?

She sighed again. It was growing dark, and she couldn't wait to make camp. She disliked thinking about magic. She disliked it almost as much *seeing* it. She preferred tangible things that she could fully understand. Things she could either fight or manipulate. She couldn't do either to the gray shapes she saw whenever she let her guard down, nor could she resist her strange, portentous dreams.

The road, currently devoid of other travelers, made her feel as if she was in a dream. The solitude made her feel vulnerable. She glared in Anders' direction. He was no doubt leading them right into a trap, yet everyone seemed to be going along with it on the off chance they could save Àed. Anna didn't care about Àed, and didn't like risking her neck for a man who couldn't possibly have many good years left to him.

She didn't think the Travelers would do any good against the Cavari either. The Ceàrdaman never truly *helped* anyone, and she would *never* forget what they had done to her.

IT WAS ALMOST NIGHTFALL BY THE TIME THEY NEARED THE meeting place. Kai found himself wishing for Garenoch, where there was whiskey a plenty, and he didn't have to deal with saddle soreness. Between his nightmares, Anders' shifty eyes and sweaty face, and the lack of any other travelers on the road, Kai felt ready to burst with anxiety. Riding with Finn was at least somewhat calming, even though they only shared a mount to prevent the Cavari from tracking them again. Still, he counted himself lucky. While he suspected she did not return *all* of his feelings for her, she at least cared about him, and trusted him enough to keep him close. The behavior was far preferable than her lashing out at him for being a liar and thief.

"Just a bit further," Anders instructed, riding ahead of the pack.

"Wait," Iseult ordered.

No one argued with his tone, drawing their horses to an abrupt halt as they reached him. Kai glanced around the darkening scenery. There were old farmsteads nearby, but none appeared inhabited, judging by the lack of candle and firelight in the growing dusk.

Anders glanced back over his shoulder, his eyes wide enough to show too much white. "We have not reached the meeting place yet," he argued.

"You will find Niklas," Iseult instructed, "and you will bring him here."

Kai exhaled in relief. He much preferred meeting in a location of his party's choosing.

"He will not come," Anders argued, moving his pleading

gaze past Iseult to Finn. "Surely you will not pass up this opportunity to help Àed."

Kai bristled at the suggestion. Anders was trying far too hard to lure them to this meeting place.

He watched as Finn flicked her gaze to Iseult, then back to Anders. "We meet here, or not at all," she agreed.

He observed the scene with interest, wondering what had transpired between her and Iseult. Had she seemed hesitant to follow his orders, or was it just his imagination? Come to think of it, the pair had spoken little to each other over the course of the day, save their private meeting at midday.

"I'll try to find him," Anders sighed. "But do not be surprised if I am . . . *unable* to return."

"That will not be necessary," a voice spoke from behind them.

The unicorn danced nervously beneath them. Kai turned toward the voice to find one of the Ceàrdaman approaching. The Traveler wore shapeless gray robes, the fabric seeming to float around his body in the receding sunlight. As he walked, he removed the hood from his bald head, fully revealing his sharp, ethereal features.

The Traveler was nearest to their mount, Kai realized with a start. *Too* near. He hopped down from the saddle and stepped forward, prepared to intercept him. Also seeming to sense the danger, Iseult urged his horse toward the Traveler. Before Iseult could reach them, the Traveler faded from sight, then reappeared behind Kai. He turned just in time to see the Ceàrdaman lift his hand and blow a cloud of shimmering dust onto Finn, still atop the unicorn.

She gasped, inhaling the dust, then slumped forward in

her saddle. Before she could fall to the ground, Iseult had his feet on the ground to catch her.

Moving faster than he thought himself capable, Kai grabbed the Traveler from behind and held a blade to his throat. "What did you do to her?" he growled.

The Traveler snickered, seemingly unworried by the blade at his throat. "Not to worry, my lad, she's simply gone on a short journey. I have faith that she will return unscathed."

He pushed the blade more firmly against the thin skin of the Traveler's throat. "A journey to *where*?" he demanded.

"It's alright," Anders interrupted, rushing toward them after dismounting his horse. "He wants her alive," he explained, gesturing toward the Traveler. "She'd be of no use to him dead."

Kai was about to demand further explanation, but was too late. Iseult had laid Finn gently on the ground with Bedelia to watch over her. He marched toward Anders, death gleaming in his eyes.

A war horn sounded from the nearby settlement, drawing Kai's gaze past the Traveler. Stout shapes rushed forward, raising axes and swords over their heads.

Kai debated slitting the Traveler's throat right there. He must have planned the location all along, ordering Anders to lead them *past* where he waited in hiding, instead of to an actual meeting place. That way, they didn't have to trust Anders enough to attend the actual meeting. They only had to be curious enough to get close.

He shoved the Traveler to the ground as the shouting warriors neared, quickly glancing toward where Finn lay to see Bedelia and Anna standing over her with weapons drawn.

If the Traveler truly did not want Finn dead, he sure had an odd way of showing it.

~

FINN SLOWLY OPENED HER EYES, CRINGING AT THE MASSIVE pounding in her head. She lay on a stone floor in a massive chamber, the walls glowing with candlelight. Someone knelt over her, vibrant red hair shimmering in the flickering light.

"Branwen?" she muttered, trying to force her eyes to focus.

The woman over her snorted. "Hardly."

Finn blinked rapidly, and slowly the woman's face came into view. Her features were sharp, but feminine. Her vibrant cornflower blue eyes starkly contrasted with her red, waist-length hair, a thick wild tendril trailing over her black diaphanous dress.

"Who are you?" Finn groaned, slowly reaching a hand to her aching head as she sat up.

The woman stood and moved out of the way. "I could be your friend, or your enemy," she said cryptically as she began to pace, trailing her dress across the stone floor. The clatter of her boots echoed around the chamber, drawing attention to the otherwise eerie silence of the space.

Finn wanted to stand, but still felt dizzy. "Where are my friends?"

The woman stopped pacing and raised a red brow at her.

"You're truly worried about mere mortals? Not like any of the Dair Leanbh I've even met."

Finn's heart began to race. She took a deep breath, then crawled to her feet, but swayed once she got there. She stumbled over to the wall and braced herself against the cool stone. "You know of my people?"

The woman turned and smiled at her. "I know you run from them. Something has been hiding you from their sight. Hiding you from *my* sight as well, but you can hide no longer."

Finn slowly pushed away from the wall. She knew her mother had been hiding her from the Cavari. Had her mother intentionally shielded her from this woman as well, or was it mere coincidence? Though she had mixed feelings about her mother, if she'd intentionally kept this woman away, she should heed that warning.

"I don't know why anyone would shield me from you," Finn began, hoping for more information.

The woman seemed genuinely perplexed. "At first I thought my inability to track you was my father's doing, or perhaps one of your other companions, but you've been separated from them all at times, and yet, you have eluded me . . . until now."

Finn stared at the mysterious woman. She'd said her *father*, and had implied that he'd been one of Finn's companions. Could it be . . . "Keiren?" she questioned. "Is that your name?"

The woman narrowed her gaze. "I see my father told you about me. Pity, I'd hoped for the element of surprise."

Finn's mind stuttered to a halt. *This* was the woman who'd turned Àed into a tree. This was the woman who could turn him *back*. She pushed away from the wall. "I demand you return Àed to me right this moment," she snapped. "How could you do that to your own father?"

Keiren sneered. "I see Bedelia has spilled all my secrets. I'll have to see to it that she loses her tongue."

"You will not touch her," Finn hissed.

Keiren grinned, then let out a throaty laugh. She stalked closer to Finn. "You believe you can stop me? *You*? I think being a tree altered your mind, because you're dumb as a stump."

Finn stepped forward, despite her quavering limbs. Keiren towered over her, but Finn refused to cower. She looked up into Keiren's vibrant blue eyes and evenly stated, "You will *not* touch her, nor anyone else who is dear to me."

Keiren lowered her face so that it was only a hair's breadth away from Finn's. Her hot breath added to the angry flush already burning Finn's skin. "Your *friends* are currently at the mercy of my Reivers, and you are stuck here with me. You can bandy threats about all you please, but it will not save them."

Panic hit her, she felt barely able to suck air through her clenched teeth. Was Keiren telling the truth? She had the uncharacteristic urge to lash out, but no, she needed to think. She had to get out of this place and back to her companions.

She stepped back out of Keiren's reach until her back met the cool stone wall. She suspected they were in the in-between, the place between the living and the dead. The last time she'd been there all she needed to do to leave, was sleep. However, she highly doubted Keiren would allow that. There had to be another way.

Keiren tilted her head, cascading her long hair over her shoulder as she observed Finn. "There is no way out. If you'd like to return to them, you must cooperate with me."

Was she so transparent? "Never," Finn spat. Even if there was no way out, she would kill Keiren before she gave her anything she might desire.

Keiren shrugged. "Then your friends will die, and it will be all your fault."

Finn balled her hands into fists. Could she be telling the truth? She glanced around the large room, desperately seeking anything that might give her an edge, then remembered something important. She lowered a hand to her hip, searching beneath the edge of her top, then nearly gasped. The Faie Queen's shroud tied around her hips for the past weeks was no longer there.

Keiren tilted her head to the other side. "Are you prepared to hear my terms?"

Finn flexed her fingers. Bedelia claimed Keiren was the most powerful sorceress in the land. Powerful like Oighear. She'd only bested the former with the use of the shroud. Could she truly hope to beat Keiren on her own?

"Name them," she growled.

Keiren's lips curled into a wicked smile. "I require your immortality. Just a taste of it, really."

She stared at her a moment, surprised by her answer. "Why?"

Keiren's smile wilted. "That is none of your concern. You will willingly share your blood with me, and I will call off the assault on your friends."

Could it be that simple? She'd shared her blood with Kai to save his life. It had drained her of energy, but hadn't seemed to do any permanent damage . . . at least not to her. Her thoughts raced for another solution, but if her friends were currently being attacked, she didn't have much choice.

She took a step forward. "We'll need a dagger. The ritual will take some time, so you must first call off your warriors."

Keiren's eyes seemed to twinkle. Finn couldn't help the feeling that she was making a terrible mistake, but what choice did she have? Without the shroud, she could not best someone as powerful as Oighear, perhaps *more* powerful.

Keiren withdrew a dagger from her belt, then took another step toward Finn. "Hold out your hand," she ordered.

With a deep, aching breath, Finn obeyed.

ISEULT FOUGHT AGAINST HIS RAGE AS THE WARRIORS CIRCLING them began to close in, clearly Reivers judging by their primitive leather garb and long beards . . . but what were they doing this far south? Reivers were the bandits of the Northern Lands. Most Southerners would normally never even encounter them, except perhaps at sea.

Iseult lifted his sword, weighing his party's odds. Dusk had turned to dark, and he could not tell if more warriors waited further away, but things did not look good. He realized then that the Traveler had appeared to distract them from noticing the Reivers moving in from the distant farmsteads. Outside the ring of warriors that surrounded them, the Traveler that had to be Niklas stood watching. Anders was beside him. *Traitor.*

The nearest warrior narrowed his black-lined eyes before lunging and swinging his gleaming ax toward Iseult, testing him.

Iseult easily dodged the attack, stepping out of reach, then looked past the warrior to Niklas, silhouetted in the moonlight. "I never thought I'd see the day when the Ceàrdaman would lower themselves to work with Reivers. Why do they not advance?"

"They await orders from *their* mistress," Niklas replied, tapping his temple with one long, bony finger. "Whether they attack depends on the choices of *your* mistress. I am simply a casual observer."

He resisted the urge to glance at Finn's prone form, still guarded by Bedelia. She was merely unconscious, not dead, but seemed incapable of currently making *choices*.

"An observer who attacked the very person with whom you sought alliance," Iseult growled.

Niklas tsked. "As I've already assured you, she will not come to harm. My desires for alliance still stand."

Anna sidled up beside Iseult, her gaze trained on the nearest Reivers. "That powder he used sent her to the Gray Place," she explained. "It's the same thing they used on me when—"

She cut herself off abruptly, for there was no need to continue. He knew all about what had happened to her while under the Travelers' *care*.

"How do we undo it?" he asked.

"It will wear off," Niklas explained, stepping toward the nearest Reiver, a stocky man with jet black hair down to his armpits, and a beard just as long. He wore a tunic and breeches topped with a heavy fur vest, their colors drained by the full moon.

"Have you heard anything?" Niklas muttered to the Reiver.

The Reiver nodded, then gruffly replied. "She asks that we stay our hands . . . for now."

"Who is this invisible mistress?" Kai sighed from somewhere behind Iseult.

Niklas grinned more broadly, then his smile faltered. He glanced over his shoulder at the dark woods looming ominously at his back.

Iseult tensed, sensing something. More Travelers? He could hear footsteps in the woods . . . and the soft rattles of metal armor? He'd never known the Travelers to wear armor.

"Go see what it is," Niklas hissed to the nearest Reiver.

The man nodded, then charged off, heedless of any possible danger. Iseult watched as he disappeared beyond the tree line. A full minute passed.

Silence.

Niklas glared at Iseult as if this was somehow his fault, then tapped another Reiver on the shoulder. "Follow him," he ordered.

This Reiver looked somewhat hesitant, but still left the group of warriors to charge off into the tree line.

Iseult watched on curiously, a small sliver of hope trickling through his mind. With Finn unconscious, they didn't stand much chance against so many tried warriors, but if Niklas kept sending them off one by one into the woods, he might whittle down their ranks enough to make them vulnerable

Several quiet moments passed.

Iseult felt eyes on him. Before looking to the source, he stepped back from the reach of the nearest warrior. Glancing to his side, he noticed Anna with her daggers poised to fend off attacks, but her eyes were all for him, clearly trying to tell him something. Something about whatever was in the woods? Perhaps even if they managed to escape Niklas and the Reivers, they would have a greater foe to face.

Niklas growled in irritation, then tapped two more of the Reivers. "Both of you go," he demanded. "I expect at least one to return."

The two men charged off, a bit more cautious than the preceding two.

"Aren't the Ceàrdaman supposed to be all seeing?" Kai quipped. "Can you not simply peer through the trees and divine what might be hiding there?"

Niklas sneered at him. "Watch your tongue, boy. I can see through to your very soul, do not make me lay all of your secrets bare."

Kai snorted. "Some threat, that. I haven't got any secrets left for you to steal."

Iseult kept his eyes on the trees, ignoring the conversation. He wasn't sure why Kai was baiting Niklas, but if it kept the Traveler preoccupied, he would not interrupt.

The remaining Reivers, still too many to fight and come out alive, began to shift uncomfortably. None of the men sent out had returned, yet there had been no sounds of struggle.

He flexed his hand on the pommel of his blade. The wise move now was to wait.

Niklas had turned his attention away from Kai, and back to the woods. Slowly, he moved his gaze to Iseult. "I don't suppose you'd like to go and see where my men have gone?"

He remained silent. Normally he'd gladly march into the woods to face whatever enemy awaited, but he would not willingly leave Finn behind while she was vulnerable.

Niklas sighed and turned toward the first Reiver he'd spoken to, the one who seemed to be receiving some sort of mental communication from this unknown mistress. His expression questioned what was amiss, but the Reiver merely shrugged as if saying, *I don't know*, then an arrow came whistling out of the woods to pierce right through the Reiver's neck.

His eyes bulged, and he tried to inhale, but instead sputtered on blood, black in the darkness, then fell to the ground, dead.

"Close in!" one of the Reivers shouted.

Those bearing large shields moved closer to the tree line, raising the rough wooden barriers to protect themselves as a volley of arrows launched forth from the woods.

Iseult raced back toward where Finn lay and stood in front of her body, his sword raised. Anna and Kai appeared at either side to flank them, with Bedelia and Sativola protecting the rear. Their horses pranced about nervously, but had nowhere to bolt since the Reivers remained in a tight circle around them, save those who'd moved closer to the treeline.

Iseult narrowed his gaze toward the woods and the more pressing danger. Shadowy forms could be seen there, casting the occasional glimmer of dull metal in the moonlight. He'd seen such a sheen before, but knew these warriors couldn't possibly be Oighear's warriors, the Aos Sí.

He caught himself before his jaw could fall open. The warriors stepped out of the trees and into the moonlight. Their ebony hair, like spider silk, flowed out the bottom of their oddly curved helmets. The pure whiteness of their skin seemed harsh in the soft darkness of night.

As the Aos Sí drew closer, Iseult's jaw fell farther. Their leader was someone he recognized. Someone he thought was dead.

Eywen, the Aos Sí warrior who'd helped them escape Oighear's dungeon, raised his gleaming sword to the sky. As one, the Aos Sí surged forth, meeting the nearest Reivers with their blades. The Reivers charged just as ferociously, likely not understanding just what they faced.

His mind calculating the odds, Iseult turned to Kai. "Lift Finn onto Loinnir with you. Be prepared to run should you find an opening. We do not know if the Aos Sí are currently friend or foe."

Kai nodded, sheathed his daggers, then hurried back to Finn, gathering her in his arms. As if by command, Finn's unicorn pranced up to Kai and knelt. He hoisted her up to sit on Loinner, allowing her body to drape forward toward the unicorn's soft white neck. He climbed up behind her, and Loinnir rose to her hooves. Satisfied, Iseult turned his attention back to the battle.

The Reivers fell one by one, unable to stand up to the unearthly might of the Aos Sí. Suddenly remembering Naoki, Iseult's gaze darted around for her, but she was nowhere to be seen. In fact, he hadn't noticed her since Finn had been rendered unconscious. All for the best, he supposed, he didn't need to worry about protecting her too.

His visual search ended on Niklas and Anders as they hurried off together in the opposite direction, away from the battle. *Cowards*.

Iseult gripped his sword tightly, not entirely opposed to testing his skills against the Aos Sí once more. If they wanted Finn, they'd have to kill him first.

THE TWO WOMEN STOOD FACE TO FACE. KEIREN'S SIMPLE dagger sliced into the skin of Finn's palm. Crimson droplets littered the stone floor as Finn fought against the urge to cradle her hand. Deeply engrossed, Keiren sliced her own palm.

"Will this even work here?" Finn's voice quavered. She'd given Kai a portion of her immortality in the in-between, but they'd both been physically there, as least she thought they had. She wasn't sure about the actual whereabouts of Keiren's body, but she was quite sure her own physical form remained back with her companions.

She gulped. Companions that were allegedly surrounded by warriors, poised to kill should she fail in her task.

Keiren didn't seem to be listening to her. She held her bloody hand out, bright red fluid dripping profusely onto the floor, but her eyes were closed, her head tilted as if she listened to distant music.

Suddenly her eyes flew open.

Finn startled and stumbled backward, nearly losing her footing.

"Your blood," Keiren hissed. "It is *not* pure."

Finn shook her head, clutching her dripping hand. "I don't know what you mean. I'm doing as you asked, so you must call off your warriors."

Keiren glared at her, then her expression softened and her eyes slid sideways, as if focusing on something far away.

Finn watched on, darting her eyes around for an escape route. She wasn't sure what Keiren meant by her blood being impure. Perhaps because she'd already shared it with Kai?

"Those incompetent fools!" Keiren hissed, startling her. She glared at Finn again. "We will finish this conversation upon my return."

Her entire form seemed to blink in and out of existence, then disappeared entirely.

Finn stared at the space where Keiren had been. How had she managed to leave so suddenly?

Her shoulders slumped in a mixture of fear and relief, but also apprehension. Had something happened with her companions to draw Keiren away? When she returned, would she still try to take Finn's blood, or did she no longer want it?

Cradling her bloody hand, she glanced around the room again. There were several halls branching off, but where they led, she had no idea. All she knew was that she should not remain in this room and wait for Keiren to return. If their deal was off because of Finn's impure blood, she had nothing left to bargain with. She needed to find a hiding place where she could go to sleep and return to her friends before it was too late . . . if it wasn't too late already.

She chose a corridor at random and started running, but

not as quickly as she would have liked. The corridor was sparsely lit by candles in wall sconces, leaving long periods of blackness in between each tiny beacon.

Her steps echoed off the stone walls of the narrow corridor, surrounding her with soft, reverberating noise. Everywhere in the in-between seemed to look the same, just long stone corridors illuminated by torches and candles, with few cross-paths to take. She could end up running down this corridor until she collapsed from exhaustion.

Slowing her gait, she considered just curling up and attempting to go to sleep. Perhaps if she hid in one of the dark expanses, Keiren wouldn't be able to find her right away.

She clutched her still bleeding hand, debating, and wondering how Keiren had so efficiently departed. She had no idea how to attempt such a feat, but perhaps someone else in the in-between could help her. She'd met her mother here before, and Branwen. Perhaps she could find them again.

Tired and frightened, she forced her feet forward. She rounded a bend in the corridor, then skidded to a halt. Mist hit her face, moistening her skin in a sensation that felt both warm and cold at the same time. The stones at her feet were covered in moss, leading up to the end of the corridor. Had she known she'd been this close to the end of the corridors, she'd never have stopped running.

Glancing over her shoulder, she stepped out into the misty night air. Had she somehow found the way out of the in-between, or had she simply discovered a new area?

Her boots sunk into the mossy earth as she left the stone corridor behind. Lichen covered trees surrounded her, hosting the chirping of night insects. This place was somehow familiar.

She continued walking, and eventually the trees opened up to reveal a wide, still lake. The full moon overhead reflected perfectly in the dark water. If she was still in the in-between, could that moon be real? Was any of this real?

"This is not only the place between life and death," someone whispered in her ear. "This is a place of dreams."

She froze, her gaze transfixed on the milky lunar reflection. "Mother?" she breathed. She recalled her dream. Her mother standing behind her, transitioning to Oighear's icy grip pressing around her throat.

Her mother stepped around from behind her to stand at her side, gazing out across the water. She wore a long burgundy dress, the color made murky by mist and moonlight.

Finn followed her mother's gaze, then stifled a gasp. Cloaked forms stood on the other side of the lake, just like in her dream, only now there was no boat.

"Who are they?" she asked. "The Cavari?"

"They are the souls you trapped here," her mother, Móirne, explained. "They have been waiting for you here for one hundred years."

Tears trailed down her cheeks. Iseult's ancestors. He should have wanted to kill her, not help her. Not . . . she cut her thoughts off. "I have to return to my friends. I cannot let Keiren harm them."

"Silly girl," Móirne hissed. "Your friends stand little chance in this life. I cannot conceal you any longer. You shine too brightly."

Finn balled her hands into fists. "I will protect them. I

just need to get out of here." She turned her gaze to her mother's impassive face, so similar in appearance to her own, but with blue eyes and surrounded by dark hair. "Please, if I go to sleep here, will I return to the real world?"

Móirne shook her head. "You did not come here voluntarily. You must wait for the spell your body is under to wear off."

"But Keiren—" she began.

"Keiren needs you alive," Móirne interrupted. "She will not harm your body. I doubt she'll be able to reach it again. Your people have come for their queen."

"What do you mean?" Finn gasped. "The Cavari? What has happened to my friends?"

Móirne smirked. "Not *our* people, *yours*. You may be Queen of the Dair, but the Dair are rulers over all of nature. The Aos Sí have come to your call, and the call of the Faie Queen's shroud. They will follow your command."

"The Aos Sí?" she muttered, confused. "But how?"

Móirne shook her head again. "You really must stop being so dense. You've regained your memories of your past, now put them to use. You are the rightful Queen of the Dair. The Faie Queen is a lesser queen, and the human queen is as of yet inconsequential. Everyone must pick their sides. The Aos Sí will not pick the losing side again, at least those not blinded by loyalty."

"The Faie Queen?" she questioned. "You mean Oighear? She'd dead. The Aos Sí would never follow the one who killed their queen. If they have found my friends, they mean them harm."

Móirne glanced over her shoulder, a sudden worried look in her eyes. "I must go soon, but I implore you to not

be so naive." She met her gaze evenly. "You cannot so easily kill the winter."

Finn's heart shuddered. She knew it. She knew it in her heart that Oighear could not truly be dead, not after the dream she'd had.

Still . . . she'd seen her body, and there'd been no mistaking the icy stare of death.

"I must go," Móirne hissed.

"Wait!" Finn rasped, reaching out for her. "Tell me what the Cavari want!"

"I cannot help you," she breathed, "I have already said too much. They cannot find us here together." She pulled away then darted off, quickly disappearing into the mist.

Finn whipped her gaze back to where the figures stood on the distant shore, but they were no longer there. She was utterly alone. Whatever had frightened her mother was nowhere to be seen. She peered across the still, dark water, wondering how long she would be stuck in this place, and what would happen to her companions while she was gone.

With nothing else to do, she started walking through the misty woods, with no idea how long she'd be there, or where she'd end up.

CHAPTER SEVEN

*A*nna's fingers ached, tired from gripping her daggers. Her weapons seemed a feeble force against the Aos Sí. Inhumanely graceful, they'd likely skewer her before she could blink. The Reivers were strewn in bloody piles before them, making Anna grateful for the darkness. It had been a while since she'd seen so many bodies freshly killed. The Reivers had fought their best, but had not taken down *one* of the Aos Sí. Not a single one. Gazing at the approaching warriors, shimmering softly with magic only seen by her, she gulped.

Kai was on Finn's unicorn, clutching Finn's limp body against his chest, prepared to ride off if need be, though only time would tell if he'd sacrifice them all to save her.

The Aos Sí wove through the corpses toward them. Some had sheathed their weapons, perhaps a good sign, but Anna didn't trust it. They had almost reached Iseult and Bedelia, a few paces ahead of her and Sativola.

Her hands flexed around her daggers as she watched the

leader of the Aos Sí reach Iseult. She resisted the urge to run and abandon them all. Why hadn't she done that already? She should have fled as soon as the Reivers were distracted.

"My friend," the Aos Sí leader began, bowing his head to Iseult. "It is good to see you again."

Anna's jaw dropped. All of the Aos Sí looked similar enough that she didn't recognize him at first, especially since they'd been sure he'd been killed. Eywen knew when he'd escorted Anna, Kai, Sativola, Iseult, Finn, and Bedelia from Oighear's dungeons that his punishment would be death.

"I'm glad to hear you call me friend," Iseult replied. "How did you survive?"

Eywen glanced past him to Anna and the rest of their companions. "That is a tale to be told around a warm fire," he replied, "far away from the stench of bandit corpses."

His gaze lingered near Anna. On Finn, she realized, being held in a sitting position by Kai.

"Does she live?" Eywen questioned.

The Aos Sí waiting silently behind him seemed to shift as one, as if taking a collective, shuddering breath.

Iseult turned his gaze to Anna. "Under a spell, you say?"

She nodded, then cleared her throat, nervous to speak in front of the Aos Sí. "A spell I experienced myself once. She's in the, um . . . " she trailed off, not knowing if the Aos Sí would understand what she meant if she called it the Gray Place or the in-between. "She should regain consciousness eventually," she said instead.

Eywen nodded, then turned back to Iseult. "Will you allow us to travel with you until she awakens?" He looked out. "I sense something powerful nearby. It would be wise to be on our way."

"For now," Iseult replied.

Anna cringed. She had no desire to travel with the imposing Aos Sí. Eywen had saved their lives once, and had just done so again, but his fellow warriors, she had not met. At one time they'd all obeyed Oighear, and she couldn't help recalling Kai and Finn's shared dream. This could all be a trap to land them right back where they'd started, in the clutches of the Winter Queen.

ANDERS CROUCHED IN THE BUSHES BESIDE NIKLAS, WATCHING the exchange between Iseult and the strange warriors. They were too far for Anders to hear anything that was said, but he had no doubt Niklas was somehow using his magic to listen in.

He watched as Iseult nodded, then one of the armored men—no, he couldn't really call them men, they were something else—gestured to those behind him. A few raced forward and off into the trees on the other side of the road. Anders realized what they were doing a few moments later when they came back with the horses that had been startled during the battle. One of the armored . . . creatures handed a set of reins to Iseult.

Iseult mounted as the rest of the warriors retrieved their own mounts from the tree line, though it appeared not all of the creatures had horses. Once those who did were on horseback, they journeyed as a unit further west down the Sand Road.

"Do they . . . know them?" Anders inquired, turning his gaze to Niklas.

"The warriors are the Aos Sí," Niklas explained, rising from his crouch. "Though how they know your . . . *friends*, I'm not sure. I sensed there would be some sort of trouble in our plan, but I had not been expecting *this*."

"Well I'm pleased to hear you say that," a female voice snapped from behind them. "I would hate to think you had betrayed me."

Anders and Niklas both turned toward the sound of the voice. Keiren stood between two spindly trees, her imposing height dwarfing the malnourished vegetation. Her fiery red hair, far more vibrant than Anders', whipped about in the moonlit breeze.

"I see you have not gained her immortality," Niklas purred. "I told you it would not happen as you hoped."

Keiren glared at him. "You knew her blood was impure, didn't you? Why did you not tell me before?"

Niklas shrugged. "I knew things would not go as you'd planned, and that was all. I had not suspected *that* would be the undoing of your plan." He stroked his chin in thought. "She was born pure blooded Dair, so she must have done something along the way to taint it."

"Obviously," Keiren snapped. "I had no chance to ask her, as I sensed my men being cut down." She gazed past them at the distant battlefield, then walked forward. "But we'll just have to devise a new plan," she continued. "Finnur should be stuck in the in-between for at least another day. She will not be able to come after me yet, if she chooses to at all. She's a coward, but I would not like to be near in the event that she grows a spine and chooses to retaliate."

"Indeed," Niklas agreed, then turned his reflective gaze to Anders. "I'm afraid now that you've betrayed your friends, and they have been joined by the Aos Sí, you're no longer of much use."

Anders gut tightened. He'd assumed he'd die sometime during Niklas' plan, but he'd managed to survive. Was it truly over?

"So then you will finally return my sister?" he asked hopefully.

"Of course," Niklas replied, stepping away from him. "A Traveler always keeps his word. I'll notify those caring for her body to awaken her and treat her wounds immediately."

Anders' shoulders slumped in relief. He'd actually done it. He'd managed to save his sister and survived to tell the tale. He glanced back at the battlefield, glad to finally leave the life of an adventurer behind. Once he had his sister back in the Archive, he'd never leave again.

Something abruptly hit his gut, the impact followed by searing pain. He whipped his gaze back toward Niklas, then down to Niklas' blood coated hand, pushing the dagger deeper into his flesh.

In a state of shock, Anders looked to Keiren, but she was too busy examining her fingernails and tapping her boot-clad foot impatiently.

He turned back to Niklas. "But you said we were done," he croaked, his body convulsing against the pain. "I kept my end of the bargain."

Niklas smiled, then jerked out the dagger. "Your *sister* will be returned to the land of the living, not to you. You, my boy, are a loose end."

Keiren sighed. "Yes, so hurry up and snip the end already."

Anders was quite sure he'd already been snipped. He fell to his knees, still gazing up at Niklas. Hot blood coated his hands, and his vision began to go white.

Niklas and Keiren both turned away, leaving him behind as he slumped to the earth. As the pain began to ebb, replaced by delirium, he found that he was not afraid. Branwen would be saved, and he wouldn't have to fight anymore. His eyes closed of their own accord as he drifted off. His body seemed to grow cold. The ground beneath him seemed to harden, and darkness consumed everything.

"Hello brother," a soft voice said from somewhere above him, but his mind was too far gone to truly hear.

BRANWEN'S ENTIRE BODY WAS ON FIRE. HER HANDS SCRAPED at the ground, expecting to find hard stone, but instead her skin was met with soft blankets.

She struggled to open her eyes. *Anything* to replace the image of her brother bleeding out in one of the endless corridors of the in-between. She'd felt it the moment he'd arrived, and had just finally reached him when she was ripped away.

Her body convulsed in discomfort. She gritted her teeth, then her eyes flung open.

At first she only saw white, some sort of white tent over her head, illuminated by moonlight and the soft glow of candles. She writhed against the continuing pain scorching her body as her vision began to focus.

There was a woman hovering over her. No, not just a woman, a Traveler. Her head was completely bald, just like the men of her race, showing blue veins through her oddly translucent skin.

Branwen opened her mouth to speak, then painfully sucked in a long breath. Her throat burned, utterly dry and seemingly filled with grit.

"Be still," the female Traveler advised. "You have rested a long while. Your body must readapt."

"*Water*," Branwen managed to hiss, weakly lifting a hand from her bedding.

The Traveler walked away, then returned to kneel beside her, a pewter pitcher in hand. She lowered the pitcher toward Branwen's face, then trickled water from the spout into her waiting mouth.

Her throat convulsed around the meager droplets, then she began to cough and sputter, lifting her upper body, renewing her pain.

The Traveler placed a hand on her shoulder and eased her back down.

"My brother," Branwen croaked. "I saw him. I must go back."

"There is no going back," the Traveler soothed. "Your consciousness has been severed from that place. You will not go back again until you die."

She clenched her eyes shut. She thought for a moment she might cry, but her eyes seemed too dry to produce tears.

Though she already knew the truth, she had to ask, "Is he dead?"

The Traveler woman nodded. "He gave his life for yours. You should be grateful."

Branwen felt her body going limp as unconsciousness threatened.

"More water first," the Traveler urged, seeming to sense Branwen's body was close to giving out.

She lifted the pitcher and dribbled more water down Branwen's throat. It still stung like liquid fire, but she managed to gulp a small amount down.

The next dose hurt a little less, and finally the Traveler set aside the pitcher.

"What are you going to do with me?" Branwen breathed.

"You will be returned to the land of the living," the Traveler replied, "whatever that might mean to you. The Ceàrdaman always keep their word."

Branwen heard the sound of dribbling water, then a cool cloth was placed over her forehead.

"Sleep now," the woman soothed. "Your body has long to go before you can travel on your own."

Branwen's eyes had already fallen shut by the time the Traveler finished speaking. She welcomed oblivion. *Anything* to drown out the pain in her body, and the even greater ache in her heart.

CHAPTER EIGHT

*K*ai braced his arm around Finn's waist with her back against his chest, keeping her upright in the saddle. Occasionally he'd press a finger on her neck below the curve of her jaw to make sure her heart still beat. Anna claimed she would come out of this trance, yet he couldn't help but fear the worse. Niklas had doused her with that powder for a reason, trapping her in the in-between. What was happening to her while she was there?

Iseult rode ahead of them with Eywen, both silent as they scouted the shadows around them for whatever danger the Aos Sí had sensed. Kai glanced over his shoulder at Sativola and Bedelia, and beyond them, the warriors riding and walking in their wake. During the battle they had moved so quickly, it had seemed like there were more of them, but now that he could count, there were merely twenty.

"They all shine," Anna muttered from her mount beside him. "It's terribly irritating."

He turned his gaze to her, waiting for her to elaborate.

She peered at him from within the shadows of her charcoal hood. "The Aos Sí," she whispered. "They glint like steel in sunlight, and I don't mean their armor."

He nodded, understanding what she meant. "We can hardly complain though, can we? They rescued us."

She sighed. "That they did. I know we all suspected Anders of telling mistruths, but I honestly never thought he'd betray us as he did."

Kai snorted. "He's lucky he ran off with Niklas before Iseult got to him. That would have been the end of Anders."

Anna nodded, but her gaze had gone distant. Her mouth twisted into a worried pout.

"What is it?" Kai questioned softly. He glanced over his shoulder again to assess if Bedelia and Sativola were close enough to hear, but they were a bit far back for that.

He turned back as Anna frowned, then sighed. "I've been thinking that perhaps I might try to enter the Gray Place this evening, but I don't want the others to know. I don't want them to blame me if I fail."

Kai's heart skipped a beat. Secretly he'd been hoping she would offer, but he knew she'd never intentionally visited the in-between, and might not be able to even if she tried. Still, he had to ask, "Can you try to take me with you like you did before?"

Anna shook her head. "I'll need you to watch over me, and wake me should something seem amiss."

His heart fell, but he nodded. At least Anna would go. It was better than just waiting around for Finn to wake up. He turned his gaze forward to Eywen and Iseult, wondering at this new seeming alliance. Had the Aos Sí truly come all this way to find Finn, and if so, the bigger question was, *why*?

~

BEDELIA'S STOMACH CHURNED, THREATENING TO EXPEL THE meager meal she'd had earlier that day. Being around the Aos Sí brought back memories of her time as their prisoner. Memories of being locked in a dungeon, interrogated, then whipped and marched until she could no longer even stand. It had taken days in Garenoch to regain her stamina, and even now her wounds still plagued her. She'd take being bitten by another Faie wolf any day than to ever again be at the mercy of the Aos Sí.

Yet, she could express none of this. She felt she had finally earned Iseult's respect, and would not allow him to see her weakness. It was why she could tell no one that her wolf bite had started to ache again, and the black streaming through the veins of her calf had begun to spread. Keiren had claimed that the potion she'd taken to save her life might not stave off the wound's poison forever. Apparently she hadn't lied.

Bedelia jumped in the saddle as something touched her shoulder, then blushed, realizing it was only Sativola. He'd tapped her to gain her attention. She hadn't even noticed that the Aos Sí around them had turned off the road to make camp.

Camp. She shivered. Was she truly supposed to sleep right alongside the creatures who had tormented her? The creatures she'd seen slaughter the Reivers, just an hour before? Biting her lip, she guided her horse to follow Sativola's off the road.

She'd assumed they'd immediately dismount to make camp, but instead the Aos Sí continued riding into the forest. She looked to Iseult, then Anna, then Kai, hoping one of them might show concern about following them so far off the road, but none did. Kai held tightly onto Finn, and that seemed to be his only concern.

They rode on and on. It had to be near midnight. Just when she thought they'd ride on until morning, the Aos Sí at the front of the line halted their horses and dismounted.

Supplies were unpacked and fires were built while Bedelia stood with her horse, feeling out of place. Kai and the others set up a small camp of their own, but she felt out of place there too. Finn was the only reason she fit in with any of them. With Finn unconscious, she simply did not belong.

His horse tended to, Iseult moved to her side, silent as a shadow. "Come," he ordered. "Leave your horse to be tended by the others."

She nodded, halfway grateful to be saved, but also nervous about whatever Iseult might have to say. He rarely spoke unless it was important.

She left her horse with Sativola and followed Iseult into the trees, away from the Aos Sí camp. They continued walking, their footfalls accompanied only by the sound of night insects, and distant mutters from the camps. Finally, Iseult gestured for her to stop, far out of earshot of the others.

He turned and peered down at her. The dark engulfed his black hair and clothing, lit faintly by hints of moonlight breaking through the trees, making him appear as an otherwordly specter. Was he angry with her? If so, she could not for the life of her fathom why.

"How much do you know of Finn's past?" he asked abruptly.

"Her past?" she asked, surprised.

"Yes. Her far past. Her original life before the Faie war."

She shook her head. "N-nothing," she replied. "Nothing at all. I know she is one of the Dair Leanbh of Clan Cavari, and now thanks to Slàine, I know she was born to be their queen, but I know nothing else."

Nodding, he began to walk a bit deeper into the woods, and she hurried to catch up to his side.

"I will not divulge Finn's secrets to you," he began again as they walked, "nor will I divulge mine, but I would like your thoughts on a theory."

She nodded for him to go on, both relieved he wasn't angry with her, and intrigued by what he had to say.

"Eywen told me the tale of his people as we rode," he continued. "He explained that when magic faded from the land, marking the decline of the Faie War, his people fell into a long slumber. Recently when Oighear awakened, so too did they."

She watched him thoughtfully as they walked, dying to know the point of this tale.

"I believe the Dair Leanbh have something to do with the loss and reappearance of magic," he continued. "I believe *Finn* has something to do with it."

Bedelia stopped walking. "But while she was . . . gone, magic still existed. People like Ealasaid still wielded their elemental powers. It was only the Faie who left the land."

Iseult nodded again, turning to face her. "Yes, magically

inclined humans maintained their elemental powers, but mostly in hiding. I believe this to be because their prophesied queen was still among the living. I believe the Dair forced Oighear, the daughter of the rightful Faie Queen, into dormancy, and her people went with her. Finn's retreat, in turn, forced her people into a sort of half life, mere shadows of what they once were."

"So you believe this all complies with the prophecy?" she questioned, mulling over everything he'd said. "And perhaps the Faie and Dair follow their queens because their magic depends on them?"

He nodded again. "Finn was born under a certain alignment of stars, fating her to be the next queen of the Dair, yet she never assumed her role. The old queen died shortly before Finn retreated from this world, leaving her people without their main source of power, thus, they slowly faded."

Beginning to catch on, Bedelia continued, "And when Oighear was forced into slumber, the Faie's magic faded. Perhaps if she'd been killed, a new queen could have taken her place, but just like Finn, she did not die, she simply . . . retreated."

He nodded, his face showing no signs of pleasure at her powers of deduction.

"But why tell me all of this?" she questioned. "How does this change our plan?"

"It doesn't, not entirely," he replied. "But it does bring us to a few conclusions. First, since the Aos Sí have not faded away, either a new Faie Queen has been crowned, or Oighear is not truly dead."

Bedelia lifted a hand to her mouth to stifle her surprised

intake of breath. She hadn't thought of that, but if Iseult's theory proved correct . . . she must have somehow survived her wounds.

"Second," he continued, "It means that the Cavari draw their power from Finn. The only way to truly destroy them, would be to force her back into slumber."

"But we don't want that," she blurted.

"No," he agreed, "I simply want you to remain aware of that fact. The prophecy says that two queens will die, leaving one alive. However, no matter the outcome, the dead queens could be replaced with new queens to perpetuate the battle. In this, this land is doomed to be irrecoverably changed by war. *But*, if we can force the other two queens into a slumber-like state, no new queens can be named."

"And the Faie would fade away again, along with the magic possessed by humans," she concluded.

"And the Cavari and other Dair would regain their strength . . . unless Finn chooses to give her magic away. Magic can be stolen with the Faie Queen's shroud. When all of this is over, if she is willing to make that choice, perhaps that act will steal the magic of her people too, and she could live a normal life."

Bedelia's head was spinning. His plan seemed sound in theory, but actually achieving it seemed impossible. "You know," she mused, "I'd wager that's the most anyone has ever heard you say in one sitting."

She'd meant it as a joke, but he did not smile. Not that she'd expected him to.

She sighed. "You love her, don't you?"

He stared at her, his expression blank.

"Fine, don't answer me," she sighed. "I'll help with your plan in any way that I can." She turned to walk back toward camp, then stopped as he placed his hand on her shoulder. Surprised, she turned to face him as his hand fell away.

"I do love her," he admitted. "Though it makes no sense, given where I come from, and who she is."

Bedelia smiled ruefully. "In my experience, love rarely makes sense."

"That's not comforting," he grumbled.

She smirked, while inside she was bursting with pride that Iseult would entrust her with his admission. She knew for a fact he had told no one else.

"It wasn't meant to be," she quipped, then turned again to march back toward camp.

This time Iseult followed, clearly lost deep within his own thoughts. For once, Bedelia thought she might actually know just what those thoughts were.

ANNA LAY ON HER BEDROLL, STARING UP AT THE STARRY NIGHT sky. She did *not* want to go to the Gray Place, not at all, but she did want to help return Finn to her body, if only so they could get away from the cursed Aos Sí.

"You have to close your eyes to fall asleep," Kai commented, sitting on his knees beside her bedroll.

"Your job is to wake me if needed," she snapped, "not to tell me how to sleep."

"Then sleep," he sighed.

She turned on her side, facing her back to him, then squeezed her eyes shut. She could hear the Aos Sí conversing amongst themselves not too far off. There was no sound of their human companions voices, but she knew Iseult and Bedelia were nearby, guarding Finn's body, and Sativola was likely braving the Aos Sí camp in search of whiskey.

Her mind began to wander. She knew it could not be as simple as just thinking of the Gray Place and going to sleep, could it? She'd visited many times in her dreams, but they were never experiences of her choosing. Even if she could make it there, she had no idea how she'd find Finn.

The sound of Kai whittling a piece of wood with one of his blades hit her ears, rhythmically soothing. She focused on that sound, *phht, phht, phht*, while thinking of the Gray Place, and more importantly, of *Finn* in the Gray Place.

Slowly, her thoughts became distant.

Her next sudden thought was that the sound of Kai's whittling was gone, replaced by the babble of gently flowing water. She sat up and looked around, no longer in the forest she'd gone to sleep in. Strange, scraggly trees twisted up toward the full moon, partially obscured by mist. It was nighttime here too, mirroring the real world, but the darkness was somehow softer, almost as if the trees and vegetation emitted a barely perceptible glow.

She took a deep breath of the warm, damp air, then rose to her feet and looked around. She sighed with relief. She'd managed to make it to the Gray Place, but Finn was nowhere to be seen.

Though the temperature there was much more pleasant than what she'd left behind, she shivered and wrapped her cloak more tightly around herself. She repeated that this wasn't like the last time, where she'd involuntarily dragged Kai and Finn along, trapping them temporarily. She wasn't here fully, only in her mind. Nothing bad could happen, could it? The cushy moss felt so real beneath her boots, she couldn't help but question if anything else that might happen there could be real as well.

Some nearby vegetation rustled. She froze. Something chittered, then growled.

Anna's heart rate increased. Could there be beasts in this place, just as tangible as those which dwelt in the real world? She reached to her waist for her daggers, taking comfort as her palms brushed their hard pommels. She had weapons, but would mundane weapons work on creatures in the in-between? Were her weapons even real, and not merely just a projection of her mind?

She shook her head. The bush had gone quiet, but she wasn't about to let whatever was hiding there get the jump on her. She withdrew both daggers and crept toward the low shrub, her eyes keenly observing its leaves for signs of movement.

She slowed her breathing, almost upon the shrub. Should she stab the area blindly, or try to lure the beast out?

She screamed as something pounced on her back, knocking her to the ground. Her daggers flew from her grasp, and something sharp skimmed along her jaw. She was going to die in the cursed in-between and there was nothing she could do about it. This was all Finn's fault.

Just when she thought the killing blow would come, the pressure lessened from her back, then disappeared altogether. She rolled over, searching desperately for her daggers, then slumped in relief.

"How in the Horned One's name did you get here?" she sighed.

Naoki quirked her white, bird-like head, then sat like a loyal dog.

Anna sighed again. "You're looking for your mother, aren't you?"

Naoki made another chittering sound with her beak, then watched as Anna stood, brushed herself off, then retrieved both of her daggers.

"Well come on then," Anna instructed, gesturing with her hand for Naoki to move forward. "You stand a better chance of tracking your mother than I."

Naoki chittered again, then sped off like an arrow, making a beeline toward . . . well Anna didn't know what she was heading toward, but she hoped it was Finn. She took off at a run after the dragon, hoping the beast would not leave her behind.

FINN WANDERED FURTHER INTO THE DARK, BOGGY FOREST. IF it was simply a matter of waiting for the spell her body was under to wear off, all she needed to do was remain far enough away from Keiren to buy her that time. She could only hope that her mother had told her the truth, and that her companions were now safe with the Aos Sí.

She flexed her palm where Keiren had cut her. She'd been so close to giving away another portion of her immortality, not fully understanding what the consequences might be. If she gave away enough, would she eventually become a mortal woman?

She didn't really mind the idea. Part of her felt like she had lived long enough. The hole her daughter had left in her heart seemed to be slowly eating away at her, even though she refused to fully acknowledge it. She was tired, and even with the company of her companions, she was lonely. No one could truly understand the burden laid upon her, as much as they tried.

She shook her head and hopped over a low, mucky puddle, her thoughts lingering on Iseult. It was so easy for him to put up a wall between them whenever he chose. She wasn't even sure exactly what that imaginary wall was made of. He'd made it clear that he would not acknowledge any feelings he had for her beyond his duty, yet he also displayed moments of tenderness . . .

Completely absorbed in her thoughts, her foot touched down on something soft. She let out a yip of fright and tried to lift it again, but it stuck in the brown, gooey substance.

She pulled again, then frowned.

Crouching down with her other foot on moderately dry land, she began to untie her boot strings. As she picked at the knot, snarled with small brambles and mud, something warm and wet splattered on the back of her hand.

Curious, she turned her hand over to see a splotch of the sticky brown mud. *Hmm.* She hadn't been moving enough to fling the splatter on herself. She glanced up, wondering if it had dripped from one of the branches above, then another splatter hit her hand.

She gasped, then looked down to see another glob flying upward from the muck to land on her breeches. Then another.

Her heart in her throat, she tugged on her foot, but the

mud would not release her boot, and the knot in her boot strings seemed impossible to loosen.

Desperate, she groped at her waist for her dagger to cut the strings, but a big splatter of mud leapt up and smacked over her eyes. She gasped, and the sticky, smelly mud flew into her mouth.

Choking and sputtering, she fell to her side and tugged futilely at her boot, but her entire foot and calf was made slick by the mud. She gave a hearty tug, only to have her hands slip, the momentum tossing her fully onto her back. She could feel her breeches dampening as the mud climbed up her leg, engulfing it while tugging her toward the center of the muck.

She continued to fight like a rabbit caught in a snare, but the mud was too slippery. She spat out the remaining muck in her mouth and opened it to scream, but another splatter snaked through her lips, blocking her airways. She reflexively inhaled, then choked violently on the mud as it entered her lungs.

Distantly her mind registered a loud squeal behind her, but she could not focus on it in her panic. Her fright increased as something wrapped around her bicep and started pulling her away from the muck. The force at her back pulled so hard that her foot slipped out of her wet boot. They thunked to the ground, *hard*, but who, or *what*, ever was dragging her recovered and continued pulling. After scraping across rocks and sharp grass for what seemed like an eternity, the grip fell away from her arm and Finn's back hit the ground. She rolled on her side and coughed up mud until she vomited, then lay heaving, lacking the strength to wipe the remaining mud from her eyes.

"You're just always in trouble, aren't you?" a woman's voice muttered, panting from exertion.

Hot breath hit Finn's damp, muddy face, then something warm and wiggly snaked across her cheek, removing a portion of the mud. The touch came again, right over her eyes, finally allowing her to open them.

Naoki, her white feathers dotted with mud, peered down at her with spherical, lilac eyes. Gasping, Finn wrapped her weak arms around her pet dragon.

"Oh yes," the woman's voice sniped, "thank the dragon."

Finn rolled over with Naoki in her arms to see Anna sitting next to her.

"Anna?" she croaked through the grit burning her throat. "How?"

Anna rolled her eyes, then flicked brown muck from her hands. "How do you *think*? I've come here before."

Finn sat up, pushing Naoki to her lap, though the dragon was now far too large to rest there. Thinking of Naoki . . . she turned her muddy face back toward Anna. "And you brought Naoki too?"

She shook her head. "No, she was here before I was. She ran off before the battle. She must have realized part of you was somewhere else and went looking."

She looked down at Naoki again. Could it be possible for her to travel to the in-between at will? She shook her head, there were more important things to discuss, if only she could get her head straight.

"You said a battle?" she questioned, turning back to Anna. "Is everyone alright? Did Keiren interfere?"

"Who's Keiren?" Anna asked, standing to brush the mud from her breeches. Clumps of it littered her dark hair, held back in a tight braid.

Finn looked past Naoki at her feet, one now bootless with her sock dangling from her toes. She didn't feel quite ready to stand. "She's Àed's daughter," she explained. "She's asked Niklas to bring me here."

"Ah," Anna replied. "The one Bedelia mutters about from time to time? Well, we didn't see any women there, just Reivers and that Traveler. Then the Aos Sí showed up and ended the fight quickly. We made camp with them, then I came here." She peered around. "Where exactly is *here*?"

"I don't know," Finn replied, finally coaxing Naoki aside to stand. She was absolutely dripping wet with mud. *Lovely.* At least she wasn't dead. "What did the Aos Sí want?"

Anna eyed her speculatively. "You don't seem surprised at their mention."

She blushed. "I've had a few encounters since I arrived. I knew they found you."

Anna nodded. "Found us and saved us, because they want you to save them."

Finn sighed. Was it truly her job to save everyone. "Did Iseult ask you to come?" she asked, ready to change the subject.

Anna smirked. "Iseult doesn't know I'm here. I decided to come on my own, for Kai's sake." She narrowed her gaze, making Finn suddenly nervous. "You know," she continued, "you'll have to stop making these men crazy over you at some point. You'll be the death of them." She flicked a last splatter of mud to the ground. "Or *me*."

"I don't know what you mean," Finn replied.

Anna snorted, then started walking in the opposite direction of the animate muck puddle.

With a glance down at Naoki, Finn followed.

"Yes you do," Anna continued. "Kai and Iseult both love you, but you only love Iseult back. Why won't you let Kai go? He's worried sick about you right now."

She glared at Anna's back as she followed her. "Is this truly the time to discuss this?"

Anna snorted again. "Why not? Now that I've verified you're alive," she glanced over her shoulder to show Finn her smirk, "largely because of me," she continued, "my mission is accomplished and I simply need to wake up, then wait for you to wake up."

"Any idea when that will be?" Finn asked, cringing as her bootless foot found a sharp rock.

Not turning around, Anna shrugged. "I was out for days when the same powder was used on me, but the Travelers might have administered more while I was unconscious, so I don't know. Now back to my original question. Don't think that you can change the subject."

"Kai is my friend," she grumbled.

"He wants to be more than friends," Anna snapped back. "You may have been naive when you first came back to this world after being a tree, but you have your memories back now, so don't play dumb."

Why on earth was Anna questioning her about this? She was trapped in the in-between, and had just nearly *died* not even knowing what would have become of her body resting in reality. Glancing at Anna's resolute expression, she sighed, "I care about Kai. Perhaps it is selfish, but I'm glad he's still around. I'm glad *you're* around too, even if you're behaving like an angry mother badger."

Anna stopped and faced her. "Do you love him?"

Finn blinked at her for several seconds. "Shouldn't we be finding a place to hide before the mud finds a way to follow us?"

Anna crossed her arms and waited patiently.

"What do you want me to say?" Finn snapped. "That perhaps I am in love with two men at once? That perhaps Iseult makes me feel safe, but Kai understands me better? That Kai, not even knowing my full past, seems to know me better than anyone else?"

Anna raised a dark eyebrow at her.

"*What?*" she demanded, fed up.

"Well," Anna mused. "At least you've finally admitted it." With that, she turned and started walking again.

Finn hurried after her with Naoki at her heels. "So you were just prodding me to get me to admit that I might love them both? Why?"

"*Someone* had to make you," she explained. "And everyone else seems to be terrified of hurting your feelings. I wouldn't be your friend if I wasn't honest with you."

Wait. Anna was trying to be her . . . friend? Finn couldn't help but smile. She increased her pace to keep up with Anna's determined gait. "Did I thank you for saving me back there?"

Anna rolled her eyes. "No, you did not."

"Well thank you," Finn sighed. "For *everything*."

Anna glared at her, then seemed to comprehend that Finn was genuinely thanking her. She did not reply, but the small smile on her lips was acceptance enough for Finn.

~

BRANWEN'S EYES FLUTTERED OPEN. THE WHITE TENT ABOVE her glowed softly in the moonlight. How long had she been asleep?

She turned onto her side with a groan as her thoughts caught up with her. Anders was dead. There was nothing she could do to save him like he'd saved her, and according to the female Traveler, she couldn't even go back to the in-between to say goodbye.

She squeezed her eyes shut, desperately wishing to go back to sleep. Her entire body still ached, but the pain in her heart was worse. She needed to escape it.

"Will you have your brother's death be in vain?" a melodious male voice asked.

Her eyes snapped open. In one corner of the shadowy tent lurked a Traveler. He looked similar to all the rest, minus the mischievous glint in his reflective eyes.

"What do you mean?" she rasped, too tired to lift her head from her pillow. "Is there a way to save him?"

"No," the Traveler replied with a chuckle, "but there is a way for you to earn a normal life back at your family's Archive where you will be safe . . . for now. Your brother gave his life so that you may live, it would be a pity if you did not make it home."

She forced herself to a seated position, though her body stiffened, then spasmed in protest.

"What do you mean, *for now?*" she groaned, feeling nauseous. Her brother was truly dead. She had failed him, and she wasn't sure if she *could* go home. Could she return to a normal life after all she'd endured?

The Traveler shrugged. "Many will die in the times to come. I cannot ensure your safety upon reaching the Archives, but I imagine you will be safer there than most anywhere else."

She shook her head, then flinched at the sudden pain stabbing through her skull. "Tell me what you want from me," she hissed, "then be gone."

The Traveler steepled his fingers in front of his face and smiled. "I have many pieces on the game board. I have a sorceress poised to break the barriers to the in-between. I have a soulless man who will inspire a queen to help her, with the Gray Lady to show them the way. Now all I need is a wraith to provide them with a link to the other realm."

She blinked at him, utterly confused as he continued, "You see, wraiths cannot travel to the in-between, because they survive on the energy that holds the barriers in place. They are bound to the land, but possess a connection to that other place that most cannot access. If enough power is filtered through a wraith, it will inflate the barriers until they burst."

She shook her head, once again cringing at the pain. "I don't understand, why are you telling me all of this. Queens and wraiths? This has nothing to do with me."

He smiled. "You apparently have not caught on. Wraiths are formed when a trapped spirit is pulled from the in-between and given physical form. They no longer share in the connected life force of the land, rather, they are animated by the power of death, the great power that keeps the in-between separated from the land of the living."

She narrowed her eyes at him. "You're telling me that

because I was trapped in the in-between for so long, I'm now a wraith, given life by the powers of death?"

Using small motions, he gently clapped his hands together, applauding her. "I see you are as astute as your brother after all."

"Yes," she replied, feeling a sudden lurch in her gut at the mention of her brother. She gritted her teeth against her threatening tears. "Yes, I am," she continued, "which leads me to ask, why in the Horned One's name would I want to help *you*?"

The Traveler snickered. "My people made you a wraith, and they can end you just as easily. That's the entire point of creating a wraith to begin with. They are at the mercy of their creators, forced to do their bidding. If we take away that which animates you, then your brother died in vain. If, however, you choose to help us, I will release you from your contract and you can return to your family. You will still be a wraith, but you may live somewhat normally."

If she had any energy she would have leapt from her bedding to throttle him. He was threatening to kill her if she did not help him, but he'd return her to her family if she did. Part of her didn't care, but the other part knew he was right. If she died instead of trying to find a way out of her predicament, Anders' death would be in vain.

"What do you want me to do?" she hissed.

He grinned. "You will go to Finnur and tell her the truth. She will understand that I have aimed to help her all along."

She shook her head. Of *course* this was about Finn. "But that's not why you're doing this, is it? You want the barrier broken for some reason. *Why?*"

He laughed, then made his way toward the open tent

flap. "You know all you need to know, wraith. Rest while you can. You have a long journey ahead."

Branwen watched him go, then lifted her palms up in front of her face, observing them closely. They didn't look unusual. She flipped them, examining her knuckles, fingers, and wrists. They looked the same too. She pulled forward a lock of her unruly russet hair, stroking it between her fingertips. It didn't feel any different. Given all that, she assumed the rest of her was the same as she'd always been. Could she truly be what the Traveler claimed?

She laid back against her pillow, staring up at the tent blocking the moon from her view. "Oh Anders," she muttered. "You have saved me only to sentence me."

She turned on her side, further pondering her predicament. If she did as the Traveler asked . . . she sighed with a soft shudder. Was it even possible? Even after walking the long corridors of the in-between for so long, none of it had felt as dreamlike as her life did now, if you could truly call it a life at all.

CHAPTER NINE

Kai rubbed his eyes, tired from staring at Anna so intently. She breathed evenly, her eyes gently shut. If she'd found Finn, they at least weren't struggling.

He raised his gaze as Sativola approached, his plump face flushed with whatever liquor he'd managed to find. Catching his eye, Kai held a finger to his lips.

Sativola glanced down at Anna and nodded, then stumbled off to find his bedroll. Iseult and Bedelia held watch over Finn's unconscious body nearby. They'd built a small fire for warmth, as it was needed. He turned his gaze back down to Anna, wondering if he should fetch another bedroll to keep her warm.

Shaking his head, he rested his face in his hands, elbows on knees, resigned to his duty. He hoped at least Bedelia would sleep soon. It wouldn't do to have her, Iseult, and himself all unrested for morning.

A loud trill cut through the night air, and the soft

murmurs still coming from the Aos Sí camp cut off. Another trill sounded. He would have thought it was a bird if it weren't for the sudden silence from the Aos Sí. Something was wrong.

He nearly jumped out of his skin as Eywen suddenly appeared before him. Kai let out a brisk sigh. How Eywen could run so silently and inconspicuously in the bulk of that dully gleaming armor was beyond him.

"We must go," Eywen hissed, meeting his eyes briefly, then turning his attention past him toward Iseult.

Iseult was suddenly at Kai's side, cradling Finn in his arms like a sleeping child. He eyed Eywen, clearly waiting for an explanation.

"That call is used by the scouting parties of the *Dearg Due*," Eywen explained, "blood sucking Faie. Their tracking skills are rivaled by none."

"Whom do they track?" Iseult asked evenly.

Eywen stared off into the darkness. "Perhaps you, or perhaps I, the results will be the same. We must go."

Before Kai could blink, Iseult was off toward the horses, Finn's long hair draped over his cradling arm. Another trill sliced through the air, this time closer.

Kai fell to his knees. He grabbed Anna's shoulders and shook her hard enough that she'd likely slap him when she woke. "Get up," he hissed, glancing over his shoulder to see Bedelia and Sativola climbing atop their horses, their supplies strapped across their saddles haphazardly.

Anna's limbs flopped limply against her bedroll, his attempt to waken her in vain.

"Curse these blasted Faie," he muttered, then sprung up to prepare his horse.

Iseult had already climbed into the saddle of Finn's unicorn with Finn's limp legs dangling down on either side of the beasts back and her body grasped against his chest. "We need to hurry," he prompted as Kai frantically saddled his horse.

"Anna went to the in-between," he growled. "She will not wake."

Hoofbeats preceded Eywen, along with several of the other Aos Sí on horseback, some riding two to a saddle since there weren't enough horses between them. Eywen hopped down from his mount beside where Anna lay. "I have her!" he shouted. "We must flee!"

Kai cursed under his breath as he watched Eywen lift Anna into his saddle. One of the other Aos Sí helped balance her so Eywen could climb next.

Kai would have preferred to be the one to watch over Anna, but there was nothing he could do about it now. He lunged into his own saddle, took up the reins, then galloped after Finn and Iseult.

As they raced onward into the night, the Aos Sí closed in around them. The loud trills, the hunting calls of something that even scared the Aos Sí, increased in frequency as they grew near.

Eywen rode up beside Kai, clutching Anna to his chest, their long black hair intermingling in the wind. "Do not look them in the eyes!" He shouted over the deafening trills. "No matter what you do, keep riding as fast as you can. If you see running water, cross it. We need only to survive until sunrise!"

"It's the middle of the night!" Kai shouted back. This was *bad*. An icy chill went up his spine as the trilling sounds closed in. He noticed black shapes darting around the surrounding trees. Whatever these creatures were, their eyes reflected the moon in a shimmering display. He tried to look more closely as he galloped by, then remembered Eywen's words. *Don't look them in the eyes.* Easier said than done. Any of the horses could easily stumble in the darkness, dislodging their riders. What was he supposed to do if he fell?

Something leapt onto his horse's rump, and he lashed out reflexively with a sharp blow of his elbow. He met with solid flesh, and the creature fell away. He couldn't make out much about the creature, except a brief glimpse of a female, humanoid body. If it weren't for the glowing eyes, these creatures could almost pass as ordinary women . . . ordinary women who were somehow outrunning their horses.

Kai watched as one of the women jumped on the unicorn's white rump, her flowing cloak obscuring Iseult and Finn from view. The woman's body jolted, then fell away, revealing the glint of Iseult's sword.

Kai's horse stepped around the fallen creature, as another vaulted to attack Iseult's back. At the risk of possibly injuring Iseult, Kai threw his dagger into the woman's back. She fell away with a screech, but another soon took her place. *They had to be after Finn*, he thought. *Of course, they were after her.*

Seeming to come to the same conclusion, Eywen shouted, "Surround the Dair! Do not let them touch her!"

The Aos Sí closed in, fending off the Dearg Due with their blades while somehow avoiding eye contact.

Kai watched on in awe for a moment, until his back was slammed with a body, and strong arms circled his chest.

Before he could respond, a mouth flew to his neck, teeth jamming down, breaking skin. He winced, feeling the clamp of a mouth affixed to him. Blood rushed to his neck, but the woman would not let go. Unable to loosen her hold on him, he fumbled for the second dagger on his belt. Securing it, he thrust his hand back, stabbing the dagger into her side.

Still she did not release her hold. His vision darted to the Aos Sí ahead, swarmed by more of the creatures. He tore his dagger free and stabbed her again.

Beginning to feel lightheaded, he managed to withdraw his dagger and stab her one last time. Her mouth fell away from his neck as her body tumbled from the horse. Suddenly too weak to keep his seat, he tumbled to the ground after her, landing with a thud in the damp leaves. The thundering of hooves grew distant, his party, he presumed, out of sight.

He forced his eyes open, desperate to see if he was alone. His gaze was met with strange, reflective eyes. The woman spoke in a foreign tongue, then moved back to reveal several others.

Still on his back, he watched on awestricken, feeling as if he were in some sort of trance. He couldn't seem to look away from the woman whose eyes he'd met. The one woman spoke again, then several sets of hands dragged him to his feet.

The Dearg Due continued speaking as they half dragged, half carried him back the way they'd come. He recognized none of their words, save two, *Dair Leanbh*. He would have cursed himself if he could think straight. They must have been sent to capture any of the Dair, and since Finn's blood ran through his veins, they thought he was one.

~

ISEULT HAD HIS BLADE IN ONE HAND, WITH HIS OTHER ARM wrapped around Finn's waist, bracing her against his chest. He leaned forward, shielding her with his body as much as possible, trusting Finn's unicorn to safely guide them.

He'd heard legends of the Dearg Due, but had never encountered them before. They'd disappeared along with most of the other Faie. He did not know precisely why they were after Finn, but it came as no surprise.

Screeches from the Dearg Due pierced his ears as the Aos Sí fell left and right, giving their lives to protect Finn. If Iseult had questioned their loyalty before, he was not questioning it now. He would not let their sacrifice be in vain.

Squeezing Finn tightly, he slashed his blade at one of the creatures that had slipped past the Aos Sí. She gripped onto Finn's limp leg until his sword sunk into her neck. Just as she fell away, another darted in from the darkness. Slashing his already bloody blade at her face, she too fell away.

"Ride ahead of us!" Eywen shouted. "My soldiers will fight them, it is the only way!"

Iseult did not need to be told twice. Perhaps he was a less than noble man for being willing to sacrifice others for Finn's well being, but it did not matter. It was simply a fact.

He sheathed his blade and leaned forward to take hold of the unicorn's reins, sandwiching Finn between himself and the saddle. Without any prompting, the unicorn shot forward, straight and true like an arrow. She pulled away from the Aos Sí horses, while Eywen shouted orders for his men to turn and fight. It would be difficult for Eywen to defend himself while protecting Anna, but it was a distant worry in Iseult's mind. Just as the worry that he did not see Kai, Sativola, or Bedelia anywhere.

He steeled his gaze forward, grateful for the unicorn's speed and ability to deftly weave through the trees and undergrowth, far more graceful than any horse. The shrieks and trills of the Dearg Due grew distant, along with the battle cries of the Aos Sí.

Soon enough, all fell silent, save the rhythmic clomping of the unicorn's hooves. It was silent enough that he could hear Finn muttering in her sleep, though he could not decipher her words.

ANNA STAGGERED, SUDDENLY FEELING OVERWHELMINGLY dizzy. Was she waking up, or was it something else? Finn stopped walking and watched her with concern.

She stared down at the mossy earth, trying to regain her equilibrium. "I think something is happening to my body," she muttered.

Finn glanced around them, then grasped Anna's arm. "You should sit," she instructed, then proceeded to help Anna lower herself to the ground.

Naoki trotted up to see what the commotion was. She blinked her lilac eyes at Anna, then turned her beak up toward her mother, chittering a question no one would ever be able to understand.

Searing pain shot through Anna's arm. She doubled over.

"What is it?" Finn gasped. "What's the matter?"

"I think we're being attacked," she groaned.

"Then you must go back!" Finn hissed. "I will be fine. I will hide from Keiren until I awake. It should hopefully keep her attention off you."

Anna nodded, though she had no idea how to return except to go to sleep, and she didn't think she'd be sleeping any time soon with the pain coursing through her body.

"Tell Iseult," Finn began, then seemed to take a moment to think. "Tell Iseult that I will be alright, and to continue on our course as planned. I almost . . . did something stupid, I think, but I will not make that mistake again."

Anna nodded, clenching her jaw against the pain. Her vision was fading to black. Would passing out be the same thing as going to sleep here? She hoped so.

She felt a soft touch as Finn kissed her cheek. "Please be safe," Finn muttered. "I will do all that I can to protect you."

Anna wanted to ask her what in the Horned One's name she was talking about, but another wave of pain raced through her, and her vision faded entirely.

Suddenly the world came crashing back around her. She sat up with a gasping breath, but someone pinned her back down against the dry, rocky earth.

"Be still," a voice soothed. "You are alright."

She forced her eyes open, then nearly screamed.

Strange, uptilted blue eyes peered down at her, set in skin as white as snow, framed in the darkness of the real world night. Eywen pushed his black, spider silk hair behind his ear, his other hand remaining on Anna's shoulder, holding her down.

She tilted her head to observe her arm, the source of her pain in the in-between. There was a fresh bandage wrapped around the entirety of her bicep. Her shirt, stained with blood, was torn all the way up to her armpit.

She turned her frightened gaze back up to the terrifying Aos Sí. "What happened?" she croaked.

"We were attacked," he explained in a hushed tone. "Iseult escaped with Finn. I don't know where the others are."

"Why am I here with you?" she breathed. "Where's Kai?"

"I do not know what happened to him," he explained. "They attacked our camp, and it was quicker for me to take you. You would not wake."

Anna groaned and pushed his hand away to sit up. "Who attacked us?"

"The Dearg Due," he explained, glancing around the dark woods. "You have a bite on your arm. I bandaged it to stop the blood flow, but it must be cleansed."

"Dearg Due?" she questioned, shaking her head to clear away the cobwebs in her mind. "*Cleansed*?"

He nodded, and that silky hair fell forward again. "For human women, the bite of the Dearg Due can be transformative. It can make you one of them. For human men," he sighed. "They become servants to their newly beloved masters."

Anna shakily climbed to her feet, noting the single horse loosely tied to a nearby tree.

Eywen rose with her, watching her closely.

She shivered. Out of everyone she could have been left with, it *had* to be the cursed leader of the Aos Sí. She took a step forward and her knees gave out.

Eywen darted in to catch her and she pushed away, not

wanting him to touch her. She ended up on her butt in the dry pine needles, clutching her arm.

Eywen watched her with concern, no sign of malice or Faie bloodlust in his strange eyes. Finally really looking at him, she noted that he was missing several components of his armor, including his helmet, and his wrist was bleeding from what looked like a messy, gaping bite wound.

"You're injured," she commented.

He nodded. "The bite of the Dearg Due will not affect me as it does humans," he explained, crouching beside her. "I'm going to help you up now," he added, as if asking permission.

She took a shaky breath, then nodded.

He gently wrapped his arms around her torso and lifted. The grip would have never worked for a human unless he was as strong as Sativola, but Eywen lifted her effortlessly to her feet. Once she was steady, he let her go.

"We should ride on," he suggested. "Once the sun rises we will be safe, and we can search for the others."

She nodded, feeling like a snake was uncurling in her gut. What if there was nothing left of the others to find? What if they were all . . . dead? Or worse, what if Kai was now a servant to these wretched, sharp-toothed Faie?

KAI GROANED AND ROLLED OVER ONTO HIS BACK. THE HARD, cool stone seemed to bite into his skin. His neck throbbed.

Slowly, his memories returned to him. He'd been bitten by one of the Dearg Due. He had fallen from his horse and was left behind. His head lolled to the side. He cringed.

Staring back at him was one of the Dearg Due, sitting cross-legged with her diaphanous black cloak billowing around her. Her hair was long and pure white, framing a skeletal face with worm-white skin.

She blinked her reflective eyes at him, then spoke in a language he didn't understand.

"I don't know what you're saying," he groaned, wishing he had the strength to stand up and run away. With a stone ceiling above them, illuminated by a small fire, he guessed they were in a cave.

"We have been sent for you, Dair Leabh," she explained in a purring voice.

His eyes widened. That was right. They'd been after Finn, and due to his blood, thought he was one of the Dair.

"By whom?" he questioned. He reached up to his neck to find an open wound, the blood slowly congealing, but still bleeding. Would he be left on the ground to bleed out entirely?

"The Winter Queen," the Dearg Due replied. "We will bring you to her."

Winter Queen? Did she mean Oighear? "The Winter Queen is dead," he replied. "I saw her die."

The Dearg Due shook her head. "You cannot kill the winter."

This was bad. *Very* bad. "Well if you want me to make it there, I'll need my wounds tended," he groaned. If he could just get himself in better shape, then he could escape.

The Dearg Due made a hissing sound that he soon realized was laughter. "I am no fool," she replied. "The Dair are not so easily killed. Most of my kin have been slain and I must keep you weakened."

Well *shit*. He couldn't tell her he wasn't one of the Dair, she'd likely kill him right there. Yet, if he didn't tell her, he'd soon die of his wounds.

"The sun will rise soon," she said, her voice trembling. "We will stay here until nightfall. If I sense your magic, I will kill you."

He cringed and turned his gaze back to the stone ceiling above their heads. If he was expected to lie there for an entire day without care, he wouldn't make it till nightfall. His only option was to convince the terrifying creature to help him, which wasn't much of an option at all.

It appeared that he was finished. He would be left in this cave to rot, and no one would ever even know what happened to him.

CHAPTER TEN

Finn sat in a grassy copse with Naoki slumbering by her side. The sun had risen, giving the eerie landscape a more serene look, though it was still misty. How long was she going to be trapped in this blasted place? She'd tried going to sleep briefly, but when she awoke, she was still here, just like her mother had said. She wished at the very least her mother would come back and tell her more, but she hadn't seen her since she'd been chased off by . . . something.

She gently shook Naoki awake, then stood. She didn't want to remain in any one place for too long, lest Keiren find her. Naoki uncurled, then stretched her winged back like a cat.

"Ready?" Finn asked her, as if Naoki could answer.

Finn stepped forward cautiously, favoring her foot with the boot still on it, wary of sticky mud. She shuddered, thinking of the slimy attack of the previous evening. Naoki was with her now though, and that made her feel better.

Her dragon was highly perceptive, and likely to spot danger long before she would.

She sighed, picking her way around tall brambles in search of a path. Eventually they left the misty area behind, emerging into a meadow filled with small trees and brambles. The sun shone brightly overhead, fooling Finn into thinking perhaps she was somewhere back in reality, not stuck in the in-between.

She meandered on for some time, ignoring the grumbling of her belly. With her physical form unconscious, she wasn't sure how she was supposed to gain nourishment, and hoped she would not be out long enough to waste away.

She walked on, her boot and sock hissing across the grass, hoping everything had turned out alright for Anna upon returning to her body.

She froze.

There was a man sitting in the meadow ahead of her, staring up at the fluffy white clouds.

"A-Anders?" she questioned.

He turned back to her, a sad look in his honey colored eyes. "I'd hoped I'd see you here before I moved on."

She hurried to his side with Naoki trailing behind her. "What do you mean? *How* are you here?"

Anders sighed and looked down at his lap. "Niklas killed me, and I ended up here. I think this is where I have to wait until I move on to . . . wherever I'm supposed to move on to."

"That cannot be right," she argued, taking a seat beside him. "Why would he do that to you?"

He shrugged, turning his gaze back up to the sky. "I was no longer of use, but it's alright. He promised he'd save my sister." He turned toward her. "I heard her voice, you know. When I first arrived here. I heard her voice, but then she disappeared. I think she must have been returned to her body. I can't believe she was here, trapped, all of that time."

Tears burned at the back of Finn's eyes. "You didn't get to speak with her?"

Anders shook his head, then wiped a tear as it fell down his face. "No." He sniffled, then looked more closely at Finn. "Why are you even speaking with me? You must be furious that I helped trap you here."

She sighed. She'd been a little angry, but it was hard to throw stones at a dead man. "I'd say you learned your lesson," she joked, then bit her tongue. "My apologies, that was insensitive."

He waved her off. "No, no, it's alright. I'm glad, at least, that no harm has come to you. I don't know what Keiren planned to do once she had you here. Well, I know she wanted to steal your immortality to destroy the barrier between this place and reality, but I wasn't sure what that might entail."

Finn blinked at him in shock. "Destroy the barrier to the in-between?"

Anders nodded. "That is her goal, though I do not know why."

Finn turned her stunned gaze up to the sky as Naoki frolicked around them, chasing bugs in the grass. "Thank you for telling me, I suppose," she muttered. If the barrier to the in-between could be destroyed, perhaps Iseult's ancestors could be freed . . .

"I can tell you something else too," Anders began, drawing her out of her thoughts. "I know you are searching for Àed to save him. Keiren has you thinking you have to travel all the way to some island to do it, but you don't. He's in a dungeon within one of her fortresses."

"W-what?" she stammered. Bedelia had seen him being turned into a tree. Had she lied?

He shrugged. "I was within the fortress for a while. I saw him in the dungeon, though he refused to speak to me. He believed I was a traitor, which wasn't entirely wrong, I suppose."

She shook her head, still struggling with disbelief. "But you told me that only the person who put him under his spell could undo it. Was that all a lie?"

He smiled softly. "No, I told you *only the caster who has imprisoned Àed can set him free*, and it's true. There's no getting in and out of that fortress without Keiren's help. I *tried*."

She studied his features, wondering if she could really believe him. Of course, why would a dead man lie?

"So he's in a dungeon," she began hesitantly, "but you cannot tell me where, or how to reach him?"

Anders nodded, turning his gaze out toward the expanse of the idyllic meadow. "You'll have to deal with Keiren one way or another," he explained, "and at least you know what she wants, if not why. Niklas has not been quite so transparent. He works with Keiren, but I do not believe him loyal to her."

Something tugged at the edge of her memory, some important scrap of information about the Travelers, but she couldn't seem to fully form it in her mind.

The vague memory was lost as Anders cleared his throat to regain her attention.

Reaching a hand out to stroke Naoki, who had settled down beside her, head nuzzled in her lap, she turned to him.

"I know I am in no position to ask a favor of you," he began, then hesitated.

"Go on," she pressed.

He looked down at his lap. "It's Branwen. She may have been returned to the living, but I have no idea what state she's in, or what schemes the Travelers might rope her into. I was hoping . . . " he trailed off.

"That I could help her?" she finished for him.

He nodded, clearly abashed.

"I consider Branwen my friend," she explained curtly. "I would help her for that reason alone."

He sighed, turning his gaze back toward the meadow. "I suppose I deserve that."

She was silent for a few seconds, trying to remain steely, but soon enough Anders' sadness got the better of her.

"I would have helped *you*, you know," she muttered. "If you had only been honest, I would have done all I could to help both you and Branwen. I've known all along she was trapped here. I saw her once, the night Kai almost died—" she cut herself off, taken aback by the incredulous stare Anders was giving her.

"And here you were, chastising *me* for being a liar," he mused.

She had the decency to blush. She hadn't trusted Anders from the moment they met him on the road. How had she expected *him* to trust *her*?

"I see your point," she sighed. "If I can figure out where

Branwen is, I will try to help her. I will do it for her, and for *you*."

He leaned back on his elbows, seeming to now enjoy the soft breeze and the gentle sunlight on his face.

"In that case," he breathed, "I believe I can move on. I have no worries left to cling to."

She glanced up at the sky a moment, thinking how nice that would be. Looking back at Anders, she gasped. He'd become transparent, little particles of him gradually floating away on the breeze.

Naoki lifted her head from Finn's lap to gaze curiously at what remained of Anders.

Anders offered them both a spectral smile, then faded away entirely.

With a shaky hand, Finn lifted her fingers to wipe away a tear as it fell down her cheek. She couldn't help but wonder why someone like Anders had to die so young, when she'd been shackled to the earth for over a century.

It didn't quite seem fair to either of them.

"CURSE YOU!" ANNA SCREAMED. "IT'S GOOD ENOUGH!"

"It's not," Eywen said evenly.

She and Eywen had ridden, *on the same horse,* she thought grudgingly, until the sun rose. Now, not only had she spent the awkward ride balancing on the back of Eywen's saddle, but he was trying to kill her . . . or at least it felt like it.

He cupped his long-fingered hands into the stream again, wetting the bandage around his wrist wound, then dumped the ice-cold water on Anna's outstretched arm. Her breath hissed out as she gritted her teeth against the pain. The rest of her body lay on the shore, with rocks digging into her back. Her shoulder ached from extending her arm over her head and into the water, but it was the only position they'd found that would allow Eywen to thoroughly cleanse the wound on her bicep without soaking the rest of her clothing.

"Who would ever believe nice, clear stream water could cause such horrible pain?" she hissed as he doused her again.

Her teeth began to chatter from the mixture of cold water and exhaustion, and Eywen finally paused his work.

"We must make sure the wound is fully cleansed with running water," he explained. "The Dearg Due cannot cross it, lest they lose their magic for a time. It drains the magic from their bites as well."

Anna peered up at him, her head cradled in the moss growing near the edge of the stream bed. "Why are you helping me?" she groaned. "Why do you care if I turn into one of them?"

He stared down at her for a moment, then answered, "I do not want to be locked into eternal slumber."

"What on earth are you talking about?" she growled. "What does that have to do with anything?"

He sighed, then rocked casually back on his heels. "The Aos Sí awakened when Oighear, our queen, awakened," he explained. "Her magic gives us life. Once, a very long time ago, she signed a contract to restrain her magic, and she could no longer sustain us. I would not like to be put in such a position again."

Anna moved her arm out of the water and cradled it

against her side. She wanted to sit up, but feared she was still on the brink of vomiting. "I still don't understand what a Faiery story has to do with you helping me."

He glared at her, rather imposing since he was directly above her. "It is not a *Faiery story*. It was the undoing of my people. Finnur could become our new queen, and *she* would never allow her magic to be weakened."

Anna rolled her eyes. "I wouldn't put your faith in Finn. She doesn't exactly think her decisions through."

He gently took her arm and lifted it back above her head to float in the water, with her wound just above the surface. "She is our only choice. *My* only choice. I will do anything to convince her to save my people, even if it means I must save hers in return."

Another splash of icy water came. She clenched her jaw, refusing to scream. Before she could catch a breath, he doused her again.

"That should be enough," he muttered. "The coloring of your skin around the wound has returned to normal."

She sighed in relief, pulling her hand back out of the water. She waited while he dried her arm, then rebandaged the wound. Finished, Eywen stood. Anna rolled onto her side, still unable to sit up.

"Rest as long as you need," he instructed. "Once you are well, we will search for Iseult and Finnur."

"What about everyone else?" she groaned, primarily thinking of Kai.

He shook his head. "Perhaps they are already together. Finn's magic is strong enough that I can sense it. I have no way of tracking the others."

Anna frowned, but could not argue. If she was close enough, she could track Finn's magic too.

She watched Eywen as he brushed loose scraps of lichen from his tan breeches, the remaining pieces of his armor long since discarded. Without the strange armor, he looked almost . . . normal. That was, if she ignored the icy hue of his skin, and his spider silk hair.

His gaze suddenly on her, he crossed his legs and sat in the grass. "Now that I have told you my story, it is time to tell me what *you* want from Finnur."

She narrowed her gaze at him. If her answer did not suit him, would he kill her and leave her for the wolves? He was Faie, after all.

"It doesn't matter," she muttered.

He continued to watch her intently. "You have traveled with her for a long while. Whatever it is, it matters enough for you to risk life and limb to remain at her side."

She frowned, considering blaming Kai, but it would be a mistruth. "I can see things," she sighed, hoping she wasn't making a mistake. "I can see when people have magic, and sometimes I see things before they happen in my dreams. Or sometimes *while* they're happening."

Eywen nodded. "I suspected you were of Clan Liath. Queen Oighear has always been fascinated by those of your lineage."

"What?" Anna questioned abruptly. "How did you know that? And why would that snowy shrew care anything about humans?"

Eywen tilted his head in thought. "She refers to your type of magic as *the shadow*. It is your shadow self that can move into the in-between, the place you go in your dreams.

Many human mages can travel to the in-between, as can the Dair, but it has always been out of Oighear's reach. She does not *like* when things are out of her reach. She longs to have shadow magic of her own."

Anna shivered, glad that Oighear had been preoccupied with Finn, and not *her*, during the brief time they'd spent in her dungeon.

She opened her mouth to say more, but hesitated. She was not sure just how much information she wanted to share with him.

Noticing her hesitation, he gestured with his hand for her to go on. "Please, speak freely."

She sighed, then struggled to prop herself up on her elbow. "I suppose it is not my tale to tell, but I'm curious since you say Oighear cannot reach the in-between. A few nights ago, Kai and Finn shared a dream. They were visited by Oighear, and awoke surrounded by frost."

Eywen lifted his long-fingered hand and cradled his chin. "Fascinating that one of the Dair could share a dream with a human. My guess is it was a premonition, rather than an actual visit from Oighear. She is very powerful, but as I told you, the in-between, known as the dream realm to some, is beyond her reach."

Anna nodded. Feeling steady on her elbow, she took a deep breath, then pushed herself to a seated position.

"You still have not answered my question," he said softly.

She glared at him, suddenly suspicious. "Why is it so important to you?"

He tilted his head again. "I'm simply curious. Finnur has gathered a rather unique assortment of companions."

Anna watched his face for signs he was lying, but his expression remained utterly impassive.

"Fine," she snapped. "I do not want my magic, this thing you call a *shadow*. I want Finn to remove it from me."

"And you have not yet convinced her to do so?"

She clenched her jaw and deepened her glare. "She agreed to help me, but I decided it better to wait until all of this . . . strangeness is over."

"Ah," he said, nodding. "You fear being left in a world where magic is increasing by the day, without any magic of your own."

She sighed, hating when her curse was referred to as *magic*. "I only figure it's better for me to see magic coming before it arrives, so that I might run the other way."

He chuckled. "Clever girl," he mused, then stood and offered her his hand.

She ignored it and climbed to her feet on her own, though the hand up would have been helpful given her lingering dizziness.

Eywen chuckled again, then walked toward his horse, tied to a nearby tree. "Come," he said happily. "Let us find your friends."

She followed him, glaring at his back. "You know, you're in a much better mood than the first time we met you."

He laughed, looking over his shoulder at her as he untied the horse's reins. "Last time we met, I was a slave to the Snow Queen. Anyone would be in a better mood after escaping *that*."

Anna sighed, then waited for him to mount before scrabbling up into the saddle behind him. She almost reflexively put her arms around his waist, then thought better of it and clutched the back rim of the saddle instead.

The day she actually trusted one of the Faie was still a long ways off, even if this one had been kind enough to rescue her.

ISEULT PACED BACK AND FORTH NEAR FINN'S BODY, UNABLE to contain his restlessness. The cool sunlight on his face was of little comfort. Finn's unicorn, curled up on the ground in a position more common for dogs than horses, watched him warily, conveying distrust.

He sighed, then stalked toward the stream he'd set up camp beside. He'd heard legends that the Dearg Due would not willingly cross running water, so he'd chosen to stop there, even if the water might serve as a lure for other predators.

He dunked a clean black shirt from his pack into the crystal clear water, then returned to Finn. With the wet shirt in one hand, he sat, then lifted the back of her head up onto his thigh. He poised one edge of his shirt over her mouth and gently opened her jaw. The water slowly dripped in, but she did not swallow. Still, he figured a few drops of water were better than none. He would keep trying. She'd already been out for a full night and into another day, and he didn't want her to wake up in a sorry state from lack of food and water. If only he had some milk or broth to drip into her mouth for added sustenance. If only he had Bedelia, Anna, or Kai to watch his back while he cared for her.

He stroked a strand of hair from her face as he cradled her head. If only she would wake up.

With another sigh, he gently laid her head back down on the bunched up edge of her bedroll, then stood. They'd rested long enough. He would have liked to stay and search for the others, but his primary objective was putting distance between themselves and any remaining Dearg Due before nightfall. Reaching a burgh would be ideal, but they'd traveled far into the woods during their flight. It was unlikely they'd reach civilization within the next few days.

Seeming to sense his intent, the unicorn stood, then lowered its muzzle to Finn's face. To his surprise, the unicorn's fat tongue lolled out of its mouth and trailed across Finn's cheek. He moved forward to shoo the creature away, but before he could it licked her again, and Finn groaned.

Iseult fell to his knees at her side as the unicorn licked a third time. Finn groaned again, then lifted a hand to rub her eyes.

The unicorn waited, poised for another lick, then Finn's eyes shot open. She blinked at the unicorn in surprise, then turned her wide-eyed gaze to Iseult. "I'm back?" she questioned weakly.

He nodded, relief flooding through him. "We must ride on," he explained. "We are not safe."

Gently pushing the unicorn's nose aside, Finn started to sit up, but didn't quite make it.

Iseult was there with a hand behind her back before she could lose her progress. "You are weak. You must eat something, but slowly. I'll give you some bread once we start moving." He began carefully helping her to sit up when something came crashing through the underbrush toward them, and he nearly dropped her.

Whatever it was, it had stopped behind a shrub. White feathers poked out above the leaves, then a body pounced forth almost upon Finn. Iseult swung his arm back to fend it off, then relaxed. It was only Naoki. What an odd time for her to emerge.

With a warm smile, Finn held out her arms to the dragon, then explained, "She followed me to the in-between. It seems she has a similar talent to Anna."

He stared at the dragon in disbelief as it began to sniff Finn's hands and face. Seeming to sense his gaze, Naoki sat back on her haunches and stared right back at him, then they both turned their attention back to Finn.

Finn glanced around as if only then realizing she'd been moved a long way since they'd met Niklas on the Sand Road. She peered past Iseult to the rest of their small camp-site, then glanced over her shoulder at the stream. "Where are the others?"

"We lost them," he explained, his gut clenched tight. She would not like what he had to say next, and she would like even less what he planned to do about it. "We were attacked," he elaborated, "by Faie creatures hunting you. The Aos Sí distracted them for you and I to escape, but I do not know what happened to the others. They were lost in the chaos." He paused, debating just how honest he should be with her. "Some might be dead," he added.

She inhaled sharply. "W-what? What do you mean, *dead*?"

He clenched his jaw. They really needed to gain more distance before the day wore on. "We were attacked," he reiterated. "The others are either as lost as we are, or they are dead. Chances are, a few did not survive."

"Stop saying *dead*," she demanded. "They cannot be *dead*. I'm sure they are searching for us as we speak. We must wait here for them."

Naoki began to hop around, chittering her beak in a seeming attempt to halt the argument.

Ignoring the dragon, Iseult shook his head. "It is not safe. Do not let their sacrifice be in vain."

Finn shook her head rapidly, scooting back away from him. "Do not say that. We will find them."

He clenched his jaw so hard his teeth ached. He had to placate her somehow. "Our best chance of finding them is to continue on with our journey," he explained. "We can wait for them in Sormyr, safe from any other Faie that might be tracking you."

She started to shake her head again, then stopped. Her shoulders slumped. "Oighear is still alive. That's why the Faie are tracking me."

"Yes," he replied, having come to the same conclusion. "Now we must go."

"No," she argued, her voice trembling. "I will not leave everyone behind. If the Faie find them first . . . " she shook her head. "I must protect them."

He flexed his hands in irritation. This was going nowhere. It wasn't *her* job to protect everyone. He turned away from her to retrieve the unicorn's saddle from the ground, then set it gently on the creature's back, securing the belly strap before fastening the bridle around its head.

Finn sat in the grass glaring at him as he rolled up the

bedroll, then strapped the rest of their meager supplies behind the saddle.

Done with that, he marched over to her.

She glared up at him. "You wouldn't dare."

He sighed, then crouched down and lifted her up like a child. She struggled against him, but he refused to release her.

"I'm not going *anywhere*," she hissed, pushing against his chest. "I will use my magic on you if I must."

"No," he stated calmly, carrying her toward the unicorn. "You will not."

She continued to struggle as he tossed her onto the saddle, forcing her to either straddle it or fall off the other side, then quickly climbed up behind her. He hated even the small risk of her falling off, but he hated even more the risk of the Dearg Due finding them come nightfall.

Naoki pranced around the unicorn, craning her long neck up to watch Finn, who seemed momentarily too stunned to fight.

Seizing the opportunity, Iseult circled Finn with his arms and grabbed the reins, then dug his heels into the unicorn's sides. He exhaled a sigh of relief as the unicorn obeyed, and Naoki trotted after them.

"Loinnir," Finn snapped. "I demand that you stop moving right this instant."

The unicorn continued walking, despite Finn's demands.

Giving up on that course of action, Finn glared over her shoulder at Iseult. "Why is she not listening to me? Did you conspire against me while I was asleep?"

"Perhaps she does not listen, because she too wants you to remain alive," he said evenly.

Her expression softened, ever so slightly. "My life is no more important than those of our friends."

He shook his head. "I do not agree, and it seems, neither does your unicorn."

Finn huffed, turning to face forward in the saddle. "Let us at least retrace our steps on the way. Perhaps we can find evidence of their fates."

And run right back to the Dearg Due? Hardly. "No," he said out loud.

She crossed her arms and proceeded to pout.

He withdrew a piece of bread from their supplies and handed it to her, both to fill her belly and keep her from speaking further.

She took it with a glare.

He did his best to ignore her after that, though it vexed him to have her upset with him. He was at least glad they were finally moving, and that despite her threats, she had not used her magic on him.

Of course, there was still time for her to change her mind.

～

BEDELIA GROANED AS SHE FORCED HER EYES OPEN. SOFT bedding rubbed against her cheek. Her vision slowly came into focus . . . candles, plush rugs, and, she sniffed, the sea? They'd still been days away from the sea. Had her companions found her after the Dearg Due attack and carried her all that way?

She sat up in the cushy bed, her hand reflexively going to her neck to examine the bite wound there, but instead she found a fresh bandage adhered to the side of her neck with some sort of paste. She glanced down to see she was dressing in a clean, white sleeping gown.

She tugged her bare feet out of the bedding and swung them over the side of the bed. Flexing her toes, she gasped. The black lines from her old Faie wolf bite had receded. The marring of the central wound was still there, but the spreading that had taken place over the past weeks was gone.

Suddenly suspicious, she glanced around the room again. Where on earth was she?

"It's about time you woke," a female voice said from somewhere behind her, though she'd been sure there was no one in the room just seconds ago.

She whipped around, then cringed at the pain in her neck, though it was nothing compared to the sudden fear in her heart. "Keiren? What's going on? Where am I?"

Keiren's rouged lips curled into a smile, and not the usual predatory one. This one was soft and . . . concerned?

Keiren stepped forward. Her long red dress, as fiery as her hair, trailed across the ornate rugs. On anyone else the matching hair and dress would have looked odd, but on Keiren, it just looked striking and lovely. Even without the clothes, that was how Bedelia had always viewed her . . . until recently.

"I found you," Keiren explained. "You were bitten by one of the Dearg Due, and left behind by your companions."

She shook her head. "No, they did not leave me on purpose. We were separated during the attack."

Keiren took a seat beside her on the bed.

Bedelia flinched.

Keiren's smile faltered. "You were near death," she explained. "If I had not found you," she shook her head, "you would have died."

Bedelia took a deep, trembling breath. "Were you behind forcing Finn into the in-between?" she asked. "I know how much you like to torment people in dreams."

Keiren tilted her head, trailing her waist-length red hair down the side of her arm. "Yes," she admitted, "that was me, but you do not understand. I did not harm her."

"Probably just because she stopped you," Bedelia muttered.

Instead of the expected anger, Keiren remained calm, her hand reaching slowly toward Bedelia. She froze, hardly breathing, as Keiren's fingers stroked through her short hair.

"Stop toying with me," she hissed. "I know you only saved me because you want something. Healing my old wolf bite was a nice touch, though it would have been nice if you'd healed that before, since you're clearly capable."

Keiren's hand fell back to her lap. "I only pushed back the poison. The wound itself cannot be healed at this late stage, but I can continue to push the poison back indefinitely."

Ah, Bedelia thought, *so there it was. Keiren had her leverage.* "I will not betray Finn in return for your healing," she growled. "You may as well just kill me now."

Keiren sighed, then stood. She began to pace. "Did I ever tell you what happened to my mother?" she questioned.

Bedelia's eyes widened. Why bring *that* up now? "She died when you were young. It was your father's fault."

Keiren sighed again, turning to fully face her. "It was

only his fault indirectly," she explained. "When I was young, I was already very powerful, more powerful than my father. It should not have been so. Magic had been weakened at that time, and most who experienced it did not gain any sort of power until they were near adulthood."

Bedelia gripped her hands in the surrounding bedding. She wanted to tell Keiren to burn in the Horned One's den, but . . . she'd never spoken much about her childhood. Why now?

Nodding to herself, Keiren continued. "My mother was not magical, but she was never one to fear what she did not understand," she hesitated. "She should have been afraid. When I was still but a child I stole a kitten from a neighboring farm." She smiled softly. "I had always wanted a pet."

She resumed her seat by Bedelia, and it was all she could do not to scoot away. She *did* want to hear this story.

"My mother found out and took the kitten away from me," she continued. "I was distraught beyond reason. I shut myself away inside my room and cursed her. I cursed her with every drop of power I had, never realizing that I might actually be capable of harming her." She took a deep breath, then let it out slowly. "The next day she fell ill. She slipped into unconsciousness and never awakened again. Slowly, her body wasted away until she died."

Bedelia raised a hand to her mouth to hide her gasp.

Keiren smiled softly at her. "My father tried to help her, but his magic was not like mine. He never said so out loud, but I knew he blamed me for what happened. He loved my mother more than anything else. I pushed him constantly to admit that he blamed me. I just wanted him to tell me the truth, but he would not. We fought, and I lashed out, crippling his magic."

Her eyes flicked to Bedelia, then down to her lap. "I believe my mother is trapped somewhere in the in-between, because of the curse I placed upon her. I began spending so much time there because I'd hoped to find her, but she is somehow beyond my reach. That is why I want Finn."

Bedelia's back stiffened at the mention of her friend. Was she finally about to find out the root of Keiren's massive scheming?

"At first I wanted Finn to grant me a measure of her immortality," she continued. "With that, I could break any barrier the in-between has to offer. I could have broken the barrier between life and death to release my mother from her prison." She shook her head. "But that plan will no longer work."

Bedelia shook her head, unable to clear her thoughts. "But how do you know she is even there? Perhaps her soul moved on long ago."

Keiren shook her head. "*No.* I know she is there. She has to be. I have grown powerful over the years, and I've taken power from others. That power has sustained my unnaturally long life, and I will not let it go until I can set things right."

Bedelia stared at her in awe. Was this the reason for everything? Was this why Keiren was willing to betray her? She shook her head and sighed. It was still no excuse. Keiren's loss was awful, but still, she had done *horrible* things. Her childhood story did not change the evil of her actions.

She flung a glare at Keiren, ready to tell her to go rot in a swamp, then her breath hitched. Tears streamed down Keiren's face. In all of the time they'd spent together, Bedelia had never seen her cry.

Keiren smiled softly at her through her tears. "I'm glad you're back by my side." She stood, then gestured down at the bed. "You must rest. I cleansed the damage from the Dearg Due, but it can still take time to recover from their poisonous bite."

Bedelia obeyed, fearful the more violent side of Keiren would return if she didn't. Once she was back beneath the covers with a pillow under her head, Keiren leaned down and kissed her forehead, then exited the room, shutting the door behind her.

As soon as she was gone, Bedelia jumped out of bed and rushed to the room's sole window. Sea breeze hit her face as she peered out at the devastating drop, leading only to razor sharp black rocks and the angry tide.

She stumbled back to the bed and sat, glancing at the closed door on the opposite side of the room. She needed to escape to warn Finn of Keiren's intent, but how? If there was one thing she knew, it was that Keiren would not make her escape easy. She'd have to play nice with her sadistic ex-lover until she could find a way out.

She began to sweat as she slipped back into bed, her heart pounding. Parting ways with Keiren had nearly killed her the first time. She was not sure she was capable of surviving it again.

CHAPTER ELEVEN

*E*alasaid chewed her lip, peering out from the guard tower at the front of Gwythern's estate. Two days had passed since she'd sent her scouts out to the neighboring burghs. She knew it was too soon to expect them back, but still, she was worried.

The flow of travelers into Garenoch had all but stopped. The last few travelers to make it in spoke of red eyes watching them in the night, and the thunder of distant hoofbeats. One even claimed he'd seen a herd of half man, half horse creatures galloping by. Most feared it would not be long now until the Faie invaded the burgh, but Ealasaid was not so sure. Something told her that humans were not of much concern to the Faie. Perhaps they were preparing for the prophecy to reach fulfillment, as Slàine had said. Now that Finn had set things in motion, war was inevitable.

"You'll catch a cold up here," a woman's voice commented from behind her.

She turned to see Slàine approaching, dressed in her

usual black, with her gray hair pulled back into a tight braid.

Ealasaid wrapped her burgundy cloak more tightly around herself and turned her gaze back to the burgh below. "I'm fine."

Not taking the hint, Slàine stepped up beside her.

Ealasaid sucked her teeth. It wasn't that she necessarily disliked Slàine, though the woman was unbearably rude most of the time. She was more worried about her intentions. She and her assassins had attacked her, Maarav, and their other companions just to prevent Finn from fulfilling the prophecy. The assassins had failed, and Maarav had turned on them. Though peace had been made, Ealasaid suspected that Slàine blamed her for the latter.

"You'll make a good leader," Slàine commented, gazing out at the burgh beside her, "if you can manage to keep your emotions under control."

Ealasaid pushed a lock of curly blonde hair behind her ear. "I think my emotions are exactly why I'll make a worthwhile leader, though I'll admit, I still have much to learn."

Slàine smirked. "Yes, much to learn, though you've come far for a simple *farm girl.*"

The way she said *farm girl* gave Ealasaid pause. Was she questioning her origins?

"Maarav told me your people were killed, and you fled," Slàine commented, her tone casual.

She inhaled sharply, twisting her neck toward Slàine. "I fled to save them, and they were killed sometime after without my knowledge."

Slàine nodded. "So you say."

Ealasaid clenched her hands to keep them from trembling. She'd blamed herself for the death of her kin a hundred times over. She didn't need *this* woman pointing the finger of blame too.

She tried to keep her mouth shut, but her words would not stay in. She spun toward Slàine. "Are you implying that I *meant* for my family to die, or simply that I fled to save my own skin?"

Slàine shrugged. "Neither. I merely find it hard to believe that a girl with such . . . pride, came from such simple beginnings."

Ealasaid fought back tears. She'd not allowed herself to mourn the deaths of her kin, not yet, and she would not allow Slàine the satisfaction of seeing her cry.

Slàine raised an eyebrow at her. "Perhaps a farm girl after all," she mused. "Even if half the time you act like a queen. A human, magic wielding queen." She raised her hand to her chin. "Hmm, just like the one in the prophecy. How odd."

With that, she slinked away, retreating down the stairs that led up through the guard tower.

Ealasaid gazed after her in shock. Was Slàine implying that *she* was one of the queens from the prophecy? A queen that would leave her family to die?

She whipped back around, looking at the burgh, gritting her jaw against her tears. *If only her mother could see her now*, she began to think, then shook her head. Her mother would never see anything again. Was it really her fault? If she'd stayed in her village, would she have been able to protect her from An Fiach? Would she then have carried on living a normal life, away from assassins and Faie and . . .

Footsteps sounded a moment before a hand alighted on her shoulder.

She jumped, then slowly turned to see Maarav looking down at her.

His eyes widened at her expression. "Are you—" he began, but cut off as she buried her face in his chest.

He seemed momentarily startled, then slowly wrapped his arms around her. "What did Slàine say to you?" he murmured.

She shook her head and took a deep breath, but her tears slipped out despite her efforts. He began to stroke her wayward curls and she almost pushed away, but could not find the strength. It felt like years since she'd known the comfort of someone who actually cared about her . . . though she was never quite sure if Maarav's caring was genuine. He was a self-serving vagabond, after all.

Finally managing to still her tears, she pulled away. "Who do you think the third queen from the prophecy is?"

He furrowed his brow. "The third queen? Why are you thinking about that? It's just a silly prophecy."

"Just answer the question," she pressed.

He gave her an odd look, then replied, "Well, if Finn is one queen, and the Queen of all the Faie another, then I imagine whoever the human queen is, she's more powerful than all of An Solas combined."

She let out a shaky breath. *Good*. That was good. She wasn't even the most powerful magic user within An Solas, let alone more powerful than everyone combined.

He looked down at her with concern, then placed a hand at the small of her back. "Come now, I'd say it's time you ate something and warmed yourself by the fire."

She nodded and let him lead her away, though she stole a final glance back at the burgh. She hoped her scouts would return soon. She didn't want any more deaths on her conscience.

ISEULT FOCUSED ON THEIR SURROUNDINGS, KEEPING AN EYE out for any sign of the Dearg Due as the sun waned on toward evening. Naoki had disappeared, likely to hunt rabbits, so Iseult kept an ear out for her too. Anything was better than focusing on Finn's silence, and the stiffness of her back ahead of him in the saddle.

She was clearly still angry that they couldn't spare the time to search for their companions, but better angry than in the hands of the Faie.

"I suppose I should explain to you what happened while I was in the in-between," she suddenly commented, breaking the silence. Her back seemed to relax . . . *slightly*.

He didn't speak, fearing he might once again incite her ire.

She sighed. "I saw Anders there. Niklas killed him."

Good, he thought, but decided to keep said thought to himself. Had he the chance, *he* would have killed Anders, so he was a dead man either way. It didn't matter who struck the final blow.

She glanced over her shoulder at him, her gaze wary. Had she somehow read his thoughts?

She bit her lip.

No, he determined, she was nervous about something.

She turned forward again, and did not speak. The

unicorn ambled onward, occasionally dipping its snout to snare shoots of tall grass.

"What else did you see?" he pressed.

She glanced at him again, then turned her gaze away. "I saw your ancestors. The souls I stole . . . I trapped them there. I swear I had no idea. Either I never knew where they went, or the memory was left out when the others returned."

The tension in his shoulders eased at her admission. "I had suspected as much. They had to be trapped *somewhere*. The in-between is a logical choice."

"You're not angry?" she asked hopefully, her gaze still forward.

"We've discussed this," he replied, perplexed.

He felt her deep sigh against his chest. Her head turned slightly his way. "I was worried that if you knew I saw them, you'd be angry I left them there. I would have freed them had I known how, but they disappeared before I could even attempt to speak with them."

"I am not angry," he replied, still unsure of her attitude. It seemed she was no longer upset with him . . .

"Anders also claimed Àed is no longer a tree," she continued, changing the subject, "or perhaps he never was. He claimed to have seen him in a dungeon, locked away within one of Keiren's fortresses. I was thinking I'd go back to the in-between to meet with her on my terms. I don't know any other way to find her, or her fortress."

Go *back*? After he'd stood idly by, waiting so long for her to awaken, not knowing if she ever would, she wanted to go *back*?

"We'll need to find Anna for that though, I'm afraid," she

continued. "She took me there once before, and I find her help preferable to that of the Ceàrdaman. Still—"

"You will not go back," he interrupted.

She whipped her head around to look at him with her jaw slightly agape.

He sealed his mouth shut. It was not his place to tell her what to do, but . . .

Her eyes narrowed. "I *will* go back if I so choose. If it is the quickest way to find Keiren and save Àed, I will do it, and Anna will help me."

He clenched his jaw. "If that is the case, then I will prevent further contact with Anna."

Her eyes went wide with shock as her face slowly turned red. Before he could stop her, she threw her leg over the saddle and slid down from their mount.

Seconds later, he was on the ground beside her, grabbing her arm before she could whirl away.

She glared daggers at him. "I thought you said you were on my side!" she hissed. "That where I go, you will follow!"

"Not when you're needlessly risking your life," he replied evenly.

She tugged her arm out of his grip. "You cannot do that! You cannot tell me that you do not care, that you will simply fulfill your *duty* to me, only to turn around and order me about!"

He sighed. This was going nowhere. He needed to find a way to get her back on the unicorn and further away from the Dearg Due. She was panting in rage, glaring at him.

He stepped forward and grabbed her before she could step away, pulling her into his arms, their faces just a few fingers apart. He could probably throw her back into the saddle now that he had her, but . . .

He leaned his head down slowly, a little closer to her face. Her expression softened, and her rage seemed to leak away. His mouth came down nearer to hers, almost touching. "I will follow you to the ends of the earth," he whispered, "but I will not allow you to sacrifice yourself for someone else. Not even for me."

She went utterly still, staring up at him.

He stopped short. What was he doing? He pulled away, shaking his head.

Finn's face reddened, her ire returning. She huffed, then marched back to the waiting unicorn. Not sparing Iseult a single glance, she climbed up in the saddle, then crossed her arms and waited.

He sighed, then climbed up behind her.

Her back was utterly stiff like before. It seemed he would be getting the silent treatment—*again*.

ANNA STARED DOWN AT THE RUNNING WATER FROM HER perch behind Eywen in the saddle. He was tall enough that he blocked most of her view looking forward, unless she leaned to the side. She was content with the view of the water though. Eywen had explained that the Dearg Due would not cross it, and she very much wanted to avoid being bitten again once night fell.

"Someone else recently rode through here," Eywen commented. "Perhaps some of my men, or yours."

She shivered. "Do the Dearg Due ride horses?"

He chuckled. "No, they are faster on foot."

She shivered again, in some ways glad she was unconscious for the attack. "What will you do if we cannot find the rest of your men, the ones who survived?"

"If *any* survived," he replied, "my goals remain the same. I will be less useful to Finnur without my regiment, but I must still attempt to save my people, especially those still under Oighear's thrall."

Anna bit her lip, feeling almost bad for her previous thoughts of the Aos Sí, and Eywen in particular. She still found him strange and terrifying, but he seemed to have more honor than most humans she knew, especially herself.

"And what will you do?" he questioned. "If we do not find your companions, I mean."

"You said you could track Finn," she replied, "and if we're close enough, I can track her myself."

"And would you remain by her side if the rest are *gone*?" he questioned.

She glared at the back of his head. "They're not *gone*. Kai, at the very least, is a survivor, and I will not abandon him."

"Why?" Eywen questioned.

She pursed her lips, her negative thoughts about the Aos Sí fast returning. "He's my best friend, if you must know. Perhaps my *only* friend. He would do just as much for me as I would for him. It's a mutual understanding between us."

"He seems like more than a friend," he continued.

She wished she could see his face to tell if he was joking. Was he honestly asking if she and Kai were . . . involved? "I'm not interested in men in that way," she grumbled.

"Never?" Eywen questioned.

Anna balled her hands into fists. It wasn't like she hadn't

endured these questions before, but now they came from such an unexpected source. Someone she never thought she'd have to explain herself to.

"Not for a very long time," she grumbled. "And never again."

"Hmph," he replied, then a few seconds later asked, "Do you care to explain why?"

"Do you care to explain why you ask so many questions?" she snapped.

He gestured to the surrounding woods. "We have a long ride ahead of us, and we may very well be alone for most of it. *You* are my only option for conversation."

She slumped in her seat. "Well then perhaps we should continue on in silence."

Eywen's shoulders lifted and fell as he sighed. "I apologize. I seem to have offended you. It was not my intent."

Anna frowned, wishing she could see right through those spider silk tresses into his mind. "It's alright," she conceded. "I'm just worried. I didn't mean to take it out on you."

She was about to say more when a distant light caught her gaze. "There's something ahead," she hissed. "Something . . . magical."

He drew their horse to an abrupt halt. "What do you sense?" he whispered.

She peered harder, but her magical sight only went so far. She could tell when magic was near, but not if it was benevolent. "I don't know," she muttered. "It doesn't seem terribly strong, not as bright as Finn."

"Wait here," he commanded, then slid down from the horse.

"Eywen!" she hissed, but he was already walking away, his hand on the pommel of his sword. Soon he disappeared into the trees.

Nervous, she peered up through the overhead branches. The sun could no longer be seen, though a small amount of its light remained. Did the Dearg Due have to wait for full night to surface?

Cursing to herself, she scooted forward and grasped the reins Eywen had looped around the saddle grip. If he left her alone in this gods-forsaken forest, she would hunt him down and kill him twice.

The clang of metal cut through the eerie silence. Then again and again. He was fighting someone with a sword. Had he known who waited for him in the trees, or had he been caught by surprise?

Shit. She hurried to dismount, then quickly secured their horse to a tree. As the clangs of metal continued, echoed by grunts of exertion, she crept forward, twin daggers drawn. There was a thud and someone groaned. *Shit. Shit. Shit.* She raced forward toward the sounds of struggle, entering a small clearing.

Eywen fought with a black haired Aos Sí while another lay dying at their feet.

Her grip on her daggers tightened as her gaze darted back and forth, unsure of what to do. Why was he fighting his own people? She gasped as he drove his blade through the gap in the other Aos Sí's armor, driving it up through his side to the hilt. He pulled the blade out in a splash of blood, and the dead Aos Sí fell beside the first.

Anna stood there, dumbfounded.

Eywen glanced back at her, hurt clear in his eyes. He knelt beside his fallen comrades and bowed his head.

What on earth was going on? She began to back away.

"We have no time to perform the proper rites," Eywen muttered, stopping her. He stood from his bow, bloody sword still in hand.

Anna gulped, then realized she was still holding her daggers in front of her, ready for a fight.

Eywen stalked toward her. He looked her up and down, then breezed past her back toward the stream.

She took one last look at the fresh corpses, then hurried after him.

When she found him again, he was kneeling by the stream, cleaning the blood from his clothes and skin. He'd removed his shirt to dunk it into the water, revealing a large gash across his back, seeping blood.

She hesitated, not sure if she should finish her approach.

Pausing his motions, Eywen glanced back at her.

"You killed your own men," she muttered.

He turned back to the stream. "They were Oighear's men. They would have killed me first. I have betrayed my queen."

She took a step forward. "They were hunting you?"

He scoffed. "It's likely. Though I'm surprised they came so far."

She closed the distance between them, stopping to stand at his back. She was more frightened of him now than ever, but there had been such pain in his eyes. She took one more step forward, then knelt. "You're wounded."

He turned and raised an eyebrow at her. "No more questions about me killing my own men?"

She sighed. "You're not the only one who has killed to survive." She took his sopping wet shirt from his hand and rung it out, then began dabbing at his back wound.

If it hurt, he didn't show it. "For someone who fears the Faie," he began, "you seem rather comfortable touching one."

She paused her dabbing, took a deep breath, then resumed. "You bandaged my wounds. The least I can do is bandage yours."

His snow white skin seemed even more unusual against his crimson blood, soaking into the shirt with each dab.

"The wound is too deep," she observed, feeling a bit sick, "We need to stop the bleeding."

She moved her gaze to see him smiling at her. "It will be fine. Fetch some bandages from my horse. We must move on."

She narrowed her eyes in speculation, but nodded. She really didn't want to be around when more Aos Sí showed up, especially now that Eywen's wound might hamper his fighting. She stood and rushed to the horse, pawed through the saddlebags, then returned with fresh bandages and a fresh, burgundy shirt.

Eywen remained kneeling beside the stream while she bandaged his wound as best she could, anchoring it with a strip of cloth over one shoulder, and under the opposite armpit. He kept his head turned, watching her the entire time, never flinching as she touched his wound.

She tried to ignore him, but as she finished he caught her gaze. She'd leaned in too close, absorbed in her work, and now his strange eyes were only a few fingers away.

She gulped.

"My thanks," he whispered.

"Um, yes," she nodded, then quickly stood and stumbled away. Wanting to cover her stumble, she hurried back toward the horse, untied its reins, and climbed on.

With a small smile on his lips, Eywen stood, donning the long-sleeved shirt she'd left him on the bank. He left the wet, bloody one where it lay, then approached. She scooted back as he climbed up in the saddle in front of her with amazing dexterity.

She let out a sigh of relief as they started moving, glad Eywen's back was to her so he couldn't see her furious blush.

She hadn't blushed so hard in years.

THE COLD HAD ENTIRELY PERMEATED KAI'S BONES BY THE time night fell. The Dearg Due had seemed to rest off and on throughout the day. Perhaps as they slept, he could have escaped the cave, but weakness pervaded his body, making it difficult to move. The fire had eventually died, so that when night came, he was left in utter darkness. The pure black in front of his eyes made him question if he was even still alive at all.

"It is time," the Dearg Due's voice hissed, alarmingly close.

Hands wrapped around his arms, pulling him to his feet. He felt suddenly sick, and proceeded to retch up the meager portion of food in his stomach while the Dearg Due held him partially aloft.

"The Dair is weak," she growled.

He tried to laugh, but it came out as more of a groan. He hoped he'd at least managed to get some of his vomit on her. One of her hands fell away, but she was strong enough to keep him standing with just one.

A sharp and metallic odor hit his nostrils just before something soft and wet hit his lips. He sputtered and stumbled backwards, but the Dearg Due's iron grip kept him from going too far. She pulled him back to her and the touch came again on his lips, more forceful this time, and he tasted blood. He realized in horror that she'd bloodied her wrist and was trying to make him drink from it.

He lifted his free arm to push her away, but she wouldn't budge. "I don't drink blood like you!" he mumbled through mostly sealed lips.

"The blood will heal," she purred. "You are weak for one of the Dair. Perhaps a half blood."

"Yes," he agreed, still pushing her wrist away in the darkness. "Just a half blood, you may as well let me go."

Kai heard a hiss of fabric as he was whipped onto his back, his head cradled in the Dearg Due's lap. With one hand she forced his mouth open, then blood dripped onto his tongue. He coughed and sputtered, trying to shut his mouth, but in his infirm state, she was no match against her inhuman grip.

"*Drink*," she demanded. "Half Dair not so big a prize, but dead you're worth nothing."

Blood poured down his throat to the point where he felt like he was drowning. He reflexively swallowed, then coughed the excess blood out to dribble down the sides of his chin. Hot bile swelled up into his throat. He was going to be sick.

Seeming to sense his intent, the Dearg Due suddenly let go, letting his head hit the hard stone. He rolled onto his side and dry heaved, but had little left in his stomach to vomit.

Just as his breathing began to calm, his stomach convulsed violently. "What have you done to me!" he gasped, clawing at the stone beneath him.

"Healed you," she hissed. Her voice was distant, like she had retreated to the far end of the cave. "Weak Dair," she said again, her voice suddenly closer. "My sisters will be here soon and we will depart."

Sisters? He pushed off his shoulder into a seated position, then nearly fell over. He felt like fire was running through his veins, and now his hopes had been crushed. He'd thought perhaps the other Dearg Due had been killed off by the Aos Sí. Had they instead been hunting his companions?

He shook his head, somewhat coming to his senses though his stomach still threatened to rebel. No, the other Dearg Due would have been trapped in caves or other hidey holes all day just like his captor. They wouldn't have had time to hunt the others.

He flinched at another hiss of fabric seconds before she grabbed him, hauling him back to his feet. She half carried, half dragged him across the stone ground toward the smell of fresh night air. Soon enough they emerged into the starry night, but Kai could hardly notice the stars. Surrounding them were dozens of pairs of reflective eyes.

How in the blazes was he supposed to escape now?

CHAPTER TWELVE

inn and Iseult had ridden on well into the night, spotting no sign of their other companions, nor the Dearg Due. After hearing a full recount of the battle, Finn now understood why Iseult was wary of remaining in one place too long. Eywen's army of twenty Aos Sí lingered on her mind.

She bit her lip in worry. Could the Dearg Due really have eliminated so many mighty warriors? No, that couldn't be possible. The Aos Sí seemed almost immortal with their combat skills and grace. Surely they had protected Kai and the others. Even now, they might all be searching for her.

She glanced over her shoulder at Iseult, using Loinnir's gentle sway to disguise the motion. His cool gaze watched the surrounding darkness, flicking from tree to tree.

She turned back around before he could notice her. Even after he'd detailed the battle to her, and the dangers yet lurking, she couldn't entirely release her ire for his insistence they move on without their companions. She *wanted* to look for her friends, no matter the consequences.

The silence between them carried on and on. She didn't want to be the one to break it, in some way proving him the winner, but . . . "Perhaps we should rest soon. I'm sure Loinnir is tired from carrying us all of this way."

Iseult wordlessly slipped the reins into Finn's hands, slipped his left leg behind her back, then dropped to the ground behind her with the unicorn still moving.

Finn turned to see him land with bent knees, absorbing the impact of the jump. Loinnir halted, and Iseult stood staring at Finn, almost impatiently, seeming riled.

Finn sighed, then climbed down from the saddle. Iseult approached and unstrapped their only bedroll. He took a few steps away and unfurled it onto the ground, then turned to Finn expectantly.

"*You* should rest too," she grumbled, though the bedroll did look rather inviting. Perhaps she'd even be able to reach the in-between in her dreams without Iseult's knowledge.

Before she could make a decision, Naoki came crashing in, pounced on the bedroll, and curled up at the bottom.

Iseult crossed his arms and waited.

Finn rolled her eyes. "I don't see what reason you have to be angry with *me*. I'm not the one bossing people around."

"I am not angry," he replied, then turned away. "I will scout the area."

"Iseult," she said before he could take another step. He stopped, his back yet to her. Suddenly she flashed on their argument. She could practically feel the closeness of their bodies as he'd leaned in toward her.

She hesitated, wondering if she should just try to rest

and reach the in-between rather than smooth things over between them. No, she could deal with this treatment no longer. She approached him despite the apprehension in her gut. Reaching him, she placed a hand on his arm, turning him to face her.

He peered down at her from beneath his furrowed brow.

Pushing away her fears, she laid her hands on his shoulders, then stood on tip toe. She gently placed a kiss right beside his mouth, then lowered herself. "*Thank you* for wanting to protect me," she said softly. "I don't know what I would have done if I had never met you."

His shoulders tensed beneath her grip. Had she further agitated him?

His look softened. His hands slid around her waist, pulling her against him.

"Iseult?" she questioned weakly, her heart fluttering like a trapped bird.

He shook his head, then lowered his face to hers. She closed her eyes as their lips touched, just the barest hint of a kiss. She let out a sigh, then his lips pressed down on hers.

A thrill ran through her body, and her fingers reflexively raised to the base of his scalp, pushing up through his hair.

His lips left hers, while holding her in a loose embrace. Looking deep into her eyes, he lifted a hand to her face, then trailed his fingers lightly down the curve of her jaw. He stepped back, letting his fingertips slowly drop, then turned and stalked off into the darkness.

Finn watched him go, her fingers on her lips, utterly stunned. Loinnir started snuffling at her shoulder. She lifted a hand to her snout to still her, still staring in the direction Iseult had gone. Hadn't he told her he had nothing to offer her, that he would do no more than his duty to her? Such a passionate kiss was surely more than his duty, so what did it mean?

~

Anna and Eywen sat side by side, peering into the darkness. They'd forgone a fire despite the chilly temperature. While a fire might serve to keep normal predators away, it could very well draw in hostile Aos Sí, or more of the Dearg Due. Anna's stomach growled despite the small portion of food she'd eaten. It had been a long day.

They'd followed hoof prints up along the stream until it ran dry, then they'd turned north, roughly in the direction of Sormyr. They both suspected the tracks they followed belonged to at least one of their companions, just judging by the direction and the remote area. While Eywen and Anna could both sense Finn, at the moment they could only tell that she was alive, and somewhere to the northwest.

"You should get some rest," Eywen suggested. "I will keep watch."

She shook her head, gathering her cloak more tightly around herself. "You're injured, and you were up the entirety of last night saving me from the Dearg Due. You must rest first."

They both glanced at the lone bedroll, still attached to the saddle lying forlornly near Eywen's feet. Their horse's head drooped close to the ground, the only member of the small group willing to rest.

"I will be fine," he muttered. "I mean no offense, but my

senses are more keen than yours. I will sense danger long before it is upon us."

"I sensed those hostile Aos Sí before you did," she pointed out.

He turned to smirk at her, half his face in shadow. "I was distracted by our conversation. It will not happen again."

She rolled her eyes then glanced once more at the bedroll. The extra warmth *did* sound nice, especially since there was no fire. Still, she felt bad resting when Eywen needed to nurse his wounds. "I could try to venture into the in-between," she offered. "If Finn is still there, we could plan a meeting place for when she awakens."

He raised a dark eyebrow at her. "I thought you wanted nothing to do with the Gray Place, nor with your magic."

"I don't," she replied, suddenly uncomfortable. She always felt this way when admitting she had magic. "But I would be a fool to neglect a useful tool when the lives of my friends may be in danger. Whether I like it or not, Finn is powerful. If Kai or any of the others are in danger, she will be our best chance of saving them."

"And she *will* save them?" he questioned. "Should her priority not be to her queenship? To rousing an army to protect herself? Surely that is what Oighear is doing."

Anna shook her head. "That's not the type of person Finn is. She's a bit of a fool really, with no idea what she truly wants, but she's kind hearted. Kind hearted enough to treat me like a friend, even after I kidnapped her," she snorted, "*twice*."

"Twice?" he asked, astonished. "And you did not feel the wrath of her power?"

She opened her mouth to explain how Finn had lost her

memories, and hadn't even known about her power initially, then shut it. Though she'd formed a tentative trust with Eywen, he was still Faie, and there was no definitive proof that he wasn't still working for Oighear in some way. She would be wise not to relinquish any more information than she already had.

Seeming to sense the shift in her attitude, Eywen cleared his throat and stood, then knelt to unstrap the bedroll. He unfurled it just a few paces away, then turned to her. "Rest, or venture through the Gray Place. Either way, you need to lie down and warm yourself. I will wake you if something seems amiss."

She stared up at him for a moment, then nodded. She supposed after he'd saved her life, she needn't worry about him killing her in her sleep. He could kill her right then and there if he so chose. She was not too prideful to admit that her combat skills were no match for his inhuman speed.

She stood, then walked toward Eywen and the awaiting bedroll.

Instead of stepping aside like she'd expected, he tilted his head, observing her. "You know," he began, "Oighear once said that those of Clan Liath were perhaps the most powerful mages of all. You see what others cannot. It was once even believed that you could see right through into a person's heart. Is that true?"

She frowned, wondering what he was getting at. She might be skilled at sensing the intentions of others, but that was simply intuition, not magic. "Don't worry," she said after a moment. "Your secrets are safe from me."

He nodded, then stepped away, resuming his previous seat.

Not looking back, Anna crawled into the bedroll, pulling it up over her head to catch the warmth of her breath.

Eywen did not speak again, and eventually she drifted off into a fitful sleep.

～

FINN WOKE EARLY THE NEXT MORNING, HER MIND IN TOTAL fog. She sat up, glancing around until her eyes found Iseult, already saddling Loinnir.

"The Faie were lurking around us all night," he explained with his back turned toward her. "Not the Dearg Due or anything quite so dangerous, but I sensed them in great number. I'd like to leave this place before they decide to act."

"The Faie?" she questioned, rubbing her eyes.

Finished with the saddle, he turned toward her and nodded. "I could sense them, though they did not reveal themselves."

She reluctantly wiggled out of the bedroll and stood, feeling guilty for sleeping the entire night while Iseult kept watch. "Do you want to sleep some before we move on?" she questioned.

He shook his head.

She frowned. Was he acting even colder than usual? Did he regret their kiss? Did *she*? Pushing away her thoughts, she wandered away to take care of her morning duties. She was painfully aware of Iseult watching her back as she retreated, but she did not have the courage to turn and see his expression.

She wandered onward, a little farther than necessary,

feeling the need for some space. Eventually she stopped in an area where she would be shielded by dense shrubs.

After a few minutes she was ready to return to Iseult, and reluctantly started back, mired in her thoughts. Distracted, she almost didn't notice when a tree in front of her moved. Then another shifted, and she was sure her eyes weren't playing tricks on her.

She stopped walking and focused on one of the moving trees. "There's no need to hide from me," she announced.

A whisper caught her ear, but she could not quite make out what it said. She listened intently, then jumped as Iseult silently appeared at her side, leading Loinnir.

"Who are you speaking to?" he muttered, his voice barely audible.

She glanced at him, then returned her gaze to the trees. "I think there are Trow here," she whispered.

"Perhaps we should leave them be," he replied.

Finn shook her head. The Trow had helped her in the past, and if she ever truly needed help, now was the time.

"Please show yourselves," she called out. "Perhaps we can help each other."

One of the largest nearby trees shivered, then its roots pulled free from the earth, first one side, then the other. Its bark seemed to ripple, slowly forming a large face with leaf-green eyes. The Trow twitched its knobby nose, then peered down at Finn.

"Greetings, Dair," it muttered in a voice that sounded like twigs snapping.

She stepped forward. "Greetings, my name is Finn. I've met several of your kin. They helped me in the past."

The Trow glanced back and forth warily. "These are not

safe times to be speaking with one of the Dair. The Faie Queen is on the hunt. She will not rest until she finds every one of you, especially *you*."

Finn tilted her head. He had to mean Oighear. "How do you know that?"

The Trow rustled its branches in what seemed like a shrug. "The roots speak, my lady. The Trow will hide through these troubled times, and hope that we are not once again trapped in eternal slumber."

Loinnir stomped one of her front hooves against the ground, pawing up dirt. Finn turned to her, then gasped. Her glittering spiral horn had reappeared.

"One of the Aonbheannach?" the Trow gasped, observing Loinnir. His green eyes wide, he turned back to Finn. "It must be true what the others are saying. They watch you. They say you are not just any Dair."

She glanced at Iseult, then shook her head. "No, I suppose I am not."

The Trow wiggled a few of its branches. "Evrial?" he called out. "Show yourself."

Something blue and glittering fluttered up from one of the Trows branches, then floated down, hovering near Finn's face. She recognized the blue wings and gauzy clothing, though this was not one of the Pixies she'd met previously.

Evrial's small, feminine face scrunched up like she smelled something foul, then slowly, her jaw went slack. She tilted her head, observing Finn. "The Aonbheannach claims you are the Queen of the Dair."

Finn glanced at Iseult again, his expression suddenly wary.

"The unicorn spoke to you?" he asked the Pixie.

Evrial glared at him. "They have words for those willing to listen, human!" she screeched. She turned back to Finn. "Will you be going to war with the Faie Queen then? Will you put an end to the snow and ice? Freeze my wings off, it does."

Finn flicked her eyes to the Trow, waiting patiently. Perhaps this was some sort of test. "Yes," she replied. "That is my intent."

Evrial placed one tiny hand on her chin, her wings fluttering incessantly to keep her aloft. "And will you deny the Faie your magic, just as the Dair did in the past? Will we be forced to slumber again?"

She wasn't sure what the Pixie was talking about, but decided perhaps it was best to pretend she knew what she was doing. "The Trow and Pixies have both proven themselves my friends. I would not see them trapped in slumber if I can prevent it."

Evrial glanced back at the Trow. Its branches bowed forward in what seemed to be a nod. She nodded in reply, then turned back to Finn. "In that case, we are prepared to swear fealty to your cause. The Snow Queen has sent Dark Faie across the land to herd us in, yet her army has no place for tiny Pixies or lumbering Trow. If the Oak Queen will grant us her magic, we will fight for her in return."

Oak Queen, she repeated in her mind, liking the sound of the title, as it separated her from her people.

"Finn," Iseult warned. "The Faie cannot be trusted."

Evrial hissed at him. "And the *humans* can?" She turned back to Finn. "Make your decision, Oak Queen."

Finn bit her lip. The Trow could see all throughout the

forest, and so could the Pixies. They could find their missing companions, and serve as messengers. She couldn't help but feel that she was already losing the war to come, and she needed an army to protect those she cared about. The Dearg Due had proven that.

"I accept your terms," she announced.

Suddenly the forest around them erupted in a cacophony of rustling and snapping branches. Countless Pixies took to the sky, while most of the surrounding trees transformed into Trow.

"We were attacked by the Dearg Due," Finn called out to her newly acquired allies. "I bid you to seek these creatures out. Discover why they attacked my companions."

Several of the Pixies buzzed around her head, then darted off into the sky. The largest Trow nodded his upper branches toward her. "It shall be done, Oak Queen."

Iseult remained bravely at Finn's side, though she could sense his discomfort. He may not like being around the Faie, but truth be told, she was likely more Faie than human. If he wanted to remain by her side, he would have to relinquish just a bit of his pride.

ANOTHER DAY, ANOTHER CAVE, KAI THOUGHT BITTERLY, BUT AT least he no longer felt on the verge of death. The blood of the Dearg Due had started to heal the wound on his neck. He hoped that was all it would do.

The creatures in question rested within the confines of the cave, blocking both the entrance, and the small caverns deeper within. Kai wondered what they did for shelter in regions where caves were less common, but perhaps they simply kept to known routes where they knew they'd have shielding from the sun.

He glanced at the distant cave opening, illuminated by bright sunlight, then to the Dearg Due. While most rested, some were awake, softly conversing in their strange language. He would stand little chance of making it out into the sunlight before one caught him.

He moved his gaze to find one of the Dearg Due watching him, recognizing her as the one who'd given him blood. Small consolation, however, as it was her bite that made him weak in the first place.

"You should rest," she hissed, "weak Dair."

"Finding it a bit difficult at the moment," he muttered. "Why is it that we must remain sheltered all day?"

The Dearg Due narrowed her reflective gaze at him. "The sun hurts the eyes, dulls the senses, but will not kill us, if that is your intent."

He sighed, then repositioned himself against the hard stone wall. "Oh, I'd never dream of shoving you into the sunlight," he grumbled sarcastically.

The Dearg Due smirked. "As if you could overpower me, weak Dair."

He turned his gaze away from her and pretended to go to sleep. She was right, he'd never overpower her, but perhaps he could outsmart her.

He wasn't sure how he'd do that now, but he had all blasted day to think about it.

CHAPTER THIRTEEN

"*I* can't believe you actually did it," Ouve mused, standing beside Ealasaid and looking out across the courtyard.

She nodded, unable to quite believe it herself. So many magic users had come, many of whom only recently realized they had magic to begin with. A large group was gathered in the courtyard, learning additional combat skills from the assassins. Those with weaker magic were glad for the lessons. They would be persecuted for their magic like the stronger mages, but would have no real way to protect themselves, and they *needed* protection.

Many had come with word of An Fiach. The group was still active, to Ealasaid's disdain, rounding up magic users and blaming them for the increasing Faie activity.

They were all utter fools, as far as Ealasaid was concerned, and she could not wait to face them with her newly formed army. There were now more magic users in and around the estate than there had been at the battle up

North. The soldiers of An Fiach truly did not understand what powerful enemies they had made. Alone, a mage was easily dispatched, but banded together, they would be near unstoppable.

"That one is particularly strong," Ouve commented, pointing to a young man in a blue tunic and tan breeches. His short black hair left his tan neck bare. His name was Sage, a simple farmer, just like she'd been.

As she watched, the young man arced a practice sword toward Tavish, who deftly spun out of the way, not even bothering to block the clumsy blow.

"Not powerful with a sword," Ealasaid smirked.

Ouve laughed. "No, but neither am I." He turned his gaze back toward the black haired young man. "He wields fire magic," he explained, "more powerful than any magic I've seen," he flicked his gaze down to Ealasaid, "besides yours."

She stroked her chin in thought. "Should we make him, *hmm*, what should we call them . . . a *general?*"

"General is as good a term as any," Ouve replied, "though perhaps we should speak with him first, make sure he isn't some power-hungry mage out to steal your army from you."

They both turned their gazes as Maarav entered the courtyard from the main estate.

"Not that anyone would let that happen," Ouve chuckled, nodding toward Maarav.

Spotting them, Maarav changed course and approached, his black garb seeming stark in the harsh light of day. "Lady Sìoda has agreed to extend the fortifications," he explained upon reaching them. "New walls will be built on the outskirts of town." He turned to stand at her other side, gazing out at the practicing mages. "Soon you will have a fortress to suit your army."

She shivered at the thought. "It's happening so much more quickly than I could have believed. When Finn returns we will be able to protect her from this elusive other queen." *Who is not me*, she added in her thoughts.

Maarav smirked. "I wouldn't be surprised if she returned with an army of her own, given her predeliction to pick up strays." He glanced at Ouve, then back to Ealasaid. "Though you've picked up quite a few yourself."

Ouve scowled, then bowed his head to Ealasaid. "If you'll excuse me, I'll have a talk with our potential general."

As soon as he was gone, Ealasaid glared at Maarav. "You shouldn't tease him," she chided. "He's one of the few allies I've come to fully trust."

Maarav snorted. "It's easy to trust someone who is entirely smitten with you."

"He is not," Ealasaid grumbled, though she sensed Maarav was correct. "And anyway, what does it matter to *you*?"

He placed his elbow on her shoulder, leaning a portion of his weight against her. "You're just so young and inno-cent," he teased. "I don't want any of these swarthy mages taking advantage of you."

She furrowed her brow, not quite sure if he was teasing her, or if he was actually jealous. With Maarav it was impos-sible to tell. He'd been so kind with her when she'd broken down in the guard tower, then had proceeded to get blad-dered with Tavish, leaving her alone for the rest of the evening with only her dark thoughts to keep her company.

She slipped away from his offending elbow. "Why do

you think Slàine is helping us?" she questioned abruptly, her gaze trained on the courtyard. She hadn't forgotten Slàine's misplaced suspicions, and couldn't help but wonder if the woman planned on assassinating her. Slàine had already given her word that she'd help Finn, so the other queens would be her enemies by default.

Maarav too turned his gaze back to the practicing mages. "Slàine's reasons are her own. I doubt we'll truly know them until it's too late."

She whipped her gaze to him.

"Oh don't look so surprised," he sighed, glancing over at her. "Slàine raised me up to be a bargaining tool once Finn resurfaced. I've known her nearly my entire life, yet she told me none of this until recently, *after* she attacked us. I would be a fool to assume I know her true motivations now."

Ealasaid shook her head. This man was utterly insane. "Then why are we working with her to begin with?"

"Because it benefits us in the present." He winked at her. "The partnership will continue until one of us finds it a detriment."

"But what if it ends with a dagger in your back?" she muttered in disbelief.

He grinned. "Now, you wouldn't let that happen to me, would you?"

She glared at him. Could he never be serious? "And what of *our* partnership?" she asked boldly. "Are you simply waiting for a time when it becomes a detriment?"

"You're different," he explained, patting her head as one would a dog. "You're far too pretty to ever be a detriment."

With that, he ambled off, whistling a jovial tune. She briefly considered striking him with lightning, but he'd likely only tease her for losing control, even while the ground was still smoking around his feet.

ANNA GRITTED HER TEETH, THOROUGHLY IRRITATED WITH herself. She'd slept right through the entire night without entering the Gray Place. She knew it meant her body had desperately needed the rest, but she still felt guilty that Eywen, wounded and likely exhausted himself, had spent the night watching over her.

"Did you see that?" he asked from his seat in front of her in the saddle.

She silently cursed herself. Not only was she a monumental burden, she'd neglected to keep her eyes on their surroundings. "See what?" she hissed.

He pointed. "A flash of color in the leaves. I think it was —" he cut off as something dove right for his face. He ducked, and the bright red blur passed by, then looped up in the air to circle around.

"Blasted Pixies," Eywen muttered, slowly straightening his back.

"Pixies?" Anna repeated in disbelief.

She watched the red shape as it hovered back down toward them, slower this time. It stopped above their heads, just out of reach. Anna's jaw fell open. It was a tiny woman with fiery red hair that matched her diaphanous wings. The wings were impossibly thin with visible veins, more like those of a dragonfly than a butterfly.

"Travelers!" the tiny woman buzzed. "Were you attacked by the Dark Faie the evening before last?"

Anna flicked her gaze to Eywen, wondering if they should answer the little woman, or squish her.

"Don't make any sudden movements," Eywen muttered. "They may be small, but Pixies are deadly en masse."

Anna shivered at the thought of being swarmed by the tiny humanoids. "Why do you ask?" she questioned.

The Pixie woman dipped in the air, then caught herself mid-fall to hover at Anna's eye level. She placed her tiny hands on her tiny hips. "We have been sent by the Oak Queen to rescue those attacked by the Dark Faie. If you are those we seek, we shall safely escort you back to the Queen."

Anna shifted her gaze back to Eywen. "Oak Queen?"

He seemed deep in thought for a moment, then nodded. "Yes, we were attacked by the Dark Faie. How far away is the Queen?"

"A full day's journey on horseback," the Pixie explained, glancing down at their steed in seeming distaste. She turned her sneer to Eywen. "Had the Oak Queen not informed us there were Aos Sí among her companions, you would have been killed on sight."

"Then I am grateful I now serve a more magnanimous queen," Eywen replied smoothly.

The little woman accepted his response with a nod. She bobbed in the air, angling her wings just right so the vibrant red flashed in the sunlight. Hundreds of colorful flashes blinked in response from the trees above.

"Follow us, please," the Pixie instructed. She narrowed her gaze once more at the horse, then added, "And do try to keep up."

She rose back up toward the canopy, where all the other Pixies swarmed around her. As one, they headed north.

Eywen nudged their mount into motion, tugging the reins in the direction the Pixies had gone.

Anna leaned forward, hovering her chin over Eywen's shoulder. "Would you please tell me what in the gods is going on?"

"They're taking us to Finn," he replied. "It seems she has decided to claim the title of Faie Queen after all."

"But I thought Oighear was the Faie Queen," Anna whispered.

Eywen chuckled, though his laughter sounded wicked rather than mirthful. "Not for long, my friend. Not for long."

Anna gulped. Was this all happening because of that blasted prophecy? Would Finn truly go to war with the other two queens? Would Kai want to remain by Finn's side, even now?

Her fingers flexed around the edges of the saddle as she caught sight of the Pixies in the distance. It was futile to think of such questions. She was riding a horse with one of the Aos Sí, following a herd of Pixies to the Oak Queen, a woman she sometimes thought of as a friend.

In a time when so many things beyond her wildest imagination could happen, there was no point guessing what might happen next. She'd most certainly be wrong.

Bedelia crept out of bed with only a single candle to light her way. She felt fully recovered from her injuries, both old and new. If there was a time to make her move, it was now, but first she needed information.

Keiren had been nothing but cordial, perhaps even loving. Her attitude was proof of only one thing: she wanted something, and Bedelia knew she was the most convenient tool to that end. Keiren might have loved her once, but had proven her love was only worth so much. She would never stake her life on that love again, especially since Keiren was holding her hostage in a room that locked from the outside.

Her only option for escape was a thin iron nail she'd pried out of her bed frame. She had tested it earlier that day to make sure it would fit in the keyhole, and now she'd test whether or not it could turn the lock.

Crossing the room, she tugged the waistband of her newly acquired breeches up, then knelt, slowly inserting the nail into the lock. If Keiren returned now, she'd be cooked.

She cringed each time the nail clinked against the metal of the lock, then nearly collapsed in relief as she finally turned it just right, and the door swung outward.

Quickly slipping the nail into her boot, she retrieved her candle and hurried out into the hall, looking both ways to ensure no one awaited her.

Her hand trembled around the candle holder as she assessed her options. She was in the middle of a long hall she did not recognize. Though she'd been to many of Keiren's fortresses, she'd never been to this one. She had no clue which way to go, all she knew was she needed to go *down*. Judging by the height of her window, she was at least five floors above the ground.

She chose a direction at random and hurried down the long hall, taking turns blindly in the fleeting hope she'd come upon stairs. She kept her hand cupped around the candle's small flame, lest she lose her way in the darkness.

When she reached the first flight of stairs, she was so dizzy with fear she nearly toppled down them. Slowly regaining her composure, she crept down to the next floor. At the base she found a single, unlit torch in a wall sconce. With trembling hands she used her candle's flame to coax the torch to life. She blew out the candle and left it behind, using the torch to light her way. It would make her easier to spot, but it would also allow her to run more swiftly without the flame going out.

She hurried down another flight of stairs starting around the corner from the first, then nearly screamed in frustration as she reached the landing. No more stairs led downward. She'd have to find another way.

With a shuddering breath she peered down one long corridor, then another, then took off at a jog.

"Hey!" someone hissed almost instantly.

She skidded to a halt, then froze. Her heart thundered in her ears, making it hard to hear. Had she imagined the voice?

"Hey!" someone hissed again.

She whipped her head in the direction of the voice, taking a few steps back. She'd passed a dark corridor, barely registering it, but now as she peered down it, dimly lit with a few wall sconces, she wasn't sure how she'd missed it. The corridor was mostly one long cell with iron bars. Further down, she could not see.

Quickly debating her options, she hurried down the dimly lit corridor, peeking through the bars to find the owner of the voice. Finally, a figure came into view, and it was one she recognized.

"Thank the gods yer here too," Sativola sighed, leaning

his heavy frame against the iron bars. He reeked of old sweat and other more pungent smells, but didn't seem to notice Bedelia's distaste as he lifted a hand to rake through his golden curls.

"What are you doing here?" she rasped, anxious to get on with her escape.

"I was hopin' ye could tell me," he whispered. "The last thing I remember was those bloody creatures attackin' us." He lifted his hair to reveal a wound on his neck, caked with dried blood. The skin around the injured area had turned an unhealthy shade of gray.

Her stomach turned. She knew Finn would want her to save Sativola if she could, but in his current state he would only slow her down.

"This fortress belongs to Keiren Deashumhain," she explained, her voice trembling. "I'll find Finn and the others, then we shall rescue you."

"Will you?" a voice croaked from the other end of the cell, the corner shrouded in darkness.

She lifted her torch, but could not make out who had spoken. She flicked her eyes to Sativola. "Is there someone in there with you?"

"Some old, grump," Sativola explained. "Please, don't leave me here, lass. There must be a key nearby."

Before she could reply, the *old grump* hobbled forward into the light. "So ye know my daughter, do ye?" he croaked.

His silver hair was in mats, and his face hollow from hunger, but she recognized him right away. "Àed!" she breathed without thinking.

He eyed her up and down. "Do I know ye?"

She bit her tongue. She'd been hiding in the foliage when he'd been turned into a tree, so he hadn't seen her. She desperately wanted to ask him why he wasn't a tree anymore, but it would only give her away as Keiren's former ally.

"I'm getting you both out of here," she decided. She felt guilty that she'd been willing to leave Sativola behind just moments before, but she couldn't resist the allure of rescuing Àed for Finn.

Sativola opened his mouth to speak, then his eyes widened.

Sensing a presence at her back, she whipped around, then nearly screamed. One of the Ceàrdaman stood there. No, not just any Ceàrdaman, the one who'd tossed that dust onto Finn, sending her into the in-between. Niklas.

He steepled his fingers together and smiled at her, revealing glistening, sharp teeth. "I was just coming to find you. Thank you for making my task less difficult."

She backed away until her back pressed against the bars of the cell. "What do you want?" she demanded, keeping her voice low.

"Oh, I want a lot of things," he purred. "I want to help your mistress," he chuckled, "well, both of them actually. If only they could realize their goals are nearly the same."

Bedelia shook her head. "I don't understand."

He smirked. "You do not need to. I will help you escape, but you will owe me a favor in return."

Her thoughts raced. Perhaps she could get him to release Sativola and Àed to escape with her, but then she'd owe him an even larger favor. Keiren had always cautioned her against making deals with the Ceàrdaman.

"We will escape on our own," she muttered. "We do not require your help."

"I'll take that deal," Sativola interrupted. "Get me out of here and I'll do ye any blasted favor ye want. The lass was willing to leave me just a few moments ago."

Niklas raised his strange eyes to Sativola. "You are not important," he sneered, "and half dead by the looks of it." He turned his gaze back to Bedelia. "I assure you, you cannot escape without my help. Keiren has warded all of the exits to hold you in while she's away."

Relief flooded through her at hearing Keiren was away, though she had no idea how she'd get through her magical wards. "I don't believe you," she boldly replied. "I'll climb out one of the windows if I have to."

Niklas shook his head. "You know the Ceàrdaman cannot tell lies."

"But you twist your words," she countered. "You're tricksters."

He glared at her. "Let me explain things quite clearly, since you seem to be rather dense. You *cannot* escape without my help, and the Mountebank's power is not great enough to aid you. The one and only way for you to escape your prison is through death. You do not have the power to break through Keiren's wards, and none of your friends will find you here. *Ever.*"

Well when he put it like that . . . perhaps owing a favor would not be so bad. Anything was better than waiting here for Keiren to return.

She glanced back at the two men in the cell. Àed muttered something about not being a Mountebank, but seemed to have no other opinion on the offer.

She turned back to Niklas. "I will agree on two conditions," she stated boldly. "First, Sativola, Àed and I must escape together. Second, you must heal Sativola's wounds before we depart."

"I will agree to the first," Niklas quickly agreed, "but not the second. This man," he gestured behind her to Sativola, "has been touched by Dark Faie, and I will not have their stain upon me."

She glanced at Sativola, who nodded for her to agree. "Just get us out of here, lass. I'll be fine."

She doubted his assurances, but it was still a better deal than she'd hoped for. She turned back to Niklas and nodded.

He grinned, steepling his fingers back in front of his face. "Excellent. Gather whatever supplies you wish. I will ready horses for your departure." He withdrew a large iron keyring from within his shapeless robes and unlocked the cell.

She moved into the cell to support Sativola, breathing shallowly as his odor assaulted her. They waited as Àed hobbled out ahead of him, seeming about a million years old.

"Quickly now," Niklas instructed. "You must depart before dawn."

Bedelia nodded as she helped Sativola stumble out of the cell. Supplies and horses were far more than she could have hoped for, along with the discovery of Àed. Niklas wanted to ensure her survival, and perhaps her gratitude, for one reason, the favor he planned to ask. She shuddered, fearing just what that favor might be.

She could only hope her survival would be worth it.

Finn sat next to Iseult by the fire. It had been an exciting day, to say the least, and there'd been no discussion of the kiss they'd shared the previous night. She *wanted* discussion, but Iseult, even at the best of times, was a man of few words.

She stared into the flickering flames, listening intently for sounds of Faie in the surrounding forest. Iseult had seemed uneasy since she'd made her pact with the Trow and Pixies. She couldn't blame him, most did not trust the Faie, including *her*, but the Trow had always been kind to her. She'd only had one other interaction with Pixies where she'd met Corcra, a Pixie she deemed a friend, even if the Pixies' penchant for blood was unnerving.

"Do you think they'll find everyone?" she asked finally, anxious to break the silence.

Iseult shifted in his seat. "Perhaps."

She frowned. *Infuriating man.* She was sure he had more experience with romantic endeavors than she, so why could he not take the lead? Then again, she wasn't entirely sure she wanted him to. He'd made clear his role in regards to her.

She sighed. Perhaps if she explained her stance more clearly, he'd understand. "You told me once that you knew about my child," her voice quavered, "and what happened to her."

He turned to her, an uncharacteristic amount of surprise showing in his wide eyes and slack jaw, now covered in stubble from their days of travel.

She took a deep breath, fighting the pain that welled up

inside her. *You can talk about this*, she thought to herself. *You need to talk about this.* "Do you know anything about her father?"

He slowly blinked at her, then shook his head. "He was never mentioned in the histories."

She sighed. He wasn't really worth mentioning. It was one of the many memories she wished had stayed away. "I knew from a very young age that I was born to be the next queen," she explained. "I was raised with that intent in mind, though my status was not flaunted. The Dair are secretive, and the Cavari most reticent among them."

"You do not have to tell me this," he muttered. "You owe me nothing."

She sucked her teeth, resisting the sudden urge to hit him for being such a stubborn mule. "In our society," she continued, "though queens are chosen at birth, it is tradition for them to acquire a consort. Those born under a certain alignment of the stars, like me, are gifted with greater magic than our kin, so it is frowned upon if we do not have children, as they will often be gifted with a magic near as great. The child is all that matters, so the consort is chosen through power, not love."

He watched her, taking in her words, but saying nothing.

"Niamh," she began, then stopped. She had not meant to say her daughter's name. She blinked away tears, then startled as Iseult's hand alighted warmly upon her shoulder. She glanced at him, then continued, taking comfort in the modest display of affection.

"Niamh," she began anew, "was a result of the ritual to name a consort. Her father was the most powerful among our tribe, though he was nearly as young as I. The consort is named once the future queen is with child. It only took a single try."

She looked down at her lap, fighting her embarrassment. She had *no* reason to be embarrassed. It did not matter that she had never truly loved a man. After Niamh had been born, she hadn't cared to. Sugn had been her consort in name only after that.

Iseult's fingers gently squeezed her shoulder, bringing her back to the present.

She glanced at him, then down at her lap again. "I just wanted you to know, that though you may not feel you have much to offer, I am the same. I know nothing of love, and have never known much affection. When Niamh was killed, I closed myself off entirely, to the point where I grew still and became a tree. Eventually my memories left me, and life was better that way. It was better not remembering what a foolish, sad creature I am."

His fingers squeezed again, then he moved his arm around her, pulling her against his side. "You are the most loving creature I have ever known," he muttered. "You may feel you have nothing to offer, but you love *everyone* as fiercely as most only love a single person. If anything, you have *too* much to offer."

She wiped a tear from her eye. "You always surprise me when you speak more than five words at once."

"And you surprise me every single day that you do not hate me," he replied.

She turned her gaze up to him, enjoying his warmth as much as his closeness confused her. "You are not your ancestors. You have done no wrong."

He sighed. "Be that as it may, you *are* your ancestors. You lived in that time of war. A time when my people were killed one by one. Yet, you are not filled with hatred or wrath. I do not understand how you came from the tribe of the Cavari, yet somehow managed to become the person you are."

She frowned. Truly, he thought too highly of her. "Iseult, I stole your people's souls, and before that, I was loyal to my tribe. I've known more hatred and wrath than most, but those things ultimately leave you hollow. They left *me* hollow. Yet, when I was a tree, I was able to relearn how beautiful things could be. I was able to watch the birds singing just for the sake of singing. I was able to watch young couples having picnics together, and hunters laboring to feed their families."

"Most people do not notice those things," he sighed.

She smirked. "Well, I was a tree, not a person."

He laughed. "Perhaps I should become a tree. I might learn a thing or two."

"I will teach you my secrets," she replied, snuggling more firmly into the crook of his arm. "If you will teach me yours."

"Most I would be afraid to tell you," he muttered distantly.

She sighed. If he would not tell her, she would simply have to figure them out herself.

CHAPTER FOURTEEN

*M*aarav stood by Ealasaid's side while she received reports from her scouts: increasing Faie sightings in the countryside, humans disappearing in the middle of the night, never to be seen again, and a massive troop of men in dark brown uniforms crested with a red wolf across their chests, heading south down the Sand Road.

It was the latter that had Maarav worried. He knew it was a possibility that An Fiach would catch wind of what Ealasaid was trying to accomplish, but he'd hoped it would take a little longer. Not much had been heard of the notorious An Fiach since the battle up North, save the contingent that had been tracking Finn. There was no mistaking things now though. The order was still together, and had recruited more soldiers by the sound of it.

Ealasaid nodded calmly as each of her scouts reported their news, then were excused from the lavish chamber so *generously* lent to them by Lady Sìoda. The Lady, he knew, had her own scouts, but if she was not going to share information with Ealasaid, nor would she with her.

Ouve shifted at Ealasaid's other side, raking fingers through his sandy hair. He'd stood silently by like a good little second in command. Although Maarav had done the same . . . he didn't consider himself a second in command. He wasn't quite sure what he was. An advisor? Or merely an ally.

Once the final scout departed, Ealasaid slumped down into a nearby chair with a sigh. "I wonder who will attack us first," she muttered, "the Faie or An Fiach."

"The Faie have no reason to attack us, do they?" Ouve questioned. "Plus, they seem disorganized, like animals. Just stealing people and livestock on the outskirts."

Maarav scoffed. "Tell that to those who used to live in Migris. The Faie were organized enough to leave not a single person alive."

Ouve turned wide eyes to him. "Truly?"

"Truly," Ealasaid sighed. "The Faie themselves may be disorganized, but all it takes is a leader strong enough to set them on a particular course."

Maarav nodded. "I'm glad you've considered that option."

Ealasaid furrowed her brow as she looked up at him. "Is there anything else you'd been secretly hoping I would consider?" she asked caustically.

He resisted the urge to roll his eyes. What had her angry with him *now*? "Only that An Fiach will be more prepared than they were in the North. Word has likely spread of what magic users can do when they band together. They will come with a plan, and will not be so easily defeated."

A flurry of knocks sounded at the door, and all three turned toward the sound.

"Come in!" Ealasaid called out.

Maarav shook his head and placed his hand upon his sword. Fool girl was far too trusting.

The door swung inward to reveal a mage, the one Maarav had noticed Ealasaid watching with interest, hunched and panting.

Ealasaid stood abruptly, facing the mage, clearly alarmed. "What is it, Sage?"

Sage panted a few more times, then lifted his head. "A contingent of uniformed men were spotted to the north, and strange warriors to the east. They look almost human, but their skin is white as milk, and they wear armor that seems to be poured of freshly molten metal, too beautifully curved to be made by hammer."

"The Aos Sí," Maarav muttered. "Iseult spoke of them."

Ealasaid glanced at him, then turned her gaze back to Sage. "What else?"

"They are both heading this way," he explained. "They will each close in within a day . . . likely at the same time."

Maarav had the sudden urge to pick Ealasaid up, run her outside, and throw her on a horse. What was he thinking making her the head of an army? He had hoped to be thoroughly fortified by the time an attack came. At this rate, they would be slaughtered.

"Are we sure they both intend to attack?" she asked, her trembling hands belying her calm voice.

"I do not know," Sage breathed.

Maarav cleared his throat. "An Fiach has no other reason to march toward a burgh filled with magic users, but the

Aos Sí are questionable. As far as we know, their queen is dead. Anyone could be leading them now."

"Well," Ealasaid began thoughtfully. "Perhaps this timing is fortuitous. If they approach at the same time, they might battle each other, leaving only the victor to attack us, if attack is even the Aos Sí's intent."

Maarav noted Sage and Ouve both looking at her like she'd grown a second head, then smiled. "I like it. Though An Fiach hunts down magic users, their primary enemy is the Faie. An army of Aos Sí will at the very least prove distracting. Judging by Iseult's description of the Aos Sí, I can guess who will come out on top in *that* battle."

Now Ouve and Sage were looking at *him* like he'd sprouted a second head. *Farm boys*, he internally scoffed.

"Good," Ealasaid replied after a moment. "I will feel no pity if every man in An Fiach falls to an Aos Sí sword, even if we have to deal with the Faie warriors afterward."

Maarav searched her face for evidence of soft-heartedness behind her words, but all he could find was a cold smile. He could not blame her for wanting revenge, but it was surprising. Perhaps someday she'd become as cold and heartless as his assassin brethren.

Ouve looked back and forth between the two of them. "But what if they both attack us first, and each other later? They might decide that another force, even one belonging to the enemy, could prove a worthwhile distraction. We'd never be able to stand against both armies at once."

"Have some faith," Maarav replied. "The Aos Sí may be frightening, but they do not possess the magnitude of magic that any of you do, and An Fiach has no magic at all. We must simply be smart and organized."

Ealasaid nodded. "Ouve, find Slàine and inform her of the incoming forces. Sage, do the same for the mages. Send scouts to move the townspeople inward toward the estate, and ask Slàine to send a few of her people to keep an eye on the Aos Sí and An Fiach. Whatever happens, we will be ready."

Ouve and Sage both seemed like they were about to piss themselves, but still they nodded and hurried to obey. Soon enough, Maarav and Ealasaid were alone.

She turned worried eyes to him. "I hope you were not lying about our magic being greater than that of the Aos Sí."

He nodded. "According to my brother, they are fierce warriors, but lacking in actual magic beyond a few minor tricks."

She let out a long breath, then took a step toward him. "And my orders? What else should I have added?"

He placed his hand on her shoulder. "We have a day to figure out the rest."

She nodded, her eyes downcast.

"And you know," he added, "as the leader of An Solas, your role is here within the estate. You will not be part of the battle unless the grounds are breached."

Her eyes jerked up to his. "I will not send anyone to fight in my place, nor will I hide from An Fiach. I ran once. I will not run again."

He sighed. He'd have to think of a better excuse to keep her out of the fight. Her magic was powerful, but she was not experienced in battle. She'd run around like a rabid wolverine in the battle up North, flinging lightning without considering she was drawing the eye of archers right to her.

"Will you fight with me?" she asked suddenly. "I—" she

hesitated, "I do not like the idea of you running off into battle where I cannot see you."

He smirked. At the very least he could use her reasoning to keep them both near the estate, ready to take down any attackers who made it through the first lines of defense.

"There is no one else I'd rather fight beside," he assured, and found, despite wanting to keep her out of battle altogether, it was the truth.

MANY TENSE HOURS PASSED. EALASAID BRUSHED A STRAY lock of hair from her face. She'd managed to pull most of it into a braid, but it was so curly that a few stray strands were inevitable, especially when faced with the harsh, chill wind up in the guard tower. She wore a winter tunic over breeches, along with a heavy cloak, but still felt the cold.

Maarav stood by her side atop the guard tower, as promised. They'd spent the day running around making preparations in hopes that they'd get some rest during the night, but luck was not on their side. Slàine's scouts revealed that neither army stopped to make camp when darkness fell. They would both reach them that night.

"They must be aware of each other by now," Maarav muttered. "Armies that large do not pass by each other unnoticed."

She chewed her lip. If that was the case, and they weren't already fighting, they might both agree to first attack the burgh before each other. Or, perhaps one would wait to see what the other would do. She half wished they'd tried to communicate with the Aos Sí to learn their intent. With

Finn no longer in the burgh, and Oighear dead, she had no idea what they might want with Garenoch.

"Torches," Maarav muttered, pointing north. "Let us hope your mages know how to follow orders."

She placed an hand over her abdomen, sick with nerves. Was this truly happening? Would An Solas meet an untimely end? Would *she*? She'd done her best to release her fear of dying when she first left her village, and even thought she had succeeded, but it all came crashing back now.

She turned wide eyes to Maarav.

He raised an eyebrow at her. "Having second thoughts on entering the fray?"

Yes, she thought, but shook her head.

He sidled up to her and put an arm around her shoulders. "It is best not to think about death. Instead think of your family and the vengeance you seek, and take heart in the mages that have come to fight for you."

She nodded several times too quickly, making herself dizzy. What if Maarav died? Who would guide her then? Would she be left at the mercy of Slàine?

She took a deep, shuddering breath. The torches were nearing the edge of the burgh, though she could not see who wielded them. She leaned against Maarav for a moment, then pulled away. She pictured her mother's face, and those of her sisters. She thought of her peaceful village going up in flames, of those she loved being tortured, then killed.

Hot rage welled up inside of her. She knew she might die that night, but not before she avenged every single person she'd lost.

~

MAARAV SIGHED AS EALASAID PULLED AWAY. HE'D DONE ALL he could for her, now he could only hope that the gods weren't cruel enough to kill a girl so young.

Footsteps sounded on the stairs leading up the interior of the tower seconds before Tavish emerged. "It's An Fiach. The Aos Sí are still in the forest to the east. They have halted their approach for now."

Maarav nodded. Hopefully it meant the Aos Sí did not intend to attack. Otherwise, they were simply waiting for An Fiach to weaken Garenoch's defenses before swooping in to finish them off.

Shouting could be heard in the distance, along with a few screams. Maarav narrowed his gaze as the first wave of magic hit An Fiach. What would have been a spectacular sight during the day was made even more so in the dark of night. Washes of flame arced outward, illuminating equally powerful bursts of ice. Yet, the torches advanced, and more people screamed. Something was wrong.

He turned to Tavish. "Find out what they're doing to guard themselves against the magic."

Tavish nodded before Maarav could give further instruction, then turned and hurried back down the stairs.

"We should go with him," Ealasaid breathed. "If they've found a way to protect themselves against our magic, we need to devise a new plan."

He grabbed her arm before she could spin away. "Wait for Tavish's return. You need to be here to relay whatever the new plan might be. All will suffer if you become lost in the chaos."

She blinked up at him, then slowly nodded. She seemed to calm herself, though he could feel electricity in the air around her, making his arm hairs stand on end beneath his shirt.

Painful minutes passed. Ealasaid remained silent while Maarav struggled to see what was happening. The bursts of magic were now more erratic as An Fiach pushed forward, intermingling with An Solas.

Finally, just when he was sure Ealasaid would flee the tower at any moment, Tavish returned.

He hunched over with his hands on his knees, attempting to regain his breath. "Cannot see what it is," he rasped. "Some sort of . . . barrier protects them. The magic just seems to bounce off."

Maarav turned to Ealasaid to see what she thought, but she'd stepped forward to the parapet.

He approached her side, leaving Tavish to recover.

Her pale gray eyes peered outward, though they didn't seem to be focusing on anything in particular. "I sense . . . something," she muttered. "*Someone* . . . protecting them." She looked to Maarav. "I can feel someone shielding them, but that someone is outside the burgh. I must locate them if we hope to prevail."

He let out a slow breath. "Focus, Eala. Can you tell who it is?"

She shook her head. "The protector is powerful, more powerful than any of our mages. That's all I can tell."

"Faie?" he questioned.

"I don't think so," she replied, glancing out to the battle.

The torches were growing closer. Their people were dying.

"I'll go with you," he decided, regretting it as soon as he said it. He should keep her within the estate, but if these men were immune to magic . . .

He turned to Tavish. "Have Slàine send her people forward, and have the mages fall back. Try to buy us some time."

Tavish nodded, then hurried down the stairs ahead of Maarav and Ealasaid.

"We'll leave through the back of the estate," he explained as they descended. "We must not be seen if we hope to make it to this unknown force unhindered."

Ealasaid's boots clicked down the stairs beside his. "I think it's in the forest to the west, opposite where the Aos Sí are supposed to be."

He nodded as they reached the courtyard, then took her hand and hurried across the grass. "Do you think you can beat whatever this thing is?" he panted as they ran.

"I have to," was her only reply.

Not terribly heartening, that.

They darted around the far side of the estate, toward the outer buildings on the southwest end. Maarav led her to an area he had earlier noted, where a building stood near the outer wall. From the building's roof, they could hop to the wall, and down the other side into the forested area beyond where it was unlikely enemies would be lying in wait.

He tugged on Ealasaid's hand to slow her as they approached their destination. A stone staircase climbed up the exterior wall, leading to a small balcony on the second story, bedecked with vine-covered trellises. Ealasaid was light enough to easily climb the trellises. Maarav hoped he could follow quickly enough to not topple the fragile wood.

"Where are we going?" Ealasaid whispered, her gaze darting around for what had stopped him.

He pointed to the stairs. "You first. When you reach the second story, climb the trellis to the top and get onto the roof. It's just a short hop to the ledge of the wall."

She whipped her startled gaze to him. "And how will we get back *down* from the wall."

He motioned for her to get moving. "There are trees. Don't worry, I'll help you."

She watched him for a moment more, then rushed off, quickly mounting the stairs, then scurrying toward the trellis as he came up after her. She climbed the trellis easy enough, then pulled herself onto the roof.

Once she was up, he tested the trellis with his hands and frowned. It was not meant to hold much weight, and he probably weighed almost as much as two Ealasaids . . . or at least one and a half.

Knowing he had little choice, he pulled himself up onto the trellis and scrambled upward. Not taking time to find proper handholds, he propelled himself toward the roof. Once he was within reach, he pushed off. The trellis toppled down, slamming against the side of the lower wall as the vines refused to loosen their grasp.

"Well so much for getting back down when we return," Ealasaid muttered.

He glared at her. "We'll worry about that later. Time is short."

She nodded. Spurred by his words, she hurried toward the edge of the roof near the wall.

Maarav tensed, hoping she would not hesitate.

Without waiting for further instruction or help, she

leapt across the gap, braving the two story fall that awaited her should she slip.

Maarav held his breath until she touched down safely on the other side of the wide ledge. He exhaled relief, pleased with her performance, then jogged to the edge of the roof and took the jump just as easily. He joined Ealasaid as she leaned against the low parapet to peer down into the forest.

"Those trees aren't anywhere near the wall!" she hissed.

It wasn't entirely true. There were a few new growth trees nearer the wall than the rest, they just weren't tall enough to reach the edge of the parapet.

"I'll drop down first onto that tree," he instructed, pointing to a sturdy looking pine. "Once I have a good hold I'll be able to catch you."

She gave him a speculative look, but before she could argue he hopped off the wall, falling like a squirrel onto the highest branches of the nearest tree. The impact stole his breath, but he managed to hang on. As soon as he could, he found a foothold on the branch below him, then twisted his body to face Ealasaid. He locked his leg around another branch just above the one he stood upon, then held his arms up toward her.

"You're mad!" she hissed, still clutching the parapet.

"Yes," he agreed, "but you're going to jump anyway."

Shaking her head, she mounted the edge of the parapet. Keeping her balance, she swung her arms a few times for momentum, then launched herself toward Maarav.

The impact of her body slamming against his stole his breath again, but he held on to her even more tightly than he had the tree.

"Can you climb down?" he asked as she panted in his ear, trembling.

"I climbed plenty of trees as a girl," she whispered, "but never quite like this."

Despite her words, she released him in favor of the nearest branch, then slowly began the climb down. Soon enough, they were both safe on the forest floor with the sounds of distant fighting.

He peered into the darkness. "Do you still sense whatever it is protecting An Fiach?"

She nodded. "Follow me."

She took off at a jog, her small feet almost silent on the pine needles beneath her boots.

He followed after her, just as silent, his eyes constantly scanning their surroundings for danger.

"It's somewhere near," Ealasaid whispered, then halted so abruptly that her boots skidded across the damp pine needles.

Maarav caught her before she could fall, then whipped around, sensing danger.

Several paces away stood a woman in a black dress with long, crimson hair. She titled her angular face at them, pretty, if slightly masculine. "Why hello," she purred. "I hoped I'd find you here."

"Do I know you?" he asked, confused at why this woman was in the woods all alone when a battle was going on.

"Not you," she replied, stepping forward. She extended a long finger, pointing past him. "*Her*."

He tried to step in front of Ealasaid, but she pushed her way to his side. "She's the one I sensed. She's protecting An Fiach."

The woman smiled. "Very good, though the battle is of little consequence to me. You're my only quarry."

"What do you want?" Ealasaid demanded.

"I want what you want," the woman replied, stepping even closer. "I want the mages to win the war to come, and you are the key to making it happen."

Maarav's hair stood on end. He could always feel when Ealasaid summoned her lightning.

She held a hand out toward the woman. "Stop protecting An Fiach or I will kill you here and now."

The woman laughed, throaty and seductive. "Quite bold, for a farm girl. I like it."

Ealasaid flicked her hand and a lightning bolt exploded near enough to the woman to spatter dirt on her boots.

She didn't so much as flinch.

"This is your final warning," Ealasaid growled.

Maarav debated just flinging a dagger into the woman's throat, but he suspected if she could deflect attacks from an entire army, she could easily deflect them from herself.

The woman flicked her long red hair over her shoulder. "I have no intention of fighting you. My name is Keiren, and with my help, you will become queen."

The name was familiar to Maarav, though he couldn't quite recall where he'd heard it. Perhaps from one of their companions?

"Finn warned me about you," Ealasaid growled. "I know what you did to Àed."

Maarav's skin prickled seconds before Ealasaid shot a bolt of lightning right at the woman, but she was suddenly no longer there.

She blinked into existence again, a few paces to Maarav's

left. "Impressive," she mused. "A worthwhile power to be sure, though few things can defeat the power of air."

Ealasaid launched another bolt at her as she blinked out of sight, then reappeared behind them.

They both whirled to face her.

She inspected her fingernails, not worried in the slightest. "The power of air is the power of illusion, the power of second sight, and the power of warding. Even if you managed to strike me with one of your bolts, it would not penetrate my defenses." She tilted her head as if listening to something far away. "Unfortunately I can only maintain so many enchantments at once." She curled the corner of her lip. "Your mages might just survive."

Ealasaid glanced at Maarav, clearly confused.

"I told you, I am not your enemy," the woman continued. "In fact, I am your greatest ally. The Aos Sí have come to kill the human queen that hopes to lead the mages to victory. They have come to kill *you*."

Maarav's breath hitched. Slàine had expressed suspicion that Ealasaid was the human queen from the prophecy, but he'd disregarded her warnings. She was powerful, but nothing like Finn.

"Ah," Keiren said, observing him. "So you already suspected?"

"What are you talking about?" Ealasaid spat. "I'm not the queen from the prophecy. If anything *you* are she."

Keiren sighed. "Unfortunately, no. I was not born under the proper alignment of stars, and I have lived for far too long for it to be possible. My magic dwindled, with all the rest. Then, eighteen years ago, something changed. My power began to return full force, even more so." She looked

Ealasaid up and down. "You look about eighteen. Is the anniversary of your birth ten days from this evening?"

Maarav watched Ealasaid's jaw go slack. She hadn't mentioned that her birthday was coming up.

"Y-you're lying," she stammered. "This is all a trick."

Keiren shrugged. "If you say so. Denying it will not change what must be done. Oighear the White yet lives, and she has sent her Aos Sí to kill you. If she fails, Finnur will come for you next."

"She would never," Ealasaid gasped. "Finn is my friend!"

Keiren clucked her tongue and shook her head. "She is no one's friend. She is the Oaken Queen, and she possesses the Faie Queen's shroud. She will give her magic to the inhuman races until they extinguish human life entirely. Our only hope of survival is our human queen. Your very existence supplies us all with greater power."

Ealasaid began to back away, then it was as if she hit an invisible wall.

"You must accept your birthright," Keiren explained, then waved her hand in the air.

Ealasaid stumbled back, as if the wall had disappeared, and Maarav was so stunned he almost didn't catch her.

As soon as she'd regained her footing, she pulled away from him, wiping at the tears in her eyes. "If all you say is true, then why attack the mages? Why side with An Fiach?"

"I told you," Keiren hissed. "My powers are those of illusion and defensive magic. I stood little chance of entering your estate on my own amidst all of your mages and assassins."

Ealasaid wiped her wet cheeks and shook her head, but did not reply.

"What is it that you want, exactly?" Maarav asked. "If the Aos Sí are coming for her, then we need to see to preparations."

"I want to help," Keiren explained. "I will be a valuable ally. Now that Finnur has the added power of the shroud, and Oighear has regained her full health, you need all of the allies you can get."

Maarav readied himself to reply, but Ealasaid held up her hand.

"Come with us to the northern end of the burgh," she demanded. "Call off your men. Then we will speak."

Keiren smirked. "They are An Fiach. Now that they have the scent of mages, they will not relent."

"Then we have nothing more to discuss," Ealasaid snapped, then turned to march off.

"I can, however—" Keiren began, halting Ealasaid's retreat.

Ealasaid turned back to Keiren with a hopeful eye.

Keiren began again, "I can, however, shield your mages instead of An Fiach. You want those men dead, do you not? You want to receive your vengeance."

"How do you—" Ealasaid began, but before she could finish, Keiren started tapping a finger at her temple as if saying, *think*.

"Powers of air, remember?" she explained. "I can see many things that others cannot, and I can explore the in-between, the realm of dreams. I know your desires."

Ealasaid looked like she wanted to reach out and slap the woman, but balled her fists at her sides instead. "Fine, protect my mages, then we will talk."

Keiren grinned, then joined Ealasaid as they walked toward the sounds of battle.

Maarav followed, staring at their backs. He didn't like that grin one bit. Women like Keiren didn't do things for the good of many, and they definitely didn't care about the desires of others.

He followed after them, wishing his brother and Finn had never left, or at the very least, that they would have taken them along on their journey.

CHAPTER FIFTEEN

*E*alasaid couldn't help the trembling in her hands as she took in the moonlit battle field. The shielding Keiren had promised her mages had been unnecessary by the time they reached them. Once the shields had fallen from An Fiach, they'd attempted to retreat. Perhaps some of them had made it, but not many judging by the corpses littering the muddy streets.

Her eyes fell upon a corpse she knew, one of her mages, an older female. She quickly averted her gaze.

Keiren stood silently at her side, and Maarav at her other, both towering over her.

"We should return to the estate," Maarav muttered, "assess our losses."

"Yes," Keiren agreed, "let us be off."

Ealasaid whirled on her, fury blurring her vision. "This is all your fault!" she screamed. "None of them would be dead if it weren't for you!"

Keiren smirked. "*You* gathered the mages together. You knew An Fiach would come."

"But you protected them!" she growled. Yes, perhaps An Fiach would have come either way, but they would not have attacked so boldly, and would have turned back when they realized what they were up against.

Keiren rolled her eyes. "Yes, I gave the men a fighting chance. This is war, my girl. You must be prepared for much worse. You will face the Aos Sí next, and they will not need a ward to protect them."

Ealasaid balled her hands, longing to hit Keiren. Anything to rid herself of the horrible feeling eating up her insides. The horrible feeling that said it was all *her* fault. She did know An Fiach would come, and she had gathered the mages together regardless.

"Ealasaid!" someone called out, drawing her attention away from Keiren.

Ouve trotted toward them, bedraggled and bloody, but *alive*. "We were worried when we couldn't find you at the estate," he panted upon reaching them. "Ealasaid, I don't know what happened, but we won!"

She peered around at the bodies, illuminated by the moon and still burning fallen torches. "Did we?" she questioned distantly.

Maarav stepped to her side and wrapped his arm around her. "You need to rest," he muttered. "Let us leave the funeral pyres to the soldiers."

The trembling returned first to her hands, then to her entire body. She was grateful when Maarav turned to Ouve and instructed him to find Keiren a room at the inn. They could deal with her later.

She allowed herself to be led back to the estate, trembling incessantly. This was all her fault. She'd grown too big for her boots, and now everything would come crumbling down.

"Don't let them see you cry," Maarav whispered, his arm still wrapped around her.

She felt too numb to reply, and instead continued moving along, counting the bodies as she passed.

ONCE THEY WERE BACK WITHIN THE ESTATE WALLS, BEYOND the view of mages and assassins, Maarav scooped Ealasaid up into his arms, her limp legs dangling. She did not cry. She did not speak. Looking down upon her sad, still face, he feared something had broken inside her. She'd seen battle before, in Uí Néid, and she'd seen the bodies in Migris, but this was different. These were people she knew.

A few of Lady Sìoda's guards eyed them as he made his way back toward their allotted quarters, but did not speak, probably glad the battle never made it to them. He debated telling them to just wait for the Aos Sí, but kept his mouth shut for Ealasaid's sake.

Soon enough they reached the proper building and entered, passing his room and heading straight toward hers. Upon reaching it, he set her down to her feet. Her trembling body wavered, unsteady as he opened the door. Fearing she might collapse, he swept her up again into his arms and carried her inside.

Leaving the room dark, he set her on her bed, lying her flat, then returned to the door and closed it.

"Some leader I turned out to be," she muttered at his back.

He shut the door softly then returned to her, kneeling at her bedside. "You saved them all by finding Keiren and negotiating with her. You did a fine job."

Her eyes glistened as she stared up at the ceiling, her curly hair popping out from her braid to splay across her pillow. "She's wrong though. I'm not powerful enough to be," she hesitated, "*queen* of the magic users, or whatever she thinks I am."

He lifted his hand to stroke a puff of hair out of her face. "It doesn't matter what she thinks you are. It does not change your course."

She turned her head toward him. "And what is my course?"

He smiled. "To band the mages together before they can be picked off one by one, and to teach them to protect themselves from whatever comes next."

"The Aos Sí," she sighed, turning her gaze back up to the ceiling.

"Yes," he replied, the danger heavy on his mind as well. "We should at least hear what Keiren has to say. We may not be able to trust her, but if we can use her power to save our own, we must at least consider the option."

"Just like with Slàine?" she asked weakly.

He nodded.

She groaned, lifting a hand to rub her eyes. "I feel like we're in a den of vipers. Make one wrong step, and everyone dies."

He stroked her hair again. He didn't like seeing her so morose, but was glad she was coming to terms with reality.

This was the way war worked. She needed to be prepared for it.

A soft knock sounded at the door. Patting Ealasaid's shoulder he stood, crossed the room, and opened it. Ouve and Sage waited outside.

"We just wanted to make sure she's alright," Sage explained.

Maarav glanced over his shoulder at Ealasaid. She was upset and tired, but likely still capable of protecting herself. He turned back to the two boys.

"Stay here with her," he instructed. "I need to find Slàine and tally the losses. Then we must prepare for the next attack."

Before he got far, gentle footsteps sounded behind him, then Ealasaid appeared at his side. "I will come with you. If I'm going to be a leader, then I must lead."

He couldn't help his satisfied smile. He was not sure if Keiren's claims were correct, but he half hoped they were. She would make a good queen. Much better than the land had seen in several lifetimes.

KEIREN PACED AROUND THE CONFINES OF THE SMALL ROOM she'd been given at the inn. She had half a mind to burn the place down. Then they'd *have* to let her stay within the estate.

She sighed, then slumped onto the small, hard bed. At least she'd convinced the farm girl to work with her. If Ealasaid ever came to terms with the power that waited within her, she would be a force to be reckoned with, rather than the scared little thing she was now. She might even prove capable of breaking the barrier to the in-between, though she doubted it. The ritual was very clear, and could only be performed by one with immortal blood. She suspected Finnur had already shared that gift with someone else, it was the only explanation for the mortal taint in her blood now. She shook her head in dismay. Finnur could no longer give her what she needed, *but* if she could be convinced to perform the barrier breaking ritual herself . . .

She smiled faintly. Ealasaid could aid in that endeavor. The prophecy was very clear. Two of the queens would die. If she could mold Ealasaid into a true threat, they could force Finnur into helping them.

She stood and began to pace once more. *No*, that wouldn't work. Finnur cared not for the prophecy, all she cared about was protecting her small group of companions and finding Àed.

She smirked at the thought. Yes, the task of finding Àed should keep Finnur quite busy. Too busy to build an army.

Soon Finnur would be forced to see things *her* way.

A knock sounded at her door. She glared at the simple wood adorned with a single brass knob and lock. She focused her senses on whoever was outside the door, attempting to determine if they meant her harm, yet she felt . . . nothing.

There was only one person she knew that felt like nothing.

She strode across the room and opened the door, unsurprised to see Óengus standing on the other side. His silver hair and beard were neatly groomed, though he looked thinner than he had before, and *older*.

She sneered. "I thought perhaps you had died."

He smirked, then pushed his way into the room. "What are you doing here?" he questioned, turning on his heel to face her as she shut the door.

She raised an eyebrow at him. "I could ask you the same question. Have you come to grovel at my feet and beg for forgiveness after abandoning your task?"

His gaze darted around the small room, then back to her face. "I was too late. I witnessed Finnur claiming the shroud. She's too powerful for you to take advantage of now."

Keiren laughed to hide the rage that washed up within her. If only she'd gotten to Finn sooner. "How little you know," she purred, feigning confidence. "Finnur may be powerful, but she is like a child in a den of wolves. Oighear hunts for her, and soon the human queen will as well. Now, give me one good reason to let you live."

He laughed, then sat on the bed, lounging.

She clenched her fists. The fool really did have guts, right to the very end.

"Would you truly kill the Snow Queen's spy?" he asked, one silver eyebrow raised.

"Oighear?" she questioned. "Is that where you've been hiding?"

He nodded. "I found her after she faced Finnur, and Finnur won. I grew tired of waiting for *you* to return my shadow."

"And the Snow Queen is capable of helping you?" she asked, genuinely interested.

He smiled, but she'd noted his brief hesitation. He was unsure if Oighear would truly help him.

She grinned, then approached him. She reached out a hand as if to stroke his cheek, as one would a prized horse.

He glared at her hand, then stood and stepped back.

She laughed, pleased to have regained control of the conversation. Few could verbally spar with her effectively.

"I'm going to let you in on a little secret, dear Óengus," she crooned. "The only way for your shadow to be returned to you, is to break the barriers of the in-between. Fortunately, that is exactly what I plan to do, with your help."

He narrowed his gaze at her. "Go on."

She fought the urge to gloat. She'd never met the Snow Queen personally, but it still felt good to steal her spy away.

"Tell me what the Aos Sí plan," she suggested, "and I will ensure your survival until the barrier can be broken, and we *both* receive just what we want."

He tilted his head in thought. "Tell me what you're planning with the human queen, and you will have your answers in return."

She strode over to the door and locked it with the heavy iron key she'd been provided, then strolled toward the small fire in the hearth. She positioned a wooden chair near the flames and sat, then looking at Óengus, gestured to a second.

With a hesitant look at the locked door, Óengus crossed the room and sat.

The night was truly looking up.

Night had come again, and Kai couldn't help but admit

that he felt spectacular. *Physically,* at least. He could stand no longer being held captive by the Dearg Due.

During the night, they marched him ceaselessly, their pace slowed by his human constitution. Other than flinging the occasional insult, they did not speak to him.

He flinched as some sort of bug fell from the trees above and landed on his shoulder near his neck, but his hands were tied behind his back so he couldn't swat it. He wiggled uncomfortably, then nearly stumbled as a tiny voice whispered in his ear, "Do not be alarmed, and do not answer me, just listen."

Was he hallucinating? The small weight on his shoulder felt horribly real, as did the tickle of something pressing against his neck.

"We have been sent by the Oak Queen," the voice buzzed, "but we cannot hope to face the Dearg Due and live. You must listen to my words carefully."

His eyes flicked to the surrounding Dearg Due, but none of them seemed to notice the tiny creature pressed against his neck, hiding beneath his hair.

"Soon you will approach a stream," the voice continued. "This is your only hope. They do not like to cross running water. It absorbs dark magic, leaving them weakened."

He resisted the urge to nod. If whatever was on his shoulder planned to help him, he would not argue.

"Tell them you must relieve yourself," the voice continued. "When you go, veer to the right of the path."

"I must relieve myself," he said out loud, stopping in his tracks.

"Keep moving, weak Dair," the most familiar of the Dearg Due hissed.

He did not obey. They'd allowed him the luxury previously . . . with a small escort.

"Hurry up," one of the other wicked women hissed, then said a few words in their language.

Three of the women, including his constant verbal abuser, hustled him to the left, but remembering the small voice's words, he veered right.

"I think I spotted a snake over there," he lied.

Grumbling under their breath, the women escorted him right instead.

He stumbled through the dark underbrush, taking his time finding a place to *relieve himself*.

"Far enough," one of the women said, grabbing his arm to stop him.

"Keep going," the voice whispered in his ear. "You must be closer to the water if you hope to escape."

"Those vines are poisonous," he said out loud. "I don't want to catch a rash."

The women spoke in their language, then shoved him. "Here or not at all," one hissed.

The shove was half-hearted, but he took advantage and exaggerated his stumble, making his way farther in the direction chosen by the voice. He thought he could hear running water.

The women caught up to him, and one grabbed his arm. "Back to the path," she ordered.

"I guess it's now or never," the tiny voice sighed. "On my command, *run*. Cross the water and do not stop."

His heart skipped a beat. Now or never. The creature on his shoulder twitched, and he felt a flutter against his neck.

"Now!" it rasped.

He tugged away from the Dearg Due and took off at a sprint as all noise was drowned out by the sound of fluttering wings. Flashes of color glinting in the moonlight caught his eye, but he did not slow his pace. The Dearg Due screeched behind him, then his feet splashed into the water of the stream.

He continued across, the water almost engulfing his hips, slowing him down. The creature on his shoulder clung to his hair painfully. Something splashed into the water behind him, but he was already out on the other side. His clothes dripping and heavy, he started to run again.

"Keep going straight!" the voice whispered in his ear, entwining itself in his hair as the creature fought to not be dislodged.

He obeyed, fighting against the burn in his lungs and the icy chill in his legs.

"Left!" the voice hissed.

He could hear more screeching and splashing as he obeyed. The Dearg Due were crossing the water in pursuit.

"They will not be as fast now," the voice whispered, hitching from his bouncing gait, "nor as strong. Just a little bit further."

He ran until he thought he would collapse, then the voice hissed, "Stop! Do not move!"

Despite his instincts telling him to run, he skidded to a halt and froze. The trees around him began to move, shuffling in around him. Their rough bark pressed against him on all sides, enclosing him fully.

"They will not be able to sense you through the trees," the voice whispered. "Just stay still and do not speak until they move on."

He would have nodded, but the trees were pinning him so completely that any movement was near impossible. He did his best to calm his breathing as the Dearg Due screeched all around him.

He'd never been a fan of the Trow, or Faie in general, but right then, he could have hugged them . . . if only he could move.

BEDELIA HELD TIGHTLY TO HER REINS, FLINCHING AT EVERY sound emanating from the midnight marsh. Her horse's hooves suctioned in the mud with every step. The moon cast an eerie glow about the shadows of night. She recognized where she was now, deep in the Southlands near the coast. Days of swampland lay before her.

She glanced at Àed atop his horse. Silence had stolen his tongue since their escape. Her gaze passed him, reaching Sativola, slumped in his saddle. If they got stuck in the mud, or slipped into a hidden bog, he would be of no help. Even though she had dressed his wound and forced water down his throat before they left, he'd grown more ill since then. They probably should have stopped to rest, but she didn't want to stay in the murky marsh any longer than necessary. Not to mention Keiren would search for them upon her return to the fortress, unless Niklas decided to aid them further by delaying her.

She jumped as an owl hooted above her, then shook her head at her own foolishness. *Why* had Niklas decided to help her in the first place? What could he possibly want from her? She had no power like Finn or Keiren, nor was she important enough to anyone to be used as a bargaining tool. It didn't make any sense.

Sativola erupted in a fit of coughing, then squinted up at the slowly rising sun. "Is it brighter today than usual?" he rasped.

She glanced up at the sun, barely high enough to shine light at all, and obscured by the ever present murk of the marshes.

"Not really," she replied, casting a speculative eye over his hunched form.

He groaned, then pulled his borrowed hood up over his curls. She hadn't been able to find something large enough for him in the short time she'd taken to gather supplies, but she'd figured the thick brown cloak was better than nothing. For herself, she'd unfortunately been unable to find her usual cloak or weapons, but Keiren had supplied her with breeches and a cream colored tunic, and she'd found a heavy green cloak for warmth. She'd also discovered a bow in a small armory, though it was larger than the one she usually used. She would be slow to fire an arrow should the need arise. Àed had taken nothing but a light gray cloak and a small ration of food.

Sativola let out a loud, shuddering breath. "I feel like my insides are twisted, and my mind is full of fog."

She frowned. She'd been bitten by the creatures who'd attacked them too, but Keiren had *cleansed* her wound. Was the poison similar to what had affected her in her wolf bite? If so, Sativola was likely to die in the marsh without Finn around to find a tincture for him.

"I'm sure you just need rest," she lied, "but we must ride

throughout the day. I want to be far away when Keiren returns."

She swallowed at a sudden lump in her throat. It wouldn't matter how far away she was. Keiren always seemed able to find her unless she was with Finn, and sometimes even then. Her only hope was that Keiren would remain away long enough for her to find Finn and Iseult once more. If they had survived the attack, they would be heading toward Sormyr, which meant they were somewhere to the North. If her horse lasted, she might stand a chance of finding them again. She glanced at Sativola. That was, if *he* didn't slow her down.

Just as she thought it, he slipped from his saddle and thudded into the mud. She hopped down from her horse, catching Sativola's mount before it could bolt. Holding a tight rein on his horse and hers, she glanced at Àed, who watched her dispassionately. Giving up on the idea of his help, she rushed to Sativola's side, tugging the horses along behind her.

Sativola groaned and rolled onto his back, coating his cloak in mud. "I think I'm dyin', lass," he gasped.

No, no, no, she thought. He couldn't have chosen a worse time. They needed to get out of these blasted marshes. She looked over her shoulder at the horses. Without Sativola's massive weight on one, they might remain fresh enough to carry her out of danger . . .

She groaned, dismissing the idea. She hurried to tether both horses to a nearby scraggly tree, then rushed back to Sativola. She sat on her knees in the mud beside him, then gently lifted his head into her lap.

While he groaned in pain, she pushed his sweaty curls

aside and lifted his bandage to observe his neck, then nearly gagged at the smell coming from the wound. It was as if the skin was rotting, and the gray coloration had spread down to his collarbone and up to his jaw.

"Is it bad?" he panted.

"N-no," she lied. "You just need to rest. I will try to find us some dry wood to build a small fire."

She gently set his head back on the mud, then stood to search for wood. She knew deep down that she should just leave him. If he was going to die anyway, there was no point of sacrificing her own life to make him comfortable. If Keiren returned to the fortress, it would take her little time to find them and drag her back to her remote tower. She knew if that happened, she would not find the opportunity to escape again.

She glanced back at Sativola's large form, lying in the mud. He was nothing but a sailor who'd hired on into a bad situation, yet, he'd always been kind to her. He'd always been kind to everyone, even though he drank far too much whiskey.

She knew in that moment she couldn't leave him behind, even if Àed wasn't present to rat her out to Finn. She couldn't use her fear of Keiren as an excuse. At one time in her life, she had considered herself a warrior, ready to face any fear that came her way.

Perhaps it was time to get that feeling back.

ÓENGUS LOUNGED BY THE WARM HEARTH IN THE DESERTED farmstead, its previous residents long since departed.

Whether they left because they feared the Faie, or because the unnaturally cold weather made their crops fail was of little consequence. He had a place to stay outside of the burgh, where he wasn't likely to be noticed by anyone who might know of him.

He held up a crystal in the flickering light of the fire. He was yet to use it to communicate with Oighear. Part of him wanted to lie to her, to side once more with Keiren, but then again, Keiren had toyed with him for far too long. If he told Oighear about Ealasaid and her army of mages, she would likely join her Aos Sí warriors when they attacked. Keiren might be killed, giving him one less option. Conversely, if he proved his loyalty to Oighear, she might just return his shadow in exchange for his continued service.

There were too many ifs. Perhaps if he was the type of man to care about the lives of those within the burgh, he'd want to fight against the Faie taking over the land, but he did not care. He thought the victory of the Faie an inevitability. Humans might be killed off entirely for all he cared. All he wanted was to achieve his mission, regain that which he once willingly gave away, then he would gladly join the lowly townsfolk in their mass grave.

He lifted the crystal again, gazing into it with a heavy sigh. Perhaps if he'd cared about the difference between right and wrong, good and evil, he would not be in this predicament to begin with.

CHAPTER SIXTEEN

*a*nna couldn't help her excitement. After a fitful night's rest and a quick morning meal, she and Eywen remounted their horse to follow the Pixies on the final leg of their journey. According to the tiny creatures, their *Oak Queen* was not far off, and they would reach her shortly.

She could only hope Kai was with Finn, or at the very least that the Pixies had found him too, and were leading him along. She even surprised herself by hoping some of Eywen's warriors had been found. He'd abandoned his evil Faie Queen along with most of his people, just to fight for what he thought was right. He deserved at least a little luck by now.

A small flurry of Pixies circled back toward them, which was nothing new considering their tiny wings carried them much faster than Anna and Eywen's horse could walk.

"Wait here," several of them buzzed in unison.

Nodding, Eywen drew their horse to a halt. The Pixies

flew back in the direction they'd come, disappearing into the trees.

Feeling suddenly nervous, she tapped Eywen's shoulder. "You don't think this is a trap, do you?"

He turned and smiled at her. Two days ago she would have found the smile unnerving. Now, it just seemed normal, like the smile of a friend.

"If the Pixies wanted to kill us," he began, "they would have done so by now. We would have been powerless against such a large flock."

Just as he spoke, another *flock* zoomed overhead.

Funny, she thought, she hadn't realized any of the Pixies had fallen behind them.

"Anna?" a voice questioned, and she nearly toppled out of her seat.

She glanced over her shoulder to see Kai, a little dirty and bloody, but otherwise *alive*. Later, she might be embarrassed about the girlish shriek she let out, but now she could not be bothered. She hopped from the saddle and raced toward him, throwing herself into his arms.

"I'm so glad to see you alive!" he laughed. "My captors only kept me alive believing I was one of the Dair, so I feared the worst."

She pulled out of the hug, gripping his biceps as she looked him up and down. "I remained unconscious for the entire attack," she explained. "Eywen kept me safe." She glanced over her shoulder toward Eywen, but he had ridden almost out of sight, as if to give them privacy.

Kai visibly relaxed, letting out a long breath. "I was so afraid when he offered to take you. His horse was ready to go, and I thought it your best chance of survival."

"You made the right decision." Her hands slipped from his biceps. "Besides, I would have been captured with you had you decided otherwise." She took his hand and guided him to walk forward. "According to the Pixies, we've almost reached Finn and whoever else they have found. I must admit, not all Faie are as horrid as I once thought."

Her eyes trained on Eywen as they approached, still atop his horse beneath the shade of a large elm. In her mind, most Faie were still horrid, but not *all*. A few kind individuals made up the difference.

As they reached Eywen, he slipped off his horse, facing them. "The two of you can ride," he offered. "I could use the walk."

"Nonsense," Anna said happily. "We will all walk together."

Eywen smiled warmly at her, then tugged the horse's reins to lead the way.

Kai leaned in close to her shoulder as they walked. "Don't tell me that you've not only developed a taste for men," he whispered, "but for the Aos Sí as well?"

She scowled at him, her mood suddenly souring, though she was unable to remain sour for long. She was just too blasted excited to see Kai alive.

He laughed at her expression.

She knew more teasing was forthcoming, but she'd welcome it, because her best friend was alive, and that was all that truly mattered.

EALASAID LOOKED OUT OVER THE BURGH AS MORNING

dawned. Acrid smoke hit her nostrils, even from her high vantage point in the guard tower. She couldn't bear to think of what that smoke meant.

Though An Fiach had sustained the majority of the casualties, many mages had fallen while Keiren was protecting them, a moral lapse that she could not forgive, even as Keiren offered to help them face the looming threat of the Aos Sí.

Her lip trembled, but she fought back her tears. *So many dead*. She didn't know most of their names, but those she did were almost too much to bear. Some of the fallen mages had been with her since she'd first joined An Solas, and others, like Tavish, she'd known for what felt like ages.

She shook her head at the thought of Tavish. She'd seem him possibly mere moments before he'd died. They'd sent him back into battle while she'd snuck out the back of the estate with Maarav, and he'd died alongside her mages. He'd been more willing to fight and protect her friends than the other assassins, and he'd paid for his heroism with his life.

She scowled at the sun, obscured by the smoke of so many funeral pyres. All along she'd thought she wanted revenge, but it had left her soul even more torn asunder than before. Now she was supposed to lead those who remained against an even greater threat. She knew she needed Keiren's help, but could she trust it?

A hand touched her back. *Maarav*.

She turned to face him, looking for signs of grief in his expression, but he showed none. Did he feel nothing for their fallen companions? He'd known Tavish most of his life. Could he truly feel nothing at his death?

"We need to speak with Keiren before the Aos Sí approach," he urged.

She gazed into his gray-green eyes. Was she truly alone in her grief?

He placed a hand on her shoulder. "All you can do now is ensure they did not die in vain. They fought for a cause. Do not let it slip away."

"How do you handle it?" she breathed. "Every single death feels like I've lost a part of my soul. How can you deal with this unbearable weight?"

He pulled her into a hug and she stiffened. She could *not* break down. Not now.

"You learn to focus on the living," he explained, still embracing her. "People will always die. It is simply a fact. Sometimes it feels like the grief will kill you, but it doesn't. You continue living, even if you feel you no longer deserve life. Those pieces of your soul will remain missing, but eventually, you will not notice them as much."

She felt her body relax, like an ocean wave crashing onto shore, then calmly dissipating. "Every time I think you are one thing," she muttered, "you prove yourself to be another."

He pulled away to reveal his smirk. "I have never lied about what I am . . . at least not much."

She snorted. "Yes, if being elusive does not count as lying, you've been rather up front, though I still do not understand your motives."

"And you likely never will," he laughed. "I fear sometimes I do not understand them myself. I've dabbled in the game of war for many years, but never truly cared about the outcome."

"And now?" she asked, quirking an eyebrow at him. "Do you care which way this war goes?"

"Well, we've come this far," he teased. "I may as well see it through, my *queen*."

"Oh don't say that," she sighed, then began walking toward the stairs. "I do not deserve, nor do I want the title, no matter what Keiren says."

"I don't know," he replied, moving to walk by her side. "I think I like it. I've never been so *close* to a queen." He stopped walking to waggle his eyebrows at her.

She punched him in the arm, though his words sent a nervous tingle through her gut. "What do you mean by *close?*" she asked boldly.

"Well look," he replied, gesturing to the ground between them. "I'm standing *right* next to you."

She rolled her eyes and started walking again. *Insufferable man.*

He followed after her, whistling cheerfully despite the fact that the air in his lungs was tinged with the smoky corpses of people he knew.

She would have liked to adopt his carefree demeanor, but every time she thought of the dead, she felt like she might vomit. Her upcoming meeting with Keiren inspired much the same feeling. The woman had tormented Bedelia, and turned her own father into a tree.

Of course, Bedelia, Keiren's spurned lover, was their only source of information. While Bedelia's judgement was questionable, the fact that Keiren had protected An Fiach while they slaughtered Ealasaid's mages was not.

MAARAV WALKED AHEAD OF EALASAID INTO WHAT HAD become the designated meeting room. Perhaps as a *queen* she should have walked first, but he was no fool. Keiren was just as queenly as any female leader he'd ever met. Putting her, Lady Sìoda, and Ealasaid in one room was a recipe for disaster.

Lady Sìoda already waited within, seated in an ornate wooden chair that could only be referred to as a throne. She was flanked by five of her guards, up from the usual two. Her plump face was set in rigid lines, dutifully ignoring Keiren, who stood near the window, free of guards to protect her . . . not that she needed them.

"Do not tell me my estate will be invaded even further," Sìoda growled, flicking her gaze to Keiren.

Keiren simply smirked. She was as tall as Lady Sìoda, perhaps even taller, but willowy with bones seeming as frail as a bird's. She would not use her size to seem imposing like Sìoda tended to do, yet Sìoda was clearly frightened.

Perhaps Keiren had magicked her way in.

"You should be grateful the magic users laid down their lives for you," Keiren chided.

Maarav found it unnecessary to point out that the entire attack was brought on by Keiren. In reality it was bound to happen at some point.

Sìoda glared at Keiren, then turned her gaze to Ealasaid, her expression softening ever so slightly. Could it be possible that Sìoda was actually warming to a *filthy mage*?

Ealasaid strode forward. "No," she answered, her gaze on Sìoda. "Lady Keiren is the only new addition . . . for now. She has some ideas to protect us from the next attack."

"An attack that will only come because of the mages," Sìoda hissed.

"You are too short sighted," Keiren interrupted before Ealasaid could once again smooth Sìoda's ruffled feathers. "This is not a matter of magic users against humans. It is a matter of humans against Faie. If you believe for a second that you would stand any chance of survival without Ealasaid's help, then I bid you to travel out into the countryside. When you come running back, terrified of dark shapes in the night, I will not say *I told you so*."

Maarav raised his eyebrows at her. She might even be worse at diplomacy than Slàine, and that was saying something.

Sìoda opened her mouth, then closed it, clearly at a loss for words.

Seizing the opportunity, Keiren flicked her waist-length crimson hair over her shoulder and paced toward Sìoda's throne, black dress swaying like silk. She placed a long-boned hand on the backrest. "Our new queen should sit here," she decided. She turned a glare down to Sìoda. "Please *move*."

Sìoda stood. "How dare you!" she hissed. "This is my estate. I will say who sits where!"

Keiren remained utterly calm. "Where is your husband, Sìoda? Still hiding under his bed from the scary mages and Faie? I don't think *he'd* have an issue relinquishing leadership to someone actually capable."

Sìoda gasped. "You know nothing of my husband! Have you sent spies into my estate?"

"You're contradicting yourself," Keiren replied, slinking away from the throne, "and you know full well you are out of your depth. Even so, we will protect you as long as you stay out of our way. Refuse, and you will be left in the woods for the Faie." She whirled on her. "What say you?"

Ealasaid turned worried eyes to Maarav. *Should we intervene?* she mouthed.

Before he could answer, Sìoda hissed, *"Fine!"* She stormed toward the door, aiming a venomous look at Ealasaid. "This isn't over," she muttered, then let herself out of the room.

Maarav lifted a hand to hide his snicker. Having Keiren around would definitely be entertaining, at the very least.

"You know," Ealasaid began, approaching Keiren, "I've spent ample time fostering a civil relationship with that woman, and you've ruined it in a single conversation."

Keiren waved her off. "She's a vile, worthless woman. You are a queen. You should have thrown her in the dungeon ages ago."

"If I'm to be a *queen*," Ealasaid sighed, "which I haven't agreed to, that's *not* the type of leader I would choose to be."

Keiren raised a brow at her. "Then it is lucky for the non-magical humans that you are the one the stars chose. Had they chosen *me*, the weak would not survive."

Maarav placed a hand on Ealasaid's shoulder before she could speak. Things would soon take an ugly turn if Keiren continued to so *honestly* spout her point of view.

Ealasaid's shoulder beneath his hand lifted as she took a deep breath. "What do you mean, *the stars chose me*? Before we discuss anything else, I'm going to need a more thorough explanation of why you believe I'm this chosen queen, and how you happened upon the information in the first place."

Keiren sighed, then began to pace. "Queens of nations are chosen through marriage or heredity. They are only linked to their people as far as the laws they make, and what they do in regards to their kingdom. *Magical* queens are different. They are chosen by birth. Something in the stars decides that they are special, granting them with enormous power, as well as a link to their people. So many magic users are suddenly popping up across the land solely because you exist."

Maarav remained silent, taking in the new information. Ealasaid seemed content to do the same, though he wouldn't be surprise if she burst out in argument any moment.

"Oighear the White was born to be Queen of the Faie," Keiren continued, "though many don't regard her as such because she did not initially claim the role out of deference to her mother, who was ironically not a true queen. Her mother's power came from a Faie relic, the shroud of the Faie Queen, but I digress. When the Cavari tricked Oighear into limiting her rightful power, the Faie linked to her began to fade. *This* was the true end to the Faie War, and the reason the Faie grew sparse. The Faie are nearly pure magic, and most could not sustain themselves without their queen. Most faded away for nearly a century, then Finnur returned, and somehow, so did Oighear. I do not know if the return in magic was due to Finnur's return, or if she returned *because* of the magic, but I do not see it as terribly relevant to this conversation." She paused and stared at Ealasaid. "Do you understand now? Oighear and Finnur were both chosen in the same manner as you."

"But if that's true," Ealasaid countered, "and this whole

prophecy thing is true, that means that Finn and I both can't survive."

"Precisely," Keiren agreed. "And Finnur is more powerful than you, and has the Faie Queen's shroud, which is why you need *my* help."

"And let me guess," Maarav interrupted, "this has nothing to do with your vendetta against Finn? You wouldn't possibly be attempting to turn us against her for your own gain?"

She glared at him. He was used to women glaring at him, but this one had a certain measure of *I will quite literally kill you* behind it.

"I have no vendetta against Finn," Keiren explained, "except that she is an immortal being who will crush humans with her power. Perhaps you know her as a friend, but you do not understand what her people are capable of." She paused, then looked him up and down. "Well, perhaps *you* do," she added cryptically, "which boggles my mind further as to why you and your brother would both ally yourselves with her."

He raised both eyebrows in surprise, and took an instinctual step back. Was this woman truly all-seeing?

She smirked. "I cannot read minds, if that's what you're thinking. At least not most."

He let out a long breath. Ealasaid was looking at him strangely in response to Keiren's revelations, but he wasn't about to explain to her that Finn had cursed his people over a century ago, stealing their souls, and the souls of any who carried on the bloodline.

Keiren smiled victoriously, making him half believe she

could read his mind. She turned back to Ealasaid. "Any further questions?"

Ealasaid glanced at Maarav, then back to Keiren. "Hundreds, but I suppose they can wait. Let us focus on the Aos Sí while I mull over all you have said."

"Ah yes." Keiren clapped her hands together. "I had nearly forgotten." She began to pace. "Oighear is not with them, that I can see, so their magic is limited. Still, they are the greatest warriors this world has ever known, able to cut down even the fiercest fighters in the blink of an eye." She frowned, her steps faltering as she seemed to think of something distant. An evil glint sparkled in her eye, then her pacing resumed.

"Given these facts," she continued, "a full magical assault will be necessary. Surely Oighear has sent them to test you," she turned on her heel to eye Ealasaid, "and we will not disappoint her. You must prove yourself a worthy adversary, for surely you will face her before you face Finnur."

Maarav shivered at the thought. Keiren was a bit scary, but Oighear frightened even Iseult, and Iseult was a much braver man than he.

"We can do that," Ealasaid agreed, "though I have no intention of *facing* Finn. She has been nothing but kind to me."

Keiren rolled her eyes. "We can address your disillusionment later. For now we must assemble your mages. We will post them along the walls of the estate, out of reach of all harm but the Aos Sí's arrows. For that danger we will use my wards. The mages will assault the Aos Sí with magic until they either die, or retreat."

Ealasaid shook her head. "But there are too many people

outside the burgh. We cannot risk the Aos Sí claiming their lives to draw us out."

Keiren finally moved her gaze to Maarav, though he suspected she was only including him because she thought he'd be on her side. In some ways, he was. He would always protect those he knew over strangers, but he wasn't *quite* cold blooded enough to leave them to die if there were another choice.

"Ealasaid is right," he agreed. "Even if we weren't concerned with their lives, there is a certain need for diplomacy. If we all hope to survive, we must not further the divide between non-magical humans and mages."

Keiren tapped her finger against her rouged lip in thought. "I suppose you're right. In that case, the mages will await the Aos Sí along the border of the burgh. I will protect them as best I can, though some will inevitably die."

Ealasaid opened her mouth to argue, but Maarav shook his head. This was the best plan they were going to get. As long as Keiren was willing to protect the mages, they might stand a chance of survival. If they *did* survive, they would seriously revisit the discussion of fortifying the burgh. If there was an outer wall, none of this would be an issue, and they might even survive without Keiren's help, which he had no intention of depending on in the future.

Ealasaid sighed, then nodded. "I suppose there is no way to move forward without risking lives. Though *this* time," she flicked her eyes to Maarav, "I will be out fighting with my people."

With a nod to Keiren, she turned on her heel and left the room.

Maarav was about to follow, but Keiren sidled up to him, placing a hand on his shoulder.

"You should exert your influence on her more often," she crooned. "She listens to you, and must be made ruthless if she hopes to survive."

He stepped away and her hand fell from his shoulder. He leveled his gaze at her. "I like Ealasaid just as she is, and I can be ruthless enough for the both of us."

He didn't mean it as a threat, but Keiren seemed to take it that way. "Let us hope it is enough," she muttered, then left the room ahead of him.

He watched the empty doorway for a moment before departing. He sincerely hoped his brother was having better luck on his quest. Then again . . . if by some twist of fate Finn was to become their enemy, he should wish them ill.

He shook his head and strode down the hallway. He was not sure what he would do if Finn and Iseult turned against them. He was used to looking out for himself above all others, and while he had no intention of altering that habit, he wasn't sure who he would choose second. Iseult was his brother, but Ealasaid, was, well *Ealasaid*. A hard-headed farm girl who would have already gotten herself killed if it weren't for him. Could he truly abandon her when the time to choose came?

Leaving the meeting room behind, Keiren diverged from the path Ealasaid had taken ahead of her, then hurried down a flight of stairs.

She sincerely hoped Óengus had told her the truth

about Oighear, and that she would not be approaching the burgh with her Aos Sí. She did not sense any great power nearing, but would not be surprised if Oighear was capable of hiding her presence. The power of ice could do many strange things, and hiding a single caster was no great feat. Ealasaid was not yet ready for such a confrontation, and Keiren would not have her most valuable pawn perish so soon.

She reached the bottom of the stairs and looked both ways, catching sight of a few mages hurrying out toward the courtyard. They would all prove useful pawns, really, and so it benefited her to keep them alive.

Once the mages had all exited to the courtyard, she darted across the entry room and down the next hall, peeking into rooms as she went.

Eventually she found what she was looking for, and dove into a darkened room with an ornate, full-length mirror.

She silently closed the door behind her, leaving herself in near darkness, but it was no matter. She was used to lurking in the dark.

Approaching the mirror, she held out her hand, waving it in front of the reflective surface. The glass seemed to ripple, then Niklas' sharp features and bald head slowly came into focus.

He smiled, showing his sharp white teeth. "Does all go according to plan?" he questioned.

She nodded. "Yes, and *this* plan better go more smoothly than the first. I received word this morning that the Aos Sí will attack the day after tomorrow. We will defeat them, and in doing so, I will earn Ealasaid's trust."

Niklas snickered, raising one of his long-boned hands to

his lips. "I do hope your confidence is warranted. The Aos Sí may surprise you."

She narrowed her gaze at him. "Do you know something I do not?"

He shook his head. "No, my people can see little where the prophecy is concerned, but there has been little word of Oighear lately. None seem to know what she plans."

Keiren scowled. She too could see little where the prophecy was concerned, something that vexed her more and more.

She glanced over her shoulder. "I should go. I don't want anyone to catch me lurking around the estate, but that sty of an inn doesn't have any proper mirrors."

He smirked, then whispered, "Good luck," before fading from sight.

With a heavy sigh she crept toward the door, opening it a crack and peering both ways before exiting.

With any luck, she wouldn't be staying in that dirty little inn much longer.

"Do you think they're close?" Finn asked excitedly.

Iseult did his best to offer her a smile, but he'd never been talented at forcing emotions he did not feel. While he would be glad to see the return of some of their companions, he did not like working so closely with the Faie.

Finn seemed to trust them. He never would.

They had reunited with a few of Eywen's surviving Aos Sí who had been tracking them. They now waited patiently for the return of their commander, if he still lived. Iseult hoped he did. Eywen had already proven he'd lay down his life for Finn, and so, he could be trusted more than the Pixies or Trow.

"The Pixies have returned," one of the Aos Sí muttered.

Iseult turned just as the vibrant swarm flew into the clearing, then dispersed as the individual Pixies darted about, finding perches in the trees. A moment later, Kai, Anna, and Eywen walked into the clearing, leading a single horse behind them.

Before Iseult could caution her that they could be Faie charmed, or worse, enthralled by the Dearg Due, she raced forward and flung herself into Kai's arms, nearly knocking him off his feet.

Iseult approached in time to hear him mutter, "Glad to see you awake."

After a moment of squeezing, Finn pulled away from Kai, then hugged Anna, who patted her back awkwardly.

In her excitement, Finn pulled away from Anna and began to dive toward Eywen, then seemed to think better of it. Iseult thought Eywen almost seemed sad at the exclusion, or perhaps he was simply projecting his own emotions.

He wanted Finn to hug him too, but at the same time, he knew he must push her away. The kiss the other night had been a mistake, a brief break in his normally iron resolve.

Grinning, Finn took a step back from their newly found companions. "Tell me everything," she demanded. "What happened? Where were you?" She hesitated, glancing around the clearing. "Where are Bedelia and Sativola?"

As Kai and Anna both shrugged, Eywen stepped forward. "If you'll excuse me, I'd like to speak with my remaining soldiers."

Finn fluttered her hands in the air, clearly flustered. "Of course! My apologies." She stepped aside for him to pass, and he did so with a bow.

Kai began recounting his adventure as Finn led both him and Anna to sit on a nearby log, dragged into the clearing for that purpose. Likely drawn by the sound of voices, Naoki trotted into the clearing, a freshly killed crow hanging by its neck from her beak.

Iseult leaned against a tree, withdrawing his attention from the conversation, though his gaze remained on Kai. Was something different about him? Iseult had a keen sense for the Faie and their magic. Kai did not seem Faie charmed, but there was definitely *something* off.

Keeping his speculations to himself, he began to pace the perimeter of the clearing. It was unfortunate Bedelia and Sativola were still missing. They needed to move on toward Sormyr before more dark Faie were sent after them. Hopefully if the Pixies' search proved fruitless, Finn would allow them to move on without their final two companions . . . though he would regret the loss of Bedelia.

He ducked as a small swarm of Pixies flew perilously close to his head, then cursed under his breath. The tiny creatures *had* proven useful, and perhaps would continue their use in the future, but he was prepared to be rid of them for the time being.

The only Faie-like creature he could truly bear was Finn.

CHAPTER SEVENTEEN

The little Pixie shook her head. "No sign of any others, my queen. Some dead Aos Sí, but no humans."

Iseult watched as Finn sighed, then turned her gaze to him. "What do you think could have happened to Bedelia and Sativola? If they still live, and aren't behind us, then how could they travel so far ahead of us in such a short span of time?"

He pursed his lips. He thought it likely Bedelia and Sativola were dead, and their bodies had been hidden. The Pixies scouted from the air, so would only notice what was visible below them. If the bodies had been buried or dragged to a cave, they would easily miss them.

Of course, he could not say that out loud.

"Perhaps they continued on toward Sormyr," he consoled, hoping to inspire her to do the same. They'd spent too long in the forest already. He had no doubt the Cavari would strike again, as well as the Dearg Due. They needed to reach civilization where they could at least blend in with a crowd and buy themselves time to escape.

Finn nodded, her expression somber, then turned back to the tiny woman hovering in the air. "We will depart immediately," she sighed, "but please, continue your scouting."

Iseult's shoulders slumped in relief. The sooner they reached Sormyr to confirm their final companions were indeed lost, the sooner they could move on to defeating the other two queens. He did not like that these other women were being given more time to assemble their defenses, but he supposed in a way Finn was doing the same. If the Pixies and Trow could gather more benevolent Faie, and if Eywen could recruit more of the Aos Sí, Finn might just have the most frightening army of all.

After exchanging a few more words with Finn, the Pixie flew away. Anna, Eywen, and Kai entered the clearing, finished with saddling the remaining horse and unicorn, being led by the three other Aos Sí. Unfortunately, with only the two mounts between them, travel would be slow.

Finn moved to join the others, her head hung low, shielding her face in a veil of long hair. "The Pixies will continue to search for Bedelia and Sativola, but we must move on."

Iseult watched as Kai and Anna each put a consoling arm around her and led her toward Loinnir.

"You should ride," he heard Kai say. "You've had a rough few days and need the rest."

With a final glance at his surroundings, Iseult followed them. That Finn allowed herself to be so easily coerced onto Loinnir's saddle meant she really did need the rest. She was looking thinner than ever, with dark bags beneath her eyes. Come to think of it, he couldn't recall the last time he'd managed to convince her to eat more than a few bites. He did not know if it was worry about their companions that stayed her appetite, or perhaps the haunting memories of the past. All he knew was he was glad to have Kai and Anna back. They were her friends. They knew how to cheer her up in a way that Iseult would never understand . . . as much as he wished he could.

Sativola had lost consciousness, putting them no closer to escaping the marshes. Àed sat across from Bedelia at the fire, munching cured venison. He watched her with a keen eye, and she was quite sure he'd managed to divine all of her secrets by now, even though they'd barely spoken.

The murk in the swamp had increased as the cool air of evening set in. If something crept up on them, she'd never see it, so she was glad for the relative silence, even though it made her uncomfortable.

"So," Àed began, "Ye know both Finn, and me daughter." His cornflower blue eyes shot daggers at her.

She gulped. Yes, he *definitely* knew all of her secrets.

"Yes," she replied softly. "I was traveling with Finn when we were attacked. Keiren and I have a . . . past. She found Sativola and I unconscious and brought us here."

He took another bite of venison, slowly chewing as he eyed her up and down. "Ye were attacked by the same creatures as the lad," he nodded in Sativola's direction, "yet yer wounds don't fester, and yer well fed."

She bit her lip, unable to think of anything else to tell him but the truth. "I believe Keiren was trying to get back in my good graces, likely to get to Finn."

"Ye were there on that island," he observed.

Her sharp inhale gave her away before she could lie. How had he known?

"Why are you no longer a tree?" she blurted. "I told Finn what happened. I swear it. We were coming to rescue you when we were attacked."

He chuckled, completely catching her off guard. "She was coming to save me, was she? Silly lass." He shook his head, a rueful smile on his face.

Bedelia was growing more confused by the moment. He wasn't going to ask her *why* she was on the island?

"I never was a tree," he sighed, gazing into the fire. "Ye'd think someone who knows me daughter as well as ye seem to, would know her magic is mostly illusion. That's not to say she isn't powerful, but turning men into trees is not a talent she possesses."

"But why create an illusion for no one to see?" she asked, then hung her head. She was such a fool. "The illusion was for me," she sighed. "She wanted *me* to think you were turned into a tree, and perhaps she wanted Óengus to think the same. She knew one of us would eventually tell Finn."

Àed nodded. "It was a ruse to lead Finn astray, nothing more. As was kidnapping the lot of us, I imagine. I do not know what she wants from Finn. All I know is she hopes to prevent her from fulfilling her true role. Keiren is buying time for . . . something."

Bedelia bit her lip. She felt almost guilty telling Àed something Keiren had told her in confidence. Then again, perhaps Keiren had planned even this. Perhaps she'd ordered Niklas to aid in their escape so Bedelia could tell Àed what Keiren planned . . . but why?

She shook her head. She was not a dumb woman, but Keiren's schemes could boggle even the greatest of scholars.

"Say whatever it is yer thinking," Àed instructed.

Bedelia sighed. "Keiren wants to use Finn to break the barrier to the in-between. She believes her mother, your late wife, is trapped there. She told me about how she died . . ." she trailed off.

Àed hung his head for a moment, then snapped it upward. "Something approaches," he whispered, climbing to his feet.

He remained hunched as he walked, as if his entire body throbbed with pain. She watched as he hobbled toward their horses, then held out a hand toward Bedelia, gesturing for her to join him.

"Quickly," he hissed, waving his hand.

She hurried over toward him. He held out his withered hand to her, and after a brief moment of consideration, she took it.

"Be still," Àed ordered.

She obeyed, not asking questions because she could now hear what he'd sensed. Rhythmic suctioning noises approached as something large made its way through the sticky mud.

Her heart raced. The mist seemed to shift as the creature entered the small clearing. It was *massive*, with craggy green skin and yellow belly scales. It walked upright like a man, but the body was all wrong, almost like a giant, fat lizard, covered in patches of the sticky brown mud. It paused and whipped its head in their direction, scenting the air with bulbous nostril pods. Its eyes were mere slits, occasionally opening wide enough to reveal pure milky white orbs.

It sniffed again, then thudded toward Sativola.

Bedelia tensed, and Àed squeezed her hand, *warning* her.

The creature hunched down toward Sativola, cradling its small arms against its chest. Smacking its wide mouth, it took a deep whiff, then recoiled.

It grunted to itself, then straightened, moving its ugly face in each direction as it scented the air. It turned and seemed to look right at Bedelia with its slitted eyes, then took another deep whiff.

That's it, she thought. *We're done for.*

The creature seemed to shiver, turned to give Sativola a final whiff, then hobbled away.

Bedelia let out a shaky sigh and received another warning squeeze from Àed. He was right, they weren't safe yet. She could hear more thuds from other nearby creatures. There must have been an entire herd of them combing the marshes.

They remained still for what seemed like hours, until the last of the creatures could no longer be heard. Finally, Àed released her hand and she slumped to her knees on the soggy ground.

"What in the gods were those things?" she breathed. She'd been to the marshes before, but had never seen such creatures.

"Ballybog," Àed muttered, returning to sit by the barely simmering fire. "Nearly blind, so they use their noses to guide them. I've enough magic left in me to obscure our scents, so it's lucky those were the creatures we encountered."

She flexed her hands to stop their shaking, then stood to join him as he restoked the fire. "Why did they ignore Sativola?" she questioned.

"He's been touched by Dark Faie," he explained. "The Ballybogs may be frightnin', but they're not evil. Most Light Faie don't like the stink of the Dark."

She shivered at the thought, grateful Keiren had cleansed her wound even if it made her more appealing to the Ballybogs.

Àed leaned over, peering down at Sativola. "Lad won't last the night in his condition." He turned back to Bedelia. "What did ye say bit him?"

She shrugged. "The Aos Sí knew what they were, but I can't recall the name. They appeared to be women, but with long white hair and reflective eyes. They ran faster than horses."

"Hmph," was Áed's only reply. He sat in silence for a few minutes, then finally looked up at her. "I'll make ye a deal," he began, "since ye *did* get me out of that dungeon."

She nodded for him to go on.

"I'll do me best to keep ye alive in these marshes," he explained, "and we'll find Finn together, but we'll not tell her anything of where we've been and what we know until we can figure out what me daughter is up to."

"I don't want to lie to her," Bedelia began, her old guilt rearing up in her heart.

Àed narrowed his gaze at her. "Omissions are not always lies, especially when they're for someone's own good."

She frowned. Perhaps that was true, but . . . "Don't you

think though that it's best for her to have any information we can give her?"

Àed turned his gaze down to the fire. "Keiren kept us both alive for a reason," he began. "If that reason is only to use us against Finn, we will tell her everything, but if that reason is because she still has a heart under all that pride and spite, well, I intend to save her."

Bedelia blinked down at him, utterly shocked. She supposed she was his daughter, but after she'd kept him nearly starving in a dark cell all this time . . .

He turned his gaze up to her. "Ye'll understand someday, lass, if ye manage to live as long as I have, that villains are not born, they are created, and they can always learn to love again." He slouched down to rest his elbows on his knees. "I know I did."

She took a shaky breath, then nodded, though he didn't seem to notice. His words echoing in her head, she walked around the fire to check on Sativola. Could there truly be hope for Keiren, and if so, did she want any part in saving her?

FINN LAY IN HER BEDROLL, STARING UP AT THE STARRY NIGHT sky, enjoying the soft sound of Pixies snoring in the surrounding trees.

She liked the Pixies, and the Trow for that matter. They seemed so close to nature, not caring for the affairs of man or Faie beyond what affected them directly.

Still, she couldn't understand why they had chosen *her*. Perhaps she was just a better choice than Oighear.

She pulled her bedding up to her chin, then turned her face to the side. Loinnir munched on dried grass just a few paces away, her constant guardian as of late. Was she the reason the Cavari had stayed away since their last encounter?

Footsteps crunched up behind her. "You should be resting," Iseult muttered.

She turned to gaze up at him. "I thought Eywen and Anna were keeping watch."

He crouched beside her. "That you are aware of who's supposed to be on watch means you have not slept at all. You're going to make yourself ill."

Oh, Iseult, she thought, *just when I grow used to your silence, you turn around and throw me off balance once again.*

He sighed as she stared up at him, then crossed his legs to sit more comfortably. "We should reach Sormyr in three days," he explained. "Perhaps then you will be able to rest."

She shook her head. "It is not fear for my own safety, or even yours, that steals my rest."

He watched her face, clearly waiting for her to go on.

She sighed, unable to think up the right words. How could she explain the uneasy feeling that had taken over her existence? She felt perhaps she never should have returned to the land of man, or maybe she never should have existed at all. Why had fate been so cruel as to make her Queen of the Dair, when she wanted nothing to do with her people? She would give anything to have been born into a normal life as a farmer or a seamstress.

Iseult reached forward and pushed a strand of hair out of her face.

"Why do you do that?" she questioned. "Why do you push me away, then do things like *that*?"

He let his hand fall back to his lap. "Sometimes you make me forget myself. I do not think before I act."

She sighed. "Do you truly wish to know why I cannot sleep?"

He nodded.

"I cannot sleep," she sighed, "because I fear the only way for this to end is for me to die." She pulled a hand loose from her bedding and held it up before he could argue. "I think you and I both know I do not belong with any of you. I was born with a purpose so utterly . . . inhuman. A purpose I still do not fully understand."

He didn't argue with her, and instead waited for her to finish, his expression blank.

"I learned something when we saw the Cavari," she continued. "I remembered the moment I became a tree. I took all of them with me. The Cavari slowly faded away because I put their magic to sleep. They were strong, so they lasted a while without me, but could not last indefinitely."

He nodded, surprising her. "Eywen believes the same happened with the Faie when Oighear was laid to rest. They faded away. Some were given power by the Travelers, and so were trapped within the Blood Forest."

"You knew?" she breathed. "You knew the Cavari returned because of me?"

He nodded. "Not initially, but I began to suspect that might be the case when they attacked Garenoch."

"Then why haven't you killed me?" she asked in disbelief. "You could have ended all of this before it began."

"Perhaps if I had only just met you when my suspicions

arose," he began, "and if I had not sworn on my mother's grave I would set things right. *Then* I might have tried to kill you. But my fight is not with the Cavari. Vengeance is an empty reward. I want to free my mother's soul, and those of our ancestors."

"Yet you will not let me do just that," she muttered. "We should have figured it out when I first found the shroud."

He shook his head. "As I've said before, I will not weaken myself. Not yet."

"But what of your ancestors?" she pressed. "I *saw* them in the in-between. Perhaps even your mother was there. I cursed everyone of your lineage, so her soul must have gone there when she died. I could have—"

He held a finger to her lips to cut her off. "I would not forgive myself if you freed them, and it harmed you in some way. Perhaps my loyalty should be to my ancestors, but you are flesh and blood. You are here right now."

"I *stole* their souls," she repeated. She'd never truly gotten over that fact. She was more monstrous than Oighear or Keiren could ever hope to be.

"They stole your child," he replied softly.

She shook her head. "That does not make it right."

"No," he agreed, "it simply is. It is painful to think about for us both, but it cannot be our primary concern. The Dark Faie hunt for you, as do the Cavari. You must not allow yourself to become distracted."

"But I want nothing to do with any of it," she whispered.

He smiled and shook his head. "I believe you were born for a reason. I also believe something like fate placed you in my path, just when I had nearly given up hope."

She sniffled, then forced a small smile. "Perhaps fate hoped to punish you."

He chuckled. "Perhaps, though if she did, she has failed miserably."

Finn felt a measure of her tension melt away. She hadn't even realized the magnitude of her guilt until she actually started talking about it. There was still more to face, like the guilt of her daughter's death, but she was still not prepared to acknowledge so much.

At least now she had most of her friends back, and she silently vowed she would find the others. After that, she *would* atone for her crimes against Iseult's people. If he could bravely face his past and move forward, then so could she.

He sat with her until she finally fell asleep, not speaking, but his presence alone was enough.

KAI STARED UP AT THE STARS, UNABLE TO REST. THOUGH HE was glad to be back with Finn and Anna, memories of the Dearg Due haunted him. Were Sativola and Bedelia currently in the same situation he had been, or were they simply dead? Kai hadn't been overly close to Bedelia, and though he'd known Sativola a long time, they weren't truly friends, but the loss still stung. It just as easily could have been any of them.

He reached a hand up out of his bedroll to touch his neck. The bite had healed into a thick mound of scar tissue, hidden by his hair.

He hadn't told Anna or anyone else about the bite,

though he wasn't sure why. Upon hearing his tale, Finn had decided the Dearg Due refrained from biting him since he had Dair blood within him, and the creatures wanted to keep him alive.

Most had seemed to buy the story, but Eywen had been eyeing him speculatively ever since. The Aos Sí had cleansed Anna's bite with fresh running water, and Kai couldn't help but wonder what would have happened to her had Eywen not been around, and if the same thing might still happen to him.

He flashed on the horrifying evening the Dearg Due forced her blood down his throat, gagging at the memory. The blood had healed him, but what else had it done?

He tugged his bedroll up and forced his eyes shut. Iseult and Finn had stopped conversing nearby, though he still sat beside her. Something was different between the pair. Iseult was still as sulky as ever, and Finn watched him like he might bite her at any moment. Perhaps they'd had a fight.

Iseult did tend to inspire them.

One of the Pixies in the tree over head began muttering in its sleep. He could not make out the words, but it was rather ... cute.

He *never* thought he would actually find any of the Faie *cute*, but perhaps that was part of their defense. Lull their enemies into a false sense of ease right before shoving needles through their eyeballs.

Suddenly feeling like he didn't want his eyes looking straight up at the sky anymore, he turned on his side. He could see the campfire not far off, illuminating Anna and Eywen, taking first watch. Beyond them rested the other three Aos Sí.

Anna's affinity for Eywen was even more strange to Kai than his own ability to find some of the Faie endearing.

He sighed and forced his eyes shut, but couldn't help feeling that Finn would soon turn the entire land on its head. If humans could befriend Faie, and magic users could live out in the open without hiding their powers, *anything* was possible.

CHAPTER EIGHTEEN

*A*nna woke the next morning to a cacophony of tiny voices. She peeled her eyelids open to watch dozens of vibrant little creatures flitting about overhead. It seemed the Pixie ranks had quadrupled overnight.

She sat up, then almost screamed. The surrounding woods were *alive* with magic, shining so brightly it gave her an instant headache.

She began to scramble out of her bedroll, desperate to stand, then froze as a pallid hand lowered down in front of her. She gulped, then looked up to see Eywen standing over her.

She took his hand, allowing him to help her up. She was glad he didn't shine as brightly as the other Faie.

Now that she was in a position to run if she needed to, she narrowed her gaze to look past the dizzying array of Pixies. In the shadows she spotted creatures the size of small children scurrying about, some covered in bushy hair, and others with scales or craggy skin.

"Where did they all come from?" she breathed, fighting the slight tremble threatening to overtake her body.

Eywen chuckled beside her. "Word that the Oaken Queen has made treaties with two of the Faie races has spread. They will continue to come, if only to escape the Snow Queen."

Anna lifted a hand to her brow and shook her head. "How are we supposed to get into Sormyr will all these Faie flocking to Finn?"

He snorted. "She can try to send them all on errands, but she'll be hard pressed to keep them away entirely. They are safest when they are near her."

Anna frowned, unable to take her eyes off the scampering Faie. "Perhaps it's time for me to go elsewhere," she muttered. Eywen she could handle, but *this* . . . it was all too much.

She turned to find Eywen watching her intently.

"What?" she questioned before whipping her gaze back to the surrounding Faie.

"She needs you," he explained. He gestured behind them. "She needs each of you."

She followed his gesture to see Kai and Iseult attempting to calm a very excited Finn. Eywen's three remaining warriors stood behind them, glaring at the nearby Faie as if they might attack any moment. More Faie flitted about behind them.

Anna shook her head, then trained her eye on the nearest Faie. "She practically has an army now. I'd venture to say she needs none of us, except perhaps Iseult."

Eywen sighed. "You and your friends are the only connection she has left to humanity. She was once . . . " he trailed off. He glanced over his shoulder at Finn, then back to Anna. "I never met her. She was merely a child when Oighear signed the treaty to limit her powers, but I've heard the stories. She was a member of Clan Cavari, feared by all. Her grief propelled her toward horrible deeds." He glanced at her again. "Looking at her now, I cannot imagine her doing any of those things, and I believe it is due to those she met in this land upon her return."

Anna pursed her lips, then moved a step closer to Eywen as one of the Trow hobbled a little too close to where she was standing. "So you're saying we make her . . . human?"

"In a way," he replied. "At the very least, you give her a reason to show compassion. She cares about each of you. I believe that caring will shape the type of queen she becomes."

"Well," Anna began, trying to calm herself, though every nerve ending in her body was telling her to run, "I suppose even with the Faie coming in droves, the safest place for any of us is around Finn. At least with her nearby, the Faie aren't likely to eat us."

"That is true," Eywen agreed with a playful smirk, "at least for most of us."

With that, he turned and walked away, leaving Anna to hurry after him lest she be left alone in the woods suddenly filled with magic.

FINN COULDN'T BELIEVE HER EYES. WHAT IN THE GODS WAS she supposed to do with all these Faie? She'd already sent Pixies toward Garenoch and Sormyr. The first were to scout from a distance, just to ensure Ealasaid and Maarav had not run into trouble. She didn't want the Pixies to venture too close to Ealasaid's magic users, only to be mistaken for enemies and attacked. The second group were to assess the state of things in Sormyr. If it had been ruined like Migris, there was no point in venturing there. Really, now that she knew Àed was no longer on the island, there was no point in venturing to Sormyr at all, except to hide from the Cavari.

She stroked her chin in thought as Kai and Iseult continued to pack up camp. Eywen was marching toward her with Anna at his heels. They would be ready to leave soon, and she needed to make a decision.

Eywen reached her, greeting her with a deep bow. "What is our next task, my queen?"

Finn blushed, glancing past him to Anna, who supplied her with a teasing grin.

"Honestly," Finn began, "I do not know. I do not want to continue the journey toward Sormyr, only to find it ruined. We'd lose too much time, especially since all we really need there are supplies."

"South are the marshes," Iseult explained as he approached. "Just small villages surrounded by expanses of dangerous swampland. We'll find little there."

She nodded, wanting to ask Iseult what *he* thought she should do, only she wasn't sure if queens should show such weakness of mind in front of their subjects.

Oh well. "What would you suggest?" she asked. "How much time would we lose venturing to Sormyr for supplies?"

He glanced at the surrounding Faie, quieter now as they

began to settle in to their new surroundings, then looked back to her. "Three to four there with our current lack of horses," he began. "I suppose our choice depends on what you would like to do now that we no longer need a ship. We could return to Garenoch, but I think it wise we first procure information on our enemy's whereabouts."

She sighed. "*Which* enemy?"

Iseult glanced at Eywen, then back to her.

Catching his meaning, she nodded. They might have decided to trust Eywen, but they still did not need to discuss the Cavari in front of him, lest the information trickle back to Oighear.

Not seeming to take offense, Eywen stepped forward. "If I might make a suggestion?"

Finn nodded, grateful for the help.

"There is an ancient fortress just west of here," he explained. "It is small, but we could wait there for the Pixies to return from their scouting missions. With our numbers growing so quickly, we could easily fortify the area against further attacks."

Finn reflexively looked to Iseult, then forced her gaze away, internally chastising herself. Could she make no decisions on her own?

She gazed at the surrounding Faie instead, weighing her options. She knew another attack from the Dearg Due was likely, now that they'd lost both her and Kai, and running hadn't worked terribly well last time. The unknown fates of Bedelia and Sativola still weighed on her. She didn't want to lose anyone else.

She turned back to Eywen. "That seems a sound plan. We will travel there immediately."

"Finn," Iseult interrupted. "Are you sure remaining in one place is the best course of action? If Kai can be *tracked* again, we will be far from civilization and the relative safety it might offer."

She frowned. "But our numbers are greater now," she gestured out at the Faie. "I imagine they will provide us with as much, if not more safety than a human city. In a human city, we would not be able to benefit from the protection they might offer."

He flicked his gaze to the Faie, his expression giving away nothing as he turned back toward her. "I do not agree," he said simply.

Kai approached with Loinnir and Eywen's horse, reins in hand, all supplies neatly strapped to their backs. "I for one would not mind delaying our arrival to Sormyr."

Iseult glared at him, but Kai stood his ground. Finn knew Kai had good reasons for not wanting to return to the city of his birth, reasons Iseult was not aware of . . . not that it would change Iseult's opinion.

"It's settled then," Eywen decided. "I will send my remaining men to scout the fortress and clear it of any dangers."

Finn turned her worried gaze to Iseult as Eywen retreated. He moved to her side. Seeming to catch the hint, Kai and Anna ambled away together, granting them space.

"I hope you know what you are doing," Iseult muttered. "The lesser Faie may not stand against the Cavari. They feared them during the Faie War."

She nodded. "I do not expect them to. I only hope they can ward away the Dearg Due and other Dark Faie. I must face the Cavari on my own."

He looked down to meet her gaze. "If it weren't for Loinnir—" he began, but she shook her head.

"I know," she agreed. "And I *do* fear them. They are a force to be reckoned with . . . but so am I."

A shiver went up her spine. She could only hope her words would prove true. She was terrified of facing her people once more, but if Iseult could face his past, and stand up to fight for what he believed in, so could she.

What kind of queen would she be if she couldn't?

A FEW HOURS PASSED AS THEY TRAVELED ON FOOT, LEADING the two horses with the supplies behind them. Iseult would have preferred Finn ride, but she seemed to value his opinion less and less. Still, despite his foul mood, he couldn't help but feel moderately impressed with the distant fortress ahead, even though he still believed Sormyr their best choice. He gazed up at the high walls in the distance, noting that they seemed structurally sound, despite being speckled green with moss and vines.

The fortress stood on the border of the marshes. By his estimation, the boglands likely butted up against the unseen back portion of the fortress wall. The part they could currently see circled the courtyard and single structure within.

Eywen's Aos Sí had scouted ahead to ensure there were no enemies lurking. The three warriors came their way, their glistening black hair floating in the breeze. Eywen stepped forward as they arrived. The tallest of the warriors with eyes nearly black in color announced,

"There is little danger, save a few marshland creatures lurking about."

Iseult began to assess what they would need in his mind. Candles or lamp oil, fresh water, and more food than they could likely hunt in the marshes, unless everyone was keen to survive off stringy swamp rodents.

As if he knew Iseult's thoughts, Eywen commented, "We can send the lesser Faie to search for supplies. There are enough abandoned farms along the Sand Road that most things should not be difficult to come by, though food may need to be purchased."

"With what coin?" Kai muttered, approaching them from behind with the supply bearing mounts. "I know *I* ran out long ago."

Ignoring Kai, Iseult turned back toward the fortress. "You speak as if we'll be enduring here for months."

"Some of us may," Eywen explained, "especially if we intend to move on to Sormyr. My men can disguise themselves well enough, but the other Faie will need a place to gather. This is as good as any. Better than most, really, as humans in these parts tend to keep to themselves."

"And it is far from Oighear's domain," one of his nearby men added.

Iseult's mind flashed on the days he'd spent with the Snow Queen, glad to be far from that place. At least *that* was a positive.

"Let's go inside," Finn decided. "We can make further plans once everyone has had a chance to rest. If the Pixies find Sormyr in ruins like Migris, this may be the *only* respite we'll find."

She walked toward the fortress walls, giving Iseult no

choice but to follow. He noticed she seemed somehow more resolute now, less frightened. What had changed? Had their late night conversation actually made a difference in her way of thinking? If so, was it a positive one?

He stalked after her, his hand hovering near the pommel of his sword just in case the Aos Sí had missed spotting any hidden dangers. His boots sunk into the moist, loamy ground with every step. It was no wonder the fortress had turned half-green.

They reached the space where the gates had once stood, though now the iron was rusted, and one half of the gate hung askew. That would need to be remedied if they truly intended on staying there for any length of time.

Finn wove her way around the fallen gate to enter the overgrown courtyard. Iseult followed closely after, observing the remnants of statues that still remained, along with the faint carvings on some of the stones that comprised the walls. The carvings seemed strange to him, swirling in odd patterns uncommon to any architecture he'd ever seen.

Upon closer observation, the statues, once human figures, were just as unusual, made from smooth stone carved into ornate clothing interwoven with flowers and leaves. He passed a decapitated statue head, once a woman with long flowing hair, bedecked with a crown of holly. He continued to put the fallen shapes together in his mind. They were all nature deities.

"To whom did this fortress belong?" he questioned, glancing back at Eywen and his men.

"To the Druids," Eywen explained, stopping to gaze up at the castle. "No one else would desire a fortress so remote."

Iseult took a step away from the nearest statue. The Druids had remained after the Faie faded away, only to be slaughtered by those who feared magic, and more so the Faie's return.

"We should not stay here," he muttered, peering down at one of the toppled statues, likely broken by humans intent on destroying their fears. "Dark deeds tend to leave stains on places such as this."

Eywen continued walking. "The Oak Queen has nothing to fear from the spirits of Druids, I assure you."

Iseult glared at his back, then continued walking since Finn had already reached the fortress entrance. He was not sure if spirits truly remained, but could only hope Eywen was right.

He watched as Finn pushed against the massive door, composed of heavy, moisture-rotted wood studded through with iron. She continued pushing until Kai and two of the Aos Sí moved to help her.

Slowly, it creaked open, revealing the leaf-strewn stone floor leading inward.

Iseult stole a final glance toward the gates, outside of which most of the Faie had decided to wait, then strode forward to enter the structure alongside the others.

They were in the Great Room, dimly lit by rectangular windows set high up in the walls. Moss had crept inside, along with curling vines, creeping up walls scorched black by a fire long in the past. A few burnt remnants of furniture remained, but the room was otherwise vacant.

The smell of smoke became prevalent as the tallest Aos Sí entered the castle with a crudely-made torch in hand.

"See if there are any Henkies among the gathered Faie," Eywen muttered to one of his men.

"Henkies?" Finn questioned, staring up at the impossibly tall ceiling in awe.

"The folk that live in the knolls," Eywen explained. "They're prone to gambling and mischief, but also quite good at cleaning."

Iseult couldn't help his smirk. Here they were, on the run from Dark Faie and the Cavari, and Eywen was worried about rounding up Faieries to clean the ancient Druid castle.

Two of his men turned back toward the exit, presumably to round up the Henkies.

While Finn and Eywen walked toward the nearest hall to explore more of the abandoned castle, Kai moved to Iseult's side.

He cleared his throat, then whispered, "Please tell me I'm not the only one horribly unnerved to exploring a Druid fortress with scores of Faie waiting for us outside."

"You are not the only one," Iseult replied, then increased his pace to catch up with Finn and Eywen, leaving Kai to take up the rear with Anna.

As he neared Finn, concern pervaded his mind. The Faie might be useful when it came to scouting, and perhaps to cleaning, but that didn't mean they were safe to be around. Perhaps they feared Finn enough to behave, but there was no saying what they might do if they got Kai, Anna, or himself alone.

BEDELIA AND ÀED LED THEIR HORSES ON FOOT THROUGH THE muck. It was too risky to ride, lest the extra weight cause one of the horses to slip and become stuck . . . though there wasn't much they could do for Sativola's horse, with Sativola's belly draped over its back with arms and legs anchored with spare shirts on either side. It wasn't a comfortable position, but it was all they could manage, and barely that. He had never regained consciousness, and he might be dead soon anyway, if he wasn't already. Bedelia had been too afraid to check his pulse since they'd started traveling that morning. Àed held the reins of Sativola's horse along with his, not seeming to care one way or another about his unconscious ward.

"Is there nothing we can do for him?" Bedelia asked, even though she already knew the answer.

Àed scowled, then paused to spit in the mud at their feet before ambling on. "Lad will be dead soon, then it will be yer choice whether we carry his body out for the proper rites."

Bedelia shook her head, then nearly slipped as she hopped over a puddle, misjudging the footing on the other side.

"I hope Finn doesn't blame me for his death," she sighed.

Àed chuckled, surprising her. "Finn could never be angry at ye fer long, whether it's yer fault or no. If it helps, ye can tell her ye valiantly rescued us both from the swamps."

She hung her head, not feeling valiant in the slightest. She'd only been spared harsh treatment because Keiren wanted something from her, and had only escaped because Niklas helped them through Keiren's wards. Then once they'd entered the swamps, Àed had proven himself the savior, not her.

Sativola groaned, the first sound he'd made since the previous night.

They abruptly stopped walking. Handing her horse's reins to Àed, she hurried toward the right side of Sativola's horse, where his head dangled. She moved his curls out of his face, then recoiled. Skin that should have been flushed from his position was mottled and pale, showing every blue vein beneath the surface between patches of purple bruising.

"What in Tirn Ail am I doin' strapped to a horse?" Sativola groaned.

Fighting a wave of guilt at transporting him like a sack of supplies, Bedelia hurried to untie the shirts holding him in place. His top half free, she hurried around Àed to the horse's other side, released the final binding, then held Sativola steady as he slid down to his feet.

Surprisingly, Sativola stepped away from her and stretched his arms, remaining erect while hitting her with a foul whiff of his rotting odor. He stretched his neck from side to side, then lifted his gaze. Pure, milky white eyes gazed back at her.

"Step back, lass," Àed commanded, grabbing her arm to pull her toward his side.

She stumbled backward, her gaze riveted to Sativola's mottled face.

"He's not himself any longer," Àed hissed, pulling her further away with one hand, while struggling to manage the three horses with the other.

As two of the horses started to panic, Bedelia took their reins from Àed, leaving him with his calmer horse.

Sativola took a staggering step toward them as they retreated, then another.

"Sativola?" she questioned.

He tilted his head to the side, then snarled. "My mistress beckons. Give me my horse."

She flicked her gaze to Àed. "What should we do?"

Àed shook his head, continuing to back away, putting the horses between themselves and Sativola. "I think he's gone, lass, under the thrall of the creature that bit him."

She inhaled sharply. Would this have been her fate had Keiren not cleansed her bite?

"Get on yer horse," Àed instructed. "We'll have to risk the mud, unless you want to kill him here and now."

Sativola took a few more shaky steps forward, causing the horses to dance nervously.

"But we can't just leave him," she argued, backing further away. "There must be something we can do."

"Get on yer horse," Àed ordered. "He's a Faie creature now, just like any other in this swamp." Following his own advice, Àed scurried up into his saddle, trotting his horse a few paces away before turning back around to keep Sativola in his sights.

Before Bedelia could make up her mind, Sativola lunged, startling the remaining two horses. One reared up, nearly striking her with its front hooves. She dove aside, landing hard on her shoulder in the mud as the horse took off, leaving the other behind.

Sativola rushed her as she struggled to her feet. She shoved him aside, nearly gagging at his pungent smell. He slipped in the mud and fell with a loud *thwap*, giving her enough time to calm her remaining horse and climb into the saddle.

She trotted far out of reach, then turned her horse to face Sativola as he slowly struggled up from the mud. "If you'll just calm down," her voice trembled, "perhaps we can still help you." *Please listen*, she silently urged. *Don't make me kill you.*

Sativola stared at her with his pure white eyes. Could he even understand what she was saying?

"Leave it, lass," Áed growled. "Trust that I can see things ye cannot. He's *gone*, and he ain't comin' back."

She felt tears burning at the back of her eyes. If he was truly gone, she'd failed. If Finn or Iseult were there, they could have figured out a way to save Sativola where she could not.

She walked her horse over to join Àed as Sativola began to stumble toward them.

"You're sure he can never come back?" she asked, glancing at the old conjurer.

He nodded. "Aye, lass."

She sighed with deep sadness. Sativola slowly hobbled toward them, grunting animalistically under his breath. Perhaps she could not save him as Finn might have, but she could at least prevent his suffering. She retrieved the bow she'd strapped to the back of her horse, grateful that Sativola's had been the one to run off.

She tested the oversized weapon as Sativola slowly slipped and slid toward them. She withdrew an arrow from the quiver laced near her stirrup and threaded it onto the bow, aiming the weapon at Sativola.

He didn't even seem to notice.

She glanced at Àed, who nodded. "It's the kind thing to do."

She pulled back the arrow, carefully aiming directly at Sativola's heart. She needed it to be a clean kill. If he struggled, it would haunt her dreams. Of course, she was sure to be haunted either way.

She took a deep breath, then loosed her arrow.

CHAPTER NINETEEN

*F*inn paced across the freshly scrubbed stone floor of the Druid fortress, enduring the ache in her feet from all those hours of walking. Last night's rest had been scant. Even her bones were tired. Rain pattered outside, hopefully not enough to delay the Pixies. She knew they should be returning soon, first the ones sent toward Sormyr, followed by those sent to Garenoch.

She was anxious to hear word of Ealasaid and Maarav, and even more anxious to discover if the Pixies had found Bedelia and Sativola.

"How are you still on your feet?" Kai asked, lounging on the floor with his back pressed against the nearest wall, casually sharpening one of his daggers. The gleaming metal flickered in the flamelight from the fireplace.

She scowled at him. Iseult was outside in the rain with Eywen, checking over the rest of the fortress, Anna had slunk off somewhere on her own that morning, and had been gone for hours, and Naoki had gone off to hunt, leaving Kai and Finn alone in the large chamber to wait out the storm. Kai had instantly settled in by the fire, but Finn felt unable to relax and enjoy its warmth.

He raised an eyebrow at her, then patted the stones beside him, inviting her to sit.

She approached, hands on the hips of her dirty breeches, and peered down at him. "Aren't you worried?"

He shrugged, then continued sharpening his blade. "This is far better than being stuck in a cave with the Dearg Due."

She frowned, then moved to sit beside him, leaning her back against the wall. "I'm sorry they took you," she sighed. "That was entirely my fault."

He stopped sharpening, turning his face to smirk at her. "I only have your blood because you saved my life. You've nothing to apologize for." He set his dagger aside. "Plus, the only reason they even kept me alive was because they thought I was one of the Dair. *Weak* Dair, they called me," he added with a snort.

She smiled at the name. "How could they tell you were weak?"

"Well their bite almost killed me—" he cut himself off, then cursed.

"Bite?" she gasped, her heart suddenly in her throat. Why hadn't he said anything before? She moved to her knees so she could turn and peer directly at his face.

He cringed. "I hadn't wanted to worry you with that part."

"Where is it?" she demanded. She reached her hands toward him, prepared to search against his will. "Let me see it. Eywen said their bite wounds require cleansing."

He gently batted her hands away. "It's fine. It healed."

She pulled her hands back, then attacked him with renewed vigor, pushing him to the floor. "Where," she struggled, "is . . . it!" she demanded.

On his back, he held her partially aloft in vain. She would not relent until she saw the bite mark for herself. Perhaps Eywen would still be able to treat it, healed or no. She maneuvered to pin his arms down, then pushed his sleeves up one by one, checking the flesh of his biceps, since that's where Anna had been bitten. Finding his arms unharmed she pushed his hair aside to check his neck, then gasped. A mound of scar tissue nestled near the base of his neck, just high enough to be hidden by his hair.

He sighed and his body went limp against her prodding. "Are you pleased now? You can see that it's healed."

Examining the healed wound closely, she reached out a finger and touched it. "The bite of the Dearg Due is supposed to possess the victim to become a willing slave," she muttered, then sat back, releasing him. "Do you feel any different?"

He sat up, scowling at her. "I told you I feel *fine*."

"Then why hide the bite?" she questioned, unable to quell the nagging doubt within her. She would not lose *another* friend, especially not Kai. She needed to protect him. "I know you haven't even told Anna," she pressed. "She would have told me if you had."

"Anna can keep a secret," he argued.

Finn shook her head. Anna wasn't much for secrets. She preferred to blurt out uncomfortable truths right to your face. "If she thought you might be in danger, she would have told me."

Kai rolled his eyes, repositioning himself to sit against

the wall. "I just didn't need anyone worrying over me," he explained, "and I didn't need Iseult killing me in my sleep on the belief that I might be a threat. I truly do feel fine. Better than fine, really."

"Better than fine?" she pressed. "What do you mean?"

He raked his fingers through his hair, a sign she recognized well.

"There's something else!" she accused. "Spit it out."

Lowering his hand, he scowled at her. "How do you do that?"

Sitting before him, she crossed her arms and waited, unwilling to give away the subtle clue. If she did, he'd probably never rake his fingers through his hair again, then she wouldn't know when he was hiding something.

"Fine," he snapped, then lowered his voice, "but you have to promise to keep it to yourself. And *definitely* don't tell Iseult."

She nodded encouragingly, hoping Iseult did not choose that moment to return.

"When one of the Dearg Due saw that I was near death," he began, keeping his voice low, "she forced her blood down my throat. It healed my wound, and I have felt wonderful ever since." He twisted his mouth in distaste. "Except when I remember the disgusting moment," he added.

"Hmm," Finn replied, wondering at his story. Could it be that the Dearg Due's blood had healed the wound before it could do any damage, or was it something else? Eywen had explained that the Faie could not be enthralled by the Dearg Due, so perhaps it was *her* blood that protected him from those particular effects.

Still, she could not be sure.

"I think we should ask Eywen," she decided.

His eyes widened. "You said you wouldn't tell anyone!"

She crinkled her nose, thinking he was being quite silly, but she *had* promised. "Fine, I won't tell him. I'll just casually ask him more about the Dearg Due. I fear even with my memories returned, I know very little of them. I won't bring you up at all."

His shoulders slumped with a heavy sigh. "I suppose that's acceptable. I *would* like to know more about the possible consequences, though I fear I'm probably a rare case, as a human magically infused with Dair blood."

She nodded, then turned at the sound of footsteps. Eywen and Iseult entered the room, both dripping wet.

"The Pixies have returned," Eywen explained. "I fear they bring ill tidings."

With a final worried look at Kai, Finn jumped to her feet and hurried toward them. Eywen offered her his wet arm, which she took after a moment's hesitation. He led her back through the doorway, with Iseult close behind.

She heard Kai curse and climb to his feet just as they left the chamber, too impatient to hear the news second-hand.

KAI FOLLOWED ISEULT INTO THE NEXT CHAMBER, THEN OUT into the central courtyard. A fine mist still drizzled from the sky, darkening it, though nightfall was still hours away.

Ewyen still led the way with Finn on his arm, toward an alcove created by the outer wall, and what remained of stables.

Underneath a jutting line of stone meant to support

wooden beams huddled three Pixie women, one with red hair, one purple, and one blue.

Finn and Eywen crouched before them, with Kai and Iseult hovering over their backs.

"Greetings, Oak Queen," buzzed the purple-haired Pixie. "My clan has returned from the Gray City. The city still stands, but is heavily guarded by men in brown uniforms. We overheard them calling themselves An Fiach, and mean to hunt the Faie."

Kai scowled at the mention of the group. So *that's* where they ended up. He supposed it made sense after Migris had been destroyed. Sormyr was the largest of the great cities.

The red-haired Pixie took a step forward, staying just shy of the lightly drizzling rain, though it was clear all three had been flying in it. "My clan returns from Garenoch," she explained. "The burgh suffered an attack, but seems to have triumphed. The mages gather there, an entire army of them! They are led by a girl with curly blonde hair, often seen with a crimson haired sorceress at her side."

Finn gasped. "A crimson haired sorceress? What was her name?" she asked, then before they could answer, she blurted, "Was it Keiren?"

Kai frowned. Keiren? The one who'd trapped Finn in the Gray Place? Why would Ealasaid be seen cavorting with *her*?

"I do not know, my queen," the Pixie answered. "I did not want to risk my clan in getting too close, as you bade us be cautious."

Finn's head bowed in thought as the third Pixie stepped forward. "My clan scouted the woods to the southeast," she chirped, and Finn lifted her head with interest. "Last night we spotted a clan of Dark Faie traveling this way. We do not know their intent, but imagine they will reach us not long after night falls."

"Not just the Dearg Due," Eywen explained, having heard the report previously, "but Redcaps and Ratchets."

"Redcaps and Ratchets?" Kai questioned.

"Goblins in the human tongue!" the Pixie chimed. "*Nasty* creatures, along with their feral dogs."

"Traveling with the Dearg Due?" Finn questioned, rising to her feet.

"Aye!" chirped the Pixie.

Feeling anxious, Kai moved his hand to check the nearest dagger at his belt, then realized he'd left it inside, forgotten due to Finn's pestering. Though he had others on his person, he wouldn't be forgetting a single one again. He'd never seen a Goblin before, but had heard horrifying folk tales. They were only about half the size of a man, but ruthless to the core.

After a moment of seeming thought, Finn tossed her long, damp hair behind her shoulders and began to braid it. "We must prepare to face them," she turned to look down at the three Pixies. "Inform the other Faie, and ask the Trow to root themselves near the gates to disguise the entrance. If the Dearg Due will only travel by night, we should have enough time to prepare before they reach us."

"I'll find Anna," Kai interrupted, worried about his friend.

Finn turned to him, hesitated, then nodded. He knew she'd been considering his bite, and what it might mean to once again face the Dearg Due, but luckily she let it go and turned back to Iseult and Eywen.

Kai turned and ran across the soggy ground of the courtyard. He'd leave the strategy talks to those more war-minded than himself. He was more worried about what he'd do when the Dearg Due inevitably made it over the fortress' tall exterior walls. He would not attempt to run this time, nor would he allow them to take him captive again, even if it killed him.

Anna watched Finn and the others in the courtyard, crouched on her perch atop the fortress roof. She'd noted the moment Eywen had noticed her, but for some reason, the Aos Sí had not given her away.

She was grateful. She needed a break from the constant shining magic of the Faie. Especially Finn, now shining more brightly than the rest.

The cool drizzle of rain was a welcome refreshment on her hot cheeks, heated from her arduous climb onto the roof.

She shifted her weight to her left, her right leg tired from crouching. Her perch was flat enough to sit, but she wanted to be ready to dart out of sight should anyone notice her. She needed space, and she'd had none for a very long while.

She watched as Kai trotted away from the others. She had been unable to hear anything that was said, but the situation had apparently grown quite dire, judging by everyone's expressions. She'd have to corner Kai and have him recount the conversations . . . or perhaps Eywen.

She wasn't sure why she had grown to trust him, but she

felt a certain kinship with the Aos Sí warrior, perhaps because he seemed to be the only one who understood her burden.

He had not judged her for wanting to rid herself of her *magic*. In fact, she suspected he wanted to be rid of his own inherited burdens just as much as she did.

She continued to watch as Finn nodded, then walked off with Iseult, leaving Eywen by himself.

He glanced up at her, gave her a subtle salute, then strode toward the broken gates of the fortress.

Once he'd ventured out of sight, she flicked back the hood of her cloak to reveal her tight braid, wetting her neck with errant droplets, then stood.

She could feel the unease in the air. Every instinct she had told her to run and hide, but she'd accepted she was no longer that type of person.

She had no idea when she started caring about what was right, but she was prepared to fight for it now.

Perhaps her newfound *magic* had changed her more than she'd like to admit.

~

"Prepare yourselves!" Keiren snapped. "This is sure to be one of the first battles of many, but the fates have not gone easy on you."

Maarav watched Keiren as she paced across the grassy courtyard, speaking to the gathered mages. She'd topped her black dress with a fur-trimmed black cloak far finer than anything Lady Sìoda owned. He glanced at Ealasaid beside him in her simple breeches and heavy winter tunic.

She looked regretful about allowing Keiren to address the mages before the Aos Sí descended upon them.

"The Aos Sí will be among the most formidable enemy you'll ever face," Keiren continued, raising her voice to address the entire crowd. Her crimson hair whipped about in the wind, slowly dampening from the light rain. "They are strong!" she shouted. "But you are stronger!"

The mages muttered amongst themselves, but seemed bolstered by the speech.

Maarav could have done without it, especially since he'd barely be a part of the fight, unless the Aos Sí breached the fortress. He and the other assassins were outmatched against the Faie Warriors. Their only chance was in the ranged attacks of the mages, along with the archers already stationed behind the parapets atop the surrounding wall.

Maarav would have liked to join them, but he'd never been good with a bow. Plus, Keiren had instructed him to remain near Ealasaid to ensure she would not hesitate at a crucial moment. He was glad to accept the task, even if it came from Keiren.

He would have accepted it from anyone.

"To your stations!" Keiren shouted. Maarav watched as her gaze fell to Ealasaid. "Make your queen proud!"

The mages cheered. They'd taken to the idea of Ealasaid as their new queen happily. She'd saved them from inevitable persecution, after all. She'd banded them together, making them strong. None of them need fear An Fiach now . . . unless Keiren betrayed them and switched sides.

The thought weighed heavily on Maarav. If this was all a ruse, and she chose to protect the Aos Sí . . .

He shook his head. There was no use dwelling on it now, and Ealasaid had already turned to enter the guard tower.

He hurried to follow her up the stairs, admiring her silhouette in her new breeches. She'd finally admitted that fighting in a dress was less than wise, though she'd threatened to strike him with lightning when he'd stared at her new clothes.

He was staring for all he was worth now. If this was going to be one of the last sights he saw, he'd remember every detail. Unfortunately, she soon reached the top of the stairs, and he was forced to emerge beside her.

Several of the assassins already waited atop the guard tower along with Sìoda's men, all armed with long bows capable of firing arrows across great distances.

Maarav nodded to Rae, one of Slàine's best archers, then made his way to the short stone parapet separating them from the rest of the burgh.

More mages stood on the rooftops below, protecting the non-magic citizens of the burgh that had earlier been herded toward the estate. Those wise enough to think straight had retreated to the woods on the western side, hoping to avoid the battle altogether. If the burgh was lost, they would have to fend for themselves in the wilds, but it was better than being skewered by an Aos Sí sword.

Drumbeats sounded in the distance, just as the Aos Sí army came into view, their strange armor glistening in the murky sunlight.

A few townsfolk remaining on the outskirts of the burgh screamed and ran back toward the estate, while the mages below signaled to each other to be ready.

The battle was about to begin.

With a heavy sigh, Maarav took up a nearby bow. He'd never been adept at ranged combat, preferring techniques where his speed gave him more of an advantage, but he'd give it a try. He couldn't just stand idly by while Ealasaid rained lightning down upon those who would dare oppose her.

A prickle crept up his spine, and he turned to see Keiren slinking up behind them. With a smirk, she moved to Ealasaid's other side, then moved her arms skyward, lifting the black furred edges of her cloak.

Nothing perceptible to the human eye happened, but Maarav could sense a shift in the air. Suddenly the cool breeze no longer hit his face, and the light drizzle had abated. He peered upward to see the tiny rain drops pattering off an invisible barrier.

Keiren was holding up to her end of the bargain, for now. Only time would tell if they would hold up to theirs.

EALASAID CLENCHED HER FISTS AS THE AOS SÍ APPROACHED IN the distance. She'd felt it the moment Keiren had raised her ward, and innately knew that it was a one way barrier. Nothing could come in, but their magic and arrows could go out.

It almost wasn't fair to the Aos Sí, but it also wasn't fair that the unearthly warriors would attack a burgh full of humans, so she figured they were even.

A hand alighted on her shoulder, and she turned to look up at Maarav. He held a bow in his free hand.

"Promise me you'll stay up here," she blurted. "No running off into the battle."

He glanced at the approaching Aos Sí, marching in organized lines, then back to her. "My girl, do not fear. I am a coward at heart. Protecting you is the only thing that steels me for the coming battle."

Her heart skipped a beat. Though it was true she could never tell when he was joking, she didn't think he was joking now.

Her bravery renewed, she turned to watch the Aos Sí's progress, then squinted her eyes as a chill wind hit her face, carrying with it tiny flecks of ice.

"No," Keiren muttered. "This cannot be right."

Ealasaid flicked her gaze to the tall sorceress, wondering what had gone wrong. Hopefully it wasn't the ward.

Keiren turned wide eyes down to her, showing an emotion she never thought to see in the fiery woman's expression. *Fear.*

"Is it the ward?" Ealasaid gasped. She glanced around at her mages. They were strong, but without the added protection, they might not be able to defeat the Aos Sí.

She turned back to Keiren to see her shake her head.

Another gust of icy wind hit the ward. The already murky sky grew dark, and snow began to fall.

"I did not see this coming," Keiren explained. "She must have blocked it from my *sight*. I was not aware it was a skill she possessed."

Ealasaid shifted impatiently, wishing Keiren would just spit it out. The Aos Sí were nearly within reach of the outer mages, their forms now appearing hazy in the snow.

"What in the Horned One's name are you going on about?" Maarav spat.

Keiren visibly shivered, then sighed. "Prepare to meet Oighear the White. She has traveled here with her Aos Sí warriors. There will be no escape."

CHAPTER TWENTY

"*A*ttack!" a mage on the building directly below the guard tower shouted.

Dizzy with sudden panic, Ealasaid peered down to see it was Sage, unaware of the increased threat despite the snow collecting in his black hair. The mages atop the buildings around him let loose their magic.

The first row of Aos Sí stopped marching and held up large silver shields at just the right moment, deflecting most of the attacks.

Ealasaid jumped at the sound of thirty arrows being loosed at once. The volley of arrows rained down from the wall to her right, hitting even more of the Aos Sí than the magic had.

She sucked in a sharp breath through her teeth. Even those who were hit continued marching, entering the range of more mages.

Chaos broke loose. Waves of fire and ice shot through the snow, hitting the Aos Sí and finally managing to down most of those in the lead. The earth erupted at their feet, and unnatural winds forced some to their knees.

Ealasaid raised her arms to add her lightning to the fray just as the snow increased tenfold, nearly obscuring the battle from her sight.

"She brings the snow!" Keiren shouted of the sudden maelstrom.

Ealasaid realized with abrupt horror that the snow was now penetrating Keiren's ward, unlike the rain earlier. It whipped tendrils of her hair loose from her braid, stinging her cheeks and nearly blinding her.

"How is it getting through!" she shouted.

The clang of metal rang out below, along with shouts and screams as the mages launched into full battle.

Keiren partially lowered one arm to shield her face. "Her magic is greater than mine! I may still be able to keep out the Aos Sí's arrows, but I cannot stand against her! You must face her!"

Ealasaid felt as if her heart had suddenly turned to ice right along with their surroundings. Oighear was the Queen of the Faie, an ancient, seemingly immortal being. Ealasaid's magic would stand no chance against such a force.

"There must be another way!" Maarav shouted from her other side.

Keiren shook her head, then turned her gaze down to Ealasaid, her vibrant blue eyes squinted against the snow. "You were born for this. The stars would not have chosen someone too weak to fight. You are stronger than you know."

Ealasaid wrapped her arms tightly around herself. They were surrounded in a cloud of white. The flecks of ice continued to sting her face, penetrating her body with cold. Despite her heavy tunic, she began to shiver.

She turned to Maarav. "Send the mages down to help the others. If the snow stays this thick, we cannot hope to fight from here. Our arrows and magic might hit our own people."

He shook his head. "I vowed to stay by your side. I meant it!"

"Look!" Keiren interrupted.

Ealasaid followed her gaze outward. The snow had parted just enough to reveal a white-clad figure, riding atop a massive animal. The animal definitely wasn't a horse. Its hair, covering its lupine body, matched the perfect white of the woman's fur cloak. As Ealasaid watched through the snow, the creature lifted a muzzle the size of her chest and scented the air.

She tore her gaze away from the terrifying creature to dart upward and meet the woman's eyes. There was no mistaking it, even across the distance and through the flurries of snow, the woman was staring right at her. Slowly, a smile spread across her pale lips.

Shouting startled Ealasaid, drawing her gaze. The Aos Sí, still mostly obscured by snow, had nearly reached the gates. They warred with assassins and mages alike. Many fell on both sides, but the white cloaked woman continued to advance. With the slight improvement in visibility, the mages atop the walls were able to throw their magic into the fray, but it would not be enough. The Aos Sí slowly advanced.

Ealasaid knew without a doubt that she had to stop the

Faie Queen before it was too late. If Oighear so chose, she could freeze them all where they stood.

"*No*, Ealasaid," Maarav urged, reading her expression. He moved to grab her arm, but she pulled away.

"I can get you down there," Keiren interrupted, her focus mostly on holding her wards in place, "but then you will be on your own."

"No!" Maarav shouted again.

"Keep him here!" Ealasaid shouted as Keiren lowered one arm toward her.

Before she could say any more, she was swept up on a current of air and carried over the wall, down to one of the snow-speckled roofs below. She landed gently on her feet beside Sage.

He whirled on her, hands raised as if expecting an attacker, then slowly lowered them. "What are you doing!" he shouted over the clamor of the nearing battle. "Get back up there!" He gestured frantically to the guard tower.

She shook her head. "If I do not return, you must keep the mages together. Do not allow An Solas to fall!"

Before he could argue, she hurried toward the edge of the roof, ignoring Maarav's shouts from above. She would simply have to trust Keiren would keep him from interfering, and hope that if they lost, he would escape safely.

As Sage turned his attention back to the Aos Sí, she lowered herself from the roof.

She dropped to the ground, bending her knees to absorb the impact of the fall. She was in an empty, snow-filled alleyway, but the fighting was so close, she knew she could run into the Aos Sí warriors at any moment. She had to reach the Faie Queen before that could happen.

She took off at a run, praying her mages could hold the Aos Sí off for just a little while longer. Her breathing seemed deafeningly loud to her ears, drowning out the sounds of her boots crunching in the freshly fallen snow.

If she couldn't reach the Faie Queen, if she couldn't *stop* her, all of the mages would die. Maarav would die. She knew it with utter certainty. They might stand a chance against the Aos Sí, but with Oighear's added magic, all would perish.

She skidded to a halt as two Aos Sí warriors darted into the alley ahead of her, cutting off her only clear path toward Oighear. Their strange, artistically curved armor was covered in frost, though they didn't seem to feel the cold as she did. They eyed her for a moment, their glistening black hair whipping around in the icy wind beneath their helmets, then charged.

She reacted instinctively, lashing out at them with her lightning. It surged around them in silver brilliance, so bright it nearly blinded her. She held up an arm to shield her face. Her lightning had never struck so powerfully before.

Her heart thundering in her ears, she lowered her arm. Both Aos Sí lay in the snow, dead.

"Impressive," a female voice commented behind her.

She whipped around to face the Faie Queen herself, fortunately without her lupine mount.

Her glistening tresses, as pure white as her skin, were pulled back into elaborate braids, studded throughout with twinkling gems. Her pale skin seemed to sparkle in the snow, making her appear as an unearthly goddess.

Truly, she was beautiful, and Ealasaid wanted nothing more than to destroy her before it was too late.

Oighear began to prowl around Ealasaid in a wide circle, pacing through the snow like a predator.

Ealasaid's breath hitched as the direness of her situation hit her. Though she had planned on facing Oighear, she'd thought to do so on the battlefield where perhaps small advantages could be gained.

Now that Oighear had found her, she would be facing the Faie Queen alone. She tried to summon her courage, but froze with fear. She was barely able to shift her feet, slowly spinning to keep Oighear in her sights.

Oighear chuckled. "My, you're just a child, aren't you? To think, you were fated to be queen of these mortals. Fortunately, they will not need a queen once they're dead."

"W-what do you want from us?" Ealasaid stammered, her teeth beginning to chatter from the cold.

She clenched her stiff fingers into fists. She was such a fool. How had she ever thought she could face Oighear on her own? She should have at least brought Sage down from his perch on the roof. He was an incredibly powerful fire mage after all. Fire should go against snow, not lightning.

Oighear clucked her tongue. "So disappointing," she muttered. "I had hoped to face a true queen. A true Queen of Wands could have been excellent practice before my final battle with Finnur."

"Queen of Wands?" Ealasaid questioned through chattering teeth, hoping to buy herself time . . . but time for what? At least the snow in the distance had died down as soon as Oighear had become preoccupied.

"The fated Queen of the Mages," Oighear explained,

completing another circle around Ealasaid. "You are she, are you not? The Queen of Wands?"

Was she? She'd only just found out, unbelievably, that she was one of the prophesied queens. Perhaps it had all been a lie, and Keiren had planned to send her to her death all along.

"Pity," Oighear muttered, finishing another circle to stop a few paces in front of Ealasaid. She raised her arms out to her sides, draping her white fur cloak so that it appeared almost like wings.

Ice formed in the air and swirled around Ealasaid. She wrapped her arms around herself as her teeth chattered more rapidly.

Oighear raised a white eyebrow at her. "Will you not even put up a fight?" she questioned, then tsked. "I should have killed you sooner, right along with your parents."

Ealasaid gasped, all thoughts of her impending doom rushing from her mind. "What are you talking about? An Fiach killed my parents."

Oighear's pale pink lips curled into a wicked smile. "Such weak minded fools. They prove eager pawns for any sorceress who might choose to use them. I've been hunting for you since I first awoke, but arrived at your village too late." She shrugged. "I'll admit, I was angry. Your family paid the price. An Fiach questioned and tortured them for information about you."

"You're lying!" she shouted. She shook her head. *No.* Oighear was simply trying to make her suffer before slaying her. Or maybe not. How had she known about what happened to her village?

Oighear's smile broadened. "Am I lying? I ordered An

Fiach to keep your mother alive. I tortured her in my dungeons for weeks, hoping her daughter would care enough to sense her mother's distress and save her."

Hot tears streamed down Ealasaid's face, turning icy cold by the time they reached her chin.

"Liar!" she screamed, lashing out with her lightning.

Oighear held up a hand, deflecting the bolt with a shimmering barrier of ice. "There we go," she chimed happily. "There's the fight I'm looking for. You know," she began to pace, "your mother refused to breathe a word about you, even after *weeks* of pain. When I finally killed her, she muttered your name, lamenting the daughter who abandoned her."

Rage washed through her. Her body felt shredded into a thousand little pieces from the inside out. She screamed, lashing out again, only to have her lightning bolt deflected.

No, no, no! her mind screamed. Frozen tears stung her face. She instinctively threw lightning bolts one after another with every ounce of power she possessed, and still reached for more. She would obliterate Oighear from the face of this retched land. Her body grasped for more power, and for a moment, there was nothing, then white hot energy was all around her. It rained down from the sky, and up from the earth. It poured in from *everywhere*.

"Now we can have a proper battle!" Oighear snarled, her face distorted through the pure white light. She lifted her hands and launched a blast of ice shards at Ealasaid.

Ealasaid sliced her hand through the air, deflecting them with something she could no longer call lightning. It was solid *power*.

Oighear cackled gleefully, launching more ice at Ealasaid.

She deflected the attack, then lashed out with one of her own, then another.

Their attacks increased until their surroundings were pure white with energy and snow. She felt her power hit up against Oighear's, like she'd smacked into a solid wall.

With another scream of rage she began to push, but Oighear pushed back. They warred against each other, evenly matched. Ealasaid could feel Oighear through the clash of white, could feel her triumph as her snow began to break through Ealasaid's defenses.

The glow of triumph faded in Oighear's eyes when Ealasaid pushed back with a vengeance.

Oighear renewed her efforts with vigor, but their powers continued to simply pulse between them.

Feeling close to exhaustion, Ealasaid rallied what little strength was left in her to push harder, forcing herself past her limits. She could barely feel her body anymore, she was so consumed with the pure power.

Oighear met her with equal force, and their magic collided in a radiant explosion, knocking Ealasaid from her feet. Her back hit the snow. She tried to sit up, but couldn't move. Her vision sparkled with dazzling lights, then all at once, went black.

EALASAID WAS UNSURE HOW MUCH TIME HAD PASSED WHEN she finally regained consciousness. She felt herself lifted out of the melting snow into someone's arms. Her first instinct was to lash out, but she was completely drained, unable to even flex her limbs.

"She will be alright," a woman's voice explained, "but she'll need to rest."

"What happened to her?" A man's voice asked close to her ear. Suddenly she recognized the arms around her. Maarav was carrying her, and the woman's voice was Keiren's.

In her head she was crying out in gratitude that they lived, but nothing came out of her mouth.

"She faced Oighear the White and did not perish," Keiren explained. "She has earned her birthright."

"I don't care about birthrights," Maarav muttered. "And know this, sorceress. If you ever stand in my way again while she's in trouble, I will kill you."

Keiren snorted. "You will *try.*"

That was the last thing Ealasaid heard before she drifted back into oblivion, lulled by the warm comfort of Maarav's arms.

ÓENGUS CRADLED AN UNCONSCIOUS OIGHEAR IN HIS ARMS, his back pressed against a nearby building. He barely breathed as he watched Keiren and Maarav carry Ealasaid away.

Something like guilt caught in his throat. He'd been spying on Ealasaid as she gathered her mages, secretly reporting back to Oighear. He was the reason Oighear had come along with the Aos Sí. He'd convinced her that with

Keiren at Ealasaid's side, the mage threat was too great, and Oighear needed to act.

It had all gone mostly according to plan. He'd *spied* for Keiren, assuring her Oighear would not be part of the battle. Oighear did not want to risk that they would run. Now, likely half the mages had been killed, and Keiren would be desperate for the upper hand, giving him more to work with, so why did he feel this horrible, wracking guilt?

He looked down at the pale woman in his arms as Maarav and Keiren's voices retreated. She had tortured that poor girl's parents. He was not beyond killing, in fact, he'd often reveled in it. He even understood why Oighear had pushed Ealasaid to the extent that she did, wanting a proper challenge.

Yet, when Ealasaid fought back, he found himself wishing she'd kill Oighear. He also found himself wishing he'd chosen a different queen to help with his problem from the start. Perhaps it was just human nature, wanting to side with his own kind rather than something Faie. Really, it should not matter. Once his shadow was returned, he'd have no issue meeting his death soon after. Yet, the thought lingered in his mind that he could have spoken with Ealasaid back in Port Ainfean instead of sending his men after Finn . . . only he hadn't known who she was at the time.

He sighed as he began to walk through the snow with Oighear in his arms. He needed to catch up to the retreating Aos Sí, surely panicked that perhaps their queen had fallen. He shook his head. Here he was, rescuing Oighear from death, yet a second time. Still, he could not help reviewing his choices.

Yes, he would have liked to ask Ealasaid for help, but she

seemed a good person, and would not want to help a bad one. Just as Finn would never want to help him with how he'd hunted her. The only choices left to him were Oighear or Keiren. Two women whose hearts had been twisted nearly as much as his.

No, he'd chosen his path, the only one he really could.

MAARAV RESTED IN THE OVERSTUFFED CHAIR, HANGING HIS head in his hands. He'd carried Ealasaid back to her room at the estate. Her body had been icy cold, lying there in the trampled snow. Her skin was so pale, he'd feared she was dead, or would be soon. He'd removed the wet outer layers of her clothing, sliding a loose, dry dress over her damp underpinnings, then had wrapped her up in layers of blankets and built a fire. After several hours of sleep, her skin had regained color.

He shook his head. *Foolish girl.* She'd made him promise to remain by her side, then had broken that promise before he'd even had a chance to keep it.

Yet, even as he watched her, waiting for her to wake, he dreaded the moment she would. The news would devastate her.

An Solas had survived, but just barely. Many had perished, including Ouve. Without Keiren's shields, Maarav had no doubt they *all* would have died, even after Ealasaid drew the Snow Queen's attention.

The Aos Sí were like nothing he'd had ever seen, unbelievably graceful and quick . . . and difficult to kill. Their strange armor seemed to reflect a measure of the magic hurled at them, and it left few openings for arrows and swords. Their onslaught had proven too much for Keiren's wards, and she'd only been able to protect those nearest to her, including Maarav . . . though he'd tried his hardest to escape her.

He sighed. Perhaps if he'd been thinking more clearly, he would have relented on trying to escape. He could have instead used that energy to protect those who Ealasaid held most dear.

He lifted his head and looked down at her pale face, framed by blonde curls crimped awkwardly from the braid she'd worn. He sighed harshly. There had been no other choice. He'd been utterly incapable of waiting idly by while she rushed off to face the mighty Faie Queen.

Truly, the girl had ruined him. He'd always been a pragmatist at heart, and nothing Ealasaid did was practical.

Still, she'd faced the Faie Queen and lived. He had no doubt the confrontation was the reason for the Aos Sí's retreat. A retreat that saved all of their lives.

She groaned, prompting him to hop to his feet. He hovered over her, waiting for another sign of life.

Her eyes fluttered open. She squinted up at him, bleary eyed. "Maarav?" she questioned weakly. "How did I get here?"

"We found you freezing in the snow," he explained softly, taking a seat on the edge of her bed. "You're back within the estate."

She frowned. "Did we win?"

He fought to hide his cringe. "Many have died, but I think we are safe . . . for now. Whatever you did caused the

Faie Queen's retreat. She was not there when we found you."

She lifted a hand to rub her eyes, then let it drop back to the bed. "Help me sit up, please."

He did as she asked, propping her up with pillows before resuming his seat.

She wiped at her eyes again, then trailed her hand tiredly down her face. "I'm the reason my family was killed," she explained. "Oighear was searching for me. She tortured them to learn my whereabouts."

"She told you this?" he questioned.

She nodded, then cringed like the movement hurt her. "I was so afraid when I faced her. I froze, but she wanted a fight. She told me what she did to them, what she did to my mother. It's all my fault. If I'd been less of a coward, I would have stayed to protect them."

"You *left* to protect them," he corrected.

She shook her head. "What happened while I faced Oighear?"

He averted his gaze. Did she really need to know?

"*Maarav*," she pressed.

He met her tired gray eyes. "Not long after you left, the snow abated, but the Aos Sí did not relent. They made it into the estate and wore down Keiren's wards . . . " he trailed off. "She could not protect everyone."

She sunk down into her pillows. "How many?"

"How many what?" he questioned, though he knew exactly what she was asking.

She stared him down. "How many *dead*?"

He considered lying to her, but she'd learn the truth

soon enough. There was no way he could keep it from her. "Over half," he replied.

Her mouth sealed into a tight line. He watched as she took several deep breaths, then asked, "How much over half?"

"Ealasaid," he said softly.

"Tell me," she demanded.

"Two thirds at least," he sighed, foreign emotions welling up within him. Loss. Regret. *Guilt.* "Many of Slàine's assassins fell along with the mages." He met her gaze. "Ouve is dead too." He regretted it as soon as he said it.

Her breath hissed out. She shook her head. "We should never have come here. Creating An Solas was a fool's errand. I gathered them all to die."

Maarav shook his head. "They would have died on their own, one by one. At least this way they were able to fight for themselves. Many are still willing to fight."

"No," she snapped, her eyes suddenly fierce. "I cannot do this any longer. We must send them all away. They must return to hiding what they are."

As soon as she'd spoken the door burst open. Maarav hopped to his feet. He was just about to release a dagger from his hand when he recognized the intruders.

Sage stumbled into the room, his dark hair still matted with sweat and blood. He'd been out since the battle ended, searching the dead for any who might still have life in them. Beside him stood another mage, an older woman whose name Maarav did not know.

"You can't do that!" Sage blurted. "You cannot give us a taste of freedom, only to force us back into hiding."

"Now is not the time!" Maarav growled. The little pests must have been eavesdropping outside the door.

"*Maarav*," Ealasaid interrupted.

He turned his gaze to her.

"Let them speak," she said softly.

"It's not your fault that so many died," Sage said, not waiting for further permission. "It's because of you that so many of us were strong enough to survive. Most of us hid our magic, never using it, but with your help we have grown so much stronger. I know, even now, we can continue to grow."

Ealasaid shook her head. "Then you will do it without me. You don't need me to band you together."

"And the next time the Faie Queen attacks?" he questioned. "Will you not be here to face her?"

Maarav watched as Ealasaid bit her lip. Was she truly reconsidering? Did he even *want* her to? Running away didn't sound half bad, but he knew she'd regret it.

After a moment of thought, she shook her head. "She attacked us because of me. She may have retreated for now, but she will come for me again. Everyone is safer without me."

The woman who'd entered with Sage stepped forward. Her simple clothes were just as stained and bloody as his, and her long red hair matted. Clearly she'd taken part in the battle.

"Permission to speak, my lady," she muttered, eyes downcast.

Ealasaid nodded. "Go on."

The woman finally raised her gaze. "Lady Slàine told us of the prophecy, of the importance of standing against the

Faie Queen. I'm not here to fight for myself, or to be able to use my magic freely. I'm fighting to protect my family. To protect *everyone*. If you are capable of standing against the Faie, I will gladly give my life to support you."

Ealasaid seemed at a complete loss, and Maarav believed he knew her well enough to guess exactly what she was thinking. Without her, some of the mages might be saved, but so many others might die. Oighear was not likely to relent.

"Give her some time to consider your words," Maarav said softly.

Sage turned toward him, then nodded. He took the woman's hand. "Let us go. We've done all that we can."

With that, they both exited the room, leaving Maarav and Ealasaid alone once more.

He walked across the room to pointedly lock the door, then resumed his seat on the edge of her bed.

Ealasaid buried her face in her hands. "I don't know what to do," she groaned. "I try to lead, to do the right thing, but I only bring death and ruin." She dropped her hands to the bed and stared at him. "What do you think I should do?"

He smiled softly. "I would have you do whatever it took to save *us*, and to the Horned One with everyone else," he chuckled, "but you are a much better person than I, and braver than I could ever hope to be. The best person to make this choice, is *you*."

She sighed. "If you are as cowardly and selfish as you claim, why are you still here? Now that we know the Faie Queen came for me, the safest place for *you* is far from my side."

His smile broadened. "My girl, you faced the Faie Queen

and lived to tell the tale. The only other person who has done that is Finn. The safest place for me, is close to one of you."

Finally she smiled, ever so slightly. "Then why not remain with Finn and Iseult?"

He laughed and raked his fingers through his dirty black hair. "Finn may be strong, and Iseult may be my kin, but neither of them are *any* fun."

She smirked. "So is that it then? You've remained by my side because you want me to protect you?"

He leaned forward, putting his face near hers. "No," he whispered. "You're also pretty cute, especially when you're angry." He lingered just a hair's-breadth from her lips, then pulled away.

She scowled at him. "You're infuriating."

"I know," he replied, glad to have cheered her, if only temporarily.

She sighed, suddenly serious. "I truly don't know if I have it in me to face Oighear again. Part of me feels like we should find Finn. Together, we might stand a chance against her."

He shook his head and leaned back. "We don't know where Finn is, and we cannot waste the time it would take to find her."

"So I continue risking the lives of the magic users . . . the ones that remain?" she questioned. "I'm not sure if I can do that."

He smiled. She was so very different from him. So pure of heart. He wasn't sure how she managed it after what had happened to her, and what she'd now learned about her family.

"Where is the Ealasaid driven by vengeance?" he questioned. "You were obsessed when your target was nameless soldiers. Now your target has a face."

She shrugged, looking utterly miserable. "I suppose I've finally realized that it means nothing to fight for the dead. Only the living care about being saved."

He leaned forward and brushed a finger beneath her jaw, raising her chin. "So save them, and let them save *you* in return."

She took a deep, shuddering breath. "I suppose it's too late to turn back either way, though I do still wish we could find Finn and the others."

He shook his head. "If I know anything about my brother and Finnur, they've already found battles of their own. Battles with even greater odds stacked against them, and even greater foes than the Aos Sí."

Ealasaid smiled, though it remained small and pained. "I suppose you're right, and I imagine neither of them are lying in a fluffy bed right now."

He raised an eyebrow at her. "You nearly froze to death."

She stared him down until he finally rose and offered her his hand. "I've felt worse," she quipped as he pulled her to her feet, then had to support her lest she fall.

"In that case," he began as he helped her toward the door, "the night is young. Let us see if Lady Sìoda can top freezing half to death."

Ealasaid snorted. "I'd rather face Oighear. Bring me to Keiren instead. I have to thank her for holding up her end of the bargain."

"You're beginning to trust her," he commented, holding

her up with an arm around her lower back as they emerged into the hall.

"Now now," she replied. "If you assassins have taught me anything, it's to trust *no one*, not even friends."

"That's my girl," he joked, as they made slow progress down the hall. "Soon enough you'll be as ruthless as Slàine and I combined."

She snorted. "That's what I'm afraid of."

He chuckled, hiding the sudden lurch in his gut. He could admit, if only to himself, that he was afraid of such a fate too. Truly, he didn't want her to change, but he wanted her to survive even more, and sacrifices needed to be made.

CHAPTER TWENTY-ONE

*a*nna hurried down from the stone roof of the dilapidated fortress, carefully treading across the wet surface. Reaching the edge, she slipped down, dangling from her fingertips, then dropped onto the lower parapet. Glancing both ways, she turned and hurried toward the nearest entrance. The heavy door was braced open against the interior door, like many of the entrances, in an effort to air out the must. She began to hurry in, almost running into Iseult as he emerged.

"The Dearg Due are coming," he said simply, barely glancing at her, then as he continued past added, "be ready to fight by nightfall."

She cursed under her breath, watching his back as he strode confidently away. She should have just stayed on the roof in the peace and quiet, away from the Faie.

Naoki came darting out of the chamber a moment later, nearly barreling into her. Before she could even react, the dragon looked both ways, then scurried after Iseult.

With a sigh, Anna entered the now empty chamber, thinking about what she'd heard of the Dearg Due. With a shudder, she instinctively glanced about the massive chamber for anything threatening. Nothing apparent, she hurried across the stone floor, her boots yielding a slight echo around the barren space, and into the hall. Glancing into the empty chambers along the way, she eventually reached the stairs and quickly descended. She emerged into the main entry chamber, where she found Kai sitting on the floor, readying his weapons.

His features slackened in relief as he spotted her. "There you are, I've been looking everywhere for you. One of the Pixies sighted a band of Dearg Due and other Faie heading this way last night. They're likely hiding from the sun now, but will reach us come nightfall. We must prepare."

She looked him up and down, wondering if he truly was alright after his lengthy encounter with the frightening Dark Faie. "And what are *we* supposed to do to prepare? Not even the few Aos Sí we have can stand against them. It will be up to blasted Finn to save us. At least she's not unconscious this time."

He sighed. "Finn *and* the other Faie. Many have gathered outside the gates, ready to fight for their new queen."

She scowled, then strode across the room. "Pixies and Trow," she scoffed, "and other small furry creatures. I can't imagine they'll be of much use."

Kai trotted after her, following her outside. "Well they blasted better be," he muttered, "else we're cooked."

She stopped in the soggy grass and gazed out toward the broken gates, now obscured with freshly rooted trees. No, not trees, *Trow*. She peered around the courtyard for Eywen, hoping he hadn't trapped himself outside the walls.

Her shoulders slumped in relief as the Trow parted enough to readmit him to the courtyard, though she quickly stiffened them, internally chastising herself for worrying about one of the Faie. Ewyen had saved her life, and her concern was generated from gratitude. At least, that's what she told herself.

She glared at Kai who was watching her curiously, then approached the Aos Sí warrior. "How much time do we have? Are you sure they won't travel until dark?"

Eywen nodded. "They won't travel until dark, and were roughly three hours away when spotted last night, at least according to the Pixies. The Goblins do not travel as swiftly as the Dearg Due, but that's not to say the latter will not leave the former behind. Although, we do not know for sure that they intend to attack."

"They attacked us last time," Kai scoffed, "I do not see why they'd do any different now."

Eywen nodded his agreement, his pale face creased with worry.

Anna agreed too. Even if the Dearg Due did not attack, she had no intention of letting them get close enough to speak. "What is our plan?" she asked.

Eywen glanced toward the Trow, having closed the opening they'd made for him. "The Faie will be our first line of defense," he explained. "Finnur will attempt to use her magic from atop the outer wall . . . though she seems unsure."

Anna smirked, knowing Finn's magic was unpredictable at best. "And what are the rest of us to do?"

Eywen glanced between her and Kai, his deep blue eyes calculating. "Nothing," he decided. "If I had more of my men, we might be able to launch an organized attack. As it is, we will defend Finnur in the event the Dark Faie breach the fortress walls. You may both join in that defense if it pleases you, though our fates may be all but sealed by then."

"That's what I had planned to do regardless," Kai replied, eliciting an eye roll from Anna.

"Someone approaching the wall!" one of the Aos Sí shouted from the nearby parapet.

"I thought you said we had a while," Anna hissed.

Eywen nodded, his gaze on the other Aos Sí far above them. "I did."

"ARE YOU SURE THIS IS A GOOD IDEA?" BEDELIA QUESTIONED, leading her horse toward the distant fortress.

"She's in there," Àed muttered, "and the Faie are gathered 'round. She might need our help."

Bedelia bit her lip, tugging her horse along as it tried to grasp at tufts of grass. She strained her eyes, peering around the outskirts of the fortress. She could see movement, but it was if her eyes could not quite train on anything. Yet if Àed claimed there were Faie around, she believed him. "You could be sensing the Aos Sí as well," she whispered. "They were with us when we were attacked."

Àed ignored her, muttering something about *Pooks and Pixies*.

She barely heard him as she spotted a humanoid figure

approaching them. "Eywen," she breathed in relief, undeniably happy to recognize the friendly Aos Sí.

He wore a plain burgundy tunic and dark breeches instead of his strange armor, and his silken hair was pulled back from his face, showcasing his pointed ears. He stopped a few paces away, eyeing both of them skeptically.

He took another step closer, looking Bedelia up and down, then gazing directly into her eyes. "Were you bitten?" he questioned.

Suddenly she realized the cause for his suspicion. He was worried that she might be infected like Sativola had been. At the thought, she fought back a sudden wave of emotion.

"My bite was cleansed," she explained. "And this is Àed," she gestured to the grumpy old man beside her.

Eywen eyed them both for a moment more, as if debating whether or not they'd be allowed to advance.

She was about to argue with him, then spotted Kai and Anna approaching behind him.

"My eyes must be deceiving me!" Kai called out. "Did you somehow make it to Àed's hidden prison and back while we've been here counting our fingers and toes?"

Bedelia smiled, cast a wary glare at Eywen, then gave him a wide berth as she moved past him toward Kai and Anna. "He wasn't as far off as we'd thought," she explained.

"She found me in the swamps," Àed loudly interjected, "not in a dungeon. We got to speakin' and realized we were searchin' for the same people."

Bedelia quickly schooled her expression to hide her surprise. "Y-yes," she stammered. "I woke up in the marshes after the attack. Àed found me there."

SARA C ROETHLE

"How did you cleanse your bite?" Eywen asked skeptically, slinking up beside her. "There's not much fresh running water in the marshes."

Anna, quiet until then, looked her up and down. "She's fine," she decided. "We should all get back inside the walls before the Faie attack."

"Attack?" Bedelia questioned, a sudden sick feeling in her gut.

Eywen nodded, trusting Anna spoke true about Bedelia not being infected. "You are right," he agreed, ignoring Bedelia's question. "She does not seem to be transforming, and she would be by now. We can continue this conversation from within the fortress walls."

Eywen turned to lead the way.

Àed and Bedelia began to walk, tugging their horses behind them. Anna moved along beside Bedelia as Kai sidled up to Àed. "You know," Kai whispered conspiratorially, "we were planning on rescuing you."

Àed snorted, though Bedelia didn't miss his wry grin. He and Kai were clearly on decent terms. "Ye better focus on rescuing yerself lad, if the Faie are comin' to attack."

Anna nodded, then turned toward Bedelia. "Yes, you could not have chosen a worse time to return."

"We're sorry for the imposition," Bedelia explained.

Anna shook her head. "Not for us, for *you*. We may all be dead come nightfall, and if not, we'll likely starve not long after."

Bedelia startled as the trees barring the entrance began to move, forming a path just wide enough for them to walk single file. She cautiously watched Anna's back as she went through the path first. She and Kai had been closer to

Sativola than the others, yet neither had yet asked about him.

Of course, they weren't yet aware that she and Sativola had ended up in the same place. Should she even tell them? Eywen already seemed suspicious of her, and she didn't want to explain why she'd had to kill their friend.

Of course, Iseult might see through any lies she tried to tell regardless, and she would entirely lose his trust, and Finn's too.

She knew she should be worrying about the upcoming attack, but it simply wasn't her primary concern. Her fear of the Faie had been replaced by another fear, the fear of losing her friends. Now that she knew how true friendship felt, she'd rather die than go back to how things were, long before she met the strange tree girl in the woods.

ISEULT COULD HARDLY BELIEVE HIS EYES AS EYWEN, KAI, AND Anna re-entered the fortress grounds, with Bedelia and Àed tugging along their horses. Truly, he hadn't expected to see either of their missing party members again.

Finn exited the fortress beside him, catching sight of Àed and Bedelia a moment later.

"How can this be?" she muttered, stunned.

Iseult walked by her side as she approached the group, their boots squishing on the soggy ground. He felt just as stunned as Finn . . . and suspicious. How had Àed and Bedelia ended up together? Had Bedelia come in contact with Keiren?

Reaching them, Finn gave Bedelia a fierce hug, muttering, "So glad you are safe." She pulled away and turned her astonished gaze down to Àed, who was looking about one hundred years older than he had before. Both of them stared at each other at a seeming loss for words.

"Ah stop lookin' at me like I'm somethin' special," Àed said finally, waving Finn off.

She laughed, then threw her arms around him. "I see you decided not to wait around for me to save you. How did you escape?"

He patted her back, then pulled away. "That's a tale fer another time. I hear ye have Dark Faie headin' our way." He eyed Eywen askance, then took a step further away from him.

"Yes," Iseult confirmed, glad to be back to the task at hand. Their reunion wouldn't matter if they soon perished. "The Faie will hold the outer gates," he explained. "We will attack from atop the fortress wall, if we are able, then retreat should Finn's Faie fail."

"I have a bow," Bedelia interjected, " . . . but only a single quiver of arrows," she added bashfully.

"A few of my men can supply you with more," Eywen offered, then gestured for her to follow.

She accepted and followed him away, though she glanced over her shoulder longingly at those left behind. Another of the Aos Sí came and took the two horses to the roughly assembled stables where Loinnir waited with Eywen's horse.

Iseult watched Bedelia retreat, wishing he could question her about Keiren, but knowing he should keep his mind on the current dangers.

He turned his attention back to those who remained.

"Do what you will with the remaining time," he explained. He landed his gaze on Anna. "If you *see* anything, I'd appreciate you letting me know."

She nodded at him, then led Kai away, leaving Iseult and Finn with only Àed. Iseult watched as the old man looked Finn up and down.

"Yer different, lass," he commented. "And yer shining so bright ye won't be able to hide any longer."

Finn frowned, but replied, "I no longer wish to hide."

Àed smiled, then turned his gaze to Iseult. "I guess I should have stuck with ye up North, seeing as ye found her first."

Iseult couldn't help his small smile. "Yes," he agreed, flicking his gaze to Finn. "Though I imagine she'd have found both of us if we'd just stayed put."

Àed chuckled, then turned his attention back to Finn. "Well why don't ye show me around this fortress and catch me up on what I've missed. Perhaps there's something here that can help against the Dark Faie."

"Yes," Finn agreed happily, turning to lead the way. "It was home to the Druid's after all." She gazed down at Àed warmly as he walked by her side. "Perhaps you'll notice something we missed."

Iseult followed after them. Even with night fast approaching, he felt a measure of his worry lifted away. Now that Àed and Bedelia were back, Finn could finally focus on her enemies. She hadn't asked them about Sativola, and he wasn't about to remind her that he was still missing. She had enough on her mind already.

He would, however, ask Bedelia about it if he got the chance. Something seemed amiss to him, and he did not believe for a moment that Bedelia had come across Àed by chance.

~

FINN WAS OVERJOYED TO HAVE ÀED AND BEDELIA RETURNED to her . . . if only it had been under better circumstances. They would either be two more people for her to protect, or two more people to watch her fail. It would be dark soon. Their fates would be decided.

The forthcoming battle weighed heavily on her mind as she led Àed and Iseult into the main entry chamber of the fortress, shutting the heavy wood and iron door behind them. She knew she would need to use the shroud and all of her alleged power to defeat the Dearg Due and Goblins, and whatever else might accompany them, but she wasn't entirely sure if she was capable.

She'd used her powers for destruction before, but they were unpredictable, likely linked to her emotions. They only ever seemed to surface when someone she cared about was in danger.

She shook her head as she stopped and turned to Àed. *Everyone* she cared about was about to be in danger. The time to use her powers was now.

"I cannae see anythin' of use in here," Àed commented, gazing around the barren space. "Except for perhaps the ghosts of the past. This place gives me the shivers."

Finn smiled down at him, fighting the overwhelming urge to hug him again. She knew she must focus on the task at hand, but . . .

She dove in and hugged him, catching him off guard.

"I'm filthy, lass!" he shrieked. "Yer goin' to get the stench of the swamps on ye!"

She pulled away, not at all caring about the stench. "Lets look out back," she suggested. "There's an overgrown garden, perhaps the Druids hid some supplies there."

"They were killed long ago," Iseult commented as she began to walk toward the back end of the room. "I doubt their supplies could have lasted."

"Perhaps magical artifacts though," Àed suggested. "Ye never know."

Finn suspected he was simply humoring her, but she continued to lead the way regardless. They couldn't just sit around and wait for the attack if there was even the slightest chance the Druids had left behind something that might help them.

She journeyed through the adjoining corridor down to its end, then pushed a heavy door open into the gardens she'd found earlier that morning.

She stepped outside and surveyed the overgrown vegetation. A few plants still bore fruit, though most had been choked out by the same heavy vines covering the exterior walls.

As overgrown as it was, the garden instantly instilled her with a sense of peace. It was bordered by a tall stone wall, though not as tall as the outer walls of the fortress. One could scale it easily enough.

Iseult remained at her side as Àed began to inspect the garden. "When did you find this?" he asked quietly.

She turned toward him. His expression was unreadable like always, but there was perhaps a hint of something else there. Worry? Unease? She could not tell.

"This morning," she explained, "while you surveyed the rest of the grounds with Eywen. It was almost as if it called to me."

"I can see why!" Àed called from across the space. He was tugging at a particularly dense cluster of vines. He gave a final hard tug, causing them to snap, flinging him down into the grass.

Finn rushed toward him, worried he was hurt, but halfway there she stopped in her tracks. Àed's action had revealed a small stone pillar, covered in archaic writing and topped with a large green gem. The gem seemed to pulse with light.

She had only stared at it for a moment when Iseult placed himself between her and the gem, facing the pillar as if it might attack. "Stay back," he ordered. "We know not what it might do. It could be a trap."

Àed hobbled to his feet, then approached the pillar, ignoring Iseult's warning.

Her hands on Iseult's arm, she leaned to peer around him.

Àed hovered his withered hand over the glowing green gem. "There's some magic within it," he explained, "though I cannae tell its purpose."

Finn watched as the pulsing green glow created patterns on Àed's face in the growing darkness. Her instincts told her the magic wasn't malevolent, but she also had no idea what good it might do them.

Her gaze lingered for a moment more on the stone, then dropped to the stone pillar supporting it. She walked around Iseult and took a few steps closer, then knelt. She traced her fingers along markings etched into the stone.

She realized with a start that she recognized the language. "It's a charm stone," she explained distantly. "Minor in power, but said to bring its holder a connection to nature deities. It's very old."

Àed tilted his wizened head as he observed her. "How do ye know that, lass?"

Remaining on her knees, she pointed to the pillar. "The inscription is a prayer to Druantia, a forest goddess. This pillar is an offering to her, a way of drawing her magic into the garden."

Iseult knelt beside her, then shook his head. "There are no words there." He reached a hand out to run down the pillar. "It's only smooth stone."

Perplexed, she stood and placed a hand atop the glowing gemstone. The plants shivered around her, and a voice echoed in her head, *Greetings, Oak Child.*

She gasped, then looked back and forth between Àed and Iseult. "Did either of you hear that?"

They both looked at her as if she'd sprouted a second head.

It's been a long time since one of my children reached out to me, the voice continued. The stone was growing warm beneath her hand, but she feared if she released it, the voice would rescind.

Only the strongest survived, the voice continued, *those like you. The strongest of the Druids became Dair, true Children of the Oak, but the Dair do not come here anymore.*

She tilted her head, confused. She knew there were other Dair besides her tribe, but had started to believe they did not return along with her people, as they were yet to reveal themselves.

They live, the voice answered, reading her thoughts. *They hide, awaiting a true queen to return them to the earth, as they are meant to be.*

"Finn," Iseult began, but she held up a hand to silence him.

The rain began to fall again, dampening her hair and making the gemstone slick beneath her palm.

"I don't understand," she said out loud. "Why are you telling me this?"

You seek your magic, do you not? the voice questioned. *Magic to fulfill the prophecy, to grant rebirth to the land. Three magical queens will come to live in the same time, and their blood shall grant a rebirth.*

"I want to protect my friends," she said out loud. "*Whatever* that might entail."

Iseult and Àed both watched her intently, but did not speak.

To protect is not your destiny, the voice replied. *It is not your place to decide the fates of mortals.*

Finn shook her head. "I don't care about destiny. I *will* protect them."

Even if you bring chaos to the land?

She narrowed her gaze at the green stone beneath her hand. It might have been selfish, but she cared more about those within the fortress than any without.

"Yes," she answered. "Even then."

So be it, the voice replied.

Finn felt as if a presence had suddenly left her. As she tuned back into reality, she could hear shouting on the other side of the fortress. The last hints of sunlight blinked out of existence behind the tall fortress wall.

"Someone approaches the gates," Iseult observed, tilting his head to listen. "We thought we had at least some time after dark before they arrived."

Finn slowly lowered her hand from the stone, which had gone dark. She turned her gaze to Iseult. "I think my people were once Druids," she explained, still perplexed, "but they became what they are now to survive. They made a choice to no longer fulfill the purpose for which they were born."

Àed watched her cautiously. "Well Druids or no, we should see who approaches. If it's the Dark Faie, we must be prepared."

She nodded. Feeling as if she were in a dream, she peered down at the darkened stone.

Iseult placed a hand at the small of her back. "We should go."

She nodded again, then allowed him to lead her back toward the fortress door. The voice's words lingered in her head. *Three magical queens will come to live in the same time, and their blood shall grant a rebirth.*

It went in line with Slaine's prophecy, except that the voice had said nothing about two dying so the third might live. Perhaps it meant that none needed to die. Or, perhaps it meant they *all* did.

She walked back into the fortress with Àed and Iseult right behind her. Part of her knew there would come a time when she had to become like her people in order to fight them, to be *strong*.

That time had come.

CHAPTER TWENTY-TWO

*K*ai waited atop the fortress wall with Anna. She'd seen something magical coming their way, but whatever it was had not moved close enough to be spotted with their eyes. In the stables below, protected by the wall, Finn's unicorn snorted and stomped, clearly agitated. He briefly wondered if the animal would prove useful against the Dark Faie, but quickly dismissed the idea. It wasn't like they could bring the unicorn up on the wall, and putting her outside of it would be akin to sacrificing her. It would be best to just leave her in the stables where Finn could reach her if necessary.

Tired of peering into the growing darkness, Kai turned his sights further along the wall. Eywen, his few Aos Sí warriors, and Bedelia stood a few paces away, bows held at their sides for what good it would do them. The Dearg Due were impossibly fast, and seemed impervious to pain.

Their only real hope were the Faie that Finn had recruited. They were allegedly in the surrounding forest below, lying in wait, though Kai could not see them. For all he knew, they had all run off.

"Where in the blazes is Finn?" Anna asked, glancing over her shoulder with abrupt, irritated movements. Her black braid was slick with moisture, and droplets slid down her sharp cheekbones.

Kai turned at the sound of echoing footsteps leaving the fortress behind them. Finn, Iseult, and Àed hurried across the courtyard.

A loud trill cut through the evening air, whipping Kai's gaze forward. "I thought the Pixies said they were hours away," he gasped.

Anna looked at him, perplexed, and he remembered she'd been unconscious for their previous encounter. She would not recognize the hunting call.

"It's the Dearg Due," he explained. "They're coming."

As one, the Aos Sí lifted their bows.

Kai focused on one end of the wall as Finn, Iseult, and Àed reached the top of the adjacent stairwell, then hurried toward him and Anna.

His attention on Finn, Kai jumped as something crashed down on the wall behind him, then relaxed upon hearing the chitter of Naoki's beak. He glanced over his shoulder at the small dragon, though he supposed she couldn't really be considered small anymore. She seemed to be growing by the day, and was nearly the size of a small pony now.

He looked back at Finn as the group reached them. Everyone remained silent, tension thick in the air.

Finn peered into the darkness, her long hair blowing freely in the cool breeze. Kai admired how the moonlight glinted in her dark hazel eyes, before joining the others in scouring the darkness for signs of the enemy.

Àed moved past Finn toward the parapet, squinting to see further into the darkness. "I can sense them not far off," he muttered.

Standing behind Finn, Iseult placed a hand on her shoulder. "Are you ready?"

She nodded, then lifted the bottom edge of her tan tunic to untie the Faie Queen's shroud from her waist. She lifted the ragged, dirty fabric in her hands.

"They're closing in," Anna hissed, her eyes darting from shadow to shadow.

A group of Pixies flew up out of the darkness to hover around Finn. "We are prepared," one of them chimed. "We will attack on your signal."

As Finn nodded, Kai spotted dozens of reflective eyes within the deeper shadows of the nearby trees.

"I don't believe this is the hunting party the Pixies spotted," Eywen observed, sidling closer to them with his eyes trained on the trees, bow at the ready, "unless they left the Goblins behind. Goblins have a particular stench about them that carries on the wind. My nose tells me they are nowhere near."

"Why aren't they attacking?" Kai whispered.

"Perhaps because Finnur is awake this time," Eywen replied. "Or perhaps they wait for reinforcements."

"Comforting," Kai muttered, though it was anything but. He couldn't help wondering if the particular Dearg Due who'd attacked him was out there right now, staring at him from the trees.

"Something else is coming," Anna hissed. "Something . . . big."

"I am ready," Finn muttered, barely loud enough for Kai to hear. She clutched the shroud so tightly her knuckles turned white. Naoki sat behind her on her haunches like a giant obedient dog.

An earsplitting shriek echoed across the dark marsh. Kai's blood ran cold. The cluster of Pixies hovering around them cried out.

"What was that?" he gasped.

The Dearg Due watching them from the trees seemed to shift.

"Bows at the ready!" Eywen shouted.

Iseult unsheathed his sword, though little good it would do them unless the Dearg Due scaled the wall . . . which they might. At the thought, Kai unsheathed his daggers. He would not go down without a fight.

The shriek sounded again, followed by the sound of breaking branches, no, breaking *tree trunks*. The *snaps* thundering toward them were too loud to be smaller branches.

Clenching his daggers, Kai's gaze darted toward the rustling treetops, their upper leaves illuminated by moonlight. Whatever this massive beast was, it was heading this way.

The shriek sounded again, then a burst of fire blasted forth from the trees far left of the Dearg Due.

"Fire-spitter!" Eywen called out to his men. "Everyone! Down behind the parapet!"

Kai didn't have to be told twice. He took hold of Finn and dove to the stones beneath their feet, just as a wash of flame hit the wall, splashing over their heads. Naoki chittered in fear, curled up against Finn's side with her long neck folded back against her body.

The heat was almost unbearable. Kai broke out in an instant sweat as his body pressed down on top of Finn's, with Anna and Iseult right beside them. He couldn't see Àed, but could hear him cursing somewhere near his feet. Most of the Pixies had dropped to the ground for safety, but Kai believed he counted a few less than there were before.

"It's a Caorthannach!" Eywen shouted. "Aim for the eyes!"

Now that the flames had passed, Kai lifted his head just enough to see Eywen climbing to his feet with his men and Bedelia.

Kai released Finn, then stood, crouching low in case he needed to duck behind the parapet once more. He leaned forward to peer over the edge, just as something heavy thudded into the base of the wall.

He braced himself against the quaking reverberation, then looked down at a long, serpent-like creature, grunting while scratching at the base of the wall with long, ink-black talons. The creature was nearly tall as a horse, but as long as five, with four spindly legs topped with pointed black scales. It jerked its lizard-like head up to meet Kai's gaze, then puffed smoke through its nostrils, just as the first volley of arrows hit it, most of them bouncing off its hard scales.

"Tell the Faie to wait," Finn frantically instructed the Pixies. "Let us try to defeat the creature with arrows. Any on the ground will not stand a chance against its flames."

The Pixies buzzed away to deliver the message, unnoticed by the great serpent.

"Fire again!" Eywen shouted. "The eyes are its only weakness!"

Snarling in agitation, the creature crouched, ready for a pounce.

"Down!" Kai shouted, pulling Finn down well beneath the wall. Everyone was crouched as the creature's snout appeared at the top of the wall, spewing flames over their heads.

The heat washed over the crouched group, then died away. The fire-spitter, as Eywen had called it, couldn't leap high enough to pull itself over the wall, so it was trying to roast them alive instead.

"I must do something," Finn said from beneath him. "Let me up."

Kai obeyed, and they both rose.

Bedelia and Eywen's men fired their arrows again. One hit the serpent's eye, erupting in a gush of blood. The creature went wild, crashing up against the side of the wall as it wailed in pain and pawed at the arrow in its eye, eventually tearing it loose.

It bellowed up at them in rage, then launched itself upward. Before Finn could stop her, Naoki launched herself forward. In that split second Kai knew Finn's little dragon was about to get cooked.

He pulled Finn down just as the next wave of flame came, but Naoki opened her mouth and spewed forth a massive torrent of water. Kai could hardly believe his eyes as the water hit the flame, dousing it, then poured down the outside of the wall with a loud hiss of steam.

The creature below shrieked, then Naoki launched herself forward, spewing more water down upon it.

"What in the Horned One's name just happened!" Bedelia shouted, crouched beside the Aos Sí.

Kai darted toward the parapet and looked down at the now soaked serpent. Its entire body hissed with steam, and heavy coughs emitted from its massive maw like it had inhaled water. Slipping and stumbling, it darted back into the trees.

They had a moment of reprieve, then the trills of the Dearg Due came again. He had nearly forgotten about them.

Taking advantage of the distraction, dark shapes with pure white hair darted out of the trees, moving like they were made of liquid. They were the next wave of assault, he realized. The Dark Faie were organized enough to plan a proper attack.

Finn's Faie appeared to intercept them, some flying down from trees, and some seeming to materialize from the earth. Little humanoid forms with the lower bodies of goats, and wide faces with round, milky yellow eyes expertly hurled rocks at the Dearg Due's faces, then darted away before the evil creatures could catch them. Lumbering Trow snatched some of the Dearg Due with their large branches, wrapping them up and crushing them until they stopped moving. Pixies darted in and out, stabbing at eyes and tender skin with tiny branches and needles. Kai continued trying to follow the movements, but it was utter chaos below them.

Even with the Faieries' efforts, Kai spotted some of the Dearg Due closing in on the wall, then beginning to scale it. He lifted his daggers to defend himself as the first Dearg Due reached the top. His dagger slashed across her throat, flinging blood in a crimson arc. She fell away from the wall as he stared at his dagger in disbelief. How had he moved so quickly? Another creature appeared at the top of the wall, darting toward Finn. Kai's hand snapped out and flung her off, sending her plunging back down the way she'd come.

Finn looked at him, stunned. "How did you move so quickly?"

Before he could reply, another of the creatures appeared atop the wall. Finn, clutching the shroud, seemed frozen.

Kai tried to fight her off, but she thrust herself downward, knocking him to the stones. Finn screamed as another of the Dearg Due attacked her, but Kai couldn't see what was happening as the first impossibly strong Dearg Due pinned him to the ground.

Hot breath hit his cheek. "We meet again, weak Dair," the creature hissed. "Or not Dair at all? Liar."

He fought against her, but he couldn't dislodge her.

"Had I known you were human," she hissed, "I would not have given you blood. I will fix my mistake."

With sounds of fighting all around them, he cried out as her fangs sunk deep into his flesh near his collarbone.

Blood poured down, pooling in his hair, flowing beneath his neck. He spared his last thoughts for Finn and Anna, assuming they'd soon meet the same fate.

FINN SWUNG HER ARMS WILDLY AT ANOTHER ATTACKING Dearg Due, connecting with hard flesh to send the creature screaming back off the wall. Panting, she stared down at the seemingly useless shroud clutched in one of her fists, then snapped back into motion. Whipping her head to Kai, her heart jumped up into her throat as she spotted the Dearg Due atop him, her loose black clothing and shimmering white hair blocking his face and body as he struggled beneath her. The sharp tang of blood hit Finn's nostrils.

Before she could act, Iseult appeared and slashed his sword across the creature's back, cutting deep into her flesh. Finn caught a flash of white bone glinting in the moonlight as the Dearg Due shrieked, arching her back. She sprung up and darted back down the wall to join her kin fighting the other Faie.

Kai sat up, his face frighteningly pale. Clutching his bloody neck, he glanced at Anna as she crouched beside him to tend his new wound. Another Dearg Due darted toward them, but Àed rushed forward, hitting her with a small burst of shimmering magic before Iseult swooped in and finished the job with his sword.

Finn clutched the shroud, her mind panicked. The light Faie were dying at the base of the wall, and her friends would soon be overcome. She needed to help them fight, but how? She had thought she was prepared, but now that the moment was upon her, she seemed unable to act. More of the Dearg Due leapt atop the wall above the Aos Sí and Bedelia. Eywen and Bedelia leapt forward to meet them with blades drawn. Finn was mesmerized for a moment watching the pair swing their blades in well-practiced arcs, Eywen faster and more graceful than Bedelia, but no more fierce.

Finn gritted her jaw. She had to do something. This was *her* battle. Sensing a presence at her back, she spun around, then stared up at the Dearg Due perched atop the parapet.

The creature tilted her head at Finn, trailing long tresses over her shapeless black clothing.

"Greetings, Oak Queen," she hissed, then launched herself at Finn.

Finn reacted without thinking, taking one hand off the shroud to shove away the Dearg Due. She felt a wave of magic rush through her as she touched the creature.

The Dearg Due stumbled to the stone floor, then began to scream. Her face turned up toward Finn, the moonlight revealing flesh turned green and yellow with rot. The skin of her cheeks began to drip from her jaw bone, splattering on the stones where she crouched.

Finn backed away, knowing she'd caused the rot. She'd done it before. Why did her magic have to be like this? So unpredictable and . . . *frightening*.

She fought the urge to gag as the Dearg Due continued to shriek in agony. Her cries ended abruptly as Iseult shoved his sword through the creature's back and into her heart.

Anna swung her daggers in a precise sweep, slashing away another Dearg Due that had gone after Kai, still recovering as he bled through a hastily made bandage. Finn turned just in time to see Naoki slash her beak across an already bloody face, knocking the creature down only to pounce and bite her neck, crushing it in a splash of blood.

"More coming!" Eywen shouted from further down the wall.

Finn lifted the shroud again, determined to do better as the next onslaught came.

A war horn sounded below them, drawing her attention to the far end of the battlefield. Stepping out of the tree shadows, more creatures revealed themselves. They appeared like twisted old men the size of children, with hide-like skin and patchy hair on their heads. What Finn could see of their clothing was roughly made, and did little in the way of modesty. *Goblins*.

Her Faie were already being overcome by the Dearg Due. She had to act now, or the Goblins would finish them off.

Her hands trembled as she lifted the shroud. She focused on the earth near the tree line, willing the roots to shoot up and ensnare the Goblins. Her entire body began to shake from her intense concentration, but nothing was happening.

She jumped as a hand touched her shoulder, then Anna's voice whispered in her ear. "You may not feel it now, but you are surrounded by magic. For all of our sake, *use it*. We will watch your back."

Finn took a steadying breath. She could do this. This was what she was born for.

Yet holding up her shroud, she focused all her energy on the Goblins, and magic flowed through her. The earth shot up in splashes of soil beneath the Goblins' feet. She almost lost her concentration, but persisted. Brought on by her magic, sudden memories shot through her like a knife. *The day her daughter, Niamh, was born. The naming ceremony, performed by just Finn and her mother, instead of the entire tribe. Her swearing to protect her daughter with every ounce of magic she had. Magic that was meant to protect all of the Dair, not just a single child, but she didn't want to protect them, only Niamh. Relations with her people had gone sour ever since that night.*

Tears streaming down her face, she snapped back into reality. She'd sworn to protect her daughter because no one else would. Despite her strong parents, Niamh been born with stunted magic. In the world of the Cavari, only the strongest survived.

With emotion welling inside her, she renewed her assault on the now panicked Goblins. Roots shot up out of the earth, not only ensnaring them, but crushing them. Though they were on the other end of the battle, she thought she could hear their bones snapping beneath the pressure of the roots.

The Dearg Due continued scampering to the top of the wall. Her friends and the Aos Sí, when not otherwise engaged, would pick them off as they arrived to ensure her magic would not be interrupted.

Now that her magic was flowing so strongly, she couldn't seem to stop. The Goblins who'd escaped the crushing roots ran off, shrieking into the night. However, more and more of the Light Faie below were dying, unable to stand up to the seemingly invincible Dearg Due. Finn longed to attack the dark creatures, but was unsure if her magic would hit the wrong targets.

She tried to focus on the base of the wall, where the Dearg Due continued to climb while others fought the Light Faie. She could tell her friends were growing weary. If she did not do something soon, they would be overcome. Her eyes flared. An idea had popped into her mind.

She approached the edge of the wall, looking down. White gleaming hands were dotting the wall on an upward climb as far as the eye could see. Still holding the shroud with one hand, she extended the other downward. If she could make the roots climb up the wall, she could ensnare the Dearg Due long before they could reach the top.

As she focused, a green tinge began to encase her vision. A vibrant glow emanated from her outstretched hand, then a voice cut through her mind, the same voice that had spoken to her in the overgrown garden.

Do you still desire only power? the voice questioned. *You must make your final choice on what you will become. Will you follow down the destructive path of your people, or choose the peace your ancestors knew.*

Finn's eye caught the glimmer of white hair surfacing at the top of the wall a few paces over. Seconds later the Dearg Due stood on the ledge with bloodlust in her reflective eyes, her long white hair blowing a bit in a breeze that had kicked up. She looked almost bodiless in her black clothing against the night. Finn's friends did not come to her aid, too engaged battling the numerous Dearg Due continually sprouting up on the wall.

Finn instinctively aimed her hand at the creature, blasting her with magic. White flesh turned dark and began to rot, falling away from the Dearg Due's bones. She shrieked, sounding more animal than humanoid, then flung herself away from the wall, back down to the chaos below.

The voice sounded again. *What do you choose?*

I need power to save my friends, Finn answered silently. *If peace means sacrificing them now, I do not want it.*

Destruction begets destruction, the voice replied. *You will choose the good of the few over the good of many?*

"Always," Finn hissed, then lashed out with her power. She'd made her choice, and would shirk the fears that had sealed away her magic. If she'd only chosen power over peace in her first life, her daughter might still be alive.

Gazing back down at the base of the wall, one hand on

the shroud and the other thrust downward over the wall, she summoned her magic full force. Roots shot up from the ground along the wall base, ensnaring and crushing the climbing Dearg Due. A cacophony of screams hit her ears over the sound of thundering earth, diminishing slowly as each met their fate.

Overcome by the sight, the Dark and Light Faie below stopped fighting each other, staring up at Finn in awe.

Waves of power lifted Finn's hair away from her face. Though her friends were near, maybe even staring at her with the same awe as the Faie, at that moment she never felt more alone, standing with her body leaned forward against the parapet, surveying the countless Faie below.

"Submit, or you will perish!" she shouted, her voice echoing across the sudden silence.

A few straggling roots shot upward, crushing the last few Dearg Due still clinging to the wall, then silence ensued. Finn scanned the moonlit darkness, watching the Faie as they simultaneously turned their gazes behind them.

Finn noticed other dark shapes lingering in the tree shadows. All at once, they emerged, revealing their cloaked forms to the moonlight. *The Cavari.*

This was it, this was the moment Finn had been waiting for. She would not ask for Loinnir's help again. If she was going to truly face her people, she would have to do it now.

The cloaked forms approached the wall with the Light Faie scurrying away to form an open path.

"Finn," Anna whispered, bringing her back to the present, but with eyes still on the Cavari. "This is the moment I saw in my dream. I'm sure of it. This is the moment I'm supposed to save you from. We must run away from them. No good can come from interacting."

Finn barely heard her as she stared down at her people. The people who had wanted a queen, and were given only a mother who wanted to protect her child.

She let the shroud fall to the stones near her feet. She would face them with her power alone, or not at all.

"I have claimed my birthright," she called out. "You wanted a queen, and you have found her!"

"Finn!" Anna hissed. "They want to kill you!"

"Let them try," she growled, then lashed out with her power.

If her power was what sustained them, she could not kill them unless she died, so she needed to make them submit. It was the only way. Her magic cut across the earth below, knocking the Light Faie on either side of the Cavari off their feet, but the Cavari seemed untouched.

Finn inhaled sharply. She would *not* let them hurt her friends, nor anyone else, *ever* again. She called upon every shred of power at her command with all that she was or could ever hope to be, then rained it down upon the Cavari.

For a moment she thought she had failed, then one by one, the cloaked figures fell to their knees and bowed their heads. One turned its gaze upward, pushing its hood back to reveal her face.

Anna and Kai both gasped as Finn's mother, Móirne, gazed up at her. "I had wanted better for you!" she called back. "But you have claimed your birthright, and now we must follow."

"If you had truly wanted better for me," Finn replied calmly, raising her voice to carry down to all below the wall, "then you should have been brave enough to step away from our people and show me the way."

Her mother bowed her head, unable to argue with the truth.

Finn had appreciated her mother's attempts to protect her, but the loyalty had only been partial, not enough to part ways with their tribe. She shook her head lightly. Partial loyalty would never do. She would protect those who stood at her back, no matter the cost.

"Finn," Anna cautioned, moving to stand at her side. "This is a mistake, I can feel it in my bones."

Finn shook her head. "Any other choice would have seen us all dead. Perhaps this was the wrong choice for the land, but I only care about those standing with me now. I can only seal away their magic, by sealing away mine. If I did that, I could not protect you from the threats still to come."

A cold feeling settled in the pit of her stomach as she peered down at the Cavari and Light Faie, the remaining Dark Faie long since retreated. For now, she had won, but she knew it was only temporary.

Eywen moved to Finn's other side, gazing down at the kneeling Faie and Cavari. "You have found your army, and your fortress, my queen. What will you do next?"

She shook her head. She wanted neither, but this was the fate she'd been dealt. "I will expand my reach," she muttered, "and I will crush anyone who would dare threaten my friends. I'm done hiding from my fate."

Eywen bowed his head. "As you wish, my queen."

Sensing eyes on her back, she turned. Kai and Iseult stood side by side, watching her, the former slightly hunched, clutching his bloody bandage against his neck. She could see the worry in both their expressions.

Her gaze met Iseult's. "Now is the time to prove if you truly meant what you said."

He watched her for a moment, then nodded. "To the ends of the earth, for better or worse."

She nodded, accepting his words, then turned back to the Cavari below.

Her new path had been chosen. There was work to be done.

Iseult cradled his left arm, injured in the battle, as he walked with Finn across the dark courtyard, with Naoki slinking tiredly behind them.

There were a million things Iseult wanted to say. *You can't reign over all the Faie. We should move on to Sormyr, to human civilization. Do not trust the Cavari.*

He would have liked to say all those things, but she never once looked at him as she strode across the soggy grass. Her light brown hair hung limp down her sides, weighed down by the heavy rain. Her tunic, breeches, and visible skin were all stained with blood and grime. With her frail frame, she looked like someone who had been lost in the marshes for weeks, not eating, not sleeping, just fighting to survive. He supposed her actual situation had not been much different.

The tired Aos Sí warriors remained atop the wall with Àed to keep watch, even though many of the Faie, along with the Cavari, had retreated . . . for now. Kai, Anna, and

Bedelia had retired ahead of Finn and Iseult to nurse their wounds.

Iseult glanced at Finn. The important thing was that they had survived the battle. Hearing the brush of his boots in the soggy grass as if his steps were numbered, he couldn't help but feel that it was the beginning of the end. Everything would come crashing down for them soon, like the waves on the shore of his homeland.

He followed Finn through the open door of the entry room. A fire was burning in the hearth. Perhaps Bedelia had lit it, as she was the least injured. The roaring flames gently illuminated the space, though the heat mostly slipped out the open door and high windows. Naoki hurried ahead of them and curled up close to the flames, seeming to fall asleep almost instantly.

Halfway across the room, Finn stopped and turned toward him. "Iseult, I'd like to sit in the garden for a while," she said softly.

He looked her up and down. "You should warm yourself first. You may fall ill otherwise."

She shook her head and turned away, continuing across the space toward the corridor leading to the garden.

With a heavy sigh, he caught up to her. When they arrived at the door leading to the garden, he held it open for her, then trailed her out.

The overgrown garden was soggy from the rain, with thick, waxy leaves reflecting the moonlight. Finn walked forward toward the small pillar topped with a green stone, crossed her legs, and sat.

Unsure of her intent, he stood at her back for several silent seconds.

"She spoke to me during the battle," Finn finally explained, her gaze on the pillar. "The Druid goddess, I mean. She wanted me to make a choice, and I chose to be like the Cavari. I chose the power to protect my friends."

He moved forward and sat on the damp earth beside her, slowly lowering his injured arm to his side. He suspected some muscle damage from one of the Dearg Due slamming into him, but nothing overly serious.

Finn turned to him. "It was the only way to protect all of you," she explained, as if justifying her decision. "The Druids were peaceful, connected to the earth, but they were not fighters. All they could do was hide, and it got most of them killed. I'm tired of running away."

He watched her sad expression, hoping she would explain further. When she did not, he asked, "What does this decision mean to you?"

She wiped her damp hair away from her pale, tired face. "It means that I'm just like the Cavari, but I have no choice. If Oighear is still alive, I must have the power to fight her." She looked sadly to the pillar. "The goddess spoke to me during the battle, but I cannot hear her voice anymore. I no longer feel the same connection to the earth that I once did."

"But you can control it," he prompted. "Surely that means you are still connected."

She shook her head. "The earth is not meant to be controlled. It's why I struggled with my magic before. I hadn't chosen my new path. I could have chosen that connection, and lived in peace, but I chose power and control. The peace I longed for, the reason I became a tree, is gone." She turned her gaze to him. "You should run far

371

away from me. I am no longer the person you thought you knew."

He sighed. For a wise, ancient being, she truly understood very little. He leaned forward, wrapping his good arm around her waist to gently pull her toward him.

She moved willingly, pressing her hip against his, then twisted to lean against his chest. He wrapped his arm around her clammy skin, wishing he had more warmth to give.

"I will not run," he muttered. "I told you once that I believe fate brought us together. There are things stronger than war, stronger than queens and entire nations."

She buried her cheek against his damp chest, hiding her face from him. "What things?" she asked after a moment.

"Loyalty," he replied softly, "and friendship . . . love."

She pulled her head away from his chest to look up at him. "And which of those things do *we* have?"

He smiled, realizing that if there was ever a time to be honest, it was now. She was teetering on the brink, and he needed to bring her back.

"All of them," he answered. "We have all of them."

"Will you help me?" she asked, surprising him. "Help me to not drown in power," she clarified. "I may have chosen the path of my people, but I—" she hesitated, lip trembling. "I do not want to be like them," she finished. "I do not want to lose who I choose to be, when I become what I must."

He pulled her gently to lean back against him. Tears in her eyes, she obliged.

"All you ever had to do was ask," he muttered, kissing the top of her head.

They stayed like that for a long while, until Kai and the others came to find them.

Everyone was wet and exhausted, ready for sleep, but someone still needed to stand watch. Eventually, Iseult left Finn in a warm room by a fire, with Kai and Anna to watch over her, and with Naoki snuggled at her feet.

For Iseult, all was as well as it could be. Finn still seemed to be Finn, despite her decisions. The Cavari would still need to be dealt with, along with all the Faie, but at least they had a unicorn in the stables if negotiations got out of hand.

As he walked across the silent courtyard toward the wall, he couldn't help but wonder what his mother would think of him now. She'd sent him on a mission to free their souls, but instead had not only his soul, but his heart, entrapped by the woman who had stolen them.

He listened for sounds of the Faie outside the gates as he ascended the staircase toward the top of the wall. He heard none, but when he reached the parapet, he observed some smaller Faie dragging the inhuman bodies of their kin away. He wondered if they would mourn the dead like humans do, and was surprised to feel sympathy growing in his chest.

Finn may have stolen his soul and taken ownership of his heart, but she had somehow given him more emotion than he had ever hoped to feel. Perhaps she'd returned his soul long ago without him knowing. It was the only explanation he could think of as he looked up through the drizzling rain, and felt a single hot tear slip down his cheek.

THOUGH THE BATTLE WEIGHED HEAVILY ON HER MIND, FINN finally managed to rest. A fire had been built in one of the smaller rooms of the fortress, and three bedrolls laid side by side for her, Kai, and Anna.

She'd been more than happy to have her two friends near, and especially relieved to learn the Aos Sí had fetched clean running water to clean Kai's wound, and that he was expected to recover fully.

She drifted in and out of sleep, reveling in the fire's warmth and taking comfort in Kai and Anna's gentle snores. Everyone had been utterly exhausted, including her.

Eventually she fell asleep fully, only to awake in a misty marsh, overlooking a large lake, shining with moonlight.

She took a deep breath and exhaled. How on earth had she ended up here? Was it somehow Anna's doing? The night air was warm here, with no sign of snow, though she knew *anything* could happen in the in-between.

"We've been waiting for you to come here on your own," a voice said from behind her, whipping Finn around.

A few paces away stood Keiren and . . . Ealasaid?

Finn stared at them. "W-what are you two doing together?"

Keiren smirked, then smoothed the fabric of her flowing burgundy dress. "I thought you two should address each other," she explained, gesturing to Ealasaid, "one *queen* to another."

Finn snapped her eyes to Ealasaid, who blushed, wringing her hands in the skirts of her ornate emerald gown. She certainly *looked* the part of a queen with her blonde curls freshly groomed and pulled away from her face.

Finn resisted the urge to blush as well upon glancing down at her dirty breeches and the fresh tunic she'd donned before bed. "I don't understand," she replied.

Keiren rolled her eyes, but before she could speak, Ealasaid stepped forward. "Keiren has been helping me," she explained. "She helped me realize that I'm the final queen from the prophecy. Oighear is still alive, and she attacked Garenoch."

Finn gasped, flicking her gaze between the two women, still not fully understanding.

"Keiren showed me how to come here," she gestured around at the dark twisted trees. "We'd hoped you would come here in your dreams, and we were right."

Had she truly managed to reach the in-between on her own? She narrowed her gaze, training it on Keiren. "Why not just douse me with dust again?" she asked bitterly.

Keiren rolled her eyes again. "I tossed aside my original plan as soon as I learned your blood was not fully immortal, even though it was when you first returned to this land. Out of curiosity, who did you share it with? Whose mortal blood has tainted you?"

"She gave it to Kai," Ealasaid answered. "He was near death, and she saved him."

Finn flinched at the sting of betrayal. She peered at Ealasaid in disbelief. "I told you that in confidence."

Ealasaid cringed. "I apologize, but Keiren has become a friend. She wants to help me protect the mages."

Finn shook her head in disbelief. Could Ealasaid truly be so foolish? "This *woman*," she began, pointing at Keiren as she took a step forward, "has been stalking me since I arrived in this land. She *abused* Bedelia, trapped me in the in-between so she could threaten our friends with Reivers, and turned her own father into a—" she cut herself off, given Àed was not stuck as a tree on a distant island, but safe inside her fortress.

Keiren tilted her head, observing her like a hawk. "There are two sides to every story, my dear, and you do not know my father as well as you think, but that is beside the point. Ealasaid and I have become allies, along with Maarav, and *you* are a threat to us."

A threat? Finn shook her head. "What are you talking about? Ealasaid and I are friends!"

Ealasaid blushed. "Yes, we are," she agreed, "but there's also the prophecy to think about. If you and I are two of the prophesied queens, then one of us must die." She looked down at her feet. "I do not intend to sacrifice myself."

Finn glared at Keiren. She'd obviously been whispering in Ealasaid's ear for quite some time now to have her acting so differently.

"I don't care about prophecies," Finn snapped, maintaining her glare. "I care about protecting my friends from Oighear," she turned her gaze to meet Ealasaid's, "and about protecting *you* from An Fiach."

Ealasaid dropped her gaze back down to her feet. "Then our goals are the same, and we must simply hope the prophecy does not come true. Either way, I think it's best you do not return to Garenoch for the time being."

Finn frowned. Had it truly come to this?

Keiren smiled smugly. "We know you have allied yourself with the Faie, and now have accepted the Cavari under your rule. Both are our enemies."

Ealasaid looked up with tears in her eyes, as if to verify with Finn that what Keiren said was true.

Finn didn't know what to say, so she simply stared back at her.

"The Cavari killed so many of An Solas," Ealasaid accused, her voice trembling. "They were drawn by *you*. We cannot risk another attack now. I must think of *my* people. They have to come before our friendship."

Finn almost laughed. Here she had chosen her friends over the good of all, while Ealasaid was prepared to do the opposite. Truly, Ealasaid had more right to call herself a queen.

"I will not return to Garenoch if you do not desire my presence," Finn agreed cordially. She turned her gaze to Keiren. "And I'll have you know, now that Bedelia and Àed are both with me, I will strike you down if you *ever* come near us again. You may have fooled Ealasaid, but you will never fool me."

Keiren's eyes widened in a brief moment of surprise, then she resumed her smug smile.

Finn flexed her hands, infuriated. She'd hoped the news of Àed's escape would faze her more.

"In that case," Keiren replied calmly, her smile still in place, "I will leave you with a final warning. Don't expect your people to follow someone who willingly tainted her own blood with mortality. Don't expect the Faie to either. You're building your army in quicksand, and your friends will be the first to sink."

With that, she took Ealasaid's hand, and the two women disappeared, leaving her alone in the dark marsh. She sat and wrapped her arms around her knees, mulling over all that was said, but focusing on *how* Keiren knew what had happened only hours before, and why the wicked sorceress was *helping* Ealasaid.

Keiren had claimed her plans had changed, and that perhaps she no longer wanted Finn's not-so-immortal blood, but that didn't mean she didn't want to use her in some other way. She needed to speak with Àed about it, and perhaps Bedelia. One of them might have a better idea of Keiren's hidden intent.

She sighed, then curled up on her side in the scratchy grass. She closed her eyes, more than ready to return to her body.

Just as she was about to drift off, she sensed a presence behind her. She quickly turned over and sat up, then exhaled in relief. It was only her mother, though perhaps, she should not feel relieved just yet.

Móirne seated herself on the ground a few paces away, wrapping her loose black robes around her legs. She stroked a long lock of dark brown hair behind her ear. "My apologies for bringing you here," she began. "I was unaware others might be waiting for you."

Finn wrapped her arms around her knees and peered at her mother curiously. "I was wondering how I came to be here accidentally. I didn't think it was my doing. What do you want?"

Móirne turned her blue eyes down to her lap. "To apologize. What you said to our people . . . you were right. I should have parted ways with the Cavari as soon as we awoke, rather than hiding in the shadows, feebly trying to protect you from afar . . . yet now here I am, once again meeting with you in secret."

Finn sighed. "It is not your fault. One hundred years ago, I ran away from my duties, away from *them*. I left you to fade away with all the others. You owe me nothing."

Móirne rose and repositioned herself to sit directly in front of her. Her hand reached out, landing gently on Finn's, still wrapped around her knees. "I must warn you, while the Cavari bowed to your power tonight, they will strike at you the first chance they get. They will never accept you as queen, not after you stole their magic away for so long."

Finn nodded. She'd suspected as much. "I don't need, nor want, them to accept me. I only need them to fear me enough to do as I say . . . for now."

Móirne gazed at her curiously. "What are you planning?"

Finn observed her mother, wanting to trust her, but knowing she could not. Immortal beings were not immune to acting selfishly out of fear, and her mother was more scared than most.

Reading her expression, Móirne sighed. "My apologies, I should not have asked. I only hope you will not anger the Cavari enough to revolt."

She schooled her face to remain calm, though sudden rage washed through her. She didn't want to make the Cavari angry, she wanted to seal their power away forever, even if it required losing her own magic in turn. She just had to time things wisely. For now, she needed the power to defeat Oighear once and for all. If Keiren and Ealasaid wanted to stand in her way, she would defeat them too, as much as the thought of facing Ealasaid as an enemy pained her.

"Your face betrays your thoughts," Móirne commented, drawing her back to the present.

Finn turned her face away to peer out at the calm, moonlit lake. Her plan meant stealing her mother's magic too. Perhaps she would even fade away again.

Perhaps Finn would too.

It was a risk she had to take if she was going to end things once and for all.

"I wish things could be different," she muttered.

Móirne sighed, gazing out at the lake alongside her. "As do I. After so many years, that is the only thing that hasn't changed."

Finn nodded. Perhaps she and her mother were more similar than she thought, but it didn't matter. It was far too late to save either of them.

CHAPTER TWENTY-THREE

*E*alasaid's eyelids slowly fluttered open. She groaned, lifting a hand to shield her eyes from the nearby candlelight against the stark surrounding darkness.

After a moment, she lowered her hand, then turned her head to the side. Maarav sat in a wooden chair at her bedside.

"You really stayed the whole time?" she asked.

He nodded, his black hair dropping forward to frame his face. "You were entering the in-between with a sorceress we only recently met. *Of course* I stayed to watch over you."

She sat up, glancing around the room. "Where is Keiren, anyway?"

He gestured to the closed door behind his back. "She left after suggesting I let you rest. How did it go?"

She slumped back against her pillow, debating her answer. *Not as planned?* She sighed. "Keiren has a tendency to rile people with her words. I feel we are now on worse terms with Finn than when we started. I only wanted to make sure she didn't plan to kill me now that I'm part of the prophecy." She bit her lip. "*And* to tell her she probably should not come back to Garenoch."

Maarav eyes narrowed in confusion, causing instant guilt to clench Ealasaid's gut. She hadn't discussed *that* part of the plan with him. It had all made so much sense when Keiren first suggested it to her.

"*Why?*" he asked finally. "Finn is a powerful ally."

"She's also allied herself with the Faie," she sighed.

"Did *Keiren* tell you that?" he pressed.

She nodded. "And Finn did not deny it. She's also accepted the Cavari into her ranks, even after what they did to An Solas. They are *monsters*, yet she still agreed to bargain with them."

He shook his head, seeming to mull things over, then met her gaze. "And Iseult? Is he still with her?"

Ealasaid shrugged. "I believe so. No one has said anything to the contrary. I suppose I can ask Keiren since she has the *sight*."

He shook his head. "No, I do not want to place Keiren's attention upon him, nor would I advise you to trust anything she says. You must remember who Finn and Iseult are. They are your friends. Don't let Keiren twist them into enemies."

She frowned. "I thought you didn't *have* friends."

The edge of his lip curled upward. "No, but *you* do. There is a difference between standing strong, and simply making enemies where once there were none."

She scooted up, repositioning her pillow against the wall at the top of her bed. Was he right? Had she made an enemy of Finn, who would perhaps be one of the worst enemies to make? She hoped not. She did not agree with her siding with the Faie, but Finn was still Finn, wasn't she?

"I suppose you're right," she sighed after mulling it over. "Perhaps we can contact Finn again to set things straight."

He snorted. "I don't see much chance of that with Keiren as your mediator."

She stared down at her laced fingers in her lap. "That's true. She destroyed what little good will I had fostered with Lady Sìoda, and now has done far worse with Finn, but . . . " she trailed off.

"But," he continued for her, "she is also powerful, and a necessary ally, especially against Oighear's Aos Sí."

Despite his words, she didn't feel any better. Still, more mages had begun to arrive in Garenoch, even after news of the battle had spread. If they were going to continue to grow their ranks, more battles would come, and Keiren's wards would be necessary to protect them. She could save countless lives.

She closed her eyes and lifted a hand to rub them. "When did things become so complicated?" she muttered.

She heard the scrape of chair legs, then felt the bed shift as Maarav sat beside her. He took her hand, lowering it back to her lap. "They became complicated when you were born," he replied, "at least, according to Keiren."

She opened her eyes and turned to him, then smirked. "I disagree. I think they just became complicated when I met *you*."

He laughed, giving her hand a squeeze. "Come with me to the garden," he suggested. "I've something to show you."

She narrowed her eyes in suspicion, then glanced toward her dark window. "But it's the middle of the night."

He nodded. "Yes, the perfect time to not have to answer questions from one hundred different mages."

Still suspicious, she nodded.

Her hand still in his, he stood and playfully tugged her out of bed. Once she was on her feet, he dropped her hand and walked across the room, fetching her cloak from a hook on the wall.

Realizing she was in her baggy white night clothes, she wrapped her arms around herself and blushed. She'd gotten into bed before he'd entered the room, and had planned on remaining there until he left. The gown she'd worn in the in-between had merely been an illusion created by Keiren.

With a playful smirk, he approached, then wrapped her deep green cloak around her shoulders.

Grateful for the cover, she opened her arms, then wrapped the cloak more firmly around herself. Once she was covered, she sat on the edge of the bed to don her boots, then stood.

Looking her up and down with a nod, Maarav gestured for her to lead the way toward the door, which she unlocked and exited quickly, glad to have her back to him to hide her continued blush.

He followed her into the hall, then shut the door behind them. "To the gardens," he instructed.

Sighing heavily, she led the way. Although she wouldn't mind going back to sleep, she was secretly glad for the distraction. Her interaction with Finn weighed heavily on her mind, almost as heavily as the lingering effects of their battle with Oighear and the Aos Sí.

Reaching the end of the hall, Maarav nodded to the two

assassins standing guard there. The extra precaution had been a recent addition, with so many new mages coming in.

One of the black-clad assassins, a younger woman, opened the door for them.

Ealasaid took a deep breath as she stepped out into the cool night air, coating her throat with refreshing moisture. She sensed another rain was not far off.

Maarav emerged beside her, then the door was shut behind them, revealing another assassin standing outside.

"So much for privacy," Maarav muttered under his breath, placing a hand against Ealasaid's back to guide her forward.

Ealasaid glanced around the surrounding dark gardens as they walked, occasionally darting her eyes upward to the few stars showing through the clouds overhead, then back down to watch her footing in the darkness.

"Will we even be able to see whatever it is you want to show me?" she asked.

"You'll see well enough," he replied, then pointed for her to turn down a narrow corridor created by neatly trimmed shrubs. How the gardeners had found time to maintain it during all of the chaos was beyond her.

They both turned down the corridor, her shoulder nearly touching Maarav's arm in narrow space. Soon reaching the end, he stopped in front of a large rectangular slab stationed upright, with hardy winter flowers planted around its base. The slab was thick enough to have four full faces, rather than just front and back, and stood nearly as tall as she did, but other than its size, she could see nothing remarkable about it.

"You brought me out in the middle of the night to show me a nicely shaped rock?" she asked skeptically.

He took her hand, then knelt, gently pulling her down beside him. "Take a closer look," he instructed.

Now consumed with curiosity, she peered closely at the stone, realizing there were names etched into its surface. She lifted her hand to trace the names with her fingers, slowly reading through them. At first she was not sure what it all meant, until she began to recognize a few.

"They're the names of my mages," she gasped. "The ones who died in battle."

She turned toward Maarav to see him nod. "It's a commemoration of those who gave their lives for An Solas. Those without magic are included as well."

She turned back to continue scanning the names, spotting Tavish about halfway down. Lowering her hand, she peered up at the large stone. The list of names didn't even take up the first entire face, and there were still three more to be filled.

She turned sad eyes to him. "There's room for so many names."

He nodded. "Yes, but at least now they will be remembered, if only in a small way."

She turned back to the stone, gazing at it in awe. "How was this erected so quickly?"

He chuckled. "That's what happens when magic users set their mind to something."

Though the names hurt her heart, she smiled. "Whose idea was this?" she asked distantly.

"Mine," he replied.

She whipped her gaze to him in surprise. "*Yours?* You, an assassin, would memorialize the dead?"

He shrugged, almost seeming embarrassed. "I haven't been an assassin for many years, and you've perhaps made me a bit sentimental."

She shook her head, still smiling. Just when she thought she knew him, he always surprised her. "Maybe it's just your advanced age," she quipped.

He scowled at her. "Don't make me regret doing a nice thing. I may never do one again," he frowned, "and I'm *only* a few years older than you. It's not like I'm hobbling around with a cane."

She shook her head, turning her attention back to the stone. She was glad he'd shown her at night, when they were alone and no one would be around to judge her reaction. Even though it was a small trifle in comparison to losing a life, she enjoyed having Ouve and Tavish's names to look at on the stone.

She leaned over and gave Maarav a kiss on the cheek, then pulled away.

"Oh no," he teased, wrapping his arms around her waist and pulling her down into the grass with him. "I'll need more thanks than that."

Leaning on her elbow with her body pressed against his side, she smiled, then leaned down and gave him a proper, full kiss, lingering for as long as she pleased.

As she finally pulled away, he raised a surprised brow at her. "And here I believed you to be modest," he joked.

She snorted at him, then rolled away to rise to her feet. "I've more important things to be concerned with than modesty."

He smirked up at her for a moment, then stood. "In that case, I suppose you wouldn't mind a warm body beside you for the rest of the night?"

She chuckled, then began to lead the way back toward their rooms. Picking up her pace to keep ahead of him, she was glad the darkness hid the blush that belied her cool air. "I wouldn't go that far," she teased in reply to his question. "Queens are only supposed to sleep next to their kings, and you and I are not married."

He hurried to catch up to her side, taking her hand to halt her brisk pace. "But we could be," he said.

She turned and blinked up at him. Was he kidding? If he was kidding, he was about to experience the full power of one of her lightning bolts.

As if reading her thoughts, he added, "I am entirely serious, Ealasaid."

She continued to stare up at him. What could she say? That she was too young to get married? That she had too many other things to worry about to even consider it? What did she *want* to say?

She looked at her feet, then forced her eyes up to meet his heavy stare. "Alright?"

He smiled. "Is that a question, or an answer?"

She narrowed her eyes at him. "Both?"

"Alright," he replied with a laugh, "and mine is just an answer. I've no questions left."

She laughed, then stood on tip-toes, leaning her hands against his chest to kiss him.

Hand in hand, they continued their short journey back toward their rooms.

Ealasaid couldn't seem to gather her thoughts as they

walked. She was happy, that she knew for sure, but she wasn't sure of the other implications such a bond might establish. Oddly enough, only one question came to her mind.

With the assassin guard now in view, she stopped just out of earshot. "This doesn't mean Slaine will become my mother by way of marriage, does it? I mean, she's not your *real* mother."

He laughed, clearly caught off guard by her question. He took her hand and started walking again. "You should be glad," he joked. "It might just keep her from trying to kill you."

She laughed, though she suspected his statement might just have some truth to it.

FINN AWOKE THE NEXT MORNING TO FIND ONLY KAI IN THE small room with her, waiting with arms crossed and his back leaned against the wall. His fresh bandage stood out stark white against the tanned flesh near his collarbone, just above the collar of his loose, dark blue shirt.

"You have a surprising visitor," he explained, noticing her open eyes.

She sat up in her bedroll, cringing at the growl in her stomach. She could not remember the last time she'd eaten.

"Visitor?" she questioned blearily.

He nodded. "She arrived with the dawn, though I'm not sure how she found us."

She crawled out of her bedroll and stood, wondering what Kai was talking about. Had Keiren come to see her in the flesh? It would be no surprise that she could magically travel so quickly, but why?

"Who is it," she questioned, straightening her breeches and donning her ratty green cloak atop her tunic. She tried combing her fingers through her hair, but it was a snarled mess from the previous night's wind and rain.

He smirked. "Come and see."

With that, he turned toward the door, opened it, and exited.

She furrowed her brow in confusion, then followed. The corridor Kai had taken led out into the main entry room where her allies had gathered.

Iseult stood off to one side of the room, discussing something with Eywen, while Àed leaned against the stone wall near the fire. The other three Aos Sí warriors, whose names Finn would most definitely need to learn by this point, sat in the middle of the floor with Bedelia, sharing meager portions of their remaining bread and cured meat.

Finally her gaze fell to Anna. Naoki, having woken earlier, pranced around her feet as she spoke with another woman.

Partway across the room, Kai turned, then gestured toward their guest with a sarcastic flourish.

Her jaw dropped. "Branwen?" she questioned, more to herself though both she and Anna turned toward her.

She hurried across the room toward them, then stopped to look Branwen up and down. She appeared healthy, and in good spirits. Her long, red hair, a much more common shade than Keiren's, was freshly brushed, and her simple brown dress appeared clean and new.

"How are you here and not in the in-between?" Finn balked, a bit suspicious.

Anna smirked. "I was just asking her the same question."

Branwen offered a hesitant smile, crinkling the corners of her honey brown eyes. "The Travelers saved me," she explained. "Or Anders did, really. He paid the price for my life."

Finn wasn't sure whether to hug her, or send her skittering out of the fortress. "What do the Travelers want?" she blurted. "Why did they send you?"

Branwen looked down at her feet, then back up to Finn. Everyone else in the room had stopped conversing, their eyes on the new spectacle.

"I would like to speak in private about that," Branwen muttered.

She had barely mentioned the word *private*, when Iseult crossed the room toward them.

Finn couldn't help her smile. After everything that had transpired, he still wanted to protect her. "Let us retreat to the garden," she suggested.

Branwen nodded, then waited for Finn to lead the way. Iseult followed behind them.

She glanced over her shoulder at Branwen as they walked, a million questions ready on the tip of her tongue. How had she found them? How was she even still alive? Finn knew the Travelers saw more than was visible to the human eye, future, past, and even hidden intents, but why send Branwen to her?

She sighed as she pushed open the heavy door to the garden, then walked outside.

The sun glittered down on the moisture slick leaves,

giving the garden a feel of magic. The Pixies seemed to appreciate it too, as they had moved into some short trees and shrubs. Their vibrant colors could only be seen in flashes as they flitted about, gathering small acorns and other things for sustenance, which brought another worry to Finn's mind. Her party would need more supplies quite soon.

She turned to Branwen as she stepped out into the garden, looking up at the colorful flashes of the Pixies in awe. "Odd," she muttered, "that things could seem so much more magical here on solid earth than they did in the in-between."

Iseult walked past them toward the garden wall. Reaching it, he leaned his back against the slick stone and gazed upward at the tree branches, giving Finn and Branwen a semblance of privacy.

Branwen eyed the Pixies, then Finn.

"Why are you here?" Finn asked softly.

Branwen's eyes dropped to her boot-clad feet. "I suppose there's no point in lying to you," she began, "you already know where I was trapped, and that my physical body was near death. I don't know just what Anders did to save me, but whatever he did, it inspired the Travelers to bring me back."

Guilt welled up inside Finn. She knew Anders' actions were not her fault, but she felt awful for Branwen, who'd never hurt anyone, yet ended up being used by the Cavari because they sought her. Then they'd left poor Branwen for dead, trapped mentally in the in-between. Now her brother was dead, and Branwen was a Traveler pawn.

She placed a hand gently on Branwen's shoulder. "Did

you see him die, or did the Travelers inform you of his fate?"

Branwen's eyes remained trained on her boots. "They told me, but I did see him briefly before I was pulled away. I saw him when I arrived in the in-between. Someone had stabbed him in the gut."

"I was in the in-between too," Finn explained. "I saw him, after . . . " she shook her head. "I saw him after he was sent there, just before he faded away. He was happy that he was able to rescue you. That was all that had mattered to him."

Branwen finally lifted her honey brown eyes, now rimmed with tears. "He was such a fool," she half laughed, half sobbed.

Finn nodded. Some of the others might not have forgiven Anders, but she did. If the situation had been reversed, and it was Iseult or Kai being held hostage in the in-between . . . well, she would have betrayed a great many people to save them.

She took Branwen's hand and led her to sit upon a toppled stone from the wall, large enough to comfortably seat them both.

"Tell me why you're here," she instructed. "Not that I'm displeased to see you, but I know by now the Travelers do nothing for free, and they've been attempting to manipulate me from the start."

Branwen took a deep breath, then began, "I met a Traveler named Niklas. He explained to me what I am now, a *Wraith*."

Finn did her best to keep her expression impassive. She

knew what Wraiths were. Branwen was no longer connected to humanity. She was barely even alive at all.

"He said I'm animated by the energy that holds the in-between together." She glanced at Finn, then back down to her lap. "He said you would have reason to break that barrier, and that you would want to use me to do it."

Finn shook her head. "I'm not sure what you're talking about."

Branwen glanced at Iseult, waiting quietly across the garden, then back to Finn. She whispered, "He told me that anyone, or anything, trapped there can only be released by demolishing those barriers, and that I'm the tool needed to do it."

Finn tilted her head in thought. *Anything trapped in the in-between . . .* She turned wide eyes across the garden to Iseult, then quickly looked away. Niklas *knew*. He knew about the souls of Iseult's ancestors, and that she wanted to free them. He'd sent Branwen to help her with that task, but why?"

Noticing that Finn had caught on, Branwen nodded encouragingly. "The Travelers want the barriers broken too. They are helping you to help themselves."

That gave Finn pause. She knew better than to trust *anything* the Travelers wanted.

"And what will they give you in return?" she asked suspiciously.

Branwen smiled sadly. "They will allow me to live a normal life, at least as normal as I can, with my family. The Travelers created me as I am now, giving me only the choice of obeying their orders, or dying fully. Truly, I would have almost chosen death if it weren't for Anders' sacrifice. If I cooperate with the Travelers I can return to my family, and my brother won't have died in vain."

Deep in thought, Finn focused on the stone topped pillar near where Iseult stood. The stone on top dully shone in the sunlight, but no unnatural glow emanated forth, nor did she sense the presence of the Druid goddess. Her choice seemed to have somehow sealed her fate. What would it mean now if she chose to break the barriers to the in-between? Iseult had asked that his soul not be returned yet, but things were growing increasingly dangerous. He could have died in the battle the previous night, and she was not sure what would have happened to him had he perished. She was not sure what would happen to his ancestors when she set them free. Would they fade away like Anders had, moving on to the next life, or spiritual realm, or wherever the dead went once their bodies had perished?

She shook her head, then pushed her long tangled hair out of her face. Branwen was watching her, waiting for an answer to her silent question. Would Finn help her, or not?

She patted Branwen's hand where it rested in her lap. "We'll figure all of this out together. If you like, you may remain with us until that point, but for now I must focus on finding supplies, and deciding where we'll be going next."

Branwen glanced around at the garden, then up the tall wall of the fortress. "Why not just stay here? This seems a safer place than most."

Finn nodded. The thought had crossed her mind more than once. They'd proven the fortress could be protected against attack, and they really didn't have anywhere else to go. Ealasaid did not want them back, something she realized she still needed to tell Iseult, and if they went to Sormyr, they'd have to face An Fiach. If they decided to travel back North, they'd have to take the long loop of the Sand Road, and would once again pass near Oighear's domain, something she wanted to avoid until she was ready.

As their conversation had all but abated, Iseult approached, seeming out of place in the serene garden with his black garb and weapons at his belt. "We have much planning to do," he said upon reaching them, peering down at Finn. "Now that the Cavari are . . . under your command, we must figure out where we go from here."

"Yes," she agreed, taking the hand he offered her to stand. "There is *much* we must discuss." She turned as Branwen stood. "Anna can help you get situated should you choose to stay here with us. Hopefully we can acquire an extra bedroll and some clothing for you."

Branwen nodded appreciatively. "I will stay. It feels good to be around friends again, even if those Faie warriors are terrifying."

Finn smirked. She too had once found the Aos Sí terrifying. Now she didn't view them as different at all. They were friends, just like everyone else staying within the small fortress, and just like some of the Faie outside the walls too.

Though she regretted becoming more like the Cavari, and less like the Druids, she knew she'd made the right choice. Her friends were most certainly worth fighting for.

WITH HIS BACK LEANED AGAINST A WALL BY THE FIRE, KAI waited inside the fortress for Finn, Iseult, and Branwen to return from the garden. So much was changing so quickly, he truly wasn't sure what his place was any longer. His new bite had been cleansed with fresh running water gathered by the Aos Sí, so he did not have to fear any ill effects beyond what he'd already suffered from his first bite . . . if he could call the effects ill at all. Though his bandage remained on his new bite, it had all but healed, something that had his thoughts spinning. His reflexes had also been increased, which had been made evident during the battle. He knew the extra healing and speed weren't from the blood Finn had shared with him, they were from the Dearg Due. He'd witnessed himself how one of the creatures could sustain severe wounds and not only survive, but recover fully within a few hours. Now he seemed to be sharing that ability, and he was not sure what else it might mean for him. However, of one thing he was sure: he wouldn't be telling anyone about it. The last thing he needed was Finn prying further into his condition, or worse, for Eywen or Iseult to decide he might be a threat.

He examined the others around him, wondering how they viewed the current scenario. Eywen and the other Aos Sí seemed pleased. They had chosen a strong queen, able to protect them from dark forces. Anna seemed, like, well, *Anna*. The perpetually sour look on her face remained, though it softened slightly when she was interacting with Eywen, something Kai did not understand at all. She did not like the Faie, nor did she like men, at least she hadn't as long as Kai had known her. He was well aware that he knew little of her past before their meeting. She refused to speak of it, and he had always respected that, but now he found himself curious given how she was acting.

His gaze next found Bedelia and Àed, conversing

quietly, another odd situation. As far as he knew, the two had not known each other previously, but he still found it doubtful that they met up in the marshes by chance, far from where they'd been attacked by the Dearg Due. To add to the mystery, Àed had not divulged how he'd escaped his daughter's clutches, nor had Bedelia mentioned Keiren further.

He sighed. Then there was Sativola. Still missing, and likely dead. The Pixies had never found his body, nor any sign of what had happened to him, but Kai doubted the Dearg Due would have kept him alive.

Echoing footsteps preceded Finn's re-entry into the room, followed by Branwen and Iseult.

Finn opened her mouth to speak, but was cut off as a heavy knock sounded on the door. No, not a knock, more like the thud of an object than the rap of a hand.

Two of the Aos Sí warriors hurried toward the heavy wood and iron door to see what the commotion was about. The Trow still barred the gates outside, so anyone coming in would have had to go through them, or over the high walls.

Kai stepped forward as the door opened, curious.

Outside stood several Bucca, small Faie that stood upright like men, though they had the lower bodies of goats. The creatures blinked their large yellow eyes up at the Aos Sí, then screeched and scattered as Naoki came barreling forward from the courtyard at the sight of the open door. She shoved past the Aos Sí, coming inside to trot past Kai to greet Finn.

"What is that!" Branwen shrieked as Finn knelt to greet Naoki.

Kai rolled his eyes and turned his attention back to the open door as Finn explained Naoki to Branwen.

The Bucca had returned to the opening, dragging forward large canvas sacks to leave at the Aos Sí's feet. Seemingly done with their delivery, the Bucca stole nervous glances into the entry room, then scattered.

Kai stepped outside past the Aos Sí to watch the Trow barring the gates as they moved aside to let the Bucca pass. With a laugh, he turned back and lifted one of the sacks, carrying it inside as the two Aos Sí hefted the others.

Once inside, they spilled the contents of the sacks onto the stone floor to find blankets, bandages, and various food products. Some of the food would keep well, but there were other items like fresh baked pies and soft cheeses that had been thrown haphazardly into the sacks to mash up and coat the other supplies.

"The Bucca are skilled thieves," Eywen explained with a smirk, peering down at the supplies, "but they're not incredibly bright."

Kai couldn't help but laugh. In fact, everyone started laughing, he even caught Iseult snickering for a moment.

Eywen knelt down and lifted one of the less broken pies, standing to take a deep whiff of what looked like blueberry filling. "Who's for a bit of dessert?" he asked.

Everyone raised their hands.

Kai shook his head, hardly able to believe that this was now his reality. He couldn't believe that he had Faie blood running through his veins, Anna had magic, and they were all camping out in an ancient Druid Fortress. It seemed like a dream, especially since it had all started so simply.

It seemed like it had been years since he and Anna

decided to kidnap a girl who was once a tree, sending them all barreling forward on a life or death adventure, where perhaps the very fate of the land rested in their hands.

He noticed Finn smiling at him as Eywen began doling out slices of pie with his belt knife. He smiled back, a million thoughts racing through his mind. She was so different than what she'd started out as. Sometimes she was even a bit scary.

Even so, watching her smile and interact with their friends, some new, some old, she was still *her*. His life could have gone in many different directions the day they met, but as he watched her messily eat her pie with childlike enthusiasm, he found he would not have wanted to end up *anywhere* else.

KEIREN STALKED THROUGH THE HALLS OF HER HIDDEN fortress, deep within the marshes. She hadn't intended for Bedelia or her father to escape, but *especially* not Bedelia. *Especially* not after Óengus had betrayed her. Truly, she had no allies left, save Ealasaid.

She stared down at Bedelia's deserted bed, wishing she'd never returned to the tower to check on her at all. Niklas was supposed to feed her and make sure she was well, not release her, sending her on her way with three of her stabled horses.

She whirled as someone entered the room behind her.

Niklas glided in like he hadn't a care in the world, trailing shapeless robes behind him over the ornate rugs.

"*Why* did you release them?" she growled.

Niklas tilted his bald head to the side. "I wanted a favor," he explained with a shrug.

She glared at him.

He tsked at her as he moved to her side. "Do not fear, it will all benefit you in the end."

She scowled at him. "I tire of your secrets, Traveler. Either you let me in on your full plan, or our partnership is over."

Niklas tsked at her again, then turned to peer out the window over the bed. "Do you know where the Ceàrdaman come from?" he asked abruptly.

She turned her startled gaze to him. "Of course not, *no one* does."

He smiled softly, still gazing out the window. "We come from the in-between. We were created as its guardians, spirit guides meant to help living souls transition to the next stage of their existence."

She shook her head in disbelief. The Travelers never lied, but could he truly mean what he said? "How did you come to live in this land?" she questioned, still not fully believing him.

He tilted his head, still gazing distantly out the window. "We did it to ourselves. My ancestors witnessed countless souls as they passed through our realm. Souls that had been allowed to learn, to taste food, to experience all life has to offer. The Ceàrdaman became greedy. They left the in-between, wanting just a small taste of life, but it did not go as planned. Their journey brought magic into this realm, turning silent nature spirits into Faie, and giving certain humans the power to wield elements."

"The Ceàrdaman created magic?" she gasped.

He nodded, then continued. "My ancestors tried to go back, to fix their mistakes, but their way was barred. The magic had flooded outward so quickly that it created a plug, like holding water in a tub. They became trapped in a foreign land, with no place to call home, constantly seeking those who could reach the realm that was lost to them." He glanced at her, raising his hairless brow. "Seeking out those like *you*."

She shook her head, still trying to grasp all he had told her. "So why inform me of this now, after keeping the secret for so long?"

He smiled. "Because the boundaries between worlds will soon come crashing down. The Ceàrdaman will be able to return to their rightful home. I will finally achieve what so many of my ancestors failed to accomplish . . . and *you're* going to help me do it."

She gazed out the window, focusing on dark clouds gathering in the distance. "Yes," she agreed, "if your goal is to destroy the barriers, I will help you, if only to help myself."

Grinning wickedly, Niklas steepled his fingers together, lightly tapping the tips against each other in rapid succession. "Then let us begin, we have much to do, and," he glanced over his shoulder out the window toward the gathering clouds, "a *storm* is coming."

NOTE FROM THE AUTHOR

I hope you've enjoyed the fourth installment in the Tree of Ages Series! For news and updates, please sign up for my mailing list by visiting:

www.saracroethle.com

GLOSSARY

A

Anna- descendent of clan Liath.

Àed (ay-add)- a conjurer of some renown, also known as "The Mountebank".

Áit I Bhfolach (aht uh wallach)- secret city in the North.

Anders (ahn-durs)- a young, archive scholar.

Aonbheannach (aen-vah-nach)- unicorn.

Aos Sí (A-ess she)- ancient humanoid Faie.

Ar Marbhdhraíocht (ur mab-dry-oh)- volume on necromancy

Arthryn (are-thrin)- alleged Alderman of Sormyr. Seen by few.

B

Bannock- unleavened loaf of bread, often sweetened with honey.

Ballybog- large Faie common in swamps.

Bedelia- former lover of Keiren.

Bladdered- drunk

Boobrie- large, colorful, bird-like Faie that lures travelers away from the path.

Branwen (bran-win)- a young, archive scholar.

C

Caorthannach (quar-ah-nach)- Celtic fire-spitting demon.

Cavari (cah-var-ee)- prominent clan of the *Dair Leanbh.*

Ceàrdaman (see-air-duh-maun)- the Craftspeople, often referred to as *Travelers.* Believed to be Faie in origin.

À Choille Fala (ah choi-le-uh fall-ah)- the Blood Forest. Either a refuge or prison for the Faie.

Ceilidh (kay-lee)- a festival, often involving dancing and a great deal of whiskey.

D

Dair Leanbh (dare lan-ub)- Oak Child. Proper term for a race of beings with affinity for the earth. Origins unknown.

Dearg Due (dee-argh doo)- female, blood-drinking Faie.

Dram- a small unit of liquid measure, often referring to whiskey.

Dullahan (doo-la-han)- headless riders of the Faie. Harbingers of death.

E

Ealasaid (eel-ah-sayd)- young mage.
Evrial (ehv-ri-all)- Pixie clan leader.

F

Finnur (fin-uh)- member of Clan Cavari.

G

Garenoch (gare-en-och)- small, southern burgh. A well-used travel stop.
Geancanach (gan-can-och)- small, mischievous Faie with craggy skin and bat-like wings. Travel in Packs.
Glen- narrow, secluded valley.
Gray City- see *Sormyr*
Grogoch (grow-gok)- smelly Faie covered in red hair, roughly the size of a child. Impervious to heat and cold.
Gwrtheryn (gweir-thare-in)- Alderman of Garenoch. Deathly afraid of Faie.

H

Haudin (hah-din)- roughly built homes, often seen in areas of lesser wealth.
Henkies- little purple man fairy that lives in the knolls.

I

Iseult (ee-sult)- allegedly the last living member of Uí Neíd.

K

Kai- escort of the Gray Lady.

Keiren (kigh-rin)- daughter of the Mountebank. Whereabouts unknown.

L

Liaden (lee-ay-din)- the Gray Lady.

Loinnir (lun-yer)- one of the last Unicorns.

M

Maarav (mah-rahv)- brother of Iseult, descendent of Uí Néid.

Meirleach (myar-lukh)- word in the old tongue meaning *thief.*

Merrows- water dwelling Faie capable of taking the shape of sea creatures. Delight in luring humans to watery deaths.

Midden- garbage.

Migris- one of the Great Cities, and also a large trade port.

Móirne (morn-yeh)- member of Clan Cavari. Mother of Finnur.

Muntjac- small deer.

N

Neeps- turnips.

Niamh (nee-ahm-uh)- deceased daughter of Finnur.

O

Óengus (on-gus)- a notorious bounty hunter.

Oighear (Ohg-hear)- ruler of the Aos Sí, also known as Oighear the White, or the Snow Queen.

P

Pooks- also known as Bucca, small Faie with both goat and human features. Nocturnal.

Port Ainfean (ine-feen)- a medium-sized fishing port along the River Cair, a rumored haven for smugglers.

R

Ratchets- Goblin hounds.

Redcaps- Goblins.

Reiver (ree-vur)- borderland raiders.

S

Sand Road- travel road beginning in Felgram and spanning all the way to Migris.

Scunner- an insult referring to someone strongly disliked.

Sgal (skal)- a strong wind.

Sgain Dubh (skee-an-doo)- a small killing knife, carried by roguish characters.

Síoda (she-dee)- Lady of Garenoch.

Slàinte (slawn-cha)- a toast to good health.

Slàine (slahn-yuh)- clan leader of assassins.

Sormyr (sore-meer)- one of the Great Cities, also known as the Gray City.

T

Travelers- see *Ceàrdaman*.

Trow- large Faie resembling trees. Rumored to steal children.

U

Uí Néid (ooh ned)- previously one of the great cities, now nothing more than a ruin.

TREE OF AGES READING ORDER

Tree of Ages

The Melted Sea

The Blood Forest

Queen of Wands

The Oaken Throne

CPSIA information can be obtained
at www.ICGtesting.com
Printed in the USA
LVHW011442080119
603165LV00017B/462/P